RAVES AND MORE RAVES FOR JAYNE ANN KRENTZ!

"An accomplished writer...a great author."
—*West Coast Review of Books*

"Jayne Ann Krentz entertains to the hilt."
—**Catherine Coulter, author of *The Deception***

"Jayne Ann Krentz is a must for those who enjoy romantic novels."
—*Brooklyn Record*

"What better guide to reading pleasure could there possibly be than the incomparable Jayne Ann Krentz? A genre unto herself, Ms. Krentz is today's premier exponent of romantic adventures....Mesmerizing characterizations, dazzling ingenuity, and fiery romance make the name Jayne Ann Krentz a surefire guarantee of unsurpassed excellence....Shimmering with the elegance of excellence, A CORAL KISS challenges the spirit and pleasures of the heart."
—*Romantic Times*

"Jayne Ann Krentz always gives her readers more than romance. Suspense, mystery, fantasy, and history are all woven into the meticulous fabric of characterization and plot that makes her work memorable."
—*Affaire de Coeur*

ALSO BY JAYNE ANN KRENTZ

Sweet Starfire
Crystal Flame
Midnight Jewels
Shield's Lady
Gift of Fire
Gift of Gold

A CORAL KISS

JAYNE ANN KRENTZ

GRAND CENTRAL
PUBLISHING

NEW YORK   BOSTON

Copyright ©1987 by Jayne Ann Krentz
All rights reserved. Except as permitted under the U.S. Copyright Act of 1976, no part of this publication may be reproduced, distributed, or transmitted in any form or by any means, or stored in a database or retrieval system, without the prior written permission of the publisher.

Cover design by Diane Luger
Cover art by Alexa Garbarino
Handlettering by David Gatti

Grand Central Publishing
Hachette Book Group
237 Park Avenue
New York, NY 10017
Visit our website at www.HachetteBookGroup.com

Grand Central Publishing is a division of Grand Central Publishing. The Grand Central Publishing name and logo is a trademark of Hachette Book Group, Inc.

Printed in the United States of America

First Printing: April 1987
Reissued: June 1992, January 2000, January 2004

25 24 23 22 21 20 19

Chapter One

*H*e had no right to make the phone call and he knew it. But he had dialed the number, so it was too late to hang up, even if he managed to convince himself he should. She was supposed to be a friend and tonight he needed a friend.

With a grim concentration necessitated by the pain pills he had been gulping for the past several hours, Jed leaned his head against the gleaming payphone, closed his eyes and listened to the ringing on the other end of the line. He couldn't remember feeling this bad before in his life. He hurt, he was exhausted and his mind wasn't functioning anywhere near its normal level of awareness.

Everything around him seemed to be annoying. He couldn't tune out the inconsequential. The constant background noise of the L.A. airport terminal was grating against all his senses. He couldn't seem to think straight because of the way the silly chatter of travelers, the roar of engines and the smell of hot dogs and fuel was sinking into his nervous system. Jed knew the pain pills probably amplified the uncomfortable effect, but the knowledge didn't help. He tried to concentrate more intently on listening to the phone—one ring, two rings, three. Maybe she wasn't home. Christ, for all he knew, she was with another man.

Not tonight, he thought as he gripped the receiver a little

more tightly in an effort to steady himself. *Don't let there be anyone else there tonight.*

He sought reassurance by reminding himself that Amy hadn't seemed interested in any other man during the three months Jed had known her. Not that she was all that interested in him, Jed told himself wryly—except, of course, as a friend. He found himself praying she hadn't turned up any other *friends* during the few weeks he had been gone.

She answered the phone in the middle of the fourth ring. Jed felt relief wash through him with a more comforting effect than his little white pills had had. He wondered why he had been so worried. Amy was always at home at night. Lately, when he was on assignment, Jed had found himself taking an obscure kind of comfort in that knowledge. He could close his eyes at any time and picture her sitting home alone in the evenings, perhaps curled up on the old couch in her front room with an album from her collection of early rock music on the stereo.

"Amy? It's Jed."

"Jed! Good grief, it's almost midnight. Where are you? Are you home?"

He heard the bright welcome in her clear, warm voice. Sometimes Jed thought it was Amy's voice he started thinking about first when he was headed home. He lifted his lashes with an effort and found himself eyeball-to-eyeball with the reassuring symbol of AT&T. Some things, at least, were constant in the universe—Amy's voice and AT&T.

"I'm in L.A. My plane gets into Monterey in an hour and a half." His fingers tightened on the receiver. "Amy, I hate to ask, but can you meet me?"

"Meet you?"

Maybe she was with another man there. Jed shook off the

sudden, tight anger that materialized out of nowhere. The pain pills again, he told himself. He had no right allowing himself to react to the possibility of Amy being with another man. He had no claim on her, just as she had no claim on him. They were friends. Their friendship might be odd, and unlike any he had ever had before in his life, but it was still a friendship. That was all Amy seemed to want.

"Amy, if you're busy. . ." He let the sentence trail into nowhere, unwilling to let her off the hook completely unless he was forced to do so. He wanted her at the airport—no, needed her there. He had to get home tonight and he was almost certain he couldn't drive. The pills, pain and exhaustion were hitting him too hard.

"No, Jed, I'm not busy. I can meet you. Hang on a second while I grab a pen." She was back in an instant. "Okay. Give me the flight number."

"Flight number," Jed repeated a little helplessly. "Yeah, just a second." Of course there was a flight number. What the hell was the matter with him? His brain had apparently shut down. He groped for the ticket envelope in his shirt pocket. He stared at the three digit number for a few seconds before it made sense. Then, very carefully, he read it aloud to her.

With relief, he now realized that the surprise he had at first heard in her voice wasn't a prelude to refusing to meet him. Amy was really surprised at being *asked* to meet him. Her reaction was perfectly understandable, he thought. At no time during the past three months had he asked her to meet him at the airport. He had always rented a car and driven back to Caliph's Bay from Monterey. His homecoming routine was just that: routine. He rarely violated his own rituals. When a man reached the point where he didn't pay much attention to his past or his future, he found himself dependent on his own little rules.

"All right, Jed, I've got it. I'll be there."

"Thanks, Amy. I'll see you in a while."

There was a small pause before her clear, warm voice asked hesitantly, "Jed? Is anything wrong?"

Jed looked down at the cane he was gripping in his left hand. He didn't feel like attempting casual explanations over the phone. He would work them up on the flight to Monterey. He was good at doing that sort of thing. Every man was blessed with one or two talents, and inventing convincing explanations was his. "No, nothing's wrong. I just thought it might be tough to get a rental car at this hour of the night. Drive carefully, Amy."

After they had said good-bye, Jed hung up the phone. Then, gathering his strength with an effort of sheer willpower, he pushed himself away from the phone and, using his cane to brace himself, made his way back to the flight lounge. Halfway there, he saw the flower cart. Something clicked in his fogged brain.

He had formed the small habit of presenting her with flowers when he returned from his trips. He did it partly as a thank you for the questions she never asked and partly as an apology for the answers he never offered. Another ritual.

Jed made his way over to the cart and bought a handful of yellow roses, so perfect they looked almost plastic. They weren't really Amy's kind of flower; there was nothing plastic about her. But he didn't have much choice. He cradled them carefully as he finished the trek to the waiting lounge.

He almost went to sleep waiting for the boarding call. When it came, he roused himself enough to follow the other passengers on board. A few minutes later, seatbelt fastened and with the yellow roses stowed alongside his thigh, he did go to sleep. But not before he had a last, anticipatory image of Amelia Slater waiting for him in Monterey.

She would be easy to spot in the crowd, if there was one at this hour of the night, Jed thought. She wasn't particularly tall and she wasn't particularly lovely. Taken separately, there was nothing unusually inviting about her intelligent, near-green eyes, shoulder-length, golden brown hair and soft mouth. Jed knew she was the sort of woman other women said could be attractive if she just bothered to wear a little makeup. Amy seldom bothered. Her body was slender, small on top and invitingly lush below the waist, but certainly not possessed of thoroughbred elegance or pin-up voluptuousness. Yet somehow, to Jed, her beauty was so vivid, she reminded him of one of the covers of the science fiction books she wrote—all bright hues, a promise of excitement and a barely controlled nervous energy.

The fantasy of tapping into that feminine energy in bed had been plaguing Jed with increasing frequency.

Tonight the fantasy was stronger than ever, in spite of the effect of the pain pills, or perhaps because of it. Ever since he had met Amy Slater, Jed had found himself letting her structure the odd relationship that had begun developing between them. What Amy had chosen to build was a delicate web of companionship, a loose friendship from which the sexual element was plainly missing. On the handful of occasions they had spent together during the past three months, Amy had seemed satisfied with the situation. Jed was wondering how much longer he could tolerate it. But the last thing he had wanted to do was push her.

But he had another reason for allowing the relationship to continue as it was, he reminded himself. The last thing he needed was a clinging woman who would begin to question his frequent, extended absences, his lack of plans for the future and his reasons for having reached his mid-thirties without having married. Once a man started sleeping with a woman on a regular basis, the woman usually felt she had a right to ask questions about things like that.

Jed told himself he didn't need questions—or a woman who asked them—in his life. Amy would be easy to handle as long as she didn't probe. Unfortunately, he was beginning to crave her in a way that could no longer tolerate simple friendship. Sooner or later the situation was going to explode. Jed wasn't at all sure what the results would be when it did.

His last conscious thought before he let himself be taken by sleep was a vague curiosity about Amy's reaction when she saw him limp off the plane. When he had left almost a month before, he had had no cane and no injuries to explain. Even a woman who normally never asked awkward questions was bound to wonder what had happened. He ought to get to work on the cover story he planned to tell her.

The perfect yellow roses took the full shock of Jed's not inconsiderable weight when he finally let himself sag against the left side of the seat. The flowers went down without a struggle, their plastic perfection crumpling into a squashed yellow mess.

For a few minutes after she hung up the phone, Amy sat staring out her window at the night darkened sea. Jed's call had taken her by surprise. When the phone had rung, she had assumed her father was calling to remind her yet again that he and her mother were expecting her for her semi-annual visit to the island. She had put it off long enough. It had been nearly eight months since she had visited them on Orleana. In years past she had eagerly looked forward to going out to the Pacific island every six months. Belatedly she realized it was much too late for a call from the island.

But she had been taken completely off guard when she heard Jed's voice. Jed, who never called while he was away. The first she usually knew of his return from a trip was when he showed up on her doorstep carrying flowers.

A heavy fog crouched over tiny Caliph's Bay tonight, otherwise she might have been able to see the lights of Pacific Grove and Monterey in the distance. It was a good half hour's drive to the airport, but with the fog she had better allow more time.

Not once during the past three months had Jed ever asked her to meet him at the airport when he returned from one of his consulting trips. But then, Jed never imposed, never made demands. He was content to take whatever she offered. The arrangement suited Amy perfectly.

But tonight he had broken his own, unspoken rules. He had asked a favor.

Amy shook off the odd sense of anxiety that had gripped her the instant she had heard his voice. She got to her feet and headed toward the bedroom to dress.

Following the advice in one of the many books on insomnia that she had bought during the past few months, she had been going through an elaborate routine in preparation for bed. With the usual optimism of such self-help approaches, the author of the book had suggested that the body and mind must relearn the anticipation of sleep. The theory was that a concentration on the repetitive, nightly ritual of undressing, tooth brushing, face washing, and the rest was one approach to reacquainting oneself with an expectation of sleep. It sounded as plausible as anything Amy had tried lately, and heaven knew she had tried a variety of techniques. She had just put on a high-necked, long-sleeved flannel nightgown when the phone had rung a few minutes ago. So much for this evening's little ritual of anticipation.

No loss, she told herself in resignation as she quickly put on a pair of black jeans, a bright yellow shirt and a knitted orange vest. The odds were against her having gotten much sleep tonight, anyway. She rarely got a good night's sleep lately, no matter how many books she read on the subject. No book could cure her underlying problem. No book could wipe out the memories of what had happened eight months ago on Orleana shortly before her twenty-seventh birthday.

She had been right about the drive to the airport, Amy realized some time later as she eased her compact car out of the drive and onto the narrow, two-lane highway. The fog was not impenetrable, but navigating it definitely required concentration and care.

Amy gave most of her attention to her driving, but a part of her mind couldn't stop wondering about the reason she was on the road at this hour of the night in the first place. She wondered if Jed would offer any explanation for his unusual behavior. She doubted it. And even if she had been inclined to ask, Jed was not the sort of man a woman nagged. Amy was proud of the way she never asked questions, offered suggestions or otherwise tried to impose her will on him. And Jed seemed to appreciate her circumspection. She sensed deep down that Jedidiah Glaze had his own secrets, just as she had hers, but she didn't want to examine that conclusion too closely. A part of her suspected that one of the reasons she never asked any questions was because she didn't want to hear the answers.

Jedidiah. Amy let his full name ripple through her mind. It was a good name for him. The first time she'd met him Amy had decided immediately that Jed could have been the reincarnation of an old-style fire-and-brimstone preacher. Not one of the new soft, sleek media conmen who dominated the religious airways, but a rock-hard, unrelenting Calvinist from the old school or the Old West. A man with big, strong hands and a face carved from unyielding stone. One of those men who could look you in the eye and make you believe in hell.

She had quickly realized that Jed Glaze had little interest in religion, but the initial impression hadn't vanished. The blunt, hard lines of his face were well suited to the equally blunt, hard lines of his body. He was somewhere in his mid-thirties, but his hazel eyes seemed to have seen at least an extra generation's worth of the world. On some level, Amy knew, Jed's cool, watchful gaze had been what initially attracted her to him. But the easygoing quality of their relationship was what held her. She had discovered Jed was good at relaxed friendships. And she needed someone who was content not to make demands.

Still, she found the thought of any kind of relationship with Jed Glaze odd. Amy knew that under normal circumstances she would never have gotten involved with him. He was not really the gentle, honest, and straightforward kind of man she had once sought. He wasn't the kind of male a woman knew instinctively could be domesticated, the kind who would make a good husband and father. Amy knew that even though he was good at projecting whatever facade seemed suitable to the occasion, there was an underlying darkness in him that would have threatened, even repelled her eight months before. But she was no longer living under "normal circumstances."

The simple truth was that Amy was not the same person she had been eight months before. For some strange reason the change in her left her open to viewing Jed Glaze in a different manner than she once would have done. On some level, the hardness and darkness in him actually appealed to her now. Perhaps, she thought, she subconsciously longed to have some of that dangerous internal strength for herself.

She was waiting at the airport gate when Jed finally came through the door. He was one of the last passengers off the plane and Amy had begun to wonder if she had met the wrong flight. When she saw the cane and the stark, controlled expression on Jed's face she had the fleeting sensation of having definitely met the wrong plane. It was as if she were seeing him clearly for the first time.

He stopped when he saw her. He had a small leather flight bag and a bundle of sadly crushed yellow roses in his right hand. The passengers leaving the plane behind him separated and flowed around him in twin streams as if he were a boulder that had fallen into their path.

Amy saw the grim challenge in his eyes and swallowed her shock. She hurried forward, reaching automatically for the leather bag. Impulsively, driven by a need to offer welcome and comfort, she stood briefly on tiptoe to brush her lips lightly across his. She had never before offered such a personal greeting and she was startled by the feel of his mouth. It was hard and inflexible under hers. Quickly she stepped back. Summoning a smile, Amy sought for the light, cheerful touch that had characterized their relationship for the past three months.

"You do know how to make an entrance, I'll say that for you. Want me to get a wheelchair?"

He glared at her. "No, I do not want a wheelchair. I'm embarrassed enough as it is. The thought of you pushing me in a wheelchair is a little more than I can take at the moment. I know I look like hell."

Amy arched her eyebrows faintly, studying him. He'd never snapped at her before; not once during the half dozen or so times they'd spent together. His tone of voice tonight was undoubtedly caused by his present physical condition. "That's one way of putting it."

Jed's mouth twisted wryly. "Sorry for the short temper. It's been a long day." Jed started forward as Amy walked beside him.

"I can see that." Amy smiled easily. "Where did you come from? A war zone?"

"I had an accident."

"Somehow I managed to figure that out all on my own. Jed, no offense, but you look terrible. Should I take you to an emergency room?" She found the flight bag surprisingly heavy and wondered how he'd managed it in his condition. Quickly she scanned his face, trying to assess the damage as she walked beside him to the car.

"The last thing I need is an emergency room. I've had all the doctors I can stand for a while."

"What on earth happened? Was it an industrial accident? Did something happen at the job site?" Amy asked seriously.

"Nothing that dramatic. It was a car accident." Jed frowned down at the crumpled flowers under his arm. "Here, these are for you."

"They look like they went through the same accident." Amy smiled with determined brightness as she took the crushed flowers. She was touched that he had remembered. It made her realize she'd grown accustomed to the little homecoming ritual. Maybe there were more expectations between them than she was willing to admit.

"I slept on them in the plane."

"Where did the accident take place? In Saudi Arabia?" Amy asked as she halted beside her compact and fumbled for the keys.

"What? Oh. Yeah. Saudi Arabia." Jed slid into the passenger seat with a muttered groan. He shut his eyes briefly and then opened them. "They drive like crazy people over there."

"No kidding? Well, now you're in my hands," Amy remarked as she slipped in beside him and started the engine.

"The mind boggles."

"You should have thought of that before you called me to come pick you up." She shifted into reverse and backed out of the slot with her customary élan.

Jed turned his head to look at her. In the shadows of the car his face was an intent mask. "Thanks for coming out tonight, Amy," he said quietly. "I don't know what I would have done without you. I'm in no shape to drive."

"I've noticed." She kept her tone dry so the worry wouldn't show through. Jed wouldn't want her worrying, and she was a little afraid of what her worrying about him might mean. "Any permanent damage?"

"I'm told I'm still structurally sound although it doesn't feel like it at the moment."

"Who told you that? The doctors at your company's engineering site?"

"Yeah. But what do they know?"

"Good question. Did you sue?"

"Who? The driver? Not a chance. Things work differently over there. It took three company lawyers and a hefty bribe just to keep the guy who hit me from suing *me*," Jed said laconically.

"The perils of being a globe-trotting engineer. Those of us who only sit and wait lead far less adventurous lives."

"So I'm told. How's the book going?" Jed leaned his head back and closed his eyes.

She had learned to expect such polite inquiries from him. "It's going together all right. I've finally got a handle on it."

"Settled on a title? You were calling it Untitled Opus Number Four when I left."

"Somehow I decided after you left that that sounded a bit ostentatious. The new title came to me in a blinding flash last week while I was scrubbing the shower," Amy admitted lightly. *"Private Demons*. What do you think?"

Jed considered the matter with mocking solemnity. "I like it. It's got charm, wit, pathos and the essence of a double entendre. What more could an editor ask?"

"A book that lives up to the title?"

"Some people have a lot of nerve, don't they? They'd complain if they got hung with a new rope. God, I'm tired." He fished in the pocket of his cotton slacks for a small bottle.

"What's that?" Amy shot him a swift glance as he swallowed a tiny tablet without opening his eyes.

"Painkiller. Good stuff. Worth fifty bucks on the street, the doctors told me. Maybe if I have any left I can sell them and make enough to take you out to dinner as thanks for picking me up tonight. Might as well salvage something from this trip." He shoved the bottle back into his pocket.

"I take it you do not consider this trip a resounding success?"

"It was an unmitigated disaster," he told her flatly.

Startled by the admission, Amy bit back a response. It wasn't like Jed to be so open about his business problems.

"Well, I'll have you safely on your front doorstep in less than half an hour," she assured him. "You're sure you don't want to go to the emergency room?"

There was no answer to her remark. Amy took her eyes off the narrow, winding road long enough to glance at her passenger's face. Jed was asleep. She didn't think he would appreciate waking up in an emergency room.

Half an hour later Amy turned down the main street of Caliph's Bay. The tiny, seaside community was sound asleep. There was one street light at the intersection by the post office, but other than that all was in darkness. Even Caliph's Inn, the town's one motel, had turned off its vacancy sign. Jed's small, weather-beaten house was located on a bluff overlooking the sea. Amy started to slow as she approached the turnoff, then glanced again at her sleeping passenger.

Jed was in no condition to look after himself tonight. The man was dead tired and doped to the gills with little white pills. Amy made her decision and put her foot back down on the accelerator.

A few minutes later she parked the car in the drive of her own cabin. She turned in the seat, trying to estimate the task ahead of her. Jed Glaze was all hard muscle and solid bone; there was nothing light or airy about him. There was no way she could get him inside unless he walked on his own two feet.

"Jed?" Gently she touched his arm. He didn't move, but

quite suddenly his hazel eyes were open and fixed on her face. His abrupt awakening gave Amy a jolt, and her hand fell away from his arm.

"Are we there?" The intensity faded from his gaze.

"Yes. And there's no way I can carry you. Unless you can levitate, I'm afraid you're going to have to walk."

"Right now levitating sounds easier." With a sigh he stirred and opened the car door.

Amy got out on her side and hurried around to help him. "Here, let me get your cane. Don't worry about the flight bag. I'll bring it."

Jed leaned one elbow against the roof of the car and stared at the house. "This is your place."

"I see your powers of observation haven't been completely dulled by little white pills. Come on, it's cold out here. Let's get inside."

He looked down at her as she stood illuminated in the faint yellow porch light. His hazel gaze was unreadable. "I don't want to be any more of a pain in the ass than I've already been tonight."

"Forget it. I'd rather have you here where I can keep an eye on you than send you home where you might get into trouble."

"What kind of trouble am I likely to get into at home?"

"In your present condition, you could have any one of a variety of common household accidents," she informed him as she took his arm and pried him away from the support of the car.

"For example?" He sounded only mildly interested as he allowed her to lead him toward the front door.

"For example, you could lose your balance in the bathroom and drown ignominiously in the toilet."

"It would be a hell of a way to go, wouldn't it?"

"It would definitely make for an embarrassing obituary. Watch the step, Jed."

"You've only got one bed." His protest was remarkably feeble.

"I'll use the couch."

"I can take the couch."

"You," Amy announced with gentle tyranny, "will take what you're given. You haven't got the strength to argue about it tonight."

"You may be right."

She got him through the small living room with it's old wooden floors, comfortably shabby furniture, braided rugs and collection of savage science fiction and horror art posters. Proceeding into the bedroom, Amy flipped on the light to reveal more of the same rustic furniture. There was a poster featuring a well endowed, futuristic Amazon warrior confronting a dragon on the wall over the bed. Jed came to a halt beside the bed, wavering a little. He focused first on the poster and then on the flannel nightgown Amy had left lying across the quilt.

"I sleep in my shorts," he announced.

"How terribly macho of you. Can you get yourself undressed?"

He swung his gaze to her concerned face, his heavy brows coming together in a nearly solid line. "I won't know until I try. If you want to play nurse, go ahead. I'm not proud."

She felt the heat rush into her cheeks and was startled by the degree of her own embarrassment. She moved nervously, collecting the flannel nightgown from the bed. "Forget I asked. I'll give you some privacy so you can get ready for bed."

"Ah, Amy, I'm sorry. I guess I snapped at you again, didn't I?"

"Not exactly. I think you were teasing me. But you do seem a little on the edgy side tonight."

"That's funny," he said consideringly as he fumbled with the buttons on his khaki shirt. "I always think of you as being the edgy one. King of high-strung at times. Nervy. As if you're always walking along some ledge."

Amy paused in the doorway. "I had no idea you'd been busy analyzing me."

"I spend a lot of time thinking about you. Especially on airplanes. Always a lot of time to think on an airplane."

She saw his hands tremble slightly as he reached the last button of his shirt. The man was definitely half out of it, she thought. In a few more minutes he would be asleep on his feet. Even his dark, gravelly voice was taking on a slurred, groggy quality. She had a hunch Jed didn't know what he was saying. "Be careful, Jed. Maybe you'd better sit down."

He ignored her advice, his mind obviously pursuing its own line of thought. "I thought a lot about you on the flight back today, Amy. I got to wondering."

"Wondering what, Jed?" She had picked up her night-gown, and now realized she was crushing the fabric in her hands.

"Whether you'd lose some of that high-strung edginess in bed. Be interesting to find out, wouldn't it?"

Amy's eyes flew to his face, but he wasn't really looking at her. She had the impression his attention was focused on some image in his head. "You're in no condition to find out anything tonight, Jed," she informed him briskly. "Call me if you need any help." She started to turn away, but his voice stopped her.

"I need help."

Amy turned back and saw him watching her with a steady intensity. His khaki shirt hung open, revealing the sleek contours of his chest and a wealth of dark hair that tapered down to his flat, taut stomach. His hands seemed all tangled up with the buckle of his belt. When he wavered slightly, she rushed forward.

"Here, let me do that," Amy said quickly. "You really are in bad shape, aren't you?"

"I don't know. I've got so many pills in me I can't feel a thing." He sank down onto the edge of the bed, eyeing her with interest as she knelt in front of him and pulled off his low, worn boots. "In the Middle East they're very big on subservient women."

"The Middle East has several enormous problems. The attitude toward women is only one of them," Amy informed him as she let the second boot drop to the floor. She glanced up and saw the warmth in his hazel eyes. She didn't need feminine intuition to know that what she saw in his gaze had absolutely nothing to do with sexual desire, or at least not much to do with it. She put her hand on his forehead. "Did those doctors give you anything for a fever?"

He blinked owlishly. "There's another bottle of something in my flight bag."

"I'll get it." She was on her feet before he could argue.

Inside the leather bag she found a small bundle of dirty laundry, one clean shirt, shaving gear and a bottle of tablets. By the time she got back to the bedroom, Jed had managed to slide out of his trousers and make his way into the bathroom.

When he emerged a few minutes later he was wearing a pair of snug briefs that only emphasized the fact that he was built solidly everywhere. He confronted her, bracing himself with one large hand wrapped around the doorframe. The strong, masculine contours of his body were broken not only by the underwear, but by a wide swath of white bandage around his left thigh. There was an ugly, fading bruise over his rib cage and what looked like a line of stitches slanting diagonally across his right arm above the elbow.

Amy stared in shock. "My God, Jed."

"Structurally sound," he reminded her dryly. He followed her glance to the bandage on his inner thigh. "Just barely. Let me have those tablets."

Wordlessly she handed him the bottle and watched him disappear into the bathroom to swallow more pills. When he emerged a second time he headed directly for the bed. Sinking down into it with a deep groan of relief, he tugged the covers up over his bare chest and turned his face into the pillow.

"Smells just like you," he mumbled. "Soft and warm. Do you realize this will be the first time I've ever spent a night in your bed?"

He was asleep before Amy could think of a response.

She quietly switched off the light and wandered out into the kitchen. She stood in the center of the old linoleum floor and wondered whether it was worth trying the tryptophane tablets she'd bought the day before at the health food store in town. As wound up and wide awake as she was now the odds were against her getting any sleep tonight, regardless of what approach she tried. Still, anything was worth a try.

Uncapping the bottle, she grimaced as she saw how large the tablets were. Regular horse pills. She would be lucky to get them down. She ran water into a glass and tossed down two of the pills. Her heart wasn't in the project. Still, trying something was better than trying nothing at all. There was a certain psychological value in taking assertive steps, and certainly the tryptophane tablets couldn't hurt her.

Moving back out into the living room, Amy surveyed the old lumpy couch with a resigned eye, then went to a cupboard and pulled out a sheet and some blankets. She felt odd getting ready for bed knowing Jed was in the house. But thinking of him in her bed was odder still.

The fact that she and Jed had not become lovers was her own fault, of course. While she had made it clear from the beginning that she wanted only friendship, she had never found a way to explain that friendship was what she needed and about all she could handle at the moment. Dealing with her private anxieties took most of her energy.

Jed hadn't pushed. He never pushed. He took what was offered in the way of companionship and an occasional meal and then went home. Once or twice he had invited her out to dinner. He seemed content with their arrangement, but there had been times when she knew he felt quite differently. She was always very careful around him on such occasions.

This was the third trip he had made during the three months she had known him. He'd been gone a month this time, the longest stretch yet. The first trip had lasted seventeen days and the second had lasted three weeks. When it was all added up, Amy decided ruefully, she really hadn't had that much time with Jed Glaze. They were really still just getting to know each other, so in a way it made sense that her feelings were so confused.

He came and went with only the most casual of explanations. The first time he had told her he was leaving on a consulting assignment she had wished him a good trip and offered to drive him to the airport. He had declined the offer politely, and Amy had never again volunteered. She had understood that he didn't want even a tiny, niggling sense of obligation between them.

When he had reappeared on her doorstep seventeen days later with an old-fashioned bunch of flowers in his hand, she had seen the pent-up sexual need simmering in his eyes. It was as if whatever he had done on his trip had built up pressure and tension inside him that were seeking a channel for escape. Apparently, he had decided that channel was sex.

Amy had been happy to see him, but her womanly instincts had reacted skittishly to the barely restrained sensual demand she sensed in him. She had invited him to stay for dinner, wary of the outcome. She sensed he was a volcano waiting to explode. The sensible side of her nature warned her it would be better to send him home. She couldn't handle a lover, least of all a man like Jed Glaze.

But she hadn't sent him home. Instead, she had put a drink in his hand and a nourishing meal in his stomach and then held her breath. To her relief he hadn't pounced. The conversation had been light and easy, as it always was. He had told her the usual traveler's tales of airport delays and lost luggage and asked her polite questions about her writing. But the trapped heat had continued to blaze in his eyes.

Afterward Amy had put some of her favorite early rock artists on the stereo and dug out a checkerboard. She nearly dropped the records and she felt clumsy setting up the playing pieces of the game. She knew her awkwardness was a result of the tension in the room. Jed had glanced at her face and at the checkerboard. He seemed to sense her near panic and fear. Then he had walked into the kitchen to pour himself a glass of brandy. When he returned to the living room, Amy saw that his sexual tension was under control. She had been relieved, and strangely touched that he cared enough not to press her.

But what came as the greatest surprise was her realization that her own sensual awareness was so high. Amy knew that the unusual rush of excitement was a direct response to Jed's masculine need and it startled her. It was not like her to react so strongly to a man. But the situation had been defused by checkers, brandy, and the Shangri Las belting out the immortal "Leader of the Pack."

Or perhaps Jed had controlled himself because of something he had seen in her face. Whatever the reason, the volcano burning in him did not erupt that night. The evening settled back into a sedate pattern and Jed went home around ten after thanking her politely for dinner.

Amy had stood in the doorway watching him drive off in his battered pickup. As the truck had vanished around a curve she'd closed the door, realizing his consideration of her feelings had made them much closer. She felt herself very near to the brink of a precipice she wasn't sure she wanted to explore. What sane woman willingly descended into the heart of a volcano or attempted to ride the tiger?

The second time he had returned from an assignment Amy had seen evidence of the same sensual fire in him, but Jed had it firmly under wraps. After that first dangerous evening, he had always seemed in control of himself and placidly content with the friendly, undemanding companionship Amy offered.

But tonight, Amy knew, she and Jed had come to the edge of another potentially dangerous barrier. This was the first time Jedidiah Glaze had ever openly asked her for anything more than the most casual of favors. He had come home hurt, bruised and feverish, and had needed care and comfort.

He had tried to limit his demands to a simple request to be met at the airport, but they both knew he'd needed more help than that and she had provided it.

Amy crawled into her makeshift bed on the couch with an uneasy premonition that something fundamental had begun to alter her relationship with Jed. And she wasn't certain she was prepared to deal with the subtly shifting situation.

The thought of waking up trapped in a web she never intended to weave was enough to keep Amy awake for the next two hours. The truth of the matter was, she was already enmeshed in the sticky strands of another web, one that was ruining her peace of mind. She wasn't at all sure she could handle Jedidiah Glaze in addition to the trauma left over from eight months before.

Chapter Two

Jed awoke the next morning to the smell of hot coffee and what felt like the worst hangover of his life. He immediately decided to cut down on little white pills.

He opened his eyes and found himself looking at the ceiling of Amy's bedroom. It was, unfortunately, the first time he'd seen it from this position. He took a deep breath and caught the faint, lingering trace of Amy that still clung to the sheets and pillowcase. In spite of the groggy sensation left by the drugs, his body tightened with the beginnings of a familiar hardness. He should be getting accustomed to this tight, disturbing feeling. It happened a lot around Amy.

But even as he began to contemplate the possibility of luring Amy into the bedroom, his sore ribs made their presence known in no uncertain terms. His leg began to throb, too.

"Hell."

"Is that a general comment on your present physical condition or do you always wake up cursing the world?" Amy appeared in the doorway, a mug of coffee in her hand. Her hair was up in its usual loose knot and she was wearing an emerald green shirt and black and gray plaid trousers that were cut full at the hips and narrowed down to tiny cuffs. There was a red and brass belt threaded through the waistband loops. She looked, Jed decided, very cheerful, very alive and very much like home.

It came as a dull surprise to realize he'd never really thought of Caliph's Bay as home until Amy had arrived three months before. For the past couple of years, since he'd moved here from Los Angeles, the small coastal village had simply been the place he came back to when an assignment was over. Something in him needed the remote, isolated quality it offered.

Lately he'd grown accustomed to the idea of seeing Amy when he returned. But each time he'd come back to find Amy waiting, the sexual tension in him grew heavier and more demanding. Occasionally it irritated him that she seemed totally oblivious of that fact.

"My leg hurts. And my ribs."

"Don't look at me as though it's my fault. Want some more of your pills?"

He glared at her. "No, I do not want any more pills. I feel as if I'm just waking up from a week-long binge because of those damn pills."

"Have you ever actually been on a week-long binge?" she asked curiously.

There had been that time after he'd learned Andy had been killed, Jed thought.

But the numbness he'd achieved through the bottle hadn't lasted very long, unfortunately. Nowhere near a week. Only vengeance had offered a form of relief and another kind of numbness. "No, as a matter of fact, I haven't."

"I'm not surprised." She nodded as if what he'd said confirmed something she had already decided. "I can't see you losing control like that."

"Are you just going to tease me with that coffee or are you going to do the decent thing and give it to me?"

"My, you are surly in the mornings. Say please."

"Please may I have that mug of coffee before I scream?" He held out his hand expectantly.

"Lucky for you I'm in a charitable mood today." She thrust the mug into his large hand and watched as he took a long, satisfying swallow. Her flippant words didn't quite hide the shadowed concern in her eyes. Jed decided he liked the sympathy he saw in her near-green gaze. He wouldn't mind wallowing in it for a while.

"Thank you," Jed murmured after the first taste of the reviving coffee. "I may survive after all." He kept himself propped on one elbow, the mug cradled in his fist, and took another swallow.

"How do you feel?" Amy asked gently.

"As I said earlier, like hell."

"Succinct and to the point. Want some breakfast?"

He eyed her with faint amusement. "You *are* feeling charitable today, aren't you? I get to spend the night in your bed and now you're going to feed me breakfast. This is indeed the best of all possible worlds."

Her mouth tilted at the corners. "You're an easily satisfied man."

"A simple soul with simple tastes," he agreed, and made a gallant effort to sit up on the edge of the bed. "Ah. Success." He ignored the dull ache in his thigh. Across the room his gaze fell on an airy structure made of thin brass wire. Technically, it was a bird cage designed to look like a Baroque Italian villa. But Amy had filled the delicate, exotic bird house with a healthy looking plant instead of parakeets. Green leaves poked through the colonnade, thrust their way out of the dome and peeked through the elegantly vaulted windows and doorways.

Amy saw the direction of his gaze. "What do you think? I decided it made a great planter."

Jed felt an instant flare of anger. "You bought it."

"Of course I bought it. I love it."

"I told you not to buy it. I said I'd give it to you if you wanted it."

"And I explained I couldn't let you give me something that expensive," Amy reminded him patiently. "It's a work of art."

"It's a hobby," he told her flatly.

"You must have spent hours on it."

"That's what hobbies are for. Dammit, Amy, I can't believe you paid three hundred bucks for that thing."

"The gallery owner gave me a slight discount because she knew I was a friend of the artist."

"Oh, yeah? How much of a slight discount did Connie give you?" Jed challenged.

"Ten percent. If you ask me, you're letting those cages go too cheap. That's what I told Connie, too. I think you should be charging five hundred for the small cages like this one and seven-fifty or eight hundred for the large ones. Maybe more."

Jed heaved himself to his feet. "When I decide to get an agent, I'll consult you. In the meantime, no more sneaking around behind my back buying my bird cages without my permission, understand?"

Her eyes widened innocently. "The coffee doesn't seem to be doing much for your mood. I didn't realize you have this surly side to your nature."

"There are a lot of things you don't know about my nature, aren't there?" Jed asked darkly as he made his way painfully to the bathroom.

"Probably as many things as you don't know about mine." Amy vanished from the doorway, leaving the cool jibe hanging in the air behind her.

Jed groaned, wishing he had kept his mouth shut. He was not handling his first morning in Amy's home with the finesse, tact and diplomacy a woman had a right to expect. After all, he reminded himself grimly as he planted both hands on the old cracked washbasin and leaned forward to study the rough, dark stubble on his face, he wasn't her lover. He was a politely tolerated friend she could choose to kick out at any moment.

He didn't want to be kicked out. Not just yet. He wanted to maintain the fantasy of being home a little while longer.

Jed reached over and turned on the shower, aware that he was secretly pleased Amy had liked the Baroque bird cage enough to buy it. What didn't please him was that at one point he had offered to give her the cage and she politely refused. He had recognized the refusal for what it was, a deliberate effort to keep their relationship free of various bonds, obligations and entanglements. As a gift it was too much in her eyes. When it came to presents she preferred a bunch of brightly colored flowers now and then. At the time she had refused the cage he told himself he appreciated the gesture because it had reassured him he made the right decision when he had decided to get involved with Amelia Slater. She wanted exactly what he wanted out of an affair: casual companionship and good sex. But he never quite forgot the odd sensation of rejection he had experienced the day she declined his gift.

Nor had he ever gotten the good sex. The affair had never quite gelled. It seemed to have stalled at the friendship stage.

The first time he saw her she had been intently studying the cage in Caliph's Bay Gallery. Jed had stopped in to chat with Connie Erickson, the owner, and to deliver another cage. Connie treated him as she treated all the rather eccentric craftspeople and artists she represented, with a kind of affectionate tolerance. Jed encouraged her to do so. The image of himself as an eccentric craftsman worked well for him in Caliph's Bay, a town overrun by the type. It allowed him to fit in nicely. But then, finding protective covers was another of his odd assortment of talents.

He'd spotted Amy crouched in front of the Baroque piece, examining each minute architectural detail with obvious delight. It was clear she was enchanted and her pleasure had intrigued him. Since he designed and built the cage, Jed figured he had the perfect opening line.

She had responded to his overture. He was pleased to find out she lived in town and was not just a passing tourist. A day spent together in Carmel visiting art galleries had quickly followed. After that there had been a couple of dinners together and one or two afternoon walks on the beach. She had shown an interest in his bird cages and he had found the fact that she wrote science fiction and fantasy fascinating. She didn't look the type, he had told her.

"What does the type look like?" she'd countered.

"I don't know," he'd admitted.

"Well, if it's any consolation, you don't look the type to build beautiful bird cages."

"I'm an engineer," he'd explained. "For a while, when I was younger, I also wanted to be an architect. The cages are a hobby. I don't make my living with them."

"How do you make your living?"

"Engineering consulting work. My firm has several overseas projects. I travel a lot." The lies always came easily. He had been telling them for years.

"Do you like it?"

He had shrugged, a little surprised by the question. "I don't know. It's what I do."

Amy had nodded, as if understanding perfectly. She also seemed to understand that he had said all he intended to say about his job. Her tolerant acceptance of the limits he established intrigued him, although he had other lies ready if she ever asked more questions. She never had, and Jed was pleased. He shied away from the thought of telling Amy any more lies than absolutely necessary.

Lazily, feeling no need to rush the affair and determined not to jeopardize the light, undemanding aspects of the relationship, Jed had set out to seduce Amy. But he had quickly discovered that moving beyond casual friendship wasn't going to be that easy. He soon learned there was something jumpy, almost frightened about Amy. She used the pose of friend almost like a shield to protect herself.

He was working on the problem when he had gotten the first assignment he had received since meeting her. As usual, there was very little time to say good-bye. Jed hadn't been certain what to expect from her when he told her he was leaving the country so suddenly, but he had been reassured by her obvious lack of concern. She had even offered to drive him to the airport, but he'd refused for the same reasons she refused to take the bird cage.

He hadn't been feeling as casual two weeks later when he returned. He had begun thinking of Amy on the plane and by the time he landed in Monterey he'd been craving her. It was not unusual to want a woman after an assignment, but it was new for him to want a particular woman as badly as he had wanted Amy. Knowing the need for sexual release was riding him far too hard, he had decided to make himself wait a couple of days before getting in touch with Amy. His resolution had lasted about twelve hours. He was on her doorstep the evening after he'd returned.

He learned his lesson that night. When he got home the second time he had forced himself firmly under control before casually stopping by to say hello. Her wariness was both frustrating and inexplicable, but he couldn't bear the thought of frightening her or causing her pain.

For a while he had wondered if she was simply the kind of woman who worried excessively about her reputation. Caliph's Bay was a small town, granted, but it was hardly straitlaced. It was a haven for struggling artists, writers and assorted craftspeople, not exactly the sort of community where people worried very much about what others thought. And Amy was definitely too much of an independent spirit to run her life any way but her own. After a short period of consideration, Jed scratched the theory that she was too conservative to engage in an affair.

He had gone on to Theory Number Two, which was that she might be gay. But he scrapped that notion when he remembered the deep, feminine awareness in her eyes the first time she had seen his clawing desire. All his instincts told him she was a woman who could respond to the right man. That had led to Theory Number Three: He might not be the right man. That thought had not done much for his ego.

It hadn't been easy psyching himself down to something resembling casual friendliness when he had returned from that second assignment. The fierce need for her had begun eating at him as soon as he had boarded the plane back to the States. He'd thought about stopping off in L.A. and looking up an old acquaintance who might be willing to drain some of his tension. But he had sensed that wouldn't work; another woman wasn't the answer.

He thought he'd done a pretty fair job of covering up the desire he felt that second time, but he knew she had seen the traces of sexual heat in him. Once again she treated the flames with wine and food and casual, undemanding conversation. He left the house to the strains of the Beach Boys' "Surfin' Safari." Amy's protective wall of friendship was stronger than ever. But Jed knew that his resistance to the idea of crashing through it was weakening rapidly.

Then had come this last fiasco of an assignment. Jed clenched his teeth as he stepped into the shower and concentrated on his leg. He was going to have to change the bandage when he got out. Best to keep Amy out of the room while he did it. He looked down and grimaced. Christ, that bullet had been close. A little higher and he wouldn't have had to worry about trying to seduce Amy.

Out in the kitchen Amy heard the shower go off and waited expectantly for the sound of the bathroom door opening. She didn't want to put the oatmeal on the stove until Jed was almost ready to eat. The phone rang just as she was measuring water into the pan. This time when she picked up the receiver, her intuition was accurate. Even if she hadn't guessed who would be on the line the distant static was a good clue. Private telephone service had come to Orleana Island's little corner of the Pacific about fifteen years before, but it hadn't yet reached the level of quality one expected in the States.

"Hello, Dad. Are you and Mom finished packing yet?"

"Your mother has that end of things under control, as usual." Douglas Slater's deep, hearty voice was not dimmed

one bit by the telephone line. His was a voice that had dominated the boardroom and presidential suite of Slater Aero,
Inc. for years. It held the essence of a still vigorous man
who was facing his sixties with the same determination that
he'd used to build and hold together his successful aerospace
manufacturing firm.

"I'm not surprised." Amy half smiled at the thought of her
mother's exceptional organizational talents. Gloria Slater
had brought the task of being the perfect corporate executive's wife to the level of a fine art. If she'd been born a little
later, she probably would have been an executive herself,
not the wife of one.

"Let's see, you two leave for London on the fifteenth,
right? That's next week. You must be swamped trying to get
ready." It was a desperate bid to avoid the unavoidable. Amy
wasn't at all surprised when it failed. Douglas Slater was too
shrewd to let her off the hook that easily.

"Plenty of time. Listen, honey, we've got a great idea,"
Slater announced. His tone was still jovial, but it held an
underlying insistent edge. "Your mom and I have decided
that what you need is a vacation. Come to the island this
week. You can help Gloria finish the packing, do a little
diving, eat a few home cooked meals and relax. On the
fifteenth you can see us off on the plane. Then you can stay
as long as you like at the house. Plan on a month."

"Dad, I'm really busy at the moment—"

"You need some time off, Amy," her father interrupted
firmly. "Don't you think I know the signs? Hell, I saw them
often enough in the people who worked for me over the
years. For the past few months you've been getting more
and more concerned about your writing. Too concerned. It's
obvious you're starting to feel the stress. You haven't come

to see us for over eight months. You know how you love this place. I'm worried about you. When I was running Slater Aero I saw more than one good man burn himself out just as he started to taste a little success. Selling that science fiction series last year put some real pressure on you. I'll bet you've been spending the past few months worrying about whether you'll be able to do the same thing again this year, haven't you? I've got news for you, honey: If you don't learn to relax again, you won't be able to keep up the pace."

"Dad, it's not a question of relaxing." Amy leaned back against the kitchen counter, absently massaging her temples as she tried to marshal her arguments. But even as she made the effort, she felt herself weakening. Sooner or later she would have to go back to the island. She couldn't put it off forever. "I'm right in the middle of a book and I wanted to get it finished before I took some time off."

"It would mean a lot to both your mother and me if you could manage a few days with us before we leave for London, Amy."

Amy groaned. "Come on, Dad. Mother might resort to this approach, but I always thought you were above using the old guilt trip routine."

"I'm desperate."

"You must be." There was a small sound to Amy's left. She glanced up and saw Jed leaning in the kitchen doorway, buttoning his shirt while he listened with unabashed interest. "Look, I'll think about it, okay? I'll see what I can do about my schedule."

"Call me tomorrow and let me know what you decide," Slater said bluntly. "I'll tell your mother you're thinking about it. She'll be thrilled. I'll take care of the tickets."

"Dad—"

"Listen, don't try to tell me you don't want to come to the island because of the accident. LePage was a fool and he paid the price. It was a tragic event, yes, but there's absolutely no reason to let it upset you forever. Accidents happen."

Amy froze. "I know that. It's got nothing to do with what happened to Bob. It's just that I—"

"Good. He was a nice enough guy and the whole thing was very unfortunate, but you shouldn't let it get to you. And I know you weren't in love with him so it's not as if you're pining, right? Come and see us, honey."

"Dad—"

It was too late. Douglas Slater had already hung up the phone. Amy tossed her receiver back into the cradle, crossed her arms under her breasts and glared at Jed.

"Hey, I'm innocent," he said, holding up a protesting hand. "I'm just hanging around for breakfast."

Amy smiled ruefully and turned back to the stove. "Sorry. That was my father. He's accustomed to having people do as he wants. Right now he wants me to go visit him and Mom before they leave for Europe."

"And you don't want to go?"

Amy became very busy with the oatmeal. "I don't really want to go to the island."

"The island?"

"My father's retired. For years he's maintained a second home on a little dot of an island a few hundred miles beyond Hawaii. We used to go there for every vacation when I was a kid. Now that he's no longer going into the office every day, he and Mom spend most of the year there. Mom paints and Dad's writing a book on management."

"Why don't you want to visit them?"

Amy shrugged. "No good reason, I guess. It's just that I'm right in the middle of *Private Demons* and I was hoping to finish it soon. I hate to take time off in the middle of a book. Dad says he's worried about me. But that's nothing new. He's always worried about me."

"Yeah? Why?" Jed eased himself down onto a stool and hooked the cane over the edge of the counter. He studied Amy with deep interest as she added a handful of raisins to the cereal.

"Probably because I'm the youngest. And probably because I'm classified as the black sheep of the family. You have to understand that my older sister is a board certified gynecologist, one of my brothers has taken over the running of my father's firm and is making Slater Aero even more profitable than it has been in the past, and my other brother is a successful attorney who's about to enter politics in a big way here in California. I, on the other hand, am twenty-seven years old and have spent half my adult life waiting tables and taking night classes in everything from surrealist painting to an intensive, in-depth study of the hard evidence for flying saucers."

"I get the picture," Jed said dryly. "You're not maintaining the family standards. But now you've actually sold a book. A three-part series, in fact, and you're writing another book. Doesn't that count?"

"Dad thinks I'm going to burn out on my first taste of success. Not that I'm likely to go too crazy on the microscopic advance I got for the *Shadow* series. And the advance on *Private Demons* wasn't much better, believe me."

"He thinks you're working too hard?"

"I guess." She finished stirring the oatmeal and ladled it

into two bowls. "He should talk after the way he battled to push Slater Aero to the top years ago."

"How long since you've been back to the island?"

"A little over eight months." She concentrated on taking the milk out of the refrigerator and setting it down on the counter, aware of the nervous tension that sometimes made her remarkably clumsy these days. With a little self-discipline she could control it, she knew. But when she safely set the milk down on the counter top in front of Jed, he only frowned at it.

"I usually just have coffee and a doughnut in the morning."

"Well, I usually have oatmeal and grapefruit," she declared stoutly. "Just another little item to add to our storehouse of knowledge about each other's habits and eccentricities."

"I haven't had oatmeal since I was a kid." He examined the bowl of gray cereal distrustfully.

"Throw a little brown sugar on it and it will go down as easily as a doughnut. Trust me. Besides, it's good for you. You need to regain your strength." Amy handed him the sugar bowl, plunked down the twin halves of a grapefruit she had prepared earlier and slid onto a stool beside him.

"So who's Bob?" Jed asked casually as he dug into the grapefruit.

Amy blinked. The grapefruit spoon trembled slightly in her hand. "No one important. Just a man I was seeing casually the last time I went to the island. I invited him to go with me."

"You still seeing him?" Jed appeared only vaguely interested.

"No." She hesitated painfully. "There was an accident."

"What kind of accident?"

"A diving accident. Bob was killed diving in some caves near my family's home. He didn't like the fact that my father had put the caves off limits to all visitors as well as the family. He went down on his own one night. I was the one who found his body in the cave entrance pool the next day."

"Jesus."

"Yes. It was a shock, to say the least." She carefully spooned up a piece of her grapefruit. "My father owns the land where the underwater caves are located. He's never allowed any diving in them. He doesn't even like members of the family showing the entrance to our guests. I doubt if many of the people in Orleana's one town even know where it is. If they do, they've always respected my father's wish to keep tourists away from the caves. Dad thinks its better if people don't know where they are. Some dumb tourist might be tempted to dive. Cave diving is very hazardous."

"I know. I've done a little."

She looked up in surprise. "Have you?"

"It's been a while. Not my idea of a fun hobby."

"No. I don't think it would be."

"Amy, I can imagine what it was like for you finding the guy's body. . ."

Amy managed a shrug. "It's been eight months. It all seems like a dream now." *A nightmare.*

"Were you in love with the guy? Was he more than just a casual friend?"

"Bob LePage was not my lover," she replied stonily. "He was an acquaintance with whom I had something in common: Diving. That's all."

"All right, calm down. I didn't mean to get too personal." He reached for more sugar and groaned. When Amy glanced at him in alarm he said, "I feel like I've been used for a football."

Amy seized the opportunity to change the topic. "Speaking of your diminished capacity..."

Jed winced. "I can think of better ways to describe my current condition."

"I'm a writer. I value accuracy. What I was about to say is that I think you should stop by Dr. Mullaney's office this morning and have him take a look at that leg."

"The leg's okay. The company doctor got all the glass out and told me how to take care of it. I changed the dressing after my shower this morning. It's almost healed. A few more days and I can stop wearing a bandage."

"I still think you should have Mullaney look at it," Amy said stubbornly.

He turned his head to look at her. "You're a bossy little thing, you know that?" he asked almost indulgently. "I'm only just beginning to realize it."

Amy flushed and speared her spoon back into the grapefruit. "Sorry. Your leg is your own business."

"I agree."

"I may be bossy, but there's a real streak of stubborn macho arrogance in you, you know that?"

Jed grinned, one of his quick, fleeting smiles that temporarily ruined the Calvinist minister image. "I've lived alone for so long I've never really learned to handle a woman's nagging."

"I've never believed it was too late to teach an old dog new tricks."

"Your faith in my adaptability and intelligence humbles me. Actually, I don't think you're nagging, exactly. More like fussing."

"I'll call Mullaney's office after breakfast and make an appointment."

"You do that and you can damn well keep the appointment yourself."

Amy sighed. "Jed, be reasonable. You were ill last night. You had a fever. Who knows what kind of infection you might have picked up in the Middle East?"

"I overdid things yesterday, that's all," Jed stated in a reasonable tone. "The doctors told me it was too soon to head back to the States, but I insisted. I got a little worn out and ran a slight fever. Nothing serious. I'm fine this morning."

"I hadn't realized what an incredibly bullheaded man you are."

"You never see a person's worst flaws until you've lived with him or her," Jed explained philosophically. "Until this morning, for example, I had no idea you squeezed your toothpaste from the middle of the tube instead of from the bottom."

Amy surrendered. "All right, all right, I give up. It's none of my business whether you see the doctor. And don't feel obliged to force yourself to eat the oatmeal. You can pick up a bag of doughnuts on the way back to your place."

Jed looked startled. "Kicking me out just because I resist a little of your advice, Nurse Amy?"

She smiled wryly. "Let's face it. Neither one of us is used to having a live-in mate. In a few more hours we'll probably be peeling long, painful strips off each other. Best to part while we're still on speaking terms." She hesitated, and then added impulsively, "You can come over for dinner this evening if you like."

"You've got a deal."

She saw the flickering trace of heat in his eyes and knew that this time it wasn't caused by fever. Some of the familiar, high-strung excitement she had learned to expect around Jed when he looked at her like that erupted in her bloodstream. The man did things to her senses she still couldn't quite understand.

The problem was that they hadn't spent enough time together, Amy rationalized. Jed's frequent, extended trips had chopped up the relationship so much that each time he returned she felt as if they were meeting for the first time again. The primitive, very feminine uncertainty and wariness always returned in full force each time she saw him after one of his business journeys. But so did the compelling, indescribable attraction. Telling herself that this wasn't really the kind of man to whom she should feel physically attracted didn't help.

Amy drove Jed back to his small, weathered house after breakfast. She watched a bit anxiously as he fumbled with the keys, flight bag and cane. Leaning against the car and having every intention of keeping her mouth shut, she heard herself ask, "Do you think you should spend tonight alone?"

He glanced at her quickly and then focused on the front door. "I wasn't going to spend it alone. I'm having dinner at your place, remember?" He hauled himself up the steps and shoved the key into the lock.

"I meant after dinner," Amy said stolidly. "I'm worried your fever might return."

"I can't throw you out of your bed two nights in a row, Amy." He pushed open the door and limped into the plainly furnished front room. "Come on in and I'll make you a cup of coffee. It's the least I can do after all the hospitality you've shown me."

Amy trailed after him, glancing around the familiar interior. Jed's house was the same ancient vintage as her own and the furniture had a similar seaside Salvation Army look. But Jed's home looked unlived in to Amy. There were no pictures on the walls, no plants, no cat.

The only intriguing elements were the two bird cages that stood empty on one shelf. One was a fanciful Victorian design with looping gingerbread trim and a flight of wire steps. The other was another Baroque piece, this one, according to Jed, in the French style. Both cages were charming, but a little lifeless without either birds or plants to fill them. They looked as barren as his house.

By the time Amy had finished her coffee she sensed things between herself and Jed had returned to their familiar, careful equilibrium. She knew that she, for one, would chew a hole in her tongue before she nagged him about seeing Dr. Mullaney again. To be accused of nagging when she had always taken such pains to keep her distance annoyed her.

On the way home Amy stopped at the small grocery store in Caliph's Bay, where she lucked out and found a supply of fresh clams and shrimp. Adding a sack of rice and some chorizo sausage to the rickety cart she was pushing, she mentally ticked off the items she needed to complete the paella. She still had a packet of saffron left from the last time she had prepared the dish for Jed. He had a weakness for it, she'd learned.

On the way out to the car she eyed the health food store across the street and wondered if she could get her money back on the tryptophane. Probably not. Besides, in all honesty, she couldn't swear it hadn't worked. She had slept a little better than usual last night, even if she had found herself glancing at the clock on the wall every few hours. In contrast, the herbal tea she'd been using the week before hadn't helped a bit. She decided she would give the tryptophane another try before making up her mind about its effectiveness.

Working out a logistics problem in chapter ten of *Private Demons* kept Amy busy for the rest of the afternoon. By the time she switched off the word processor for the day she was reasonably satisfied with her solution to the heroine's dilemma. The nightmare Amy had created in the book had substance, but there was a way to contain it.

A good therapist, Amy knew, would undoubtedly figure out right away that she was using the novel to try and work through the things she couldn't seem to work through in her head. Nightmares could be handled in a book such as *Private Demons*; real life was proving to be another matter.

She had finished scrubbing clams and shelling shrimp and was opening a bottle of Chardonnay when Jed's familiar knock sounded on the door. A small frisson of anticipation trickled through her nerves. Wiping her hands on the red kitchen towel, Amy went to answer the door, not quite certain what to expect from Jed.

She opened the door, took one glance at the weary way he was leaning on the cane, and knew that Jed Glaze wasn't going to be launching any assaults on her that evening. A sense of relief went through Amy. She firmly ignored the equally disturbing sense of disappointment she felt.

"You look like warmed over oatmeal," Amy declared as he moved slowly over the threshold.

"That's a fairly accurate description of how I feel. I hate to admit this, but I took your advice and went to Mullaney's this afternoon. Don't gloat. I can't take gloating just now."

"I'm not gloating, I'm relieved. What did he say?" She

closed the door and watched with concern as Jed lowered himself carefully into one of the deep, badly sprung armchairs.

"He said," Jed announced, "that everything's healing okay, but that I'm pushing myself too fast. I need," he shot a grim look at Amy's questioning face, "tender loving care. Rest. Good food. Someone to keep an eye on me for a few days. Someone, in short, to fuss over me. Did you by any chance phone Mullaney and prompt him?"

"Not me. I swore off fussing at eleven this morning. I decided I lack experience and skill in that art. But I'll admit I'm glad you had Mullaney look at the leg. I've got some very nice, very expensive painkiller here." Amy walked back into the kitchen to pick up the bottle of Chardonnay. "Want some?"

"An excellent idea. I'll use it instead of pills this evening." He leaned back in the chair as she poured the wine. When she returned to the living room he accepted the glass with obvious gratitude. Then he said baldly, "I figure I could take the couch tonight."

Amy raised her eyebrows. "You're serious? You want to spend another night here?"

Jed contemplated the wine in his glass. "I think Mullaney's a little nervous about that fever I had last night. He wants me to have someone within yelling distance in case it comes back tonight."

Amy smiled. "What am I supposed to do for you if you yell?"

"Feed me some pills he gave me." Jed touched the side pocket of his slacks. "Just what I need. More pills. I'm sorry to impose, Amy. If you'd rather I didn't stay another night, just say so. I'll be fine on my own."

"I've already told you, you're welcome to stay another night," she said softly. "And you can have the bed."

"Couch."

"You won't fit on the couch. Don't argue with me, Jed. This is my house, remember?"

"And you're bossy by nature."

"Think you can stand another night of my nagging?"

He grinned. "I brought some earplugs."

Several hours later Jed wished he hadn't been joking about the earplugs. The scream that woke him was the kind that taught a man the meaning of cold chills down the spine.

He rose from the bed in an instinctive movement that sent a shaft of pain through his ribs. Then he was through the bedroom door and into the living room, prepared for anything from an intruder to a manifestation of one of the creative horrors that abounded in Amy's books.

What he found was Amy huddled on her knees on the couch, her arms wrapped protectively around herself as she stared blindly at the red glow of the dying fire. Her fading scream was still echoing eerily in the room.

Chapter Three

*S*he knew she was drowning; she also knew she couldn't be drowning because she could still breathe. Air flowed into her lungs on command. How much more proof did she need? She longed to claw her way back to fresh air, but that was impossible. There was something important that had to be done first. So she continued to swim forward into the darkness, clutching her unwieldy burden.

The dark walls of the watery grave closed in around her, threatening to trap her forever. The water seemed to thicken and grow opaque, defying the frail beam of her light. Evidence of an old underwater slide of gravel and mud flashed into view as she swam past the hideously black entrance of a tunnel. It would be all too easy to touch off another such slide, one that would seal the passage through which she was swimming. Then she would never get back out. She would be trapped forever with the body and the locked box.

Trapped forever in an endless underwater labyrinth . . .

Amy awoke with the scream fading on her lips, jerking to her knees in an instinctive effort to rise to the surface of the flooded cave. She fought desperately to free herself of the burden that threatened to drag her down to the depths, but she knew she couldn't let go of the box.

Even as her mind latched onto reality she was aware of Jed appearing in the doorway. For an instant she couldn't speak. The effort to separate the dream from reality was too demanding. It took every ounce of her strength. But she was getting good at that part, even if she wasn't having much success stopping the dreams themselves. The tense silence didn't last long.

"Amy?" His voice was rough with concern.

"I'm sorry, Jed." She barely heard her own voice. It was just a thin whisper of sound. She shook her head, trying to inject some energy into her words. "A bad dream. An occupational hazard of writing science fiction and fantasy." Amy managed a weak smile as she turned to glance at him.

He looked very large and reassuring standing there in the shadows. He hadn't taken time to grab his cane and he was bracing himself with one large, strong hand on the doorframe. In the dim light she could see the speculative, assessing quality of his expression. There was a primitive, vibrating alertness in him that some part of her identified instinctively: Jed had appeared in the doorway ready to do battle.

Even as she watched, Jed seemed to quietly sink back into himself. It was as though he turned a key somewhere inside that switched off the battle-ready tension. Slowly he moved toward her, walking a little awkwardly without the cane.

"That's quite a mouth you've got, lady." As he neared the couch, the glow from the hearth briefly caught and highlighted the wry amusement in his eyes. "Must have been some dream."

Amy huddled on the couch, drawing her knees up under the flannel nightgown and wrapping her arms around them. "It was."

"Want to talk about it?"

She shook her head. "No, I just want to forget it."

He nodded understandingly as he sat down beside her. His

weight put a large dent in the cushions. "I know what you mean. Better to let that kind of thing fade. Talking about it only makes it worse, somehow. More real."

Maybe he was right, Amy thought fleetingly. Maybe talking about it would make it worse. She wondered how he knew that. She'd been thinking lately that talking might help, but that was probably because she knew she couldn't talk about it. Perhaps she would just go silently crazy.

"I'm sorry I disturbed you, Jed. Did you hurt your leg?"

"No." He settled one heavy arm around her shoulders and pulled her close. "The leg will survive. It's you I'm worried about. You feel like you've got steel wire running through you. All stiff and tense."

"It takes a while to come down off a nightmare." So far it had taken eight months and she was showing no signs of improvement. The thought of living with this tension for the rest of her life was appalling. Surely it would begin to fade someday.

"Do you have a lot of them?"

"Nightmares?"

"Yeah."

Her head came up. "I'm a restless sleeper. I've told you that. Me and about thirty million other Americans. I have problems with insomnia and sometimes I get these dreams. It's no big deal. I'm sorry I alarmed you."

He patted her shoulder in an absently reassuring manner. "Don't worry about it."

Something about the casual way he said that made Amy ask recklessly, "Why? Have you been awakened by worse?"

He went still for an instant and then tipped up her chin so he could look directly into her eyes. "There isn't anything worse than a woman's scream in the middle of the night. Are you sure you're okay, Amy?"

She nodded uncertainly. She was vividly aware of his warmth and strength as he held her close.

He released her chin but kept his arm around her shoulders. For a while they just sat silently on the couch. Amy's breathing slowed to a more reasonable rate as she quietly absorbed the reassurance and comfort Jed willingly offered. When she felt the world had returned more or less to normal, she tried to ease away from him. "Thanks, Jed. I'm fine now, really I am. There's no sense in you losing any more sleep. Go back to bed."

"And leave you out here alone?"

"I'm used to being alone at night, remember?"

"Maybe that's part of your problem," he murmured. He shifted, turning toward her on the couch. Sliding both palms around her throat and using his thumbs under her jaw he carefully held her still. His fingers moved on the nape of her neck with subtle, massaging pressure.

She saw the kindling heat in his eyes and a new kind of tension coiled within her. Amy knew his look for what it was, and she wasn't at all sure she wanted to deal with it now. "You're used to being alone, too," she pointed out softly.

"So maybe we've both got a problem." He lowered his head and brushed his mouth lightly against hers as if he were testing the waters.

Amy stiffened in spite of herself. Water was a bad mental image under the circumstances. Jed felt her immediate withdrawal.

"Hey, calm down," he whispered. He cradled her head in

one big hand and pushed her face gently against his bare chest. "It's just me."

"But I hardly know you," she heard herself say bleakly, wondering why she had said the words aloud. They sounded silly, considering the relationship that existed between her and Jed. He wasn't the kind of man she wanted back when she was looking for a good, gentle, kind man to love. She wanted a man who had sunlight, not shadow inside; a man who wanted a wife and a mother for his children as well as a lover. And now she had Jed, a man who was still nearly a stranger to her after three months. Six months from now he would still be a stranger. He was a man who was as silent about himself as she was about herself. Perhaps they deserved each other.

"Hush, Amy. You know me. I'm your friend, remember? You're still replaying the nightmare in your mind, aren't you? Stop thinking about it. It's the only way to handle it." He kept her face pressed into the warmth of his chest while his other hand stroked her shoulder.

Amy shivered slightly in nervous reaction to his touch. He was right. She had to stop thinking about it or she really would go crazy. Deliberately she made herself concentrate on the warmth emanating from Jed's strong body.

It wasn't accurate to say he was a stranger because there were so many things she did know about him. His scent, for instance. She inhaled deeply. She would know this scent in her mind until her dying day. The essence of him was unique, very male, captivating and even comforting. There was honest sweat, clean soap and musky sensuality all mixed together. Amy relaxed and leaned against him.

"Much better," Jed said in a voice made lazy with the

beginnings of desire. "Stop chasing around in circles in your head and let me hold you for a while."

"Your leg—"

"Feels wonderful."

"Your ribs—"

"Have never felt better."

Amy choked on a muffled exclamation that was almost a shaky laugh. "I'll bet."

"Believe me," he said, "I know what I'm doing."

He eased her down onto the tumbled sheets and blankets that Amy had used to make the couch into a bed. She looked up at him, her amusement gone as she felt the rising heat in him. He settled himself alongside her, his injured leg lightly touching her leg. There was a tautness in him now that told its own ancient story.

"Why do you always look at me like that when you know I want to touch you?" Jed asked, letting his hand rest on the first button of her flannel gown. The gesture was unthreatening but almost excruciatingly intimate.

"How do I look at you?" Her bewilderment was plain in her eyes. He felt very big lying next to her like this. His shoulders blocked out the sight of the coals in the hearth.

He shrugged one broad shoulder. "I'm not sure how to explain it. It's as if you're a little afraid of me."

"I'm not afraid of you."

"Wary, then. Cautious. Uncertain. Hell, I don't know. It's just something I see in your eyes when I get too close. Hiding a lover from me? Afraid I'll find out you've got something going on the side when I'm out of town?"

"Would it bother you if I did?"

He leaned down to nip half playfully at the curve of her

throat. When he raised his head again his eyes were unreadable. "It wouldn't be any of my business, would it?"

"No."

He groaned and undid the buttons of the flannel gown. Amy drew in her breath as his hand moved under the fabric. His fingers found the tip of her breast. "It wouldn't be any of my business, but it would drive me out of my mind."

"Jed?" Amy caught his face between her palms, trying to read his expression in the shadows.

He gave her a strange half smile. "I realized that when I called you from L.A. I thought, what if she's not alone tonight? What if she's with someone else?"

"Started worrying about who would pick you up at the airport?" she demanded, her nervous attempt at humor making her voice a little uneven. She was violently aware of the warmth of his palm as it rested over her small breast.

"There's a sadistic teasing streak in you, Amy Slater." His hazel eyes gleamed with a fresh surge of desire as his mouth closed over hers.

Amy felt the touch of his tongue along the edge of her lower lip. His desire was still under control. If she asked him to stop, he would undoubtedly do so. Now was the time to call a halt if she intended to keep the relationship confined to a safe, undemanding friendship.

But his strength was already enveloping her, promising safety and excitement and perhaps a means of release for some of the lingering tension induced by the nightmare. Amy sighed and put both arms around his neck. She closed her eyes and for the first time in the three months she had known him, began to let herself respond to the driving need she sensed in Jed.

The flame of desire she had grown accustomed to seeing

in his eyes when Jed returned from a trip was burning as brightly as ever tonight. It hadn't disappeared. It had only been held in abeyance for a while because of his injuries and the medication.

Excitement flowed through her as her body reacted to Jed's powerful urgency. She clung to him more tightly, grateful for the way the hot emotion pushed aside the tattered remnants of the nightmare. He used his rough, blunt fingertips to gently draw forth one nipple.

"You may be a little cautious at first, but I think that when you give yourself, it will be completely. My God, you don't know how much I've wanted to find out how completely." With a quick, impatient movement he pulled the flannel gown down to her waist and then swept it to her ankles. It fell in a silent heap to the floor. Jed levered himself high enough off the couch to start removing his briefs. Freed of the confinement, his fully aroused male shaft jutted outward, pressing insistently against Amy's thigh.

He was big, Amy thought wonderingly. She should have guessed that this part of him would match the rest of him. Large, solid, blunt and powerful. She suddenly felt very small and vulnerable.

Then she saw the small wince of discomfort that crossed Jed's face as he shoved the underwear down over his bandaged leg, and she reached out to touch him gently. "It does hurt, doesn't it?"

"Not nearly as much as the part of me that needs you. I've been hurting for you for a long time, Amy Slater." He pulled her back into his arms, crushing her breasts against his chest. "Christ, I've needed this. I don't think I even realized just how much until tonight."

He ran one hand down her spine, stopping long enough at

her hips to push her lower body closer to his. Amy was instantly aware of his vibrant hardness. Her leg became trapped between his muscular thighs as Jed continued to explore the full curve of her buttocks.

"So soft and sweet and sexy," he murmured wonderingly. "I don't know how I waited this long."

Jed's mouth moved back to Amy's, this time deepening the kiss until she was moaning softly and opening her lips to invite him inside. His tongue slid intimately into her with a rush, and the sizzling tension in Jed was communicated to Amy. She reacted to it almost fiercely, wanting to ease the pressure that was driving him as much as she wanted to find her own release. She held him more tightly, engaging him in a tiny duel that had no winner or loser, but only served to heighten their sensual awareness of each other. He tasted good, she thought. Hot and demanding and exciting.

"Amy, Amy, you don't know what it's been like . . ." The words faded beneath a stifled groan as Jed slid his probing fingers into the shadowed cleft of her soft bottom.

Amy shivered at the unfamiliar caress, automatically pulling slightly away. His hand tightened on her and she felt the hardness of him stir demandingly against her thigh. She sensed instinctively that Jed was becoming desperate for her. It was as if all the self-control he had exerted over the past three months had disintegrated, leaving him at the mercy of his own raging desire. His fingers moved lower, testing the damp warmth that was beginning to form between her legs.

"I knew you'd respond to me." His voice was thick with triumphant satisfaction. "I knew it. You're getting damp and hot already."

"Jed," she breathed, twisting herself against his hand as desire swept through her. She touched his shoulder, splaying her fingertips across his strong muscles, and then she felt one of his large, blunt fingers part her and sink into her. Instantly her body reacted, all the tiny muscles contracting rapidly. She closed her eyes and clung to him.

"You're so tight. Small and tight and strong. I'm going to lose my mind." Slowly he stroked his finger back out of her and when she cried out and pressed her face into his chest, he gave a satisfied, husky moan. Then he boldly used her own dampness to gently lubricate the tiny nub of desire that was hidden in the triangle of her soft, curling, golden brown hair.

"I'm the one who's going to go out of my mind," Amy whispered.

"Good." He used his teeth on her earlobe.

Amy pressed her lips to his flat male nipple, eager for the taste of him. Her lower body knotted with warmth and an aching, empty sensation. She worked her hand down between their bodies, seeking the heavy shaft that waited there. When she found it, her fingers closed around it in a gentle caress that brought a groan from somewhere deep in Jed's chest.

"Now, Amy. I know I'm rushing this. I should wait a little longer, give you more time. But so help me, I can't wait. I have to have you now."

Jed moved then, pushing her thighs apart with his hands until she lay open and ready. Amy looked up at him as he loomed over her and she saw the volcano in his eyes. His face was set in passion-stark lines. In that moment she wanted only to grant him the release he sought.

"Come to me, Jed. There's no one else for me. No one when you're away. You know that, don't you?" She lifted herself, inviting him into her warmth.

He came to her then. Amy felt the scrape of his bandaged leg against the softness of her inner thigh. The wide, solid tip of his manhood was a throbbing pressure that her body resisted at first. For a moment there was an aching, almost painful tightness that made Amy breathe more quickly. He was so big and she had never known anyone like him.

"Hold me, Amy. Take me inside and hold me. I need it. God knows, I need it." He flexed his hips powerfully, forging completely into her in one long, smooth movement.

Amy exhaled on a little whimper of excitement and feminine uncertainty. Her tautly stretched body was caught between the promise of pain and the promise of pleasure. And then she felt herself adjust slowly to the invasion. She realized that Jed was straining to hold himself still, exerting all his control to give her time to accept him.

"I should have waited," he said roughly. "I should have given you a little longer. I told myself I wasn't going to rush you."

"Hush." She touched his hard mouth with her fingertips to quiet him. "You're not rushing me. This is exactly what I want. I want you."

"Amy." He bent his head and took her mouth, entering her with his tongue just as he had entered her with his manhood. Slowly he began to move both within her, using the exciting friction to generate more of her feminine dampness. Her body responded at once. Amy sank her nails into Jed's shoulders and lifted herself to meet his increasingly fierce thrusts. The bright passion caught them both up in its blaze, flaring high and heralding even greater fulfillment. Streams of energy flowed together into a quick, roaring fire that preceded the explosion of the volcano. Amy forgot about every-

thing else in the world except the aching need that was about to be satisfied.

Jed's harsh, muffled shout was accompanied by a last, deep plunge into Amy's tight, moist sheath. Hot lava flowed. She clung more tightly, poised on a brink and aware of the taut, spiraling response of her own body. And then the sweet spasms rippled through her, over her, around her. Amy's soft cries chased Jed's panting echoes as she followed him into the temporary exhaustion of the sensual aftermath.

Silence and peace filled the room. It was the first real peace Amy had known for eight months. She knew it wouldn't last, but the respite was sweet and she savored it.

It was a long time before Jed could bring himself to move. If it hadn't been for the dull ache that started again in his ribs, he decided, he probably wouldn't have moved until morning. He liked his present position, liked having his head pillowed on Amy's soft, delicate breasts, liked the lingering dampness between her legs that deepened the sense of intimacy between them and her feminine, sensual aroma. And he liked the contentment in her body.

Her intense response to him filled him with a purely masculine combination of wonder and satisfaction. Later, he promised himself, he would give her the slow, lingering pleasure he had intended to give her their first time together. Later he would take his time. But tonight his need had overtaken him with little warning. When Amy had put up no resistance, indeed, had welcomed him, there had been nothing to stop him. Jed had taken from her what he'd been wanting to take for the past three months.

His head was already full of the things he would do to her, the things he would teach her in the future. Her startled, uncertain response to the way he had touched the sensitive valley between her curving buttocks told him that she was not a very experienced woman. But then, he had guessed that the moment he met her. Her throbbing tightness told him that it had been a long while since she had been with a man. That didn't surprise him, either. She was the kind of woman who would always be cautious about risking an affair. She had too much to give and, therefore, too much to lose.

"Jed?" Her voice was sleepy.

"Sorry. My ribs are bothering me a little."

She stirred beneath him, concern replacing the relaxation on her face. "Maybe you should take one of your pills." She touched his forehead. "You don't feel feverish."

"I'm fine." He smiled. "You took care of the fever that was bothering me tonight. What about you? Anything left of the nightmare?"

She laughed. "What nightmare? I think you've found a definitive cure."

"You think so?"

"It seems to have worked for me."

"Good. Then I suggest we run an experiment." He sat up slowly, letting his hand trail down across her breasts and come to rest on the softness of her stomach.

"What sort of experiment?" Amy punctuated the question with a catlike yawn.

"Come and spend the rest of the night with me, Amy."

Her yawn was cut off. Her eyes widened. "Jed, I don't think that's a good idea."

"Let's try it and see what happens."

"I've told you, I'm a restless sleeper. It's not just a matter of an occasional nightmare. I'm a first class insomniac. I wake up several times a night. And I toss and turn a lot. Believe me, you wouldn't get much sleep."

"I'll chance it."

She shook her head and her instant refusal to even consider the suggestion annoyed him. "No, I don't think so," she said flatly.

Jed got to his feet and reached down to catch hold of her shoulders. She was slender and light, even though she had a woman's strength. It was easy to pull her up beside him until she was standing in front of him. "Don't be silly, Amy," he said calmly. "We're going to give it a try."

"I don't . . ."

He hushed her with a kiss. "There is no good reason for you to sleep out here on the couch." When he lifted his head she didn't say anything, just looked up at him with an anxious, searching glance that told him nothing except that she was genuinely nervous about sleeping with him.

"For pete's sake," he muttered, turning her around and steering her toward the doorway with his hands on her shoulders, "why the hell should sleeping with me be so upsetting after what just happened between us?"

She ignored the question. "I'm cold."

He reached down to sweep her nightgown off the couch. The downward, twisting movement put stress on his injured leg and Jed swore softly. "Here, put this on." He dropped the flannel gown over her head.

She disappeared briefly beneath the soft material and then her frowning face reappeared as she put her arms through the sleeves. "You've got a lot of nerve calling me bossy, you know that? In fact, I think you've got a lot of nerve, period."

"Fortunately, I compensate for my drawbacks by being good in bed."

"Hah."

"You got any complaints, lady?" He had her almost into the dark bedroom now. He kept his hands on her shoulders as he guided her toward the bed.

"If I did have any complaints, who am I supposed to take them to?" she demanded as she crawled under the covers and leaned back against the pillows to glare at him.

"Always go to the source of the problem, I say." He slipped in beside her, tangling his feet with hers. "Come here and tell me exactly where I failed to meet your expectations and requirements."

"Dammit, Jed."

"Can't think of a single problem area, can you? I knew it."

She sighed. "Your ego could become a major problem."

He chuckled softly and cradled her in his arms. "If I've got an inflated ego where you're concerned, you have only yourself to blame. After the way you just responded to me, I'm bound to think I'm hell on wheels in bed. Go to sleep, Amy."

"I don't think I can," she said very seriously.

"You will."

"What makes you so sure?"

In a dramatic singsong voice he droned, "Because you look extremely sleepy. Your eyes are getting heavy. You can barely keep yourself awake. Your body is limp, relaxed, you're pleasantly comfortable. You want nothing more than to just close your eyes and go to sleep."

"I'm not susceptible to hypnotic suggestion."

"Sure you are. Creative minds are the most susceptible,

didn't you know that? And anyone who writes science fiction for a living would have to be twice as susceptible as the average person."

She shook her head a little ruefully and finally gave in to the inevitable. "All right, but it's not going to work."

She was asleep within ten minutes.

For a long time Jed lay very still beside her, not daring to move for fear of waking her. She looked very sweet and vulnerable lying in his arms. Her golden brown hair was spread in sensual disarray over her shoulders. The old-fashioned nightgown added a charming, piquant touch.

Jed realized for the first time that one of the reasons he was attracted to Amy was the odd combination of emotions she elicited from him. Every time he looked at her he felt an urge to ravish her and an equally strong need to protect her. The mixture was fraught with an emotional danger he'd never before faced.

It was a relentless curiosity that finally drove him to disentangle himself from Amy's soft body. He didn't like loose ends. Carefully he eased away from her, watchful in case she started to awaken. She stirred once or twice, but her eyes stayed closed and her breathing remained even. Jed grinned to himself. Maybe she was one of those so-called insomniacs who believed they were awake half the night when in reality they slept peacefully through most of it.

But the nightmare had been real enough, Jed reminded himself. And he knew something about nightmares.

He wanted to see what kind of writing could cause such a chilling, frightened scream. He'd read all three books in Amy's *Shadow* trilogy: *Wizard's Eye*, *Lady's Bane* and *Shadow's Master*. The last one wasn't due out for another few months, but Amy had let him read the manuscript. He'd found it different from the other two, although all three were tied together with common characters and a quest theme.

Jed knew from what Amy had told him that she'd finished *Shadow's Master* only a few months ago, just before he'd met her, in fact. The tone had seemed darker than the others, not as adventurous and lighthearted in its dealing with the perils faced by the hero and heroine. In a way it had been a better book, richer in detail and characterization, but there was no doubt there had been an uneasy edge to it that set it apart from the others.

He made his way haltingly out into the living room, absently scratching the healing wound on his right arm. Amy kept her home computer in a corner of the room near the kitchen. She also kept a bottle of brandy in a kitchen cupboard. It was an expensive brand and she tended to dole it out in tiny, carefully measured quantities. Jed headed for the kitchen cupboard first. He would have preferred a glass of Scotch, but Amy didn't keep any in the house. She hadn't kept any since the evening she'd paid him a casual visit and found him well into a bottle.

She hadn't said anything that night, but her concern and disapproval had been evident. Whenever she offered him a drink after that, it was usually white wine. Instead of taking offense, Jed had found her gentle maneuvering rather sweet and amusing.

A couple of minutes later, brandy in hand, he sat down in front of the computer. Amy had shown him how to run the word processing program and load a disk before he'd left on the last assignment. At the time he'd merely been curious, his engineering mentality coming to the fore, he supposed. Sometimes it still did that on occasion. He'd been a good engineer once upon a time. He frowned intently at the dark screen and began to fumble through a box of diskettes.

He was about to load the program when he spotted a pile of printed manuscript pages lying on one corner of the desk. Dropping the program disk back into the storage box, Jed hefted the stack of paper.

It was labeled *Private Demons*. Amy must have decided to print out what she had done so far. Jed picked up the manuscript and the brandy and ambled back to the rumpled couch. He sat down, flipped on the end table light and quickly scanned through the pages, starting from the back. He wanted to read Amy's most recent work.

The story seemed to be a straightforward sword and sorcery tale about a very normal young lady from California named Wanda Madison, who found herself transported against her will to another world to fight mysterious creatures of an even more mysterious dark power. The new world was an aquatic environment, and somehow in the transition process Wanda was endowed with the ability to live underwater.

Somebody, however, had made a serious mistake in recruiting Wanda for the dangerous task of demon fighting. Wanda spent a lot of time trying to explain the error, but it was too late. The problem was that the demons she was supposed to battle came from the darkest part of the sea. They represented a power that thrived in the deep, and any attempt to master them meant swimming into the black depths of the sunken caves where the creatures lived.

As it happened, poor Wanda had a lifelong fear of the dark. She also had claustrophobia.

It was a major disaster. Unfortunately, for Wanda and the aquatic people who had kidnapped her, there weren't going

to be any second chances. She was their one and only hope
for survival.

She forced herself to swim steadily on through
the murk, half blinded by the silt that had been
kicked up in the creature's death throes. She was
certain that at any moment her lungs would suddenly revert to normal, human lungs and she would
no longer be able to breathe water. Telling herself
that the drowning sensation was purely her imagination, she struggled forward into the cavern.

The oppressive, watery darkness was a distilled
version of all the childhood fears she had ever
known. Every instinct warned her there would be
no escape. She would be trapped forever. Still, she
kicked out awkwardly with her strange, webbed
feet, struggling to maneuver the dead weight of her
burden. She couldn't look at what she was dragging
into the darkest, watery corridor. To do so would
surely drive her over the edge of sanity. But she
could sense its leg gliding limply alongside hers as
the thick current caught it, could feel the occasional
brush of the dead hand as it floated through the
water beside her.

The eyes. If she looked at the eyes it would be all
over. The sightless, staring eyes would be full of
accusation and a curse that would follow her for as
long as she lived. She must not look at the eyes.

In that moment Wanda would have sold her soul
for a glimpse of clean light, fresh air and freedom.
The trouble was, she wasn't at all certain she would

have a soul to sell after she completed her grisly
task.

Thoughtfully Jed set aside the last page, took a long swallow of the brandy and asked himself if describing such a
scene was really enough to give a woman nightmares.
Surely someone accustomed to such writing wouldn't have
found the description unnerving. He wondered if Amy herself was afraid of the dark. There was so little he knew about
her.

He did know what it was like to be afraid of the dark, he
thought bleakly. He also knew what it was like to have it as
an ally. During the past eight years he had learned to make it
a friend, not a foe. At times his survival had depended on it.

He finished the brandy and slowly got to his feet. He
switched off the light and headed back toward the bedroom.
Amy was curled into an inviting lump under the quilt, still
sound asleep. Her hair was a dark fan on the white pillow.

Feeling gratified, as though he had a right to take credit
for her being asleep, Jed slid into bed.

As the bed gave and she was jostled, Amy started to rise
from a dreamless oblivion. A rough, masculine leg touched
hers. Subconscious panic formed from nothing, swirling to
life as quickly as a thunderstorm. Dark water surrounded her
again, and for an instant she couldn't breathe.

*This time she knew she was drowning. Then the hand
lightly grazed her thigh.*

*It was just the movement of the water around her that had
caused his hand and leg to brush against hers, she told herself. He wasn't alive. She mustn't panic. She was committed
to this now. There was no choice but to go through with it.*

But the panic swamped her completely when she felt the

masculine foot snag hers. Amy surfaced from the depths of sleep, flailing wildly at the big hands and heavy legs that were seeking to clutch her and drown her. There was no scream on her lips this time. She didn't dare open her mouth. The water would rush in and steal what was left of her air supply. Desperately she fought to free herself, struggling violently against the restraining hold.

"Amy!"

She heard Jed's voice calling her, but there was no release. She was being pinned more tightly than ever. Her arms were trapped at her sides, her legs were locked beneath the weight of a man's thigh. She couldn't move.

"Amy, stop it. For God's sake, wake up. Open your eyes. Look at me. *Look at me!*"

The harsh command penetrated her mindless panic, calling her back to reality. Amy drew a deep breath. No water rushed into her lungs. She was in bed. Her bed. It was Jed's voice she heard. Her eyes snapped open.

His face was fierce and unrelenting in the shadows. It was the face of a man who could make her believe in hell, Amy thought. Or perhaps it was the face of a man who would walk through hell to save her.

Her breathing slowed to normal. She closed her eyes and opened them again. "I'm sorry, Jed. I warned you I'm a restless sleeper."

His grip eased. "So you said. Are you all right now?"

"I'm fine."

"Uh huh." He sounded distinctly skeptical. "I think I'm going to get you a medicinal glass of brandy. I'll be right back."

"It's all right, Jed, I don't need anything." But her protest was weak and she knew it. She most definitely needed something. The panic attacks were getting worse, just like the nightmares. Jed didn't bother to respond to her mild denial. He left and she soon heard him opening a cupboard in the kitchen. When he reappeared in the bedroom a few minutes later he was holding a hefty dose of brandy in one hand. She sat up, hugging her knees under the quilt.

"I can't afford to drink that much," she said as she accepted the glass. "Do you know what this stuff costs? I have to save it for special occasions."

"This is a medical emergency. Don't worry, I'll buy you a new bottle." Jed's face hadn't relaxed. The intent look in his eyes was unnerving.

"Well, I guess it is an emergency," she agreed, sipping at the brandy. There was a long moment of silence in the bedroom.

"How long has it been like this, Amy?"

She didn't pretend not to understand. Instead she gave a small shrug. "A few months."

"How many months, Amy?"

She sighed. "About eight or so."

"Maybe your Dad's right. Maybe the pressure of your writing is getting to you."

"Maybe."

"You don't want to admit that, do you?"

"Nope. It's embarrassing. I've got one brother who can handle the pressure of politics, another who can handle the pressure of high tech corporate business and a sister who can deal with life and death. Heck, no, I don't want to admit that I'm coming apart just because I've had a couple of books published and want to write more."

"Everyone has his or her own internal limits. You have to learn to respect those limits if you're going to survive."

"I didn't know you were an amateur psychologist," she muttered, taking another sip.

"I'm not. I'm an engineer, remember? That means I know something about stress. Buildings and people can only take so much."

Amy considered that. "I'm sure you're right," she said politely.

He hesitated. "Amy, is it the writing or is it something else?"

Her head came up quickly. "Whatever it is, it's my problem, Jed. You don't have to worry about it."

"I'll make that decision."

She bit back an automatic protest, knowing instinctively that Jed would only see it as a challenge. "Suit yourself."

"Are you afraid to let me get involved?"

"You know as well as I do that this relationship has been running along very careful lines, Jed. Neither of us has gotten overly involved. I thought that was the way we both wanted it."

"Things change," he suggested casually. "Take tonight, for instance."

She didn't know what to say to that so she concentrated on the brandy. When she was finished she handed the glass back to him and tried a small smile. "Thanks. I needed that, as the old saying goes. If you're going to get any sleep tonight, I'd better move back out to the other room."

"No. You're staying here with me." He set the glass down on a nightstand and got back into bed beside her.

In his present mood, neither sweet reason nor an argument would move him. Without a word, Amy slid back down under the covers, letting the warmth of the brandy take hold. For a long time she looked up at the ceiling, aware of the weight of Jed's arm across her breasts. Some things, it seemed, you couldn't escape—things like nightmares and panic attacks and, Amy was inclined to believe, Jedidiah Glaze.

"Jed?"

"Hmm?"

"I think I'm going to go visit my parents."

He was silent, but she sensed he was waiting. Amy took a deep breath. "Do you want to come with me?"

"I thought you'd never ask."

Amy realized she had been holding her breath. She let it out in a soft sigh. "You're sure?"

"I'm sure."

"I don't want you to feel obligated or anything."

"I don't feel obligated or anything."

"If you have other plans . . ."

"I don't have any other plans. I could use the vacation."

"You're sure?"

"Shut up, Amy," he said gently. "I'm sure."

Amy began to relax. She knew it was more than the brandy. She had no choice about going back to the island. Deep down, she had known she'd have to face it at some time. But having Jed along was going to make it a little easier. There was a silent strength in him that she might be able to emulate.

It wasn't just Jed's strength she wanted to study, Amy realized. She also wanted to look into her mother's eyes and try to discover what it took to live with the shadow of murder for twenty-five years. Her mother, apparently, had learned how to do it. Amy needed that secret if she wanted to keep herself from going off the deep end.

Chapter Four

"**A**rtie, I've had it with waiting. This thing is eating me alive. Jesus, man, it's been eight months since the last try. We've got to get moving."

Daniel Renner gripped the telephone the way he did when he was making a pitch or closing a deal. He sat hunched forward on the couch, his elbows resting on his knees as he stared sightlessly at the gray carpet between his feet. He radiated intense excitement, as well as a deep, restless impatience that he seemed to have been born with. The world couldn't move fast enough for Renner. He was always looking forward to the next Big Deal.

Those restless and intense qualities had translated well into the business of selling. Daniel Renner could project an enthusiasm and a sense of integrity that was completely false but highly believable, which made him a natural salesman. He was twenty-six years old and had sold everything from drugs to securities. The days of peddling illegal substances were long gone, however. Renner had discovered there was more challenge and prestige to be had dealing artificially hyped stocks and other assorted but equally shaky securities. The day he started working as an account executive in a small L.A. brokerage firm had been the day he knew he was headed in the right direction.

Typically, he had become impatient with the life of a

commissioned salesman almost immediately. He had recently made the decision to open his own brokerage firm in a year or two, and he fully intended to do it in style. As usual, he'd consulted with his old friend from the drug dealing days, Artemus J. Fitzpatrick.

At Renner's urging, Fitzpatrick had also decided to abandon dealing dope for the highly profitable and socially acceptable business of selling major investments. The investments were seldom either profitable or advantageous tax shelters, but in the financial world no one seemed to mind those two minor drawbacks. Fitzpatrick had discovered—to his endless wonder and delight—that Renner was right: There were any number of people who would put their money into anything rather than give it to the government. Artemus Fitzpatrick took advantage of a seemingly universal human desire to avoid taxes at any cost while Renner concentrated on selling high risk stocks to gamblers who dreamed of hitting it big with the next IBM.

Renner Securities, Inc., Daniel had explained to Artemus, was not going to be another run-of-the-mill, street-front securities firm. It wouldn't even be located on a street. The very last type of client it would seek to attract was the casual walk-in variety. Who wanted the lobby filled with retirees watching their IBM and General Motors shares moving slowly across the board? That sort of thing was strictly low class.

Instead, Renner Securities was to be located a discreet thirty stories up in a glass and steel high rise that carried a solid gold address on Wilshire Boulevard. Everything would be first class, from the hand-polished oak furniture to the hand-picked clientele.

Fitzpatrick was impressed by the plans, but then he'd

known Renner since the younger man had discovered the extensive, disposable incomes professional athletes had to expend on recreational drugs. Even in those days Daniel Renner had sought a high class clientele. He had never stood on street corners worrying about getting knifed by an irate client. He had kept his operations discreet and by referral only.

Life hadn't been that easy for Artemus Fitzpatrick. There had been too many occasions when he had had to stand on street corners and worry about what kind of gun the next sleazy client would be carrying. Renner had gotten him out of that dangerous world and Fitzpatrick was forever grateful. On the other hand, Fitzpatrick had made contacts and learned a few things from his miserable life on the streets that Renner had never had an opportunity to learn.

Eight months ago Daniel Renner had discovered a need for that highly practical and specialized knowledge. He'd turned to Fitzpatrick for help. It was the first time the role of benefactor had shifted from Renner to Fitzpatrick. Fitzpatrick had rather enjoyed that shift. It was good to be the one in the know, the one who had the right contacts, the one Renner needed to carry out his plans.

"Listen, Dan, that damn box, if it exists, has been sitting there for twenty-five years, right? It's not going anywhere, so calm down. You haven't had any choice but to wait and you know it. Don't take it out on me. Eight months ago we thought we were going to get lucky with LePage. Looked like an ideal setup when he hit it off with the daughter. But deals go sour all the time, man, you know that. When that fell through there was nothing else to do except wait for the next chance. Another few days and it's next chance time. So just take it easy, pal."

"I've been taking it easy for eight months and I've had it." Renner drummed his fingers on the surface of the coffee table in front of him. "It's June already, Artie. I want to get moving."

"You've got time. The Slaters are scheduled to leave for Europe next week, right? Everything's under control. Once they're off the island, we'll have all the time we need. Stop chewing your nails. Why the hell are you so nervous?"

"Because things went wrong last time and I've got no guarantee they won't go wrong this time!" Renner exploded. He rose from the couch and began pacing the steel gray carpet. "LePage was a professional, right? He was supposed to know what he was doing, right? He was a good diver, you said. He didn't mind getting his hands dirty, if necessary. Didn't mind the rough stuff. And he knew his way around a gun. Hell, he was supposed to be a professional mercenary. Nothing was going to go wrong last time, but it did. The guy fell on his head in a pool of water and drowned. What kind of professionalism is that?"

Fitzpatrick sighed with the weary patience of one who had suffered unjust accusations all his life and had risen above them. "He wasn't my man. I hired him for you on the recommendation of an acquaintance whose business is making such arrangements. LePage supposedly had excellent credentials. Unfortunately, something went wrong. Maybe he proved unreliable or maybe he wasn't as good as he claimed. I'm told that cave diving is extremely hazardous."

"You said he was an expert!"

"Even experts have problems, I've learned. Cave diving is dangerous, especially for a man diving alone. That's why he demanded so much up front, if you'll recall." Fitzpatrick was trying to be patient.

"And that money is gone. Vanished. Who knows what the hell he did with it before he took that swim?"

"Calm down and stop rehashing it. It's over, Dan. This is hardly the sort of thing one can take to the Better Business Bureau."

"I don't want any mistakes this time."

"Since you're planning to manage the next attempt yourself, I'm sure there won't be any problems," Fitzpatrick said soothingly. "Just be patient a few more days. When the Slaters leave, you'll have half the island to yourself. No one will pay any attention to you. You'll be able to take your time and do it right. I've made sure you have good men this time. Real pros."

"What if the two guys you've hired aren't any more reliable than LePage?"

Fitzpatrick sighed again. "I've hired the best I could find, Dan. Guthrie and Vaden come highly recommended. They've been around and they honor contracts. There are no guarantees in this sort of thing. We're paying them well and they understand that the bulk of the commission isn't to be deposited to their accounts until the box is retrieved. This time you'll be on site to supervise. That's all we can do to guarantee their, uh, professionalism."

"*We* aren't paying them well, *I'm* paying them well." Renner paused in front of the floor-to-ceiling windows of his apartment. The smog was as thick as molasses outside his window. "It's got to work this time, Artie. It's got to work."

Fitzpatrick paused and then asked bluntly, "What if there's nothing in the box after all these years, Dan? Have you thought of that?"

"I've thought of it."

"And?"

"And it doesn't matter. I've got to know."

"You know what your problem is, pal? You never learned that sometimes it's better not to know all the answers."

"Give me a for instance," Renner challenged.

There was another pause and then Fitzpatrick admitted, "Offhand I can't think of any."

Renner nodded. "That's because there aren't any. It's always better to know the answers. And Artie, this answer could be big. Very, very big."

"Don't forget that twenty-five years ago people had a different idea of what constituted big money," Fitzpatrick advised blandly.

"My mother," Daniel Renner stated, "knew what constituted big money in any decade. And she was even better at figuring the value of gemstones."

Fitzpatrick sucked in his breath. "You really believe the payoff was in emeralds?"

"My father was a certified genius, Artie. I checked into it. Michael Wyman was no fool. My mother's diary says he made the deal for stones, not cash. I believe it." Renner was aware of a strange sense of pride in the unknown man who had been his father. His old man had made a deal to end all deals. Big time. Talent definitely ran in the family. The emeralds constituted Wyman's legacy to the son he had never seen and who did not bear his name. Renner wished, not for the first time, that his mother had used Wyman's name instead of her own when she named her son.

"Shit. Have you any idea what those rocks might be worth today?" Fitzpatrick's question was rhetorical. His voice contained an element of wonder.

"I know, Artie, I know. And that's not all that's in the box. The emeralds are only part of the prize. According to my mother's diary, when I have that box in my hands, I'll have a rising young politician named Hugh Slater in my hip pocket. There are pictures in that box, Artie. Compromising photos of Hugh Slater's father meeting with a known Russian agent."

"But that meeting, if it took place, would have happened over twenty-five years ago."

"So? You think the threat of exposing his father as a man who tried to sell secrets to the Russians wouldn't be enough to keep Hugh Slater in line? Come on, Artie. It doesn't matter how long ago it happened. It's potent stuff. A political career couldn't take it. With those photos I'll probably even have a handle on Slater Aero, too. Just think of it, Artie. With those emeralds, a company like Slater Aero and a guy who will probably be a senator some day in my palm there won't be anything I can't do."

"The thing I've always admired about you, Dan, is your modest ambition."

Renner laughed with the sheer excitement of the deal. He felt hot, powerful, bursting with energy. Making deals was better than sex or cocaine any day of the week. "Let's meet at the club and play some racquetball. I need to work out. Winner buys the drinks."

"Since you always win, that sounds like a pretty good deal. See you in half an hour."

Renner tossed the phone back into its cradle and headed for the door of his apartment. It was going to work this time. It had to work. All his life he'd been waiting for the first big break, the one that was going to boost him right to the top of the Southern California power crowd. When he'd found his mother's diary in her safe deposit box after her death he'd known he held his future in his own hands.

It was too bad he had found out in a scuba diving course he'd taken the year before that he wasn't cut out for the sport. Oh, he could get by in shallow water where there was plenty of visibility, but the thought of diving in the confined environment of a cave was too much. He just couldn't do it. He'd go nuts and he knew it. That meant he had to hire pros who didn't ask too many questions and who didn't mind a little rough stuff if it became necessary.

Renner decided he didn't really mind the idea of the rough stuff. It gave him a nice jolt of power to know he was in a position to pay others to handle it for him.

The island was as deceptively serene and inviting as ever. Amy watched from the window of the small twin engine plane as the dark smudge on the horizon crystalized into a lush green emerald set in a turquoise sea. There was very little sign of civilization to mar the Pacific island paradise. Commercial jets only landed there twice a week. Amy and Jed had booked seats with a small, island hopping airline service based in Hawaii.

Orleana Island was a typical Pacific volcanic formation. The steep sides of the ancient crater were shrouded in a cloak of verdant foliage. Dazzling white beaches were scattered carelessly around the skirts of the island. As the plane made its approach the small town on the southern tip came into view.

"Talk about an unspoiled tropical paradise." Jed leaned across Amy to peer out the window. "You weren't kidding. If it weren't for that little village at the tip, the place would look uninhabited. Where's your parents' house?"

"The other end of the island. You can't see it from this angle." Amy pressed back against the seat so Jed would have a better view. His shoulder brushed hers and she was deeply aware of his warm, male scent. There was a casual intimacy about the way he was leaning across her. His forearm grazed her breast and his wide hand rested lightly on her thigh. She had a sudden impulse to run her fingers through his dark hair, but she resisted. The truth was, she didn't know quite where she stood with Jed now.

There had been no repeat of the passionate lovemaking that had taken place on the couch in her living room three nights before. The next morning Jed had been as easygoing and undemanding as ever. He had teased her about serving him oatmeal again, taken over the task of making the plane reservations and then gone home. He had some laundry to do, he explained. Not knowing how to interpret his casual attitude, Amy had given him one more opportunity to back out of the trip to Orleana Island, but Jed had ignored it.

Another bird cage had been sold while he'd been out of the country, and that, Amy declared, was cause for celebration. She'd bought champagne and invited him to dinner again before they left Caliph's Bay. He'd accepted, but after dinner he'd gone home.

The relationship was definitely back to normal. Well, Amy decided silently, almost normal. Amy didn't know whether to be grateful or disappointed. Part of her insisted it was best this way. She had enough problems without trying to figure out how to have an affair with a man like Jedidiah Glaze. But another part of her wanted nothing more than to entangle herself completely in his life.

The problem, of course, was that Jed wasn't the kind of man who allowed people to get tangled up in his life. Amy reminded herself that she had been trying to maintain the same kind of distance in her own life. She had no business getting involved in a serious relationship, least of all with Jed Glaze.

Still, there was no denying that things had changed between herself and Jed. The fact that he was sitting beside her as the plane eased down onto the runway was proof of that.

"I'm looking forward to doing some diving," Jed said as the plane taxied to a halt near the small terminal building. "It's been a while since I've had an opportunity. When was the last time you did any?"

Amy kept looking out the window. Her hands twisted tightly in her lap, but she forced herself to relax them. "I did a little the last time I was here. There's plenty of equipment at the house. My mother taught all of us kids how to dive."

"What about your father?"

"He doesn't care for the sport." Douglas Slater had never done any scuba diving as far as Amy knew. Knowing that, Amy had been forced to realize that he probably wasn't the one who had committed the murder twenty-five years before. The killer had been a good diver, Bob had explained. And Amy's mother was an excellent diver. God knew she had also had ample motive. All the reasons for murder were locked in a waterproof box that rested far back in a flooded cave.

"I told Dad we'd rent a car and drive to the house," Amy said as she slid out of the seat. The tropical warmth and shatteringly brilliant sunlight hit her in a familiar wave as she preceded Jed off the plane.

"Sounds like a good idea." Jed glanced around at the shabby little terminal and the small crowd that was exiting the plane.

They found their luggage amid the small pile of bags being unloaded by the co-pilot. Jed hoisted his and Amy's.

He started toward the door with a bag in each hand. He'd stopped using his cane the day before, Amy had been pleased to note, but she didn't think he ought to be pushing things quite this fast.

"Here, let me have one of the bags. You shouldn't be carrying so much weight." She reached out to take one of the suitcases.

Jed ignored her efforts, giving her a quick grin. "I like you fussing over me at times, Amy, but there are limits. I can manage the bags just fine, thanks."

Amy stared after him as he made his way out of the ramshackle terminal. Damn him. If Jed chose to interpret her efforts as "fussing" that was his problem. She was only trying to help.

She followed him outside to another small building where they rented a car, and they were soon on their way.

Several people waved at Amy as Jed drove through town. She waved back cheerfully.

"Do you know everyone on the island?" Jed asked curiously.

"Just about. It's a small, close-knit community and my family has had a home here for nearly thirty years. We're considered locals."

"What's a nonlocal?"

Amy laughed. "Off-islanders. Tourists, mainly. Or people who haven't lived here long. Off-islanders are automatically under suspicion, I'm afraid, even if they do bring in money."

"Where do I fit into this scheme of things?"

"No problem. You're a guest of my family so you're an honorary local."

Forty minutes later Jed nodded toward a house set high above a perfect semicircle of white beach. It had just come into view as he'd guided the small, noisy, rusty rental car around a bend in the narrow road. "Is that your parents' place?"

"That's it. Dad and his business partner, a man named Michael Wyman, had it built nearly thirty years ago. They wanted it to look like a gracious old South Pacific plantation home."

"I'd say they did a good job." Jed eyed the large, handsome, two-story structure with an expert's eye.

Amy glanced at the intent expression on his face and then tried to see the house through his eyes. It was a graceful building set amid the flowering trees and palms. Shaded verandas with elegantly carved posts wrapped both levels of the structure. All the rooms, both upstairs and down, opened onto the breezy, outdoor galleries.

The windows were trimmed with decorated shutters that could be pulled closed in the event of a storm. The front entranceway was an arched set of doors that stood open to reveal the cool depths of a wide hall.

"I meant to ask you," Jed remarked as he slowed for the turnoff, "what did your dad say when you told him you were bringing along a guest?"

"'One bed or two?'" Amy said dryly.

Jed smiled fleetingly, although he didn't take his eyes off the road. "To which you replied?"

"Two."

"I can tolerate your restlessness at night, Amy. Haven't I already proven that?"

His question threw her. Since he'd left her alone for the past three nights, she wondered why he was bothering to discuss the subject in the first place. Irritated, she kept her eyes on the front doors of her parents' home. "I didn't specify two beds to save you from my restless sleep habits. I did it to save you from a lot of—um, unnecessary pressure."

"Pressure?"

"To set a date," she amplified politely.

"For what?" He sounded honestly blank.

"To marry me, you idiot!" For just an instant, Amy felt quite angry.

As the light dawned, Jed grinned again. "Does your father have a shotgun?"

"It wouldn't be all that humorous, Jed. Both my sister, Sylvia, and I are unmarried. We're the only unmarried offspring and it worries everyone. My parents, as I've explained before, tend to worry, especially about me. They also tend to get awfully excited whenever some unwary male shows an undue amount of interest in me."

"I'll keep that in mind."

"You do that." The asperity went out of her voice. She was about to inquire after his leg but changed her mind at the last minute. He'd probably accuse her of fussing. "How are your ribs?" she heard herself ask instead. She could have bitten her tongue.

"They ache a little. Not too bad. A couple of drinks before dinner should take care of the problem. I prefer alcohol to pills."

Some time later Jed stretched his aching body out on a lounger and surveyed the picturesque scene that would have done any postcard justice. From this side of the house the veranda posts framed a scene of the tranquil beach and brilliantly clear sea below the house. It was a perfect island setting.

Jed had come to a couple of conclusions since Amy had

introduced him to her parents. The first was that Amy had gotten her near-green eyes from her father. The second conclusion was that Douglas Slater didn't look like the type to dig out a shotgun if a man proved reluctant to marry his daughter.

Slater did, however, look as though he were capable of finding other ways of accomplishing his goals. Hardly surprising, Jed thought. The man had made Slater Aero a success in what everyone knew was a cutthroat business. Anyone capable of accomplishing that feat knew how to get what he wanted.

Jed felt a certain amount of respect for Amy's father right from the start. His first impression of the older man was that Slater could have passed for everyone's image of a retired college professor. He was nearing sixty and had acquired a patina of casual charm and civilized polish that hid a core of strength. His trim body and healthy color beneath his light tan could easily lead one to mistake him for a man ten years younger. His silver hair was thinning in a gentlemanly fashion and he looked at home in a short sleeved shirt, a pair of expensively cut slacks and sandals on his feet. That academic look had probably served him well in business. It would have been nice camouflage for the ruthlessness that lay underneath. Jed had a practical appreciation for people who were good at camouflage; it was one of his own personal skills.

Gloria Slater was equally interesting. She was in her early fifties and her stylishly short hair was almost completely gray. There were, however, traces of a familiar golden brown laced throughout the silver. The effect was aristocratic, Jed decided. She had fine, attractive features that had probably been through a very discreet facelift.

Through the years Gloria Slater had learned to wear her husband's success well. The perfect executive's wife, Amy had said, and Jed believed it. Gloria Slater was an intelligent woman, almost intimidatingly organized, and it was obvious she loved her husband and daughter and was devoted to the family she had created.

On his way out to the veranda Jed had seen photographs of Sylvia posing in her consulting room with her assorted medical degrees behind her on the wall. The photograph of Hugh, the lawyer and aspiring political candidate, showed a good looking, square-jawed young man sitting comfortably on a desk in front of a wall lined with law books. The framed portrait of Darren, the oldest son, showed him standing proudly in the office of the President and Chief Executive Officer of Slater Aero, Inc. It was the office his father had turned over to him two years before.

The picture of Amy showed a young woman in jeans and a bright shirt on a windswept beach. Her hair was whipping around her face and she was laughing at the camera. There were no obvious signs of achievement or success in the picture, just a happy young woman whose eyes promised gentleness, feminine mischief and excitement. Jed liked that photograph the best.

Jed was torn from his reverie when his host called to him from the teak liquor cart that had been wheeled out to the veranda. "I've got Scotch, bourbon or vodka, Jed. What can I get you?"

Jed glanced at Amy, who was stretched out on another lounger beside her mother. He grinned. "Got any wimpy white wine? Amy's been trying to wean me from the hard stuff."

Amy's head came up in shock. "Jed! I've never tried to tell you what to drink. How can you say such a thing?"

Slater glanced at his daughter's startled expression and then raised his brows at Jed.

"It's true, you know," Jed defended himself with a rueful expression. "Everytime I've been to her house for dinner I've had to drink wine. Usually white wine. She never seems to have any real liquor around. To be fair, she's got one bottle of brandy that she hides in a corner of the cupboard, but you'd think it was solid gold, the way she dispenses it."

Amy's eyes widened. "I can't believe I'm hearing this. If you wanted Scotch when you came to my house, you should have brought your own bottle!"

Jed shrugged. "It wasn't that big a deal. I thought it was kind of cute."

"*What* was kind of cute?" Amy demanded, her eyes forbidding.

"The fussing." Jed smiled at Gloria Slater. "I haven't had a woman fuss over me in years until Amy came along. I hadn't realized I missed the little demands and instructions for improvement."

Amy sat speechless while her father poured a glass of wine for Jed. "Interestingly enough, I never really thought of my daughter as the sort of woman who, uh, fusses. I always had the impression her mother and I were the ones who fussed over her."

"Oh, she's good at it," Jed said. "And I don't mind. I can handle white wine. The trick is to hold your breath and swallow fast." He accepted the glass from Slater and leaned back in the lounger. He grinned at Amy. "But she's got a few other habits I may have to modify. I've never seen anyone with such limited taste in music."

"You've never said anything about the music I play. I had no idea you didn't like it."

Gloria shuddered in mock revulsion. "I refuse to take responsibility for Amy's current musical tastes. She was exposed to classical music while she was growing up, and—"

"Hah," Amy interrupted, looking triumphant. "That's what you think, Mom. I used to sneak in my rock 'n' roll on the side."

"Then you have no one to blame but yourself for your present appalling tastes, my dear," Slater said as he finished handing out drinks and sat down beside his wife. "We did our best."

Amy cast her eyes heavenward, apparently seeking divine intervention. "I'm not here more than two hours and everyone is already picking on me."

"It's probably a conspiracy," Jed offered, aware that he was enjoying himself. He was very conscious of the fact that the Slaters were checking him out as a suitable mate for their daughter and it amused him. The irony of the situation was not lost on him. "If I were you, Amy, I'd get paranoid."

She stared at him, all humor leaving her eyes for an instant. "Maybe you're right."

Jed swallowed his wine, wondering what had put her over the edge. One moment she had been a picture of amused exasperation. The next there had been a haunted look in her eyes. One of these days, in his own good time, he'd find out what it was that kept Amelia Slater hovering on the brink.

"My daughter tells me you were recently in an accident, Jed?" Gloria looked at him with ready sympathy.

"Nothing serious. I had a disagreement with a car. I lost."

"Good lord, how awful." The older woman shook her head. "Where did it happen?"

Jed swirled the wine in his glass. "The Middle East. I was on assignment there with my company."

Douglas Slater glanced at him inquiringly. "Amy says you're an engineer?"

"That's right." Then, because he knew what the next question would be, Jed added, "Mechanical engineer." Douglas Slater, after all, would know to ask that kind of question.

"And you work for a company that has overseas projects?"

Jed relaxed back against the lounger, idly massaging his leg through his cotton slacks. "A small consulting firm that's gotten a couple of major projects recently. I've been busy. Haven't seen nearly as much of Amy as I'd like." He looked directly at Amy, who looked astonished.

The honest surprise in her face made him want to give her a small shake. Was she really so oblivious to his growing desire? Maybe he shouldn't have left her alone at night for the past few days. His idea had been to give her a little time to adjust to their changing relationship. He had been determined not to rush her now that the initial hurdle had been crossed. But she seemed to have retreated back into her nice, safe cage of friendship.

There were a few more pointed, parental questions about his work which Jed fielded easily enough while Amy tried unsuccessfully to interrupt. Jed had the impression she didn't like the way her parents were delicately dissecting his occupation and financial status, just as if he were, indeed, a suitor for her hand. He almost had the impression that she might be trying to protect him from her parents' inquiries.

Personally, he was finding the game entertaining. The last time he'd been put through this he'd been eight years younger and a good deal more nervous. To be strictly fair, though, he reminded himself that the last time it had all been for real. He and Elaine had actually set a date and the future had looked good. But then things had changed and he had learned not to look too far ahead.

"What Jed really does well," Amy declared, "is make bird cages. The most beautiful bird cages in the world. I think he ought to consider making a full-time career out of it."

Jed was surprised by her tone. She sounded as if she meant it. "And when I consider doing that," he said mildly, "I can also consider learning to live on an income that wouldn't provide enough loose change to buy wimpy white wine, let alone decent Scotch."

Gloria Slater spoke before her daughter could reply. With the grace of years of experience, she smiled and changed the subject. "Where does your family live, Jed? California?"

He should have known that question would follow right behind the financial status quiz, Jed told himself. He glanced at Amy and saw the small frown between her eyes. She had never asked him about his family. It was one of several subjects they had silently agreed not to discuss for the past three months. "My parents are dead. Killed in a plane accident a long time ago."

"Any brothers or sisters?" Gloria persisted gently.

"I had an older brother." Jed took a long swallow of his wine. "Andy died about eight years ago."

"Oh, I'm so sorry to hear that."

Gloria's comments, although well intentioned, were only the conventional reaction to old deaths in the family, Jed decided. It was Amy who looked stricken. She was sitting there in her bright turquoise trousers, yellow shirt and white woven belt with an expression of genuine shock on her face.

She didn't know anything about Andy or his parents and now she was beginning to think about how many other things she didn't know about him, Jed decided. Why was it bothering her? It hadn't seemed to worry her for the past three months. Probably had something to do with bringing a lover home to meet the family, he thought. That was bound to make a woman view a man through different eyes.

All things considered, Jed realized, he was handling this traditional little scene better than Amy. But then, she hadn't brought him here with the intention of running him through the old-fashioned gauntlet to secure parental approval. She'd brought him here for reasons of her own. Jed wondered how long it would be before she told him what those reasons were.

"Well, Amy," Gloria announced, getting to her feet in a graceful movement, "I think it's time we sent the men to the barbeque while you and I retire to the kitchen."

Amy glanced uncertainly at her father and Jed wanted to laugh. He knew she was wondering what other personal question Douglas Slater was going to ask when she was out of earshot.

"Don't worry," Jed murmured for her ears alone as she walked past his lounger, "I'll yell for help if I get in over my head."

"I'm glad you think it's funny. Oh, Jed, I'm sorry about this. I told them you were a *friend*."

"I know. Two bedrooms. Forget it, Amy, I won't leave you in the lurch. I'm not going to get scared and take to my heels just because your dad's asking me the same kind of questions I get from the IRS. I'm made of stronger stuff than that."

She batted her long lashes and dropped her clear voice

into its huskiest range. "You're so wonderfully macho. A woman could just swoon."

At least she wasn't looking nervous any longer. "You don't think it takes guts to chat casually with a man who knows you're sleeping with his daughter?"

Amy stopped batting her lashes. "Dad doesn't know we're—that we once—uh . . ."

"The hell he doesn't." Jed reached out and patted her turquoise clad thigh with absent possessiveness. "Run along and chop lettuce or whatever it is you're going to do in the kitchen. Leave the barbequing to the male of the species."

Amy stifled a groan. "I'm beginning to wonder if I made a serious error when I invited you here."

"Nope. It was probably one of your brighter moves." Jed swung himself up off the lounger and glanced over to the far corner of the veranda where Slater was arranging coals in the pit of the barbeque grill.

Amy started to leave, but paused and asked quickly, "Is your leg feeling any better?"

"One more glass of white wine and it'll be good as new. Well, maybe five or six more."

"And that's another thing," she began, "I have not deliberately tried to alter your drinking habits! I never fuss. Especially not with you."

He gave her a gentle push in the direction of the sliding glass doors. "'Bye, Amy."

She clearly wanted to argue further, but surrendered to the inevitable with rather bad grace. Jed sauntered toward the barbeque grill to offer moral support.

"Can I pour you another Scotch and water while you deal with that, Doug?"

Slater chuckled and nodded. "Sounds like a good idea.

Pour yourself one, while you're at it. As long as my daughter's out of sight, you might as well live a little."

"Thanks. I'll try not to run wild. Amy says you've had this place since before she was born?"

Slater nodded, bending over to poke at some coals. "Yeah, went in fifty-fifty with my partner, Mike Wyman. He and I were stationed here back in the fifties. That was when the Navy kept a supply depot on this island. Mike and I got drunk one night and decided Orleana Island was going to be the next Hawaii. We had visions of tourists pouring in as jet travel became popular. Land around here was dirt cheap. Still is, which tells you something about our real estate forecasting abilities. Mike and I bought up a lot of island. When we got out of the service we went into business together in California. After a few years of making money we built this place for our own use while we sat back and waited for Hilton and Sheraton to grovel at our feet. As you can see, it never quite worked out like that."

"I'll have to admit that little bunch of buildings and shops at the other end of the island doesn't exactly look like Waikiki."

Slater grinned. "From a business point of view, buying up a chunk of Orleana Island was about the stupidest move I ever made. But from a personal point of view, it was a real coup. Gloria and I don't know what we'd do without this place now. It's home. We've got friends here. Good friends, not business associates, if you know what I mean."

"The kind of people you can count on," Jed murmured.

"Exactly. And you can't beat the climate. The book on managing in the aerospace industry I'm supposed to be writing keeps me busy. If I get really bored, I do a little consulting on the side."

"Did you have another business before Slater Aero?" Jed poured the two drinks and carried them both over to the grill. He handed one to Slater and leaned back against the railing.

"Another business?" Slater asked, obviously confused. "Oh, you mean with Wyman. No, Mike and I founded Slater Aero together more years ago than I care to remember. Mike was the engineering genius of the firm but he had mush in his head when it came to business."

"You, on the other hand, had the business sense to make his strokes of genius marketable, right?"

"It was the perfect partnership. We called the firm Wyman and Slater back then. Changed the name after Mike was killed. Working with Wyman was a little like working with an artist." Slater straightened and took a sip from his glass. "Temperamental as hell. But, Jesus, he was sharp when it came to aeronautical design. Slater Aero made a lot of money over the years off some of his early work. Wish he could have lived to spend some of it. Mike liked spending money."

"What happened to him?" Jed watched the last of the sunlight dapple the water in the cove below.

"Sailing accident. He loved the sport, but was a bit reckless. Went overboard during a cruise between here and Hawaii and was never seen again. He was the only person on board. He and the ship were both lost. Mike was always taking chances. I guess he took one too many. Things were a little hectic when the news came that he'd disappeared. Everyone knew Mike was the technical mind behind the firm."

"So everyone in the industry stood around and waited to see if you'd go under without him?"

Slater shot Jed an assessing glance. "As I said, things were a little hectic for a while."

"I'll bet." Jed could imagine the guts and determination it must have taken to hold the company together after Wyman's death. Contracts would have been hard to get until the firm had proved itself capable without the technical genius.

"How long have you known my daughter, Jed?"

"About three months. But I've spent a lot of time out of the country since I met her, so we really haven't had much of those three months together."

Slater nodded. "I was beginning to wonder if I'd ever get her back to the island this year. She had a rough experience here about eight months ago."

"She mentioned a guy named LePage," Jed said carefully.

"Amy brought him here for a few days early last October. They'd met in San Diego about three weeks before, I gather. She lived in San Diego for three years before she moved to that artsy-craftsy Caliph's Bay. LePage was a nice enough guy, if you like the type."

"Meaning you didn't like him?"

"There wasn't anything to dislike, I suppose. Good manners. Smart. Gloria assured me he was handsome. I just didn't think he was Amy's type. But maybe a father never thinks any man is his daughter's type. Still, you can't protect them forever. And Amy always did make her own decisions."

"What happened with LePage?"

"Didn't Amy tell you? He insisted on trying to dive some flooded caves that have an entrance a few hundred yards out in the jungle." Slater waved his hand in a vague direction that took in much of the heavy, dark foliage beyond the house. "He hit his head somehow when he entered the cave. The blow knocked him out and he drowned. Amy found him the next morning. It shook her up." Slater looked at Jed. "Do you dive?"

"Scuba? Yeah, I've done some."

"Amy does a lot when she's here. Her mother taught her. We've got plenty of equipment if you want to do some while you're staying with us."

"I'd enjoy that."

"Glad to get Amy back here," Slater went on easily. "I was getting worried about her. Thought maybe her recent success was getting to her. Got published this year, you know."

Jed heard the fatherly pride in the older man's voice and smiled. "I know. I've read her books."

"Got another one in the works."

"I've seen the first part of the manuscript. It's called *Private Demons*."

Slater cocked one brow. "Very interesting. Normally Amy won't let anyone read her stuff until it's in print."

Jed reminded himself that as far as *Private Demons* was concerned, he hadn't bothered to ask the author's permission before reading the manuscript. But that was a mere detail. He saw no need to mention it.

He stood leaning on the veranda while Slater prepared the barbeque and wondered what private demons were swimming behind Amy's almost green eyes. Soon, Jed promised himself, he would find out. He took another thoughtful sip of Scotch

Chapter Five

Gloria Slater had not done much diving in recent years, but she still swam daily and took long walks on the beach with her husband on a regular basis. Her figure, as always, had an athletic fluidity that had softened only a little in the last decade. Amy eyed her mother's narrow waist with rueful admiration, hoping privately that she would look that good when she was Gloria's age.

"I think I like your young man, Amy." Gloria removed a large salad bowl from a perfectly organized cupboard and went to the refrigerator.

Amy tilted her head to one side, considering the comment. "I never think of Jed as young. He's in his middle thirties, I think."

"Well, that sort of thing is relative, isn't it? Believe me, from my perspective, he looks young." Gloria smiled and handed her daughter a sack of romaine. "You can tear the lettuce. Do it with reverence. It costs a fortune to have it flown in from Hawaii. I'll do the dressing." She opened the door of her spacious walk-in pantry and pulled out the makings.

Amy began work on the lettuce, wondering as she did so if Jed had ever been "young." The idea startled her. From the very beginning there had been something in his eyes that had spelled too much age and experience. That quality, she acknowledged for the first time, was one of the things that had both repelled and attracted her. It was as if she sensed that Jed might be the kind of man who would understand and possibly accept what she had done because he'd seen much worse. Irritated with the fleeting bit of self-perception, Amy concentrated on tearing the lettuce.

"Have you heard from Sylvia lately?" Amy asked, seeking a safe topic.

"Oh, yes. Got a call from her last week. She's doing beautifully. Women doctors, especially gynecologists it seems, are very popular these days. She has a full patient load." Gloria shook her head. "Amazing how times change. You should hear her talk about all the new birth techniques."

"I got a note from Darren saying he and Anne are going to Europe for a skiing vacation next December." This wasn't what she wanted to talk about, Amy thought desperately. There were so many questions she wanted to ask her mother, and none of them had anything to do with how her brothers and sister were getting along.

"He and Anne need to get away," Gloria said as she whipped the salad dressing. Her movements were precise, efficient and strong. "Darren's just like your father was at that age. Totally committed to the business."

What about you? Amy asked silently. *What were you like at that age? You weren't committed to the business or your husband, were you? You were passionately in love with Michael Wyman.*

Amy had seen the letters. They were all together in a neat little pile.

"Hugh and Glenda are going to have another baby, did he tell you?" Gloria moved back to the refrigerator.

"So soon?" *I want to know how you did it, Mom. I want to know how you pulled yourself together afterward and went*

*on with your life. How did you escape the nightmares? Or
did you have any?*

"It's good to have them close together," Gloria stated.
"And voters love politicians who are good family men.
About time you gave some thought to the matter, yourself,
Amy. A family, I mean. I know it's fashionable to have your
babies later these days. Sylvia told me about a forty-year-old
woman who delivered her first child recently. But I don't
think it's such a good idea. Time does run out for a woman."

Her own time was running out, Amy realized, in a way
she couldn't explain. She had thought it would get better as
time went on. She had thought she'd gradually put it behind
her. She knew she would never forget, but she thought it
would get easier. She was wrong.

*How did you survive, Mother? I have to know. I want to
survive, too.*

"Have you discussed a family with Jed?"

"Mom! For crying out loud, I've only known the man for
a few months." Amy ripped the last of the romaine apart.

"It's best to sort those things out in the beginning."

"I can't see Jed with a bunch of little rug rats running
around his feet." The mental image was jarring at first, then
it became amusing. Amy smiled in spite of herself. "Then
again . . ."

"You never know about a man. It's hard to tell which of
them will make good fathers."

"Sounds risky." *Did you think Michael Wyman would
make a good father? Or were you going to leave your children behind when you ran off with him? If it had worked out
as you had planned, would we have ever seen you again?*

"It is risky. That's why so many women make so many
mistakes. A woman just does the best she can under the

circumstances. Sometimes she makes an error in judgment, but she doesn't look back. She picks up the pieces and keeps going forward. Don't be afraid of the risks, dear."

The last risk I took almost killed me, Mother.

"If it were up to the men there wouldn't be any children in this world." Gloria finished the dressing with a flourish.

You took the same risk down in that damn cave as I did. What was it like for you? Could you see his eyes, Mother? Did they stare at you so intently you wondered if some part of him was still alive? Did those eyes come back to haunt you? Could you feel the brush of his leg in the water? Did his hand touch you so lightly he might have been making love to you?

"It worries me that you haven't settled down with anyone, Amy. How serious are you about Jed?"

"Jed is just a friend, Mother."

"Amy, my dear, don't pull that one on me. I've seen the way he looks at you. Possessive men give themselves away with their eyes. Has he been married before?" Gloria asked casually as she handed the dressing to her daughter.

Amy nearly dropped the bowl. She didn't know, she realized in disbelief. She didn't even know if he had ever been married. "No, I don't think so. He's never mentioned a previous marriage."

"Ask," Gloria advised firmly, laying out silverware.

"Why?" Amy realized she was beginning to feel cornered. "I've told you, he's just a friend."

"I've lived long enough to know that very few men are capable of having a simple friendship with a woman." Gloria grinned, looking twenty years younger for an instant. "It's the nature of the beast. One of the biggest mistakes a woman can make is thinking she can have a real friendship with a man. Men almost always want something more, even if they never say it or act on it."

"That's an old-fashioned view, Mom, and you know it."

"You think so? Ask any man."

Before Amy could respond to that, Jed materialized in the doorway. He glanced inquiringly at Gloria. "Ask any man what?"

Amy glared at him. For an instant she wondered if her mother had identified that look in his eyes accurately. No, it didn't make any sense. Jed would not be possessive of a woman. He wanted no strings. "Nothing. Go back outside and amuse yourself walking on hot coals or something. We'll be right out."

Gloria laughed. "Amy and I were discussing male-female relationships."

Jed nodded, folding his arms as he leaned against the doorjamb. "Always a fascinating topic."

"Amy thinks it's possible for men and women to have pure friendships. I told her I thought such true, platonic friendships were extremely rare. Men aren't built to engage in those kinds of relationships with women."

"It's a weakness in the brain, no doubt," Jed agreed.

Amy's head came up. "Are you saying she's right?"

Jed looked at her. "Based on personal experience, I'd say she is. It's possible to have a lot of female acquaintances, but not a lot of close female friends." He paused and then added deliberately, "Not unless there's something more involved."

"Sex?"

"Yeah." He grinned wickedly.

"Well, hell." Amy began tossing the lettuce with the dressing her mother had made. "If that's the case, then I

guess you're right. It's a weakness in the brain. Either that
or you and my mother are both throwbacks to another era."

Jed moved from the doorway and dropped a quick kiss on
her forehead. "Don't worry about it. I consider us friends.
Close friends."

Amy went red and was thoroughly flustered by the fact.
She shoved the salad bowl into Jed's hands. "Here, take this
out on the veranda with you."

Jed shook his head at Gloria. "And to think I've always
admired assertive women." Obediently he disappeared back
through the doorway.

Gloria's gaze was thoughtful as she watched him leave.
"An interesting man."

"That's one way of putting it."

"I think he might make a very good *friend* for the right
woman." Gloria smiled serenely and began stacking the buf-
fet plates.

Amy watched her mother and realized how much she had
always taken Gloria Slater's efficiency for granted. For as
long as Amy could remember, her mother had been a woman
whose life revolved around order. She always knew what
she would be doing in the next hour, the next day, the next
month. She had raised her children and planned her husband's social life with cool organizational ability. She had
taught Amy to dive with the same methodical approach.

Her approach to life did not make Gloria inflexible by any
means. She was brilliant at accommodating last minute
changes, houseguests or alterations in plans that had been
laid for months. She was simply a naturally organized
woman, always looking ahead to the next detail.

And that, Amy thought with abrupt insight, was how her
mother survived; she didn't look back, she kept moving for-

ward. New plans, a new life, a new direction. She could almost visualize Gloria walking away from the death scene, certain she had taken care of every detail, her mind already busy with the task of reordering her future.

But she herself kept going back, Amy thought. She was caught in some kind of time loop and she kept going back in her mind. She was trapped.

Amy faced the fact that Gloria Slater's method of survival wasn't going to be one her daughter could use. Amy would have to find another way. She thought of Jed.

Several hours later Jed lay awake in bed, his arms crooked behind his head as he gazed thoughtfully out the open window. The rustle of palms was a low murmur hovering just beyond the veranda. The big, fat tropical moon threw a long spear of light across the ocean's surface. The water itself looked black and impenetrable for the first time that day.

His ribs had felt reasonably good most of the evening, but now they were aching again. He considered getting up and taking one of the little white pills, but finally voted against the idea. Maybe aspirin would do the trick.

He swung his feet down to the carpet and padded over to the window. The scent of ocean and exotic flowers was carried on a warm, balmy breeze. It was almost unreal. For a moment Jed stood looking out, mentally comparing the beautiful, inviting darkness of the veranda to the bloody darkness of the alley where he'd taken the bullet in the leg a couple of weeks before. Then he turned and went into the adjoining bathroom to find the aspirin. As soon as he swallowed them he knew he needed something else. He wanted to share the darkness with Amy.

Her room was two doors down from his. Her parents'

bedroom was at the far end of the hall. Jed had been given what Gloria called the boys' room. There were pictures of Hugh and Darren in high school football uniforms on one wall. An elaborate trophy for first place in a wrestling competition stood on the chest of drawers. Several smaller trophies for everything from band to track had been placed along one wide windowsill. Gloria had apparently moved all the important family mementos to the island when she and her husband had retired. Jed wondered if there were any certificates or trophies in Amy's room. He doubted it. Not unless they gave awards for daydreaming or the secrets of a woman's hidden thoughts.

Jed walked back out of the bathroom, not bothering to switch on any lights. He found his jeans lying on the chair where he'd left them, stepped into them and headed for the door that opened onto the veranda. He was curious to see if Amy was alseep.

He made no noise as he moved along the gallery to her room. She would be infuriated if he accidentally woke her parents. She was playing a silly game trying to pretend he was only a friend, Jed told himself. It was time he put a stop to it. Just because he'd been trying to give her a little breathing space didn't mean things between them had reverted to their original level. Besides, there was no point pretending that what existed between them was only friendship. Her parents had known better right from the start. Jed had done nothing to alter their conclusion. In fact, he'd had fun answering the Slaters' purposeful questions that evening, although he didn't quite understand why. He could only conclude he was enjoying the unusual role he was playing.

Amy's veranda door was closed. Jed tested the doorknob cautiously. It turned easily under his hand. He quietly slipped into the room and at the same time heard a faint sound from the first floor. The front door was being opened or closed.

Amy's empty bed answered the rest of Jed's questions. She had left the house. This left him no option. He would have to follow her.

Downstairs Amy stood on the front step, inhaling the fragrant night air. At least the sky was clear, she thought as she started slowly down the steps. Last October there had been a storm brewing out at sea the night she'd gone down to the caves.

She had tugged on a pair of white jeans and a coral T-shirt before leaving the house this evening. Shoving her hands into the back pockets of the jeans, she started down the path that led through the palm trees. The scent of the water and the surrounding jungle vegetation grew thicker as she walked.

For the past two hours she had sat at her bedroom window telling herself there was no point in paying a visit to the caves. It would serve no purpose except to make her more nervous. But she had a growing feeling that she needed to pass through some sort of exorcism. Perhaps, she thought, this was the strange sensation that drove a criminal to return to the scene of a crime.

The jagged memories pushed insistently at the edges of her mind. They were always there these days, hovering in the shadows. But tonight, she decided, she was going to stop fighting them for a while. She let them fill her head, her muscles tightening instinctively in resistance.

She never knew what it was that had awakened her that night in October. Amy remembered sitting upright in bed as if reacting to a shout or a scream. Her heart was pounding and the blood was moving too quickly through her veins. But there had been no sound. She sat listening to the silence, straining to understand what it was that had brought her awake so abruptly.

Finally, she had gotten out of bed and walked out on the veranda. She saw Bob as he walked beneath her, leaving the house to head toward the jungle. He had been carrying a diving tank and a duffel bag full of equipment, and was dressed for swimming. Even as she watched in startled silence, he disappeared into the shadows. She couldn't believe he was going diving alone, especially at that hour of the night. They had already gone down in the cove that afternoon and Bob had seemed to have had his fill. Something was very strange and very wrong.

Just as she wasn't certain what had brought her awake, Amy wasn't sure what it was that drove her to pull on a pair of jeans and one of the few dark shirts in her wardrobe and follow Bob LePage out of the house. At that point she hadn't sensed real danger, she was simply compelled to follow him. The mystery of the situation dominated her thoughts as she let herself out the front door.

Within a minute or two Amy knew LePage wasn't heading for the cove. He was going into the jungle, following the path she had shown him earlier in the afternoon when he'd finally cajoled her into showing him the entrance to the caves. Amy had to move quickly to keep up with him, and a sense of foreboding filled her.

Eventually Bob halted. Holding her breath, Amy stopped some distance behind him and watched through swaying branches and drooping vines as he flicked on a small light. He seemed to be examining a piece of paper in his hand.

When he was finished, he turned to the right. A hundred

feet further on he stopped again, and now Amy was certain of his destination. He was standing near the opening to the twisting, underwater caves that honeycombed this portion of the island. Amy couldn't believe he meant to go diving in them alone.

She watched as he adjusted his equipment. Bob slung the tank on his back, buckled it and tested the regulator by taking a few breaths through the mouthpiece. Then he climbed over the treacherous lip of the rocky cave opening and carefully entered the dark water. Once he was safely in the pool he put on his fins. Amy stared in bewilderment as he vanished from sight.

Cautiously she had emerged from her hiding place and glanced more closely at the rippling water that filled the cave opening. An eerie luminescence reflected faintly up from the depths because LePage had switched on his light. It hovered in the water a moment and then disappeared as he swam into the yawning underwater passage.

Something underfoot caught her attention as she stood uncertainly near the cave opening. She reached down to pick up the piece of paper LePage had trapped under his duffel bag. It was a crude map, barely discernible in the fretful moonlight. She picked up the pencil flashlight LePage had used earlier.

The map depicted what appeared to be the first few meters of the convoluted underwater passage, itself. How could LePage possibly know what the inside of those caves looked like?

Amy jerked herself back to the present, trying to push aside memories of her own confusion, growing fear and the certainty that something terrible was happening. All the frightening images that had assailed her that night had flooded back much too quickly. For eight months she'd tried to shut out the scene, but her efforts had been unsuccessful. As she stood listening to the soft murmur of water in the cave, every haunting detail was as clear in her head as it had been the night it happened.

"Amy?"

There had been no sound until he called her name. Amy spun around, stumbling a little over a trailing vine as she heard Jed's low voice.

"Jed. I didn't hear you." She stared at him, knowing her startlement must be plain. She was tense and Jed would see that tension. He noticed such things. Until recently she hadn't realized just how much he saw. He stood in the shadows, half hidden by the swaying foliage, watching her. The midnight moon barely touched the harsh angles of his face.

"It's a little late to be out walking alone, isn't it?" He came closer, moving soundlessly through the tangle of greenery that surrounded his feet. Idly he reached out to brush aside the long, sweeping tendrils of a fern.

"It's perfectly safe out here." Conscious of the cave opening only a few feet away, Amy started forward. She hoped he would notice nothing more than the jumble of rocks that hid the entrance. "How did you know where I was?"

"I was on my way to your room when I heard you leave the house." He looked past her as she stepped closer, his gaze on the rocky formation that marked the cave.

"You were on your way to my room? Why?"

His mouth rose slightly at one corner and his gaze moved from shadowed rocks to her face. "Why the hell do you think? We're lovers, remember?"

His casual attitude flicked her on the raw. "Barely. You

haven't shown much interest since that . . . that one night, so I assumed it was a fluke."

"A fluke?"

She shrugged in what she hoped was an offhand manner. "I decided you were just letting off tension, or something. You'd had a long trip, you'd been hurt, you were sleeping in my bed. I was convenient. It all sort of went together."

"Ah, I see what you mean." He reached out to catch hold of the hand she was waving haphazardly. His strong fingers closed around hers, stilling the nervous movement. "A fluke."

"That's right." She made to brush past him. Jed didn't try to hinder her, but neither did he let go of her hand. Instead he fell into step beside her as she walked pointedly away from the vicinity of the cave.

"Tell me something, Amy, who was using whom to release a little tension that night? You were the one who woke up screaming because of a nightmare."

She gave him a quick, sideways glance. "Okay, so it was a mutual thing."

"A friendly thing."

"If you like." She nodded stiffly.

"A neighborly thing."

"Jed—"

"A casual roll in the hay between a couple of friendly, neighborly folks who both just happened to need a bit of physical release."

Amy glared straight ahead. "You don't have to make a joke out of it."

"I'm not making a joke out of it. I'm just trying to see it from your perspective."

Amy lost her fragile hold on her equilibrium. She spun

around to confront him. "I don't know what my perspective is. And I haven't the vaguest idea of what your perspective is on the subject, either. I'm not sure what going to bed with you meant. Therefore I choose to think of it as a friendly gesture on both our parts, all right?"

"Bullshit."

She blinked at the dismissive tone in his voice. "Then you tell me what it meant, dammit!"

"Why try to find words for it?" Jed asked quietly. "There's no need to pin a label on it."

"How can you say that?" She snapped. "Of course there's a need."

He led her out of the thick greenery to a bluff overlooking the moonlit cove. He paused to look down at the silvered strip of sand below. "You say that because you're a woman."

Amy set her teeth together. "So?"

"So, I'm a man and I don't feel any need to label and categorize things just yet." He wasn't paying much attention to her. Retaining his grip on her hand he was seeking the path down the small cliff.

"You're the one who said we were lovers. *Lovers*. What's that if not a label?" Amy didn't know why she was arguing. It was a ridiculous discussion in the first place. She didn't know why she was letting Jed lead her down the cliff to the beach, either.

Jed's fingers tightened around hers. "Okay, it's a label," he said soothingly. "It's sufficient for now."

"I'm not so sure, Jed." They were almost down to the beach. Amy looked at Jed's profile, aware of the way the moon made his dark hair shine. "Do you realize how little I know about you? I don't know anything more about you today than I did the day we met."

"That's not true." He sounded thoughtful, as though he was just now considering the matter. "You know that I was getting into the habit of going a little heavy on the Scotch when you first met me. I saw the way you watched me after that evening you dropped by unannounced and found me hitting the bottle. Right away you put me on white wine and limited me to two or three glasses whenever I was with you."

"Good grief! That wasn't a conscious effort to rehabilitate you, Jed. White wine is what I drink, so it's what I offered you when you came for dinner. You never protested or insisted on bringing your own Scotch."

"That's because I didn't mind." He sounded amused. They were on the beach now. "You know how much I like designing bird cages. You're always hinting I should give up working for my engineering firm and make a career out of the cages instead."

"Jed, that's hardly an example of in-depth knowledge or indicative of a meaningful relationship."

He led her along the sand. "A lot of people who know me don't know about my bird cages."

"Well, maybe that's because you don't socialize very much," she pointed out tartly.

"And that's another thing you know about me. I'm not much of a socializer."

"You seem to be doing just fine with my parents."

"Mmm. That's different."

"Oh, really? Why?"

He shrugged, his strong, bare shoulders catching the gleam of moonlight. "I don't know. Maybe because they're connected to you."

Amy dug in her heels, forcing Jed to stop and look at her.

"Tell me something, Jed. Why are you putting up with all Dad's not-so-subtle questions about your financial status? And why are you being so tolerant of Mom's questions about your family?"

"Because they're your parents and because I'm their guest. And because I'm sleeping with their daughter and they know it. That gives them a right to a few questions."

"Is that so?" Amy demanded, feeling thoroughly exasperated. "What about me? Do I have a right to a few questions?"

"I think so."

"Well, thanks a lot! I always had the impression you liked your privacy, that you didn't want me asking questions." Amy swept her hand out in a disgusted movement.

There was a heartbeat of silence and then Jed said quietly, "I had the same impression about you. If you've got a question, Amy, ask it."

They stared at each other for a long moment. The soft, warm air lifted a tendril of Amy's hair, lacing it around her throat. Jed reached out and caught it. He held the silken strand between his fingers while he studied Amy's searching eyes.

"Have you ever been married?" Amy asked baldly.

Jed shook his head, saying nothing.

"My mother told me to ask." Amy smiled in an unexpected burst of humor.

"I was engaged once about eight years ago."

"What happened?" she waited tensely for the answer.

"It didn't work out. My brother died about the same time. I had to handle some things." Jed spoke tersely. "The engagement fell apart."

"Stress," Amy said knowledgeably. She wondered just

what it was he'd been required to handle and why his fiancée hadn't been able to deal with the situation.

"Stress. What a useful word."

"Do you miss her? Think about her a lot?"

"No. But sometimes I wonder about what my life would be like if I had gotten married eight years ago and settled down to a normal routine."

Amy felt a great wave of empathy. She touched the side of his hard face. "Eight years is a long time. Surely there have been other opportunities for you to establish a family, if that's what you wanted."

"I'm not sure what I've wanted for the past eight years. I've just followed a routine that worked. Gone where I'm sent, done my job, come back and designed bird cages. Drank a little Scotch. I don't think much about the past."

"Or the future?"

"I haven't thought much about the future, either," he said.

"Oh, Jed . . ." Her fingertips trailed lightly down his throat to his bare shoulder.

"Until lately," Jed concluded softly.

"What?"

"I haven't thought much about the future until lately. But now I find I'm starting to think about it again." He pulled her into his arms, cradling her against him, burying his face in her breeze-tossed hair.

Amy wrapped her arms around his waist and rested her head on his shoulder. "Are we friends or lovers, Jed?"

"Both." He sank to his knees, drawing her down with him. His hands went to the hem of her T-shirt as she knelt in front of him, and his smile was a lazy, sexy promise. "Last time I rushed things." He kissed her nose as he slid the shirt up over her head. "I'd been wanting you a long time. You knew that, didn't you?"

Facing him on her knees, Amy's eyes softened in the moonlight. His chest was solid and warm under her palms. "A couple of times when you came back from a trip I thought you might have wanted me."

"Might have wanted you?" There was soft laughter in his voice. "I was burning up for you. And all you seemed to want to do was play checkers and old Beach Boy albums."

"We were supposed to be friends."

"And you were afraid to let the friendship grow into something else, weren't you?"

"A little," she admitted. His rough fingertips grazed the peaks of her uncovered breasts. She felt herself grow taut and sensitized. "Afterward I couldn't figure out where we stood."

"I wanted to give you some time." His palms were warm on her sides now as he stroked his way down to the fastening of her white jeans. "Maybe I wanted some time for myself, too." He leaned down to kiss the firm peak of one breast.

"Jed, there's so much we don't know about each other," Amy whispered.

"Does it matter?"

"I don't know." She drew in her breath as he unsnapped her jeans.

Jed turned her around and cradled her between his thighs with her naked back pressed against his chest. He pushed the denims off her hips, sweeping the scrap of underwear along with them.

Amy tilted her head back as his fingers stroked the inside of her bare thigh. She could feel the muscles in his legs as he gently pulled her body toward his. His manhood was straining against his trousers, pressing into the curve of her buttocks. She was thrillingly aware of the power he was restraining for her.

"You feel so good," Jed murmured. He kissed the curve of her shoulder as he leaned over and around her to part her thighs. When she was open to his touch he began to stroke the dark curls just below her stomach.

Amy shivered and closed her eyes, resting her head on his shoulder. She absorbed his warmth and felt her hunger for his touch grow. When his probing fingertips found the delicate flesh between her legs she cried out with aching wonder. Then he was parting the silken skin, tracing exquisite patterns in the hidden places. Amy gripped his muscular thighs on either side and her nails made small half moons in his skin.

"Jed, I don't understand how you can do this to me so easily." It was neither a protest nor a plea, simply an exclamation of amazement. Amy didn't fully understand her own reaction to him. She'd never responded to a man like this in her life.

"The effect is mutual." His fingertips were teasing her more intensely now. When Amy began to tremble, Jed pulled her closer to the warmth of his thighs. "Feel me, sweetheart. Feel how much I want you."

With an inarticulate murmur, Amy turned in the confines of the close embrace, pushing Jed back until he lay in the sand. He grinned up at her as she sprawled on top of him. He flexed his legs, drawing his knees up on either side of her so she was carefully trapped. His hands worked slowly, hungrily, down her back to the sweet contours of her hips.

"You like this, don't you?" Amy said half-accusingly as

she nipped lightly at his flat nipple. "You're getting off on seeing how quickly you can make me respond."

"What man wouldn't? You respond so beautifully. You're hot and silky smooth and vibrating. I can feel the shivers going through you already."

"Beast." But she clung to him, seeking the zipper of his pants. His fingers sank into her as she found what she sought and began to force his jeans down over his hips. Amy sighed. "I can feel you shivering, too."

"Shock waves. I'm about to explode."

"Just like a volcano. That's the way it was last time. Are you always like this?" She pushed the jeans off, taking the briefs with them. He was suddenly filling her hand, urgent, hard, throbbing.

"No, I'm not always like this. But it's getting to be a habit around you." Jed's eyes gleamed in the moonlight as he caught her around the waist and eased her up until she was kneeling astride him. The strong length of his manhood brushed tantalizingly against her. "Last time I was in such a damn hurry I was afraid I'd hurt you. I think I did hurt you a little."

"No." She shook her head in swift denial.

"This time you'll be in charge. Take your time, love, and take as much as you want."

Amy sighed her need, balancing herself with her hands planted on his shoulders. Slowly she eased herself down, feeling the thick, waiting length of him probing eagerly at the soft, moist entrance of her body.

"You know how to torture a man, don't you?" Jed's voice was a husky gasp as she carefully fitted herself to him. "Are you going to draw this out forever?"

"You said I should take my time." She felt a daring, feminine mischief rise inside her as she looked down into his stark face. Slowly she eased herself down another inch. He was so big, stretching her, filling her. The sensation was incredible. She was losing herself in the passion she saw in his eyes.

"When I said to take your time, I didn't mean you should make it last a week. Come here, lady, before I go out of my mind." His hands closed around her and he surged upward, driving deep into her damp, feminine sheath.

Amy cried out and fell forward, her hair spreading over his chest. As she gave herself up to the intoxicating rhythm, her fingers gripped his shoulders tightly. It was like riding a wild stallion, all muscle and driving energy. Her knees tightened around his waist and she felt his exhilarating response. For an endless time everything around her ceased to exist. There was no past to haunt her, no future to fear, only this man and this moment.

When he felt the tiny convulsions begin to shimmer through her and heard the breathless sound of his name on her lips, Jed gave a muffled shout of release, lifting himself one last time into Amy's softness.

And then it was over. The short, sweet aftermath settled around them. The rush of the light surf on the sand, the silver moonlight and the balmy air seemed to bathe Amy and Jed, creating an intimate, protected world that was impervious to external intrusions.

But as so often happens, the danger came from within. Amy's eyes were still closed, her head still pillowed on Jed's chest, when he spoke softly, fracturing the crystal thin cocoon in which Amy huddled.

"I answered a couple of questions for you tonight, Amy. I think it's time you answered some of mine."

She went still. "What questions?"

"I'd like to know what really happened the night LePage died."

Chapter Six

Jed could feel the tension overtake her body. She barely stirred against him, but he was instantly aware of the deep change in her mood. The sweet, sensual relaxation was gone as if it had never been.

"Why?" Amy's voice was hard.

"Why do I want to know what happened the night LePage died?" Jed flexed his shoulders, aware of the gritty sand beneath him. Making love on a moonlit beach had a few minor drawbacks. "Because I'm curious. Because you've told me yourself you've had trouble sleeping for the past eight months and, unlike your father, I think it's got something to do with LePage, not your writing. Because I wonder why, if LePage wasn't your lover, you're so upset about his accidental death after all this time. Lots of reasons." He wove his fingers through her tangled hair as she raised her head, crossed her arms on his chest and stared down at him. The green of her eyes was washed out by the moonlight, but he could see the watchful caution in them.

"It's considered tacky for a woman to discuss one man with another."

She was looking for a loophole, Jed knew. She was hoping to distract him with a few snappy little retorts. He decided not to let her wiggle away that easily. The best approach in a situation such as this was the direct one. "Was LePage your lover?"

Her store of snappy comebacks failed her immediately. Amy shook her head, her eyes reflecting the truth of her denial. "I've already answered that question. No!"

"Then why did you get up in the middle of the night to return to the scene of his death? That was where he had the accident, wasn't it? That was the entrance to the underwater caves you told me about."

"Jed, I see absolutely no need to discuss this."

He smiled faintly, lifting himself slowly to a sitting position. He kept a firm hold on her as he did so. "You do the imperious lady bit rather well. Just like one of the sorceresses in your books. But the act works better when you have your clothes on. Nude, you're much too soft and sexy to pull it off. Tell me what happened that night."

She shook her head more in bewilderment than refusal. "I don't understand why you've gotten so curious about me lately. For the past three months you haven't given a damn about my past or anyone in it."

"Things change."

"The hell they do. What's changed?"

"We've started sleeping together for one thing. How's that for a major change in the relationship?" He gave her a whimsical look, inviting her to soften and relax, but she didn't take him up on the invitation. He felt her test the strength of his hold on her with a subtle effort to pull up and away from him. He reacted as though he hadn't felt her muscles gently flexing, and kept her braced lightly but firmly across his thighs.

"LePage has nothing to do with our relationship, such as it is."

"So tell me about him."

"God, you're persistent."

"Engineers tend to be. Persistent and thorough. They like to know how and why something works." He paused. "Or doesn't work."

For a moment he thought she would continue to resist the light pressure he was applying. Jed was considering the best way of increasing the pressure when Amy spoke in a neutral, almost bored tone.

"I've already told you all there is to tell. He was simply a friend who liked diving."

"Did the two of you do a lot of diving while he was staying here?"

Amy nodded. "Sure. I showed him all the best places. He seemed to be enjoying himself. But our personal relationship was always casual. There are no deep dark secrets about what happened the night he died. He should never have tried to go into those caves, especially alone."

"Amy, I'm not as dumb as I look. I know there's more to the story."

Before he could stop her, she sat up and moved out of his reach. "All right! There was a little more. Not that it matters. We argued that night before going to bed." She grabbed her T-shirt and pulled it over her head.

"About what?"

She sighed. "Take a guess."

"Sex?" Jed watched in fascination as she seized the topic he offered.

"He wanted me to go to bed with him. Claimed I'd promised more than I'd delivered. Said I was a tease. I told him if he felt that way about things, he was welcome to go back to San Diego. He got mad. I guess he decided to work out his anger by going diving."

"In the middle of the night. In a cave that was marked off

limits by his host." Jed watched her closely. Amy was as tense and high-strung as she had been before he'd made love to her.

"That's when we had our argument." Amy got to her feet, hastily tugging on her jeans. "The middle of the night. Maybe if we hadn't argued he wouldn't have gone diving. Maybe that's what bothers me."

Jed didn't believe a word of her story, but he decided now wasn't the right time to call her on it. He had pushed her far enough tonight. Thoughtfully he climbed to his feet, reaching for his jeans. Before he gave up entirely, however, he decided he'd try one more goad. "You told me your father didn't want tourists to even know about the caves. How did LePage find out about them?"

Amy froze. There was a taut moment of absolute stillness before she said in a very distant, very neutral voice, "I showed him the location."

Jed knew for certain then that he had gone as far as he could for the time being. He broke the unnatural tension flowing between them with a soft chuckle. "I feel like I've been lying on sandpaper."

A flicker of relief lit Amy's eyes as she realized he was going to lay off the questioning. "Better you than me. That's what you get for playing the gentleman."

He tried to wipe off some of the sand. "It was worth it." Jed worked the zipper on his jeans and then looped his arm around Amy's shoulders with comfortable familiarity. "What made you take the walk this evening?"

He felt her flinch under his arm but her voice was steady. "Same old problem. I couldn't sleep. Thought I'd try some exercise."

"That pool where I found you looked a little treacherous."

"It is. It's the place where Bob died. It's the entrance to a network of flooded caves that run under that part of the island. They've never been charted Dad has never wanted anyone to take the risk."

"I can see why your parents made it off limits. They wouldn't want to be responsible, even indirectly, for accidents. The LePage incident must have reinforced all their concerns."

Amy nodded soberly as she walked beside him across the sand. "So many things can happen in a flooded cave. A diver could easily get lost. There would be no way to surface in an underwater cave. You'd have to find your way back to the opening. If you couldn't do that in time—" Her sentence stopped abruptly.

"A grim thought," Jed said cheerfully.

"I keep forgetting you've done some cave diving."

"Only a little. I didn't like it," he admitted.

"I think," she said slowly, "that it would be a nightmare to go into an underwater cave. You could be trapped forever What a horrible way to die."

Memories of the pages he'd read from *Private Demons* flickered through Jed's mind. Where had Amy come by her horror of being trapped in an underwater cave? he wondered. After all, LePage had died attempting to enter the cave. He hadn't died inside the labyrinth. Well, he was sure Amy wasn't going to tell him much else about it. He'd got ten about all he was going to get out of her, unless he really applied the pressure. There was no need to do that yet. he told himself. He'd give her time.

"Jed?"

"Hmm?"

"I never knew you had a brother."

"I never mentioned him."

"How could I have known you for three months and not know a thing like that?"

"I think," Jed said quietly, "that you and I have been very careful for the past three months."

Amy absorbed the impact of his words. "Yes, we have, haven't we?"

Why were the barriers breaking down now? she wondered. Something changed that night she picked him up at the airport and took him home. Something very drastic had changed.

A part of her was deeply alarmed. The carefully structured friendship had been her protection from him. She had been able to be near him without taking any risks of surrendering to true emotional or physical intimacy. But the situation had been unstable from the start, and now the barriers were crumbling.

It wasn't until Jed left her at her bedroom door that Amy began to seriously consider the full ramifications of what had happened that evening.

Jed had started asking questions. Pointed, explicit, pressing questions. Bob LePage had asked a lot of questions, too. Amy was chilled by the thought.

More similarities between the two men filtered into her mind as she got into bed and stared out the window. She had met Jed in very much the same casual manner that she had met LePage. Both men had appeared in her life shortly before she was due to return to Orleana Island. Both men talked little about themselves or their pasts. Both men knew something about cave diving.

Both men asked questions.

She had shown LePage the cave entrance because he had charmed her into it. She had unwittingly shown Jed the way.

But only one of the two men had succeeded in seducing her. It wasn't much, but she supposed she should be grateful for small favors.

Amy continued to stare out the window. Coincidence, she told herself. A few superficial similarities, that was all. Jed and LePage had nothing in common. They couldn't possibly have known each other. It had been Amy's idea to move to Caliph's Bay a few months ago. Jed had already been living there for some time. It couldn't have been a setup.

It could not have been a setup, she repeated to herself. No one could possibly know what had really happened last October. Jed was a friend and, she had to admit, now a lover. There were shadows in him, yes, but not the kind of shadows she had seen at the end in LePage.

Still, one fact remained: She was back on Orleana Island with another man who asked too many questions.

Amy knew even before she entered the water the next morning that she probably shouldn't have agreed to go diving with Jed. As she held her fins in one hand and walked backward into the surf, she felt an undeniable tension in the pit of her stomach. Tension under water could get a diver into trouble. It led to stress and that led to going through the air supply too quickly. It also led to a dangerous lack of attention to surroundings. If the tension didn't fade quickly after she was under water, Amy knew she ought to call a halt to the dive

They passed through the surf and slipped under the surface of the aquamarine water. Instantly Amy found herself in that other world she had known since childhood. The awkwardness of the tank, vest, shortie wet suit, weight belt, mask, gloves, and assorted equipment ceased to be a burden. She was free and graceful once more, able to move about in another dimension.

She listened to the sound of her own breathing through the regulator as she put on her fins. Beside her in the water Jed thrust his feet into his fins, glancing at her for directions. This was Amy's world, and he'd told her he wanted a tour. She signaled her readiness and turned to swim toward the dark reef that bounded the cove.

Jed used his fins with a lazy, powerful movement that quickly brought him alongside her. She had worried about his injured leg, but he assured her it was completely healed. He had stopped wearing the bandage, and she had briefly glimpsed the puckered scar when he had removed the jeans he wore over his swim trunks. Since the injury had been to the inside of his thigh, she could see nothing of it as he swam. One glance at him and Amy knew he was at home in the water. After her uncomfortable thoughts the night before, she didn't know whether to be pleased or wary.

The reef was like a sunny underwater garden. The light from the surface washed down through the depths, illuminating the brilliant coral, the gently undulating spines of sea urchins and a dazzling array of fish. Sandy ravines ran between the coral formations like small dessert valleys between mountains.

Amy pointed her gloved finger at a foot-long, reddish hued bigeye hiding in the reef's shadows and Jed nodded. He spread his hands in a mocking gesture of regret. The bigeye would have made good eating.

An hour before Douglas Slater had offered Jed his choice of the various trident underwater spears that were stored in the large room with the rest of the diving gear. Jed had casually examined a Hawaiian sling, the equivalent of an underwater bow and arrow, but he declined the offer.

"I'm not much of a hunter," he had explained with a rueful smile. "I'd be better off driving into town after the dive and buying dinner from one of the local fishermen."

Amy watched now as Jed turned away from the bigeye to follow a small school of exotic blue and yellow butterfly fish. She got the impression he didn't really regret his lack of ability with a speargun. She didn't regret it either. It was refreshing to be with a man who was content to absorb the beauty of the sea without feeling obliged to kill some of the inhabitants. LePage had loved underwater hunting. As Amy thought about that basic difference between the two men some of last night's uncertainty about Jed faded.

Unfortunately, her own personal tension wasn't being soothed as she had hoped. When she agreed to the dive this morning she had told herself that it would be good for her to get back into the water. This wasn't a terrifying labyrinth of caves. This was an open cove. She could swim to the surface at any time and breathe fresh air. There was nothing to haunt her along the reef.

But her breathing was still too rapid. Amy couldn't seem to relax. She was all too well aware of the slow, even sound of bubbles from Jed's regulator. He was relaxed, drifting easily as he paused to shine his diving light under a ledge of coral.

He glanced over his shoulder and saw her hovering in the water behind him. When he signaled her to come closer, Amy took another quick breath and kicked forward. She nodded when she saw the head of a small, speckled moray eel protruding from its hiding place in the coral.

Jed retreated from his vantage point and indicated he wanted to explore the nooks and crannies of the rock face that formed one wall of the cove. Amy hesitated, remembering some of its dark corners and holes that before she'd always found so interesting. Today she didn't want to get too close to anything that reminded her of an underwater cave.

But Jed was already leading the way, and Amy could see no logical reason to protest. He wouldn't understand. He'd only want to know why she was nervous about such a relatively safe exploration.

Questions. She didn't want to answer any more of Jed's questions.

Reluctantly Amy followed Jed, thinking wryly that she was supposed to be the one giving the tour. Somehow it didn't surprise her that Jed was already taking the lead. If she wasn't a little more assertive, he would take charge completely. She had a feeling it was his nature. Kicking more strongly, she caught up with him and moved slightly ahead.

Jed seemed willing enough to let her resume her role as guide. Amy moved along the cove wall, letting her guest take his time viewing the sights. While he swam down to the sandy bottom to examine a dark coral formation, she paused in the water and tried to concentrate on breathing more normally. The anxious, shallow breaths she'd been taking were burning up too much air. Awareness of how quickly she was going through her supply only increased the overall level of her tension. She caught herself staring too intently at a small lemon yellow surgeonfish and realized she wasn't paying attention to anything except the fish. It was dangerous to become unaware of one's surroundings underwater.

She wasn't afraid, she told herself. And she wasn't out of

control. But she wasn't functioning normally, either. *Stress*. As Jed had remarked, it was a useful word. It covered a multitude of sins.

She glanced down and saw Jed swimming slowly toward her. He was watching her and Amy wondered if he was noting the too-rapid escape of her exhaust bubbles.

Embarrassed by her own tension and annoyed by Jed's sudden watchfulness, Amy turned away to swim further along the cove wall. She would give him something more entertaining to watch than her breathing rate. A few more yards and she found it.

It wasn't really a cave in the rocky wall, it was more a deep indentation where a part of the old lava had been sliced out centuries before. The entrance was almost six feet across and nearly as tall. The dark opening didn't extend too deeply into the face of the cliff, but it went back far enough to provide the sensation of a small cave. A variety of flora and fauna swayed gently just inside the opening, beckoning the eager explorer.

Jed swam up beside Amy. She waved him inside the rocky opening. He studied her eyes through the mask for a moment before asking her with a hand signal if she wanted to ascend to the surface. Angrily Amy turned away from the question in his gaze, fluttering her fins in a determined kick. She would be damned if she was going to give in to this growing anxiety. She would handle it. She had to handle it.

The burst of energy sent her deep into the interior. The darkness of the rocky gouge rose to meet her, threatening to swamp her. Instantly she reversed herself, turning around in the water so that she could see the safe, sunlit cove.

Jed was swimming through the opening, swinging his light toward the back of the shallow cavern. He glanced again at Amy and she knew he was getting concerned. Her movements had been too jerky, too nervous. He was bound to wonder what was wrong with her.

Nothing was wrong, she told herself. This wasn't a cave, it was just an interesting hole in the wall. The wide open spaces were only a few feet away and she could swim to the surface any time she wanted. Those weren't his eyes shining out at her from that crack in the rock. Jed's light had just caught a little parrot fish, that was all. Calm down.

But she wasn't calming down. She was getting more anxious. Furiously Amy fought to control her runaway nerves. But memories of recent nightmares began to crowd in on her. The underwater cranny was suddenly much too confining. She couldn't see the roof of the cavern very clearly. Sunlight didn't penetrate far enough to give her a good view of the interior.

Amy heard the tempo of her breathing pick up. Good grief, she thought. She was almost hyperventilating. She had never lost control like this in the water, not even that night.

She stared at Jed as he slowly investigated the cavern, oddly furious at the ease with which he swam. He was everything a diver should be: calm, alert, relaxed. She used to be like that in the water; she had never felt the teeth of anxiety eating at her this way.

Amy hovered in the lazy current, vaguely aware that she was concentrating on nothing except Jed's movements. She was unaware of everything else around her. All she seemed able to do was stare. The gentle current pushed her slowly toward the side wall of the small cavern. Amy barely noticed. She was fixated now.

Jed was using his light to examine some of the sea urchins that clung to a rock. Amy saw the beam of light drift slowly across the colorful spines, illuminating one creature after another. The effect was hypnotic. Her focus shifted from Jed to the light. Her breathing was increasingly quick and shallow, and all she could think about was Jed's light.

Then her fin grazed a rock. The shock of the small physical contact was so great that Amy jerked violently, almost panicking. She had drifted too near the coral encrusted opening of the cavern. Her leg scraped across a rough edge of coral and almost instantly a thin stream of purple mingled and then disappeared in the surrounding seawater. She was bleeding.

Of all the stupid, idiotic things to do, she thought. There was no pain yet, but she knew that would come when she was out of the water. Amy was furious with herself. She wanted to scream with frustration and anger.

Getting out of the water became the only thing she could think of in that moment. She had to get out of the water. Her nerves had frayed to a dangerous point and now she was bleeding. Stupid, stupid, stupid.

She whipped around, swimming frantically for the wide mouth of the shallow cavern. She had to get out of the water before she completely fell apart.

And then Jed was beside her. She felt his hand on her leg, tugging gently in a signal to slow down. Amy ignored him. All she wanted at the moment was to reach the surface. His fingers closed more forcefully around her ankle. Amy glanced back, angry at his interference. She tried to wrench free of his grasp and belatedly realized he wasn't going to let go. He signaled firmly to her to slow her ascent, holding on to her to enforce the command.

He was right, Amy knew. She should slow down. Halfway out of the cave now, she had been about to dump the air

from her buoyancy compensator vest instead of slowly re-
leasing it. She and Jed weren't all that deep, but a rapid,
uncontrolled ascent to the surface was always bad practice.
She remembered reading somewhere that nearly half of the
annual diving accidents occurred in less than forty feet of
water. What was the matter with her? She knew better than
to react wildly. All she had was a minor cut on the leg.
There was no excuse for panic.

But then, she had been swimming along the edge of panic
almost from the moment she had entered the water, Amy
reminded herself bitterly.

Jed's mask was level with hers now. She looked into his
eyes and saw his grim determination. He still had a hold on
her. He was taking charge and he was giving her no option
but to do this his way. He held her steady and waited for her
to calm down and accept the situation.

Amy didn't know whether to laugh or cry. She had been
diving since she was a child and water was her second element. She had made a fool of herself today, and in front of a
man who had probably never lost his nerve or self-control in
his entire life. Strange how humiliation could achieve what
common sense could not. She took a firm grip on her nerves
and forced herself to breathe more naturally. She nodded to
Jed and they slowly started back toward the surface at an
angle that brought them in toward shore.

It was, Amy decided later, one of the longest underwater
trips of her life, even though it only lasted a few minutes.
Jed didn't let go of her until they were walking out of the
surf, pushing their masks back on their heads. Neither said a
word until they had reached the sandy beach. Then Jed
stopped. He stood facing Amy with his feet braced slightly
apart, water foaming around his ankles, his hands resting on

his hips. His hazel eyes had lost none of their unrelenting grimness.

"You want to tell me what the hell was going on down there?"

Amy, who had been feeling torn between apologizing for her foolishness and screaming at him for interfering, reacted violently to the cold demand in his voice. She forgot all about apologies and explanations.

"Nothing was going on down there until you started acting like a Neanderthal. I cut myself on the coral. I was trying to get to the surface. That was all there was to it. Are you always that aggressive underwater? You should have warned me. I don't like diving with macho types who feel obliged to take charge of the little woman. When two people go down together it's supposed to be a buddy system, not master and slave!"

"Don't give me that. You were nervous almost from the moment we went in. And it was getting worse, wasn't it? Admit it, you were acting as if it were your first dive and you were terrified. You told me you'd been diving since you were a kid. Your parents said you were good in the water. What got into you down there?"

"Nothing got into me."

He took a step toward her and tapped her air pressure gauge with a short, irritated movement. "Look at that. You were burning almost twice as much air as you should have. Christ, you're down to about five hundred pounds. And you didn't bother to call my attention to that little fact while we were in the cave? Amy, that was stupid and you know it—or you should know it."

"Don't worry," she said through gritted teeth as she stripped off her mask and gloves and began unbuckling the equipment, "I won't subject you to any more dives with me. Feel free to find another partner or feel free to use your return ticket to the States. Just don't get the impression you have a right to stand there and read me the riot act because you don't happen to like the way I handle myself underwater."

He caught hold of her shoulders, his fingers closing around the fabric of the short wet suit. Jed's eyes blazed. "That was the whole damn problem down there. You weren't handling yourself. You were losing control. I want to know why."

"I was not losing control. You just decided you knew more about diving than I did. You had to take charge, didn't you? Couldn't stand the thought of a female diving partner making her own decisions."

"Did this kind of thing happen when you went diving with LePage? Did you panic on him, too?"

A white hot fury enveloped Amy. She swung her hand in a short, violent arc that caught the side of his face with a loud crack.

For a painfully long moment Jed simply stared at her. Amy gasped, aware that she had just provided all the evidence he needed of her lack of self-control. She wanted to scream, she was so mad at herself. She stood trembling with tension, wanting to turn and run and knowing that was impossible. Jed was silent, and his eyes were frighteningly unreadable.

Clenching her fingers into fists, Amy stared at a point just beyond Jed's shoulder. "For both our sakes, don't bring up the subject of Bob LePage again. Do you understand me, Jed?"

"I understand you." He didn't say whether he intended to obey her, however. In fact, he didn't move.

Amy jerked her eyes back to his, feeling suddenly pressured from a new direction. "So? Had enough fun in the sun in a tropical paradise? Going back to California on the next available plane?"

"Is that what you want me to do?"

She moved away from him, trying to appear unconcerned with the matter. "It might be for the best. It's obvious you're not going to enjoy diving with me and, frankly, that's about all there is to do here on Orleana. That and drink Scotch."

"You're not going to get rid of me that easily, Amy."

Her head came up at the soft threat in his voice. She wanted to lash out at him again but she couldn't think of anything to say. A part of her desperately wanted him to stay, but there was another tiny, carping little voice in her head that said it might be much safer if he left.

If he left, she'd know he was just the casual friend she thought he was. It would prove he had no real interest other than normal curiosity about the caves or what happened the previous October. But if he stayed she would have to continue wondering.

"How's the leg?" Jed came closer, eyeing the thin bleeding cut just above her ankle.

Amy stepped back uncomfortably. "It's only a minor scratch."

"Yeah. Hardly enough to cause all that panic," he agreed coolly.

"I did not panic." She shoved equipment into a duffel bag.

"Pardon me, I meant it was hardly enough to cause all that *stress*." He began removing his gear. "Let's get back to the house and take care of it. No sense getting it infected. Then you really would have something to scream at me about, wouldn't you? Somehow, it would be my fault."

"Stop it, Jed," she hissed.

"Stop what?"

"Stop baiting me, dammit."

"Sorry. Maybe I'm just trying to let off a little of my own tension. Returning your slap might do the trick, but it doesn't seem like the gentlemanly thing to do."

Amy said nothing. Grabbing her equipment, she stalked up the beach to the Jeep her father had insisted they use. Jed joined her a few minutes later. He had pulled his jeans on over his swimming trunks. He stowed diving gear in the back of the vehicle, dropped into the driver's seat, and twisted the key in the ignition without saying a word.

In spite of her own foul mood, Amy glanced at his left leg. "Is your leg all right?"

"The leg is fine." He spun the wheel of the vehicle and headed for the road.

Amy lapsed back into silence. Her small wound wasn't even bleeding now. It was a long, uncomfortably silent ride back to the house.

Douglas Slater was standing in the doorway when Jed pulled into the drive. He waved a jaunty greeting and started to ask about the dive as Amy jumped out of the Jeep. When she gave him a short, monosyllabic answer, grabbed her gear and strode past him, he cut off his questions and raised his eyebrows inquiringly at Jed.

"My daughter, sir, seems a bit upset."

"Your daughter, sir, is mad as hell at me."

"You don't seem all that upset," Slater observed.

"I'm choosing to interpret the situation as a sign of progress." Jed hoisted his diving tank and bag of equipment and walked into the house.

Chapter Seven

Sunset that evening found Jed with a glass of white wine in his hand. He sipped it in hope of gaining fortitude. He would have preferred the Scotch his host had offered earlier, but Jed figured the wine was a small gesture that might help appease Amy. He only hoped she had noticed it before she had left for the kitchen with her mother. But she had hardly spoken three words to him since they had returned from the dive, so he couldn't be sure. For that matter, he couldn't be certain if she even gave a damn what he drank.

"I trust you like grilled pompano," Slater said as he began the nightly ritual of stoking his outdoor barbeque. "One of the local fishermen had a nice haul this morning. I picked up a couple of pounds from him today when I went into town."

"Anything to wash down this wine." Jed grinned and held up his glass as Slater glanced at him.

The older man returned the grin. "She's really got you going, hasn't she?"

"I've only just begun to realize it, myself." Jed leaned one elbow against the railing, swirling the wine absently in the glass. "Her temper took me by surprise this afternoon, though. Somehow I wasn't expecting it." But he should have expected it, Jed told himself. There was too much passion in her. She was bound to have a temper. It was strange to realize he had known her for three months and this was the first time he'd encountered it. She had been very careful these past few months. But then, so had he.

Slater laughed and straightened to reach for his Scotch. "Sooner or later you were sure to encounter Amy's temper. It takes a lot to rile my daughter, but when she gets angry, it's for real. I won't ask what happened during the dive this afternoon."

Jed smiled wryly. "It wasn't all that much. She did something stupid underwater and I yelled at her for it afterward. I think she's as furious with herself as she is with me."

Slater nodded. "You're probably right. She's not used to being yelled at, however. Because she was the youngest I think we all tended to coddle her. She was different from the other three. She seemed to lack any clear direction. Hugh, Darren and Sylvia all seemed to know what they wanted to do in life by the time they were twelve or thirteen. Amy sort of drifted along. It was frustrating at times. Especially when she reached her twenties and was still drifting from one silly, mundane job to another. Who'd have guessed she'd wind up writing science fiction?"

Jed abruptly thought of the heroine in *Private Demons* swimming through the black depths of an underwater cave to face an indescribable horror. Memories of Amy's increasing stress in the small cavern that afternoon mingled with what he'd read in those last pages of her manuscript. "I take it you never expected her to end up as a writer?"

Slater shook his head, smiling indulgently. "To tell you the truth, I always understood my other offspring far better than I understood Amy. There were times when Gloria and I swore she must be a changeling. But some things about her are crystal clear."

"Yeah?" Jed watched Slater's face, aware of a deep curiosity.

"She's loyal as hell, for one thing. She'd face the devil himself for someone she loved. Don't get me wrong, so would my other kids. But they'd use a little finesse. Hugh would negotiate. Darren would produce a contract so airtight, the devil himself couldn't break it. Sylvia would charm him silly."

"And Amy?" Jed prompted softly.

Slater met his eyes. "What do you think Amy would do?"

"I think she'd go for his throat." Jed paused, thinking about it. "She'd somehow know that the direct approach is the only one that works in some situations and she'd do what had to be done or go down trying."

Slater nodded. "That's Amy."

Jed would bet his last dollar she got the trait from her father. Studying the older man, Jed sensed with the intuition that had helped keep him alive the past eight years that he was right. Doug Slater had definitely passed a few of his own personal traits down to his daughter, whether he realized it or not. Jed was about to say something else when the phone rang just inside the open doors. He turned his head and saw Amy hurry out of the kitchen, wiping her hands on a towel, to answer it. She didn't look at him as she picked up the receiver.

Amy said hello into the receiver and then smiled as she recognized the voice of her sister Sylvia on the other end of the line.

"So that's where you are, Amy. I've been calling Caliph's Bay for two solid days. I was beginning to think you'd run off with some handsome little green man with pointy ears."

Amy sank down onto the cushion of a rattan chair. "It's

tough to find handsome little green men, Sylvia. All the good ones are married. What's up?"

"I was calling to give Mom and Dad the good news." Sylvia's voice was laced with sheer, feminine satisfaction.

"What good news?"

"I'm pregnant."

Amy surged to her feet. "Pregnant? Sylvia, that's impossible. You can't be pregnant!" She glanced around wildly and realized she had everyone's attention. Gloria Slater was standing in the kitchen doorway, looking astonished. Her father had crossed the veranda to look questioningly into the living room, and Jed was watching Amy with mild amusement. Amy put her hand over the phone and said baldly, "Sylvia's pregnant."

"We heard, dear," Gloria said calmly. "Let's get the rest of the story."

Amy took her hand off the mouthpiece and said very determinedly, "Sylvia, you can't possibly be pregnant. You're an obstetrician, a gynecologist for heaven's sake. How could you have had an accident?"

"Who said it was an accident?" Sylvia murmured.

"Oh, lord." Amy sank back down onto the cushion. "Don't put us through this suspense, Syl. Tell me the whole thing in one gulp."

"I'm pregnant and I'm going to get married. How's that for neat and simple, little sister?"

"I can't believe it. Who are you marrying?"

"His name is Craig Larsen. He's healthy, handsome and upwardly mobile. Excellent genetic stock. The folks are going to love him."

"Is he a doctor, too?" Amy demanded, aware that she was about to lose the receiver to her mother.

"Yes. An orthopedic man. Is that Mom I hear in the background?"

"How did you guess?" Ruefully Amy started to relinquish the phone. "Congratulations, Syl. Can't wait to meet—" She didn't get a chance to finish. Her mother already had the receiver in her hand and her father was heading for the bedroom to pick up the extension.

Amy was left to wander out to the veranda where Jed was still looking amused. She cleared her throat. "My sister," she explained.

"So I gathered."

"She's getting married."

"And she's pregnant."

Amy glanced at him and her mouth curved in spite of herself. "Apparently so. Sylvia is a lot like my mother in her organizational abilities. She likes things tidy and efficient. I should have realized the pregnancy was no accident. Knowing Sylvia, she probably refused to marry this poor Dr. Larsen until he'd proven his reproductive abilities."

Jed chuckled. "I think your parents are in shock."

"Sylvia knows how to handle them. She knows how to handle everyone. Mom and Dad will be thrilled by the time she finishes talking to them on the phone. Wait and see."

Amy was right. Gloria and Doug were not only excited, they were bound and determined to meet Dr. Craig Larsen before they went to Europe. Amy's mother was already realigning their schedule to accommodate the surprise. She sat across from Amy at the dining table, handed her the salad tongs and announced, "I think we'll leave tomorrow afternoon instead of next week. That will give Doug and me a few days to spend with Sylvia and meet her fiancé. We'll even be able to attend the wedding, which, I gather, is going to be extremely simple."

Amy's heart pounded wildly as she realized what her mother was saying. Amy couldn't leave yet. She hadn't found the key. She had to face something on the island and she hadn't figured out how or when she was going to do it. If she left now she might never be able to return and face it again.

As though he'd read her mind, her father said easily, "No reason you and Jed can't stay on here for as long as you like."

Stay alone with Jed? Amy's eyes flew to his. She found his intent gaze already fixed on her.

"Sounds like an excellent idea. I'm getting addicted to the lifestyle," Jed said. "What do you say, Amy?"

She had to stay. She knew that. And it looked like there was no way to avoid having Jed stay with her. She couldn't even convince herself she really wanted him to leave. He troubled her and raised questions that couldn't be answered, but the thought of staying without him brought no sense of relief. Somehow, she realized, Jed had become mixed up in her nightmare and could no longer be separated from it. He was part of the key.

"Yes," Amy said quietly, "it does sound like an excellent idea. I'd like to stay for a few more days."

"Wonderful," Gloria enthused, covertly eyeing her daughter's expression. "I'd much rather have someone in the house; I hate to leave it standing empty any longer than necessary."

Amy glanced down at her plate of grilled fish. Until her father had retired the house had stood empty most of the time. The Slaters had only used it a few weeks out of the year while Amy was growing up. Leaving the house empty in those days hadn't worried Gloria Slater. She was matchmaking.

"Good heavens, I can't believe we have another grandchild on the way, Doug." Gloria smiled benignly. "I hope it's a girl. What with Hugh and Darren's kids we've got enough boys running around. How like Sylvia to present us with a *fait accompli*. Baby on the way and a wedding scheduled in four days' time. I hope she knows what she's doing."

"She does," Slater said easily. "Sylvia always knows exactly what she's doing. Has since she was five years old. She inherited your talents for organization and detail, my dear."

Amy concentrated on her fish, only half listening to the conversation. It was hard to believe she had thought she could learn to handle her problems by observing the way her mother lived her life. Amy knew she wasn't anything like Gloria.

Something made Amy glance up again to meet Jed's steady gaze. He was watching her as her mother chatted about grandchildren and plans for the future, his eyes full of that assessing, perceptive quality that could be so unnerving at times. It was almost as if he could read her mind. But in a flash of disorienting intuition, it was Amy who thought she read his.

It wasn't the first time she'd had the experience, but she reacted as she always did, retreating instantly, just as if she'd been about to cross some dangerous mental barrier. There always seemed to be shadows on the other side of that barrier, shadows Jed kept locked behind iron gates.

* * *

Hours later, Amy stood in the veranda doorway of her bedroom, listening to the silence of the house and the soft sounds of the island at night. Her parents had gone to bed two hours before. Jed had wished her a pleasant good night and vanished to his own room. As far as she knew he was asleep.

As usual, it was only Amy who was wide awake in the middle of the night. She told herself she ought to be growing accustomed to it.

She stepped out onto the veranda, her bare feet making no sound on the boards. The soft warm air caught the hem of her long cotton nightgown, causing it to drift lazily around her ankles. The gown was cut with a demure scoop neck and tiny sleeves. Lightweight and comfortable, it was designed for sleeping on a warm, tropical night. It most definitely was not from Fredericks of Hollywood. Jed would have no reason to think she was trying to seduce him.

Amy moved silently along the veranda until she came to the open doors of his room. Standing quietly for a moment with the light of the moon outlining her slender figure, she peered into the darkness. If he was sound asleep she wouldn't wake him, she promised herself.

"Having trouble sleeping again, Amy?" His voice was like a dark shadow among the other shadows of the room. Until he moved, pushing back the sheet and swinging his feet to the floor, she couldn't see him. Then he was walking toward her out of the darkness, turning from ghost into man. He stopped a couple of feet away, not touching her

"I wanted to talk to you," she said quietly.

"About staying here after your parents leave?"

She shook her head. "No. About what happened in the water today."

"Ah." The single syllable emerged as a soft, satisfied sigh. He stepped through the doorway and moved to lean against the veranda railing.

"Look, Jed, if you don't want to hear this—"

"Hush, sweetheart. Keep your voice down or you'll wake your parents." He paused, regarding her stiff, uncertain figure with an indulgent eye. "Come here, Amy."

Reluctantly she went to him, her eyes never leaving his.

"What did you want to say about today?" he prompted softly.

She drew a deep breath. "That I'm sorry. I behaved like an irresponsible idiot. I shouldn't have lost my temper afterward. You did the right thing. There, I think that about covers it."

He didn't move, but she could tell he was scowling. "Is that all you wanted to say?"

"What else is there to say? I assume you don't want me to actually grovel over a minor bit of stupidity. I thought an apology would be sufficient."

"How about telling me why you reacted the way you did down there? You're supposed to be a competent, experienced diver. What upset you?"

"It's been several months since I dove." It was a lame excuse and she knew it. "Next time I'll be fine."

"Uh huh."

"Dammit I will be all right next time."

"Okay, okay." He lifted a palm as if to ward off an attack, although Amy hadn't moved. "We'll find out soon enough, won't we?"

"Look, Jed, if you've got doubts about going down with

me again, just say so. No one's forcing you to keep me company on this island or underwater. If you'd rather go back to California, you're welcome to leave tomorrow with my parents."

"Trying to get rid of me again?"

She closed her eyes briefly against the injustice of it all. "I am not trying to get rid of you." Each word was enunciated with great care. She felt Jed's big hand close around her arm and opened her eyes to find him standing very close.

"I'm glad you're not trying to ditch me," he murmured, "because I'm not ready to leave yet."

"Why not?"

"Take a guess." He tugged her lightly into his arms.

Instinctively, Amy's hands lifted. Her fingers slid up along his forearms and she heard him suck in his breath as she touched the long scar above his elbow. "Jed? What's wrong?"

"Nothing." He tightened his grip on her, intending to pull her closer.

But Amy had felt the heat around the newly healed wound. She touched him again, lightly. "There is something wrong. Come inside. I want to have a look."

"Amy, just leave it alone, will you?"

"No " She wrapped her hand around his wrist and drew him into the bedroom. He sighed impatiently but didn't argue as she pulled him through the shadows into the bathroom where she quickly flipped on the light. Instantly she saw the reddened area around the scar. "There's a clinic in the village. Tomorrow when we take my parents to the airport we'll stop in and have someone look at this."

"There's no need. It'll be fine."

She frowned at him. "Don't be silly. It will only take a

minute and there's no sense taking chances. Why didn't you tell me you were having trouble with this arm?"

"Because I wasn't having trouble with it."

"When did it start getting red like this?"

"This evening," he growled. "I'm sure it will be fine by morning. Now, if you've finished playing nurse, let's get back to what we were discussing on the veranda."

She ignored him. "You probably shouldn't have gone into the water this afternoon."

"I'm sure it's got nothing to do with the diving. Amy, normally I like it when you fuss over me, but—"

"I do not fuss!"

He smiled. "Yes, you do. You try not to, but you do it anyway. It's sweet."

"Sweet? You think I'm sweet? Is that how you see me, Jed?" She released his arm and stepped back.

"Amy, I think an unnecessary argument is taking shape here. Let's stop right where we are, back up and start again."

"Not a chance. I'm not in the mood."

"Headache?" he taunted.

She lifted her chin. "Not at all. As it happens, I suddenly feel very sleepy. Given my insomnia habits, I can't afford to ignore any sign of genuine sleepiness. I'm going back to bed."

She swept toward the door before Jed could think of a way to stop her. At the last possible instant he had a thought.

"Amy?"

She paused in the doorway. "What is it?"

"About your sister."

"Sylvia? What about her?"

He took a couple of steps toward her and halted. "Her big

announcement about expecting a baby made me realize that we . . ." He paused, searching for the right words. Finally he gave up. "That we haven t been taking precautions."

"A fine time to start worrying about it."

He heard the asperity in her voice and sighed. "I'm sorry, Amy. I should have thought about it earlier. We went along for nearly three months as friends and then, all of a sudden, we were more than that. Things just started happening very quickly between us."

"Don't worry about it, Jed. I know you don't want any strings. I paid a visit to Dr. Mullaney last month and got a prescription."

"Last month!" He was startled. "But nothing happened between us until I came home the last time."

"I know." She smiled faintly in the moonlight. "But I'm not a complete idiot. I knew something was probably going to happen sooner or later."

"And you didn't want to take any chances?"

"Neither of us can afford to take chances, can we Jed?" she asked wryly and turned to go.

"Amy, wait." He caught up with her, catching hold of her wrist. "Do you think I'd make such a lousy father?" Christ, he didn't know what made him ask such a dumb question, but it was too late to call back the words.

To his surprise, Amy didn't respond with the scathing retort he expected. Instead, she touched her finger to his bottom lip, her eyes misty with an expression he couldn't read. "As a matter of fact, Jed, I think you might make an excellent father."

He opened his mouth, but no words came out. He didn't know what to say. Before he could think of anything brilliant, Amy was gone.

He stood staring out into the darkness and thought about private demons. Amy wasn't the only one who had them.

Gloria Slater had herself and her husband packed and ready to leave late the next afternoon. Amy could only marvel at her mother's ability to accomplish such miracles, but her father had learned to take the talent for granted over the years. He was relaxed and good natured as he and Jed discussed the vehicle situation.

"Follow us into town and return that rusted out rental MacCready gave you. Then you can use our Jeep for the rest of your stay. When you leave the island, just leave the Jeep with MacCready. He'll take care of it until we return."

Jed nodded, swinging suitcases into the back of the Jeep. "All right, sounds like a reasonable plan."

Slater glanced toward the house where both Amy and her mother were taking care of last minute details. "I'm glad Amy decided to stay a while longer. She needs the vacation."

Jed hoisted another suitcase and asked bluntly, "You don't mind the fact that I'm staying with her?"

Slater regarded him assessingly. "No," he said quietly, "I don't mind. I have a feeling you'll take care of my daughter."

Jed stowed the last suitcase and turned to face Slater. "You're right. I'll take care of her."

Slater nodded.

The small island hopper plane left for Honolulu around four o'clock. Amy perched on the fender of the Jeep with Jed standing beside her and waved as the plane lifted off the runway. It took a wide, sweeping turn out over the sea and headed for the horizon. When it was almost out of sight,

Amy jumped down from the fender and slid into the passenger seat.

"All right," she announced brightly, "let's make a quick stop at the clinic. It's not very far from here." She saw the stubborn look in Jed's eyes, but she refused to be deflected from her goal. "I'm not taking no for an answer, Jed. Your arm should be looked at."

He got in beside her. "My arm is okay."

"Your arm is not okay. The scar is still red and I think it should be seen by someone who knows what he's doing. Dr. Stearn is a competent man. He's been running the island clinic for fifteen years."

"I don't doubt his competency. What I doubt is the need to have him look at my arm." Jed let out the clutch with a swift, impatient movement. The Jeep leaped forward.

"Jed, you shouldn't take chances. This is a tropical island. There are a lot of weird organisms floating around in the water."

"You know, a month ago—or even last week—you wouldn't have nagged me like this." But there was a wryly amused twist to his mouth.

"A month ago I was just your *friend*," she said sweetly. "Friends aren't supposed to nag."

"But lovers are allowed the privilege?"

"Of course. Lovers also have the right to lose their tempers the way you did yesterday after the dive," she added magnanimously. "The way I see it, you brought this all on yourself. If you don't like being nagged, you should never have made love to me in the first place."

"The logic of this is defeating me."

"Just drive. And don't forget to have Stearn take a look at your leg, too "

Forty minutes later Amy flipped through the last of the ancient magazines in the clinic waiting room and got to her feet to pace toward the screened window. What was taking Dr. Stearn so long? Perhaps the injury on Jed's arm was more infected than Amy had thought. Lani, the nurse, had gone home twenty minutes before. Through the door of the tiny examination room Amy could hear the low murmur of male voices, but they hadn't bothered to inform her what was going on.

She was about to go across the street to get some things for dinner at the small grocery store when the examination room door opened. Dr. Stearn, a man in his mid-sixties with a comfortable paunch, a wide bald spot and a bad cigarette habit came through first. He beamed at Amy. Over his shoulder she could see Jed buttoning his shirt.

"Amy, my girl, good to see you again. It's been a while. I hear your folks just left the island?"

She nodded, smiling. "They're on their way to see my sister and then they're headed for Europe. How have you been, Dr. Stearn?"

He chuckled. "Same as always. Nothing changes here on Orleana, you know that. It's one of the reasons I came to stay fifteen years ago. The rest of the world is changing too fast these days. There aren't many places like Orleana where a man can escape. People like me need islands. Thanks for bringing me some business."

Amy laughed. "You're welcome. How is Jed's arm?"

"Oh, nothing too serious. One of the stitches wasn't removed and was festering under the skin. It probably would have emerged on its own in a couple of days. Stitches are the least of your man's problems. If you want to keep him in one piece you'd better learn to discourage him from playing around with sharp knives and loaded guns. That bullet in the thigh was a close call. A little higher and he might have been singing soprano in a boys' choir."

Amy kept the smile frozen on her face as Jed came into the waiting room. She knew he'd heard the doctor's words. He looked at her, his gaze revealing nothing. He silently and methodically finished rolling up the sleeves of his khaki shirt.

Dr. Stearn turned to slap his patient on the back, giving Jed a comradely, man-to-man look. "Just keep the wound clean for a couple of days. You won't have any more trouble with it, I'm sure. I don't see any problem with diving in a day or two."

Jed nodded, his eyes still on Amy's politely smiling face. "Thanks, Stearn. I'll take care of it."

"You do that." The doctor turned to nod once more to Amy. "So long. Take care of yourself, Amy. I hear you're a big-time writer now?"

"Not exactly big time. More like very small time."

Stearn chuckled. "That's not the way your father tells it. He's very proud of you. After all those years of wondering whether you were ever going to find yourself, he's quite relieved to see you settling down to a genuine career. Even if it is something flaky like writing science fiction."

"Good-bye, Dr. Stearn," Amy said politely.

"Take your man home and give him a drink. Nothing like a little alcohol to disinfect things, eh, Glaze?"

"Thanks for the advice." Jed didn't move, though. He was staring at Amy, waiting for her to take the lead.

Amy nodded once more to the doctor, then turned toward the screen door. "Come on, Jed, I think Dr. Stearn is right. Let's go have a drink."

He followed her slowly into the late afternoon sun. When he realized she wasn't heading for the Jeep, he fell into step beside her.

"Where are you going?" His voice was tight and clipped.

"For that drink Dr. Stearn recommended. Don't worry, Hank and Rosie don't serve white wine." She moved briskly along the sidewalk, past the small shops that were being closed up for the evening. Several people nodded to her in greeting.

Jed said nothing as Amy led the way down to the waterfront. She made for the familiar, ramshackle, open air bar that overlooked the quay. The comfortably worn interior was already filling up for the evening. Several of the locals waved at Amy as she headed toward a table near the railing.

Jed sat down slowly, still apparently riveted by her calm, remote expression. Tension crackled in the air. Silence stretched between them for a long moment and then he said quietly, "Stearn has a big mouth."

Amy looked out over the fishing boats bobbing in the harbor. "Maybe I should have known all along that you weren't really an engineer. You never talked about your work. I guess I just didn't want to ask too many questions. I was afraid of the answers."

"And now?"

"Now I feel rather like a wife whose husband comes home with a venereal disease. It's impossible for her to pretend any longer that he's not having an affair with another woman. The issue is out in the open. Who do you work for, Jed? The government? The Mafia? Or are you just a free-lance mercenary?"

Chapter Eight

"I thought it would be better if you didn't know what I did for a living." Jed's voice was low and remote. He followed Amy's gaze toward the harbor.

"Better? Or was it just easier for you if I didn't know?"

"You never asked any questions."

"Maybe I didn't want to know the answers."

"Why open up the subject now?" Jed asked calmly.

"I told you. After what Dr. Stearn said, it would be a little difficult to ignore it. Good thing for you I didn't visit Dr. Mullaney after you went to him to have him check your wounds, wasn't it? It might have been Mullaney who gave me the advice about keeping you away from knives and guns." Amy's fingers clenched and unclenched nervously. Dear God, Jed might have been killed. She might never have known what happened to him.

"Mullaney bought my story about the car accident. He didn't ask any questions. But Stearn apparently did a stint as a surgeon in Vietnam. He knew what he was looking at right away."

"So here we are with the subject of your employment opened for discussion."

"What if I choose to go on ignoring it?" He sounded only academically curious, as if he were testing alternatives.

Amy thought about it. "I suppose we could go on as we are."

That seemed to startle him. "You think so?"

She said cautiously, earnestly, "It might work. It's worked this far, hasn't it?"

He smiled faintly. "You're lying to yourself and you know it. You'd probably try to ignore your own questions, but I don't think you could do it. Not now that we're more than friends. And not now that the subject is out in the open. You'll start pushing for answers sooner or later."

"You think you know me very well, don't you?"

"I'm learning."

She nodded, accepting the fact that their relationship was changing almost daily and that he was a perceptive man. But before she could speak again she was interrupted by the approach of a huge bear of a man. He bore down on the table, a big grin slicing through his full beard. His beard had once been red but it was heavily streaked with gray these days. The man's shrewd brown eyes were as vital as ever, though, and Amy found herself smiling in return in spite of the tension that had been gripping her.

"Amy, girl, where've you been? Haven't seen you for ages. Your dad said you'd postponed your trip to the island for a couple of months."

"I did." Amy got to her feet and was promptly enveloped in a tight hug. "How are you doing, Hank?"

"Same as ever." He chuckled, the sound a rich, deep rumble in his chest.

"And Rosie?"

"She's around here somewhere. Probably in the kitchen. You two staying for dinner? She'd like that." Without waiting for a response, Hank forcefully clapped Amy on the back. "Introduce me to your friend. Heard you had a visitor with you."

"Jed, meet Hank Halliday. He and his wife, Rosie, own this place. They've been running it since before I was born. Hank, this is Jed Glaze. He's . . . a friend."

Hank stuck out a paw that was as big as Jed's. "Glad to meet you, Glaze. Any friend of Amy's and all that. How long you staying?"

"Amy and I are going to be here a few more days. We haven't really made any decision about when to leave, have we, Amy?"

She caught the cool challenge in his voice. "No, we haven't made any decision."

"Careful. That's what Rosie and I told ourselves thirty years ago. Kept putting off the decision to leave and look what happened. Let me get you two something to drink. I hope you're not still drinking that water you call white wine, Amy, 'cause I don't have any on hand."

"Actually, I was thinking of something a little stronger tonight," Amy replied dryly.

"How about one of Rosie's guava juice cocktails?"

She gave in to the inevitable. "All right, I'll take a chance."

Hank looked inquiringly at Jed.

"Scotch," Jed said. "On the rocks."

Hank nodded. "I'll be back in a few minutes. And I'm going to tell Rosie that you're both staying for dinner, okay?"

Jed answered before Amy could. "Sounds good, Hank, thanks." He waited while the older man headed back toward the bar on the other side of the room. When he was out of hearing, Jed said calmly, "Where were we?"

"I believe you were telling me you didn't think I'd be able to keep my questions to myself." Amy looked directly at him. "I think you're right. Things have changed, just as you said."

He nodded. "I knew it would come to this sooner or later. I guess I hoped it would be later."

"Why?"

He shrugged, leaning back in the scarred rattan chair. "Because I've always assumed that when you found out the truth, you'd call a halt to our relationship. You're not going to like what I do for a living, Amy."

"I may not like it, but I don't think I'll end things between us because of it. Just tell me, Jed."

He seemed to come to some inner decision. "All right. I work for the government on a kind of unofficial, free-lance basis. The job with the engineering consulting firm is a convenient cover because I used to be an engineer. Now I go places and do things that have very little to do with engineering."

"And you also build bird cages," she said softly.

Jed paused. "And I also build bird cages," he agreed.

An unofficial, free-lance government agent who built bird cages in his spare time. Amy let the information wash through her as Hank returned with the drinks. She listened to the casual flow of conversation between the two men, marveling at the easy way Jed shifted gears. Jed definitely had a talent for showing people the side of him they either wanted or expected to see. She was thinking about how smoothly he had handled her parents efforts to treat him as if he were a potential husband when Hank turned to her.

"Hey, Amy, girl, you going to take him out to dive that old B-25? Most folks get a kick out of that " Hank grinned at Jed. "Orleana Island's one big scenic attraction, I guess you'd say. A bomber went down during the war when the Marines took the island back from the Japanese. It's not far off the north shore in fairly shallow water. The few tourists we get around here are usually into diving and they always want to see it."

"I'll have to get Amy to show it to me one of these days," Jed replied, glancing at her.

Amy thought of the dark interior of the old, shattered fuselage. It would be a little like going into a cave. She shivered and said nothing.

"The waters off the north shore are usually a good place to find dinner," Hank went on enthusiastically.

"I'm not much of a hunter," Jed said.

Amy looked into his eyes and knew he was lying. He hunted, all right. But Jed's game was human. She knew that in the depths of her soul. She had probably known it all along. Perhaps it was one of the reasons she'd allowed him to get so close to her. He was a man who knew how to keep shadows locked away behind iron bars and she needed to learn that skill.

"Rosie'll be out in a minute," Hank was saying. "Says she's got a pot of her special fish chowder going on the burner. Her chowder's just this side of heaven, ain't it, Amy?"

"It's terrific." She started to search for a more casual, conversational response, but found she couldn't find the words. How on earth did Jed do it so easily? she wondered. The answer was obvious. He'd had practice. He was accustomed to playing different roles. Amy was saved from the awkward situation by the arrival of Rosie Halliday.

"Amy, you little bit of a thing, you! How're you doing?

Haven't seen you in months. 'Bout time you got back to the island. Understand you've brought along a man friend. Hope he's a site more interesting than the last one. I didn't take to that one. Let me see what you've got this time. Ah ha. He's big, ain't he? Not quite as big as my Hank, but he'll do. Good, big hands. That's a sure sign."

"Of what?" Amy asked dryly as Rosie stopped beside her husband and stood, hands on her hips, studying Jed.

Rosie was not exactly small, herself. She was broad from top to bottom and her eyes were engaging blue lagoons set in a wide, laughing face. Her hair had gone almost as gray as Hank's over the years, but she didn't really change much. Rosie always had on a flowing white apron, a bright print dress and a flower in her hair. Tonight was no exception. She turned on Amy, appearing stunned by the question.

"Of what? A sign of *what*, girl? You don't know what I'm talkin' about? Big hands are a sign a man's built to match elsewhere. What's the matter with you? Don't you folks on the mainland know about this kind of thing? I thought sex education was being taught in all the schools these days."

Amy went pink. She knew she ought to be accustomed to Rosie's sense of humor after all these years, but sometimes the woman still managed to take her by surprise. "I thought it was big feet that were supposed to be a sign of . . . you know," Amy mumbled into her drink, not daring to look at Jed.

Rosie glanced pointedly down to where Jed's large feet were stretched out under the table. "Well, I'd say he's okay in the foot department, too."

Amy nearly choked on her heavily laced guava juice. Hank intervened before she was called upon to reply to

Rosie's observation. "That's enough, Rosie. You're embarrassing the girl."

"She's a full grown woman now. Don't need to shield her from the facts of life any longer, do we?" Rosie winked broadly at Jed, who was blandly watching the byplay.

"No," Jed agreed. "I think she's tough enough to handle the facts of life."

Rosie laughed delightedly and scooped up Amy's cocktail. "Come on back in the kitchen and keep me company, Amy girl. I got to fix dinner for some folks we've got staying here at the inn. Some of them are leaving tomorrow and I want to send 'em off with fond memories. We'll eat when they've finished. Hank, you can take care of Jed here, can't you?"

"You bet." Hank waved Jed toward a stool at the bar "Come on up front and talk to me while I ply everyone here with liquor." He started back toward the bar and Rosie moved off toward the kitchen.

Amy glanced helplessly at Jed. "I don't think this is such a good idea," she whispered.

"Why not? You and I were having a hard time carrying on a conversation by ourselves, as I recall. Limited subject matter. Go see if chatting with Rosie will relax you."

"Dammit, Jed, I don't need to be relaxed. Don't you understand? Hank just wants to check you out the way my parents did."

"Ah, another approval drill. But I'm good at getting through those, remember? Don't worry about it, Amy. I'll see you at dinner." He got to his feet, picked up his Scotch and sauntered toward the bar.

Amy stared after him, aware of all the things they had yet to discuss

Jed worked undercover for the government. She couldn't concentrate on anything except that single fact.

It was when she entered Rosie's small, old-fashioned kitchen that Amy suddenly realized what Jed's admission meant. If he worked for the government, then she could stop worrying about whether he was part of a dangerous conspiracy against her. Surely the Feds had no interest in what had happened on the island in October. It was a private matter. She would have had more cause to be frightened if she had learned Jed was a true mercenary like LePage.

"Here, I knew this would lure you in." Rosie thrust Amy's drink back into her hand and picked up her own. "Not many folks can resist my little invention." She stirred the simmering fish chowder, then took a small taste.

"What in the world is in this guava juice, Rosie? It goes down easily, but I think I'm getting to feel the sting."

"Delayed reaction," Rosie explained, tipping a bottle of whiskey over the chowder. She put the bottle down on the chipped counter top and took another swallow from her guava juice cocktail. "It's my secret recipe. Maybe I'll write it out for you as a wedding present."

"It might be years before I get it, then. I have no immediate plans, Rosie." Amy kept her voice cordial but firm.

"Hah. You're not gettin' any younger, you know. And the good Lord knows your parents are starting to fret about you and your sister's lack of interest in marriage."

"Well, they've stopped worrying about Sylvia." Amy found herself smiling. "She called to say the wedding's scheduled for next week. That's why Mom and Dad left for the mainland this afternoon. They want to vet the groom."

Rosie gave a great crack of laughter. "Now, ain't that just like Syl? Have everything tied up in a neat package before telling anyone about it." She waved a dripping ladle in Amy's direction. "You, on the other hand, were never that organized. Look at you—floundering around at your age, bringing a different man to the island every few months..."

"You're exaggerating, Rosie, and you know it. Jed's only the second man I've brought to the island. The one I brought a few months ago was just a... a diving acquaintance. And Jed's merely a friend."

"Sure. And if I believe that man out there with the big hands is merely a friend, you've got a nice bridge you can sell me, right? Come on, girl, we may be a little out of touch here on Orleana, but that don't mean we're stupid."

Amy groaned. "You know I didn't mean that." She leaned forward to sniff the chowder, anxious to change the subject. "That smells delicious. You said you had some people booked at the inn?"

"Yup, arrived a week ago to do some diving. We're starting to get paying customers on a regular basis these days. Some of this batch will be leaving tomorrow, but we've actually got a few more coming in next week. Hard to believe. Made reservations yet. Just as if the place were a real hotel." Rosie shook her head. "Orleana's getting downright popular. We've even got a cruise ship calling here once a week. First thing you know the place will be crawling with tourists, just like Hawaii."

"I doubt that. Not for another fifty or sixty years. Orleana's just too far off the beaten track. Don't worry, Rosie, you and Hank and Dr. Stearn and my parents will all have your privacy for a long time to come."

"I surely hope so. I don't think I could adjust to what you folks like to call the fast lane. I know Hank and Stearn and most of the other locals couldn't either. Your parents are the only ones I ever knew who seemed to be able to come and go and live in both worlds. But if you ask me, since they retired here, it's getting harder and harder for them to leave. We sure have us some good times with them here, now."

Amy felt a small shiver of an odd and totally unexpected anticipation. She didn't know whether she wanted to ask the next question, but she couldn't seem to help herself. Her fingers tightened around the glass in her hand. "Do you remember what it was like when we used to come here in the old days, Rosie?"

"Sure do. My memory hasn't gone anywhere yet. Hank and I opened this place a couple of years before you were born. Your folks and that guy who was your father's partner used to stop in here all the time." Rosie grabbed her glass and took another healthy swallow. Amy winced at the quantity of liquor that was going down the other woman's throat. Rosie was apparently one of those people who believed the cook had a few privileges in the kitchen.

"I don't remember much about those first years," Amy prompted tentatively. Why was she doing this?

"'Course you don't. You and your brothers and sister were just babies. In fact, I remember the first time your mother carried you in here. You started squalling and I put a drop or two of whiskey on your tongue. Quieted you right down."

"I can imagine."

Rosie shook her head reminiscently. "Those were the days. We were all so much younger then, so full of life. Hard to believe so many years have gone by."

Amy took a deep breath. "Do you remember when Michael Wyman died?"

"Sure do. Changed everything for your folks. We didn't

see much of them for the next few years. Occasionally they'd get out here for a week or two during the summer, but that was about it. Your dad really had a job on his hands trying to keep his company afloat after Wyman went down in his boat. And your mother, bless her heart, had her hands full raising four kids and giving your dad the kind of support he needed to survive while he kept Slater Aero alive. The two of them made a heck of a team. They stuck together under conditions that would have driven a lot of folks apart. Sometimes I think it was the best thing that could have happened to them."

"Why's that?"

"Well, it's hard to explain. But you gotta realize that your mother was only twenty-six by the time you came along. There she was, a young, good looking woman with four kids on her hands and a husband who was spending most of his time building an aerospace company. Before Wyman died and brought on the crisis, she was getting mighty frustrated and restless. Oh, she loved you kids and your dad, but I think she was lonesome, if you know what I mean. It sounds ridiculous, but raising four kids can make a woman feel mighty lonesome. But after Wyman disappeared, she really buckled down and devoted herself to keeping the family on an even keel while your dad built the business back up."

"I don't remember Wyman," Amy said carefully. She shouldn't be doing this. It was dangerous. The past should stay buried and she knew it. But she couldn't help herself. She took another sip of her drink, no longer tasting it. Her attention was on Rosie.

"I remember him," Rosie declared, sounding aggressive

"He was a born troublemaker if ever there was one. Wild. Smart as hell and knew it. Thought he owned the world and he sure as hell thought he was the important half of that aerospace company. He seemed to get his kicks from upsetting everyone. I remember the year he brought that woman with him to the island."

Amy went cold. "What woman?"

"Some blond floozy. You know the type. Thought she was Marilyn Monroe or something. Really upset your mother, as I remember."

"Why?" Every instinct warned Amy to stop, but she had given up even trying.

"That blond hustler made a play for your dad. Bold as brass. And all the while that Wyman fellow just grinned like a shark waiting for his food." Rosie frowned intently over the chowder. "This looks about ready. What do you say we get the paying customers out of the way so we can eat?"

Amy nodded mutely, picking up a stack of napkins and a handful of old stainless steel spoons. She was trembling when she went out into the main room to set a table for Hank and Rosie's inn guests.

Jed was still sitting at the bar, hunched comfortably over his glass of Scotch while he talked to Hank. He glanced at Amy when she came into the room, then turned back to his conversation with Hank.

For some time after that, Amy had no opportunity to pursue her line of questioning with Rosie. The inn guests were loud in their praise of the fish chowder, the garlic bread Rosie had fixed to go with it and the papaya and coconut salad. They asked for seconds on everything, and Amy somehow found herself serving as waitress. It wasn't the first time. More than once she'd dropped in to visit Rosie and Hank and found herself helping out. The truth of the matter was, she was a good waitress. To her parents despair, she had had a lot of practice during the years she'd been searching for her goals in life.

When the inn guests had finished and gone back to drinking at the bar, Rosie ladled large bowls of the chowder for herself, Amy, Hank and Jed. Hank turned the bar over to his backup, a thin young man who helped out part-time in the evenings.

The conversation was general at dinner, covering every thing from island storms to the best eating fish to be found in the reefs. Amy said little. Rosie was as talkative as ever, and managed to keep Amy's glass full along with her own. At the end of the meal Amy followed her back into the kitchen as the men wandered out to the bar. As she ran hot water into the sink to wash the dishes, Rosie poured herself yet another guava juice cocktail

It seemed to Amy that the more Rosie imbibed, the chattier she became. Rosie had never been reticent, but with a few drinks inside her she began to talk almost nonstop. She seemed to enjoy talking about the past.

"What happened to the floozy?" Amy asked as she dried dishes.

"Well, your dad didn't take her up on her open invitation as far as I could tell." Rosie sounded proud of Douglas Slater's willpower. "Wyman never brought her back to the island. She was just here that one time."

"How long did she stay?"

"Oh, a couple of weeks or so." Rosie finished plunging the last of the dishes into the hot water and tossed the chipped plates onto the drain board for Amy to catch and dry. "If you ask me it was deliberate. Thought so at the time and I still do "

"What was?"

"Wyman bringing that woman here. It was no secret your parents were having some personal problems of their own about that time. Having that blond bombshell around didn't help matters. But things didn't get really bad until after your dad had gone back to the mainland. Wyman and your mother and you kids stayed behind. Your dad said your mother needed a vacation."

"What happened?" Amy matched Rosie's swallow of guava juice cocktail. She was no longer feeling as though an anxiety attack was about to move in on her. In fact, the world was looking remarkably mellow now. It probably had something to do with Rosie's secret recipe.

"Well, it looked to me like Wyman made a play for your mom."

The news shattered some of Amy's increasingly mellow mood. She took another sip of the cocktail to recover. Rosie was busy pouring herself another glass. "Did he really?"

Rosie heaved a huge sigh and lowered her large body into a chair that looked like it would give out under her bulk at any moment. "I shouldn't be talking to you like this. But what the hell, you're a big girl now. And everything turned out all right in the end, didn't it? Your parents have a real solid marriage. Everyone has troubles in the early days when the kids are little and business is putting pressure on a man. Bound to be a few problems. Go grab a chair from the bar and come sit down."

Amy set her glass on a counter with great care, aware that things around her were becoming slightly unsteady. But Rosie was still in a chatty mood. Amy didn't want to cut her off now. She made her way into the tavern and saw that Jed was no longer sitting at the bar.

She glanced around the room and found him at a table with a handful of other men, including Hank. They were obviously involved in a serious game of poker. Jed picked up his cards and saw Amy watching from the kitchen doorway.

"Everything okay?" he called easily.

Amy snatched up a chair, holding it in front of her as if it were a shield. "Just fine." She turned and marched back into the kitchen.

"Jed and Hank are playing poker with some fishermen," she told Rosie as she set down the chair.

"Then we're in for a long night. If Hank's dragged your man into a poker game, he won't let go of him anytime soon. What do you say we have another drink?"

"I'm floating in guava juice as it is."

"Well, then, let's skip the guava juice and just concentrate on the secret ingredients." Rosie reached for a bottle.

It was a long time later before Jed appeared in the kitchen doorway. Amy saw him through half closed eyes. He looked very large and solid in a world that had gone very misty and soft.

"Did you win?" she demanded.

"A few bucks." There was a trace of a smile on his hard mouth as he surveyed her. He glanced at the big woman lounging in the other chair. "What have you done to her, Rosie?"

"Nothing at all. We were just reminiscing about the past." She peered at Amy. "I think she's feeling a little sleepy."

"I think she's smashed." Jed moved forward, took hold of Amy's hand and tugged her gently to her feet. She wavered there for a moment and then collapsed against his chest with a contented sigh.

"Is it time to go home, Jed?"

"Yes, I think it's time." He cradled her against him and started for the door. "Good night, Rosie. Thanks for the great meal."

"You can come back anytime, Jed. Bring Amy with you. Been a long time since I've had a nice, cozy chat with another woman who knows how to drink."

Jed glanced down at the top of Amy's tousled head as it lay on his shoulder. Her eyes were closed and she seemed to be asleep. "I'm afraid Amy's not quite in your league, Rosie. She's basically a white wine drinker."

"I can cure her of that."

"Uh huh. What did you two talk about all evening?"

"Her folks for the most part. And that Wyman character who used to own half the house. Amy had a lot of questions about him. She didn't seem to remember him, you see. She was only a baby when he disappeared."

"I hear he was lost at sea during a trip between here and Hawaii."

Rosie chuckled. "That's what they say." She nodded to herself. "That's what they say. You take her home now, Jed. Put her to bed. She might not feel too good in the morning."

"You're probably right." Jed eased Amy through the door.

Amy opened her eyes a few minutes later when she felt the breeze whipping hair around her face. She blinked, trying to orient herself. It took her a moment to realize she was seated in the Jeep beside Jed and that they were whizzing through the island night. Thick green foliage crowded close to the edge of the road. She could see nothing but a wall of green on either side of the vehicle. The fresh air revived her a bit and Amy glanced at Jed.

"Did I embarrass myself?"

"Nope. You're a very sweet drunk."

She winced. "There is no such thing. I'm going to feel this in the morning, aren't I?"

"Undoubtedly." Jed shifted gears with casual precision. He smiled.

Amy decided she liked his smile. She leaned her head back on the seat again and stared straight up into the star-studded night. "Did I tell you I'm glad you work for the government, Jed?"

"No, you didn't mention it. Why does the news make you glad? I thought you'd be . . ." He paused. "Concerned."

"I'd rather you work for the government than . . . for just anyone who was willing to pay your price." She was feeling drowsy again. It was hard to keep her eyes open. Even to her own ears her words sounded slurred.

"Who else would I be working for, Amy?"

She tried to shrug and didn't quite make it. Too much work. "Same person LePage worked for, I guess. I know you can't trust the government, but in this case I'd trust a government agent before I'd trust some damn mercenary. You know, Jed, I think I'm going to sleep well tonight. I can hardly keep my eyes open. Be nice to get a good night's rest."

Amy fell asleep, unaware of the still, thoughtful speculation in Jed's gaze as he glanced at her.

"Amy," Jed said softly through set teeth, "what in hell have you been living with these past eight months? When you're sober again, sweetheart, we're going to have a little talk. I'll be damned if I'm the only one who's going to answer questions around here."

Chapter Nine

Artemus Fitzpatrick wasn't particularly surprised when Renner nearly came unglued. The news was not good.

"What the hell do you mean the daughter's staying behind on the island? I thought you said we got lucky because the Slaters left early?" Renner was pacing, as usual. The impatience was gnawing at him as if it were a living thing. He told himself he couldn't stand any more delays. There had already been twenty-five years of delays, thanks to his lush of a mother.

It was typical of his mother to deliberately keep the truth from him, Renner decided. Vivien had never been much of a parent. She'd resented the young boy after Wyman's death, saying it was because of him she was unable to find a man to marry her. No man wanted to raise another's kid, she claimed. Renner had obliged by leaving home as soon as possible, but it had been too late for Vivien. No man, it seemed, wanted to marry an alcoholic. It wasn't until he had opened Vivien's safe deposit box after her death the year before that Renner had learned the truth about his father and the box of goodies stashed in a flooded cave. He'd also found the key in that safe deposit box. Wyman had mailed it to Vivien as a backup, and Vivien, deep in grief and anger, had stuck it into the safe deposit box along with her diary after learning of Wyman's death. It had been a mistake to give LePage a duplicate of the key, Renner decided. This time he would keep the key until he had the box in his hands.

"According to Vaden, the Slaters left yesterday afternoon. But the daughter stayed behind with that guy she brought with her. Take it easy, Dan. There's nothing we can do. We'll just have to wait it out. They're bound to leave sooner or later."

Renner glanced at his watch. "I'm booked on a ten o'clock flight to Hawaii. I'm going to be on that flight, Artie. Tell Vaden and Guthrie to expect me on Orleana first thing tomorrow morning. Maybe even this evening if I can make connections."

"I don't think that's such a good idea, Dan." As usual, Fitzpatrick knew, he was wasting his breath. "We can wait a few more weeks. Better to be sure the Slater house is vacant. That'll give us plenty of time to search for the cave entrance."

"I've had it with waiting. I'm going there myself and I'll make my decisions on the spot. Vaden's already on site, isn't he?"

"Yeah, he's staying at a little inn there called Hank and Rosie's or something equally quaint. Guthrie is due to arrive tomorrow. Look, Dan, these guys are good. They know what they're doing. It's worth it to pay them a little standing around time so that in the end they can do the job right."

"The way LePage did it?"

"Okay, so LePage was a mistake. He wasn't as good as he was supposed to be. These things happen." Artie said the words soothingly, the same way he would tell a tax shy investor that last year's shelter had been a miscalculation but this year's was going to be a sure-fire winner. The trick was to make it sound like he had taken an even bigger loss than the client and he was still able to be a man about it, not a nervous wimp.

"Waiting around to see what the woman and her boyfriend are going to do would be another big mistake, Artie. Has it occurred to you that this guy who's with the Slater woman might be connected to LePage in some way?"

"What the hell?"

"Yeah, think about it. You got to admit, in a way, it makes sense. After all, whoever he is, he made contact with the daughter, just like LePage did. Got himself in bed with the woman and in good with the family, just the way LePage did. And now he's staying on with the daughter after the parents leave. It's a little too pat, Artie. Dammit, I can't fool around any longer. Tell Guthrie I'll meet him in Honolulu and we'll fly to Orleana together. We'll go in as a couple of tourists. Vaden will work separately. Guthrie and I will pretend we don't know him. Might be useful not to have Vaden connected with Guthrie and myself. You never know."

"I think maybe you've been watching too much television, Dan."

"Just do as I say, Artie. Get the message to Vaden and Guthrie that I don't want any overt contact. Got it?"

"I got it."

"Good. I'm on my way. Oh, and tell Vaden tnat if this joker who's sleeping with Slater's daughter tries to leave the island before I get there, I want him stopped."

"Uh, Dan, what do you mean, you want him stopped?" Artie was suddenly feeling extremely cautious.

"If Guthrie and Vaden are as competent as you say, they'll know exactly what I mean." Renner slammed down the phone and stared at the hapless instrument in brooding silence. Then he swung around in an explosion of energy and went to work to finish packing his discreetly initialed, Italian leather flight bag.

Artemus Fitzpatrick gingerly replaced the receiver on his end and breathed a sigh of relief that he was only the broker in this deal. Just the middleman. Buy a little here, sell a little there, but don't get mixed up in the action, he told himself. Words to live by. He might never make it quite as big as Renner was going to make it, but there was something to be said for erring on the side of caution. The last thing he wanted to do was end up standing on a street corner again.

Amy awoke with the vague sense of having had her first full night's sleep in eight months. But the headache that kicked in when she moved her head less than an inch convinced her the price of that sleep was much too high. She'd rather lie awake half the night than feel like she did.

Her stomach stirred uneasily as Amy lifted herself up on one elbow and gazed out at the morning sunlight on the sea. She took a couple of deep breaths, waiting for things to settle. Then she concentrated hard, trying to remember exactly what had happened. She had spent the evening talking to Rosie, that much was clear. Something had been said about her mother and Michael Wyman and Wyman's girlfriend and Douglas Slater. All very complicated. Then Jed had appeared to take her home.

A few words had been exchanged on the trip back to the house, but Amy couldn't remember how much of the conversation had taken place inside her head and how much had been verbal. Her frown intensified.

"Well, if it isn't little Miss Sunshine. Think you can handle a cup of coffee?"

Amy groaned and turned her head slowly toward the door. Jed was leaning against the jamb, two mugs of coffee in his big hands.

Big hands. Rosie had made some crack about the significance of large hands. Amy flushed as memories started trickling back.

"Bathroom first." The words were a little weak, but Amy managed to sit up. The sheet fell to her waist and she discovered she was naked. Automatically she grabbed the sheet again. It didn't take much imagination to figure out who'd undressed her. "Would you please hand me my robe?"

"How long are you going to continue being shy around me, sweetheart?" Nevertheless, Jed strolled into the room, set the coffee mugs down on a table and went to the closet to pull out her lightweight kimono. He walked to the bed, holding it out for her. "Here we go. Up and at 'em, Amy. The day is slipping away."

"Let it slip. I don't think I'm up to catching it before it falls." She yanked the robe out of his hands, tucked it around herself and got carefully to her feet. "My God, I feel awful."

"That guava juice will get you every time."

"It wasn't the guava juice, it was whatever Rosie was adding to it." Amy headed for the bathroom with what she hoped was a stately tread. "I got some sleep, though. I just wish I could enjoy it more this morning."

"Anyone who's tried drinking himself to sleep can tell you that the pain is definitely not worth the gain," Jed said calmly as Amy stepped into the bathroom.

"You sound like an expert on the subject," she muttered before starting to close the door.

"Let's just say I've conducted a few scientific experiments of my own in that particular area."

Amy caught the dry note in his voice and more memories came flooding back. She peered at him from the crack in the almost closed bathroom door. "Were you conducting scientific experiments when you took that bullet in the leg?"

"I see you do remember what happened yesterday before Rosie started pouring guava juice cocktails down your throat."

"You said you were a government agent," Amy searched his face as she recalled the scene in the clinic office.

"And you said better that than a paid mercenary," Jed retorted coolly. The familiar watchful look was back in his eyes.

Amy quietly shut the door. The last of her vague memories fell into place. She had told him something about LePage.

When she emerged a few minutes later, clutching the kimono around her, she headed straight for the coffee Jed held out. She gave her full attention to it, sipping appreciatively.

"Thank you."

"You're welcome," he said. "When you're dressed, come on downstairs. I'll fix breakfast."

"I don't think I could eat."

"Wait and see." He left the bedroom without a backward glance.

He was taking charge again, Amy thought in resignation. And she was too hung over to put up much resistance. With a sigh she returned to the bathroom to take a shower.

Half an hour later, Amy found herself sitting down to two perfectly fried eggs, a pile of hash browns, toast and three strips of bacon.

"Cholesterol," she murmured weakly.

"Protein," Jed retorted. "Fortunately, your parents keep a well stocked freezer, and your mother's pantry seems boundless."

It wasn't worth an argument. Not this morning at any rate. Amy picked up a fork and gingerly cut into the eggs.

"All right," Jed said casually as he sat down across from her, "I think we've postponed this long enough. Who the hell was LePage and why have you been having anxiety attacks at night for the past eight months?"

"I got kind of chatty last night, didn't I?"

"It all would have come out sooner or later. I want to know the whole story, Amy."

"Why?" she asked simply.

"That should be obvious."

"Because you're sleeping with me on a casual basis? You think that entitles you to know all the details?"

He smeared his toast with egg yolk and took a bite. "Whatever else it is, it's not casual. Talk, Amy."

She looked down at her plate, knowing that this moment had been inevitable. She'd both anticipated and dreaded it. Perhaps she'd used the alcohol last night as a way of slipping past her own self-imposed defenses. She had said far too much in the Jeep, but that was probably because, deep down, she had wanted to say it and get it over with. She needed to take the risk of telling the truth because she needed to know how Jed would react.

"It's a long story," Amy said.

"We've got all day."

Her head came up abruptly, her body growing tense. "Have you ever watched a man die, Jed?"

He looked at her for a long moment and then finished

eating the slice of toast. "You watched LePage die? You saw him drown?"

"Worse than that." She shuddered, losing interest in her food. "I was responsible, in a way. I could have saved him, I think." She'd never actually said the words aloud. They sounded very strange.

"Christ, Amy. What's been going on inside your head for eight months?" Jed's tone was surprisingly gentle.

"A nightmare I can't seem to shake."

"Finish your breakfast," Jed said with sudden decision. "Something tells me we'd better conclude this after you've eaten."

Amy nodded. "You're probably right."

She managed to get down one of the eggs and one slice of toast before she gave up and followed Jed out to the veranda with a second cup of coffee. He settled her into a lounger and sat down across from her, his mug cradled in his hands. His gaze was intent. Amy hesitated a moment longer, gathering her thoughts, and then began telling the whole story. It was a relief to talk about it at last.

"I told you I met LePage about three weeks before I flew out here eight months ago. What I didn't know was that it had all been arranged. He knew who I was before he set up our initial meeting." Amy shook her head. "I was such a fool."

"Just tell me the story, Amy. You can skip the asides."

"The visit here with my folks went exactly as I told you. All very casual, very friendly. But he kept asking questions about the underwater caves. I told him my father refused to let anyone dive in them. He didn't argue, but he kept saying he wanted to see the entrance. He was fascinated with them. Like an idiot, I let him talk me into showing him the entrance pool. He swore the last thing he'd want to do was actually dive there."

"But that last night, he decided to."

Amy nodded struggling to deal with the memories as they threatened to overwhelm her. "Something woke me that night, Jed. Maybe the sound of the front door closing. Maybe just some kind of intuition. I don't know. I've never been sure. But I walked out on the veranda and saw him starting into the jungle with his diving gear. And I . . . followed."

Jed whistled soundlessly between his teeth. "Oh, Amy."

"I know. It wasn't the brightest thing I've ever done. But I knew something was terribly wrong. I was the one who had brought him here to the island. I had shown him the caves. I had to know what he was up to. I followed him to the caves and watched him put on his tank and gear and enter the water. I couldn't believe it. I didn't understand why the cave diving was so important to him that he would deliberately go against his host's instructions. And in the middle of the night? I assumed he was just some kind of daredevil fool. Then I found the map."

"What map?"

"He'd been studying it before he entered the water. He left it under his duffel bag when he went into the caves. I picked it up and looked at it. He'd left a small flashlight next to the map." Amy stared out at the sunlit sea. "I knew right away what I was looking at. It was a diagram of the first few meters of the caves. It had to be. Someone had sketched the opening and the water level at the surface and even drawn an arrow from the main entrance tunnel into a side cave. I couldn't see how anyone could know what the cavern looked like inside. As far as I knew, no one had ever dived those caves. But the map was very explicit."

"So explicit that you figured LePage had gone in for more than some casual sightseeing?"

"I didn't really know what to think. I just stood there waiting, knowing he'd have to come out within forty-five minutes or so. He came out in a lot less time than that." Amy fell silent, taking a fortifying sip of coffee.

"He emerged and found you waiting, right? Dammit, Amy, how could you have been so foolish?"

"Maybe because I wasn't accustomed to dealing with people like Bob LePage," she snapped.

"All right, all right," Jed soothed. "Just tell me the rest."

She took a breath. "He surfaced and found me waiting with the map and the flashlight in my hand. His hands weren't empty either, Jed. He was carrying a locked, waterproof box. When he saw me he called me a fool, too. Said I should have had the sense to mind my own business. Then he calmly climbed out of the pool and carried the box over to his duffel bag. I didn't know what to do. I just stood there, staring at him, trying to figure out what was happening. When he took off his tank and gear and knelt down beside his bag I finally managed to ask him what was going on."

Jed sighed. "What did he do? Pull a gun out of the bag?"

Amy's gaze snapped back to his. "How did you know?"

"Somehow I just saw it coming."

"Well, you're right. Unfortunately, I didn't see it coming until it was too late. He reached into the duffel bag and the next thing I knew he was holding a gun on me. He told me it was too bad I'd followed him because he was going to have to kill me. He'd like to make it look like an accident, he said. He was going to knock me out and let me drown. But if that didn't work, he didn't have any qualms about keeping it simple with a bullet. He would leave my body wedged deep in the caves where no one would ever find it."

Jed's hand was holding the mug in a grip that threatened to crack the thick pottery. His eyes were as cold as the deepest part of the sea. "Jesus, Amy."

"I know. I was doing a little off-the-cuff praying myself at the time. But I didn't get the feeling there was going to be any divine intervention." Amy shuddered, remembering her stark fear that night. "What saved me, the thing that eventually got him killed instead of me, was his greed to see what was inside the box. He had to know if the emeralds were inside."

"What emeralds?"

"That's exactly what I asked him." Amy let her head sink back against the lounger and remembered.

"What emeralds? What on earth are you talking about? Please, Bob, I don't understand any of this." She was shaking, Amy realized, but not so badly that she couldn't stand. She still seemed to have some control over her own body. Except for her eyes. She couldn't seem to raise them above the level of the gun in LePage's hand.

LePage reached out to yank the metal box closer. "The Russian emeralds, you fool. You don't have any idea what's been sitting in that cave for twenty-five years, have you?"

Amy shook her head, speechless. Keeping the gun trained on her, LePage reached back into his duffel bag and removed a small packet. With a one-handed movement he shook the key out of the packet. Then he picked it up and inserted it into the box. There was a soft, grating sound but no movement.

"Damn thing's corroded shut," LePage hissed furiously. He tossed the key to Amy. "Here, you work on it. I can't manhandle that old lock and keep an eye on you at the same time. As long as you're here, you might as well be useful." He straightened and toed the box toward her. "Come on, go to work. Unjam that lock. I can shoot it off if I have to, but I'd like to keep things quiet around here as long as possible."

Amy sank to her knees in front of the box. With trembling fingers she fit the key into the lock and began to twist it gently. Metal scraped on metal. LePage kept talking, his excitement making his tongue limber.

"Wyman made a deal with some Russian agents twenty-five years ago," LePage explained as he watched the box with avid eyes. "He was going to sell one of his designs. But he didn't want cash or gold. He wanted something light and portable and that meant gemstones. The agreement was for six first class emeralds, I'm told."

"Who told you?" Amy asked in a low voice as she wiggled the key.

"Never mind who told me. It's not important now. What's important is that I get my hands on those stones. This is the deal of a lifetime."

"What will you do when you have them? Assuming they're in here?"

"I'm going to disappear, of course. The LePage ID has been useful for a couple of years, but it's time I made a new man of myself. Hurry up, dammit."

"I'm trying." She was. It had occurred to Amy that if there really was a packet of emeralds inside the box she might be able to use them to distract LePage. It was obvious the stones were his sole interest.

"Did you know your father probably killed Wyman?"

Amy paused, staring at him. "You're lying."

He saw at once that he'd found a vulnerable point. With a low chuckle, LePage probed further, the beast in him more than happy to inflict a little extra pain. "Not according to my research."

"What research?" she demanded

"I always do my homework in these cases."

"What are you talking about? And what do you mean 'these cases'?" She was desperate, confused and now, over poweringly furious. How dare he drag her father into this?

LePage squatted down in front of Amy, the gun still trained on her. "You know what I am, honey? I'm what the romantics like to call a Soldier of Fortune. Know what that means? I get to go anywhere, do anything and make my own rules."

"You're a paid mercenary," she spat, her trembling fingers hesitating as she felt the key twist completely into the lock.

"Right. Except this time around I'm working for myself and those emeralds are the payment. The way I figure it, your father found out Wyman was selling company secrets and killed him. Unfortunately, he didn't know Wyman had already sold the stuff and taken the emeralds as payment. Slater didn't know Wyman had already hidden the box in the caves—or if he did, he couldn't find it afterward."

"After what?"

"After he'd killed him. You don't think Wyman really went overboard at sea, do you? That's just a little too pat."

You really believe my father killed Wyman?" Amy was still in shock

"That's right. I found some lead from an old weight belt down there and a few other pieces of corroded equipment. Must be what's left of Wyman. I probably could have found a skeleton if I'd had time to look. The way I figure it, he was killed, all right. The old diving stuff wasn't in the same cave as the box, though. I just happened to find it when I swam into the wrong tunnel. No, I don't think your old man knew about the emeralds. But he got rid of Wyman and that was apparently all he cared about."

"Surely you don't believe all this?" The key scraped again in the lock and this time LePage heard it.

"Open it."

Slowly Amy lifted the metal lid. It creaked. Inside the box was almost completely dry; the seals had held for twenty-five years. There was a bulging waterproof bag inside the box. Surely six emeralds didn't take up that much space.

"Come on, let me see what I've got. Open that sack very carefully," LePage ordered.

Obediently Amy undid the fastenings. What fell out into her hands first was a stack of letters. She recognized her mother's handwriting at once. Amy felt physically ill. She swallowed rapidly.

"Never mind the junk. Keep looking. I want those stones."

Without a word Amy put her hand into the plastic sack. Her groping fingers found another envelope, larger than the others, and then, at the bottom, a small packet. Her hand closed around it, knowing it was her death warrant. Once LePage had the emeralds, he would kill her.

"There's nothing else in here," she whispered.

"The hell there isn't." LePage leaned forward, yanking the box around so he could investigate the contents for himself. "They've got to be here. I'll kill the bastard if they're not "

"Kill who?" Amy kept the small packet clutched in her hand as the box was pulled from her grasp. In the darkness LePage didn't notice her closed fist as he reached into the bag.

"Forget it. Where are they? They've got to be here."

Amy was on her feet now, the packet still in her hand. She edged toward the rocky pool behind her. "Is this what you're looking for?"

LePage's head shot up, his eyes full of violent anger "You little bitch. I'll teach you to play games with me. Give me those stones or I'll kill you."

"You're going to do that anyway. I don't have much to lose, do I?" Amy held the open packet out over the yawning mouth of the pool. She could feel the hard stones inside "What are the odds you'll be able to find these if I let them drop into the water? The pool is deep and there are a lot of places where six small emeralds can get lost. It could take you hours just to turn up one of them."

"Put that packet down or I'll put a bullet through your gut You got any idea how bad that hurts? You'll lie here dying until morning. You won't even be able to crawl to the house for help."

"And you'll be on your way off the island without your payoff. A lot of wasted effort. I suggest we negotiate." Her arm was trembling as she held it stiffly out over the black water. She tried not to let her imagination run away with the picture he had painted of a slow and painful death. Already she could envision the blood pouring from her stomach. A creative imagination was a burden at times. Desperately she tried to shove the image aside.

"What do you have in mind?"

LePage was edging closer, the gun trained on her midsection. He was simmering with a violent energy that Amy could feel. For a fleeting second she saw a monster with clawed hands reaching for her. She took another step backward and her foot struck against one of the jagged rocks that rimmed the pool.

"You can have the emeralds. All I want are those letters and whatever else is in the box. You let me live and I'll let you get off the island with the stones."

LePage's mouth twisted. "Sure, bitch, anything you want."

"You'll give me your word?"

"You got it." He took another step closer.

"How can I trust you?"

"Beats me."

He was going to lunge for her at any moment. Amy could see the predatory gleam in his eyes. The pool was relatively deep, but it was lined with treacherous outcroppings. Under ideal circumstances it should be entered with great caution; these were hardly ideal circumstances.

"Come on, bitch, you've stalled long enough. *Give me that packet!*"

Amy tightened her grasp on the packet of stones and threw herself into the dark water. As she went in she prayed she remembered the general contours of the pool well enough to miss the craggy pile of rocks on the bottom. Her goal was the cave itself. If she could reach its sheltering darkness she could survive a few more minutes. The first portion of the tunnel was only partially flooded; nearly a foot of space above the water line could be seen during the day.

That breathing space undoubtedly disappeared within a few feet as the cave angled downward.

Amy was distantly astounded that she didn't hurt herself on the rocks. The dark water closed over her and she stayed underwater, kicking wildly in the direction of the yawning, black cave entrance. A vibrating splash in the water told her that LePage had followed her into the water. She heard no sound of a gunshot and wondered if the water had muffled it or if he hadn't fired.

It didn't matter. What mattered now was that he was in the water with her. She'd felt him enter the pool immediately after she had, so that meant he hadn't stopped to grab an underwater light. They were evenly matched in the darkness. At least they were until LePage finally realized he could hunt her down far more quickly with the light. Where was he? There was no sound from the other end of the rocky pool.

She was almost out of breath. In another few seconds she would have to surface. Amy's hand brushed against the wall of the cave and she knew she must be inside. It was time to find out just how much breathing space there was. Lungs straining, she pushed her way upward, using the tunnel wall as a guide. A few seconds later she surfaced, banging her head painfully against the roof of the tunnel.

There was less than a foot of headspace between the water and the roof of the cave in this first section of the passage. Something that smelled green and mossy tickled Amy's nose as she struggled to steady herself in the water and keep her nose above the water level. She realized she was still clutching the packet of stones.

Silence filled the intense darkness. She was only a couple of feet from the entrance of the tunnel. Looking out Amy could see the pale wash of moonlight on the pool's surface. Clouds were moving in, breaking up the light pattern.

Where was LePage?

There was no sound, no sense of movement. Amy waited, wondering if LePage had already scrambled back out of the pool to get a light.

But there was only the fragmented moonlight, no harsh swath of a flashlight cutting the water's surface.

What was LePage doing?

He must have had to surface by now. He was somewhere in the shadows of the rocks, listening and watching for her to reappear from the cave.

The water was deep. She couldn't touch the floor of the tunnel with her sandaled feet. It was difficult trying to keep her head above water when the weight of her clothing kept pulling her down.

Amy couldn't stay there all night. Then again, maybe she could. It was better than facing LePage's gun. But she sensed that LePage wouldn't have the patience for a long game of hide and seek. She'd seen the glitter in his eyes, felt the violence emanating from him.

Minutes passed. When there was still no sound Amy decided to risk maneuvering closer toward the entrance of the cavern. She glanced once over her shoulder into the endless depths of the cave behind her and didn't make that mistake a second time. Once was enough to send new chills through every nerve in her body.

As silently as possible Amy started to swim forward. She hit her head once more on the low ceiling of rock and then she found herself at the mouth of the cavern. There was no sign of LePage or his flashlight. Perhaps he was out there in the darkness waiting for her just as she had waited for him.

But she hadn't heard him clamber back out of the pool, Amy reminded herself. Still, she'd been underwater for a full minute or more. He might have surfaced and climbed out in that time.

She ducked down, deciding to swim underwater across the rocky pool and come up again on the far side where she could conceal herself in the shadows of the rocks.

Amy had almost reached the opposite side and had put out a hand to find the craggy wall when her toe caught on an underwater obstruction.

Automatically she tried to kick free. And then she realized what she had struck. It was a human leg. LePage's leg.

It had to be.

Amy wanted to scream. Instead she fought her way up out of the pool, slipping and sliding on the wet rocks, clawing frantically for purchase.

She was gasping for breath as she hauled herself out of the water and knelt on the ground. There was no sound behind her.

LePage was still underwater.

She searched for the flashlight, found it, and finally got the light trained down into the pool.

"He was just lying there, staring up at me from beneath six feet of water. I could see his eyes, Jed. They were wide open. He was looking at me. He was dead by then, but he was still looking at me."

Jed rose from the lounger and went to sit beside her. He put an arm around her the way he had the night she'd awakened with the nightmare. "He was dead. There was nothing you could have done and you had nothing to do with the way he died. You were trying to save yourself. He must have gone into the water after you and struck his head on a rock. He deserved what he got, Amy. He would have killed you."

"I know. I've been telling myself that for eight long months. Maybe if it had ended there, I wouldn't be having the nightmares and anxiety attacks." Amy couldn't feel the comforting weight of Jed's arm. She was too drawn in on herself, too lost in the horror she had been living with for so long. "But it didn't end there, Jed."

He went still beside her, his hand no longer moving slowly on her arm. "You'd better tell me the rest, sweetheart."

There was no reason not to tell him, Amy decided bleakly. She'd already told him everything else. He might as well learn the full truth.

Chapter Ten

"I still had the packet of emeralds," Amy explained slowly. "And there were all those letters."

"They were written by your mother?"

Amy nodded. "To Michael Wyman. They were love letters, Jed. I didn't read them all. I couldn't. My hands were shaking so badly I could barely handle them. But I read enough to find out that she was passionately in love with him and intended to run off with him. There were pictures, too. In the big envelope. Black and white photos of my father talking to a man I didn't recognize. They were annotated on the back. Somebody, probably Wyman, had written dates and times and a Russian name."

"Sounds like Wyman had set up a blackmail scam. Or maybe he'd intended to sell the engineering designs to the Russians and make it look as if it was you father who'd sold out."

Amy twisted her hands together and nodded once more. "If LePage had been right, that the emeralds were a payoff, then I had to assume the photos were meant to make my father look guilty. I don't know why my mother's letters were there."

Jed took his arm from around Amy, got up and went to lean against the railing. "Maybe he intended to use them as blackmail material, too. You probably won't ever know for certain, but it's possible your mother had changed her mind about going with him and he was planning to use the letters to force her to do what he wanted or to ensure her silence. What do you think happened that night?"

I think," Amy said carefully, putting into words a theory she'd been working on for eight grueling months, "that my mother might have killed him and hidden the body and box in the caverns My father doesn't dive, Jed. Only a good diver could have risked going into those caves to hide a body. LePage seemed very certain Wyman hadn't gone down in his boat. He was sure he'd been killed and he said he'd seen those pieces of lead and the remains of some diving equipment.'

"He had no way of knowing for certain they once belonged to Wyman."

"No, I suppose not." Amy paused, thinking of one of the scenes from her nightmares.

"So what do you figure as your mother's motive?" Jed asked laconically.

"I don't know." Amy looked down at her folded hands "Jealousy, perhaps. Wyman apparently had another love, ac cording to Rosie. Or perhaps my mother did try to break things off and Wyman threatened to blackmail her with the letters as you suggested. I don't know, Jed, but I have this terrible feeling that LePage was right. Someone killed Wyman and the only one who could have done it and also hidden the body in those caves was my mother. Jed, no one knows about those caves except members of my family."

"Wyman knew."

"Well, yes. That's logical. At one time he owned the house and the land with my father." She was quiet for a moment, thinking. "What would be left of a body hidden down there all this time, Jed?"

"Amy, you're letting your imagination run away with you."

"But what would be left of a body if there had been one?" she insisted.

"The skeleton, I guess," Jed stated matter-of-factly.

Amy looked at him, wondering at the calm, pragmatic tone of voice. *The skeleton*; eye sockets that stared forever; bony hands that fluttered in the water. She swallowed. "LePage said he was fairly certain Wyman's body had been left down there."

Jed shrugged. "All right, Amy, it's possible Wyman's body is down there. Who knows? That doesn't tell us who killed him. With six good emeralds involved, I'd say the number of possible murderers is fairly open. Hell, the Russians themselves might have decided to take the designs and the emeralds after the deal was concluded."

"Except that the stones were still in the box," Amy said quietly.

"They were in that packet you took into the water with you? You checked?"

"Yes."

Jed gave her a considering look, folding his arms thoughtfully across his chest. "And you just left them down there? Six emeralds?"

Amy stared down at her tightly clasped hands. "I didn't want to see them again. I wanted them to disappear. They represented so many horrible things."

"Mmm." His low murmur was distinctly noncommittal. "So what is the rest of the story?"

Amy took a breath. "I was in a panic. I couldn't wake my parents and tell them LePage had just gotten killed diving for a box that contained emeralds, incriminating photos and old love letters. And that he'd been willing to kill to get that box. All I could think of was that I had to hide the box and everything that was in it. I told myself that the caves were the best place. The box had been safe down there for all those years. It should be safe for another few decades."

Jed closed his eyes. "Don't tell me, let me guess. You took the box back into the caves?"

She clenched and unclenched her fingers. "I couldn't think of anything else to do. I just wanted to get rid of every damn thing in that box!"

"Even if it meant risking your neck in those caves?"

Amy looked up at him and felt a queasy sensation in the pit of her stomach. "I didn't see that I had any choice."

"Tell me exactly what you did that night."

Amy couldn't tear her eyes away from his now. "I put on LePage's tank and equipment and went into the cave. I wasn't sure what I was doing. I've never done any cave diving. But I'd read a few books on the subject. I . . . I used the reel he'd been using. I tied the line to a rock outside the cave entrance and swam as far as I dared before I found a place to stash the box. Then I turned around and followed the line back out. I had the diving light with me, and as I swam out of the tunnel back into the pool I could see him lying there in the water. He was still staring at me. Then when I tried to climb out I stumbled on the rocks and . . . and fell back into the water. I felt his leg again and I . . . Oh, God, Jed " She couldn't say anything else. Her hand moved in a vague, helpless gesture and then settled back onto her lap

Jed took one long stride away from the rail, reached down and hauled Amy to her feet. Holding her by the shoulders he said grimly, "You didn't kill him, Amy. Even if you had, it would have been self-defense."

"It's the nightmares. Why can't I shake the dreams?"

"Probably because you've been keeping this all locked up inside for months, and you're not the kind of person who knows how to deal with that kind of information. And because you've got an overactive imagination. *And because that damn box is still down in those caves.*"

She stared at him. "What's that got to do with it?"

Jed shook his head once. "Amy, you left everything as it was. The box is still there with everything in it. Don't you understand? If LePage knew about that box, someone else probably knows about it, too."

"LePage said he was working for himself. Working alone."

"Where did he get his information?"

"I don't know," Amy whispered fretfully. "Jed, I've wondered about that for months. He implied he'd gotten the information from someone but he didn't seem worried about that person coming after him. Maybe he killed whoever told him about the box. He was certainly capable of it."

"Maybe. Maybe not. There are a hell of a lot of loose ends dangling here, Amy."

"I know," she admitted.

"We've got to get that box out of the caves, sweetheart."

Her head jerked up. "No! Absolutely not. I'm not going back into the caves and neither are you."

His mouth tightened but he didn't argue. Instead he pulled her closer, crushing her into his warmth. "All right, Amy, we'll talk about retrieving the box some other time."

"The box is safe enough where it is. No one will ever find it. Not unless I show the way."

"Amy, from what you've told me you didn't spend very long in those caves that night. You were scared and in a hurry. My guess is that box isn't very far inside the entrance, right? Anyone who's willing to spend a little time could probably find it."

Amy pulled herself free of his grasp. "Why are you so concerned about retrieving it?"

"I've told you, loose ends."

Or was it the fact that six of those loose ends were emeralds? Amy thought suddenly. No, she trusted Jed. She had to trust him; she'd gone too far.

"What's the matter, Amy?" Jed's big hands moved soothingly on her lower back. "Scared you've said too much?"

She tried to pull away and Jed reluctantly let her go. "I let those stupid guava juice cocktails get to me last night. After eight months of keeping my secrets to myself, I got a little drunk and the first thing I know, I'm spilling the whole story."

"Because it was tearing you apart."

"You told me once, after that night when I woke up screaming, that it was usually best not to talk things out," she reminded him. "You said it made things more real to put them into words."

"I was talking about nightmares. But you haven't been having ordinary, run-of-the-mill bad dreams, have you, Amy?"

"No," she admitted. "I think I've been living in some kind of time loop. I can't forget what happened eight months ago. I keep reliving it in my dreams. Jed, there have been times when I thought I might go crazy."

"Loose ends."

She looked at him. "You keep saying that."

He shrugged, shoving his hands into the back pockets of his jeans. His eyes were fixed on her face, his expression very intent. "The loose ends are haunting you. You don't have all the answers. You don't know for certain who really killed Wyman twenty-five years ago. You wonder who else might know about the contents of that box. And you must have wondered from time to time if there are any more LePage types running around looking for you. Given an imagination such as yours, those kinds of questions could easily drive you nuts. Especially since you've been trying to handle it all alone."

Amy winced. "You sound like an authority on the subject."

"An authority on loose ends? Yeah, I guess I am. Sometimes you have to clean them up in order to go on living, Amy."

"I can't bear the thought of going back into those caves," she whispered.

"I'll be with you this time."

Amy was silent.

Jed listened to the telling silence and then breathed a deep, understanding, "I see."

"What do you see?" Amy had wandered over to the railing. She glanced around at him a little uneasily.

"I see it's occurred to you already to wonder if I'm another LePage."

"You don't seem overly concerned about it."

He shrugged. "I'm not. It's a logical consideration. But I think deep down you trust me. You would never have let the guava juice get to you last night otherwise."

Amy half smiled. "You don't know Rosie's cocktails. They're potent."

Jed strolled over to stand beside her, his gaze on the sea "What, exactly, was the point of trying to drink Rosie under the table last night?"

"I'm not sure. I started asking her questions about the past and she seemed willing to talk. So I kept asking questions."

"About your parents?"

Amy nodded. "She said Michael Wyman was a trouble-maker. She implied he tried to cause trouble between my parents first by siccing his girlfriend on my father. When that failed, Rosie said he turned his charm on my mother. Judging from those letters I found in the box, the charm must have worked."

"Maybe. Up to a point. Don't try to figure out all the details yet, Amy. You don't have the facts."

"I don't want them."

"You might not want the facts about your parents, but you can't ignore the emeralds. Not now when you know some-one else is aware of them."

"That someone else is dead."

"LePage got his information from someone," Jed insisted softly. He flattened his palms on the rail and leaned forward There are some similarities between me and LePage, aren't there?"

Amy hesitated and then said, "Yes."

"He set up a casual meeting with you shortly before you were due to come to the island. You thought he was a friend Someone with whom you had a few things in common When he got here he ingratiated himself with your family He went diving with you. Asked questions about the caves In short, he used you."

"Yes."

"And in the end he tried to kill you '

"Yes." Amy's voice was feather soft but very steady.

"When I started asking questions about him and what had happened between the two of you, you must have started wondering about me," Jed continued thoughtfully, relentlessly.

"When you said you worked for the government, I decided I could stop worrying."

"I could have been lying. It would be easy enough to do. I had to come up with some explanation after Stearn told you I hadn't been in a car accident."

"Were you lying to me, Jed?"

"No."

"What really happened to you on the last trip?" she asked.

"I made a mistake. I was forced to trust someone who wasn't exactly trustworthy. It cost me. But in the end I got lucky. It could have cost me a great deal more."

"Your life?" She turned to stare at his hard profile, her eyes full of silent anguish.

Jed's lips moved in a rueful smile. "Or a vital portion of my, uh, structural integrity. You heard what Stearn said. If that bullet had been a little higher..."

"You might have been singing soprano." Without stopping to think, Amy went into his arms, clinging to him. "Oh, God, Jed, you could have been killed."

"I think that might have been preferable to the alternative Stearn suggested. I don't sing very well. And if I'd had to spend the rest of my life wondering what it would be like to make love to you, I probably would have gone off the deep end."

"It's not funny!"

"Sorry. My sense of humor sometimes leaves something

to be desired." His arms were closed firmly around her and he was cradling her head on his shoulder.

"Yes, I've noticed." Amy lifted her head, smiling tremulously. Her fingers clutched the open collar of his faded denim shirt. "Actually, I think we would have gotten along reasonably well, even if Stearn's hypothesis had come to pass."

Jed looked pained and skeptical. "You think our 'friendship' would have been enough?"

"Uh huh. Especially given the fact that you're a very resourceful man. And as Rosie mentioned, you have wonderful hands."

Jed shook with laughter and Amy buried her flushed face in his shirt. It was so good to hear him laugh, she thought. So very good. Warmth and reassurance flowed over her, driving out some of the chill that had invaded her when Jed had first begun asking questions.

Jed's laughter broke some of the tension, but when the moment was past, Amy sensed the beginning of a subtle change in him. He grew quiet and a little withdrawn. He didn't mention the box in the caves again for the rest of the day, however, and Amy was profoundly grateful. She had told him the stark truth when she said she did not want to face the thought of retrieving the box.

The remainder of the morning went by quietly. Amy dug out the notepad she had brought with her and curled up on a veranda seat to outline another chapter of *Private Demons*. Jed, too, found some paper and a collection of rulers and pencils in Douglas Slater's study. He arranged everything on a table near Amy's seat and began to sketch the design of another intricate bird cage. This one, Amy noticed, was light and airy and full of graceful, curving surfaces. It amazed her somehow that a man who was so hard could produce something as whimsical as a beautiful cage for small birds.

Jed got up at one point to put some Vivaldi on Doug Slater's sophisticated stereo system. The music drifted through the open house. Amy decided it was probably the right kind of background music for Jed's designing work. She wanted to make a joke about the differences in their musical tastes, but Jed seemed too preoccupied to appreciate the punch line.

Amy felt better by lunchtime and her appetite was back in full force. She and Jed ate a quiet meal in the kitchen and then went back out onto the veranda for the remainder of the afternoon. Conversation between them diminished virtually to nothing.

There was no hostility in the air, Amy told herself as she covertly glanced at Jed's intent expression. It was silly to look for problems where there weren't any. Jed wasn't pushing her about the box. He must have accepted her decision regarding it.

But by dinner Amy knew that something had changed. Jed seemed more withdrawn than ever. He offered her a glass of wine which she ruefully declined and poured himself a glass of Scotch. He helped her shell and steam shrimp and prepare a salad, but he didn't offer a great deal of friendly conversation in the process.

Several times Amy almost asked him what he was thinking about, but she never quite worked up the nerve. She didn't want to talk about the box again and she was afraid that was what was on his mind.

It wasn't until after dinner that she began wondering if it was something other than the box that was bothering Jed.

Her vivid imagination seized the new possibility and ran with it. By ten o'clock that evening she was convinced she knew what was really wrong.

The problem was simple and straightforward, and it was based on one of her deepest fears: Jed was trying to deal with what he had learned about his lover. Amy wasn't the sweet, innocent woman of somewhat limited experience he had assumed. She had a past and that past involved one death in which she'd been involved and a possible murder by one of her parents. Furthermore, Amy had proven herself to be the kind of woman who was capable of swimming over a drowned man's body in order to hide a small fortune in emeralds.

Amy knew instinctively that it was one thing for a man to be acquainted with violence and quite another for him to accept a woman who had been involved in a questionable drowning and the disappearance of several gemstones.

Amy got very little done on *Private Demons* as the evening wore on. She could almost hear the questions Jed was probably asking himself.

At five minutes after ten Amy couldn't take it any longer. She quietly excused herself and went upstairs to bed. Jed looked up from his bird cage sketch, nodded politely and watched her walk up the stairs. He made no move to follow.

Why hadn't he followed? Amy wondered dismally as she paced her bedroom. Couldn't he even bear to sleep with her now that he knew her secrets?

She tortured herself with variations on that theme for almost twenty minutes. Then she started getting angry. Who the hell did he think he was to pass judgment on her? She was the same woman he had been so determined to seduce when he came home with a bullet wound in his leg, a knife slash on his arm and a set of bruised ribs. Nothing had changed, except, of course, that now he knew the truth about her.

Maybe Jed considered her "unfeminine."

Maybe he did find nothing attractive about a woman whose past involved death and emeralds.

Maybe he'd been lying to her all along. Maybe he had only used her to get to the emeralds.

Amy felt dizzy as her imagination went wild with all the possibilities.

Jedidiah Glaze wasn't exactly Mr. Perfect, Amy told herself forcefully as she stalked out onto the veranda. He played with guns, he spoke little about his past, he showed even less interest in the future, and he probably didn't know the meaning of the word commitment.

And heaven help her, she was in love with him.

Amy halted at the veranda railing, her whole body tensing as she acknowledged the truth at last. She was in love with Jed. She'd been in love with him for weeks, perhaps a couple of months. She should have realized her true feelings when she had gone to Dr. Mullaney and gotten a prescription for birth control pills.

At the time she had told herself she was just being pragmatic and prepared. She had seen the sensual hunger in Jed's eyes once too often, and with a woman's sure instinct had known where it was bound to lead. The thought of cutting off the relationship had never occurred to her. She had camouflaged her love for him behind a facade of friendship, but deep down a part of her had known the truth.

She was in love with Jed and now that he knew the truth about her he was already backing away from the limited, uncommitted affair they had begun.

Amy's emotions took over. She turned on one bare foot and marched toward the bedroom door. Flinging it open she stalked down the hall to the head of the stairs. She could see Jed down in the living room, still hunched over his design. He didn't look up until she spoke.

"It's not as though I was expecting marriage," she announced with cold pride.

That got his attention. Warily he raised his head to look up at her. Amy braced her hands on the banister and stared back at him with an expression of blunt challenge.

"I beg your pardon?" Jed responded.

"I said, it's not as though I expected you to marry me."

"I heard you. I don't get the connections you apparently think I should be making." He didn't move from his chair.

"You know what I'm talking about."

"Do I?"

"Of course you do," she told him through set teeth. "I'd just like to point out that you have no right to act as if everything has changed between us. I'm the same woman I was yesterday and last week. You were more than happy to indulge yourself in a little affair with me then, weren't you?"

"I sense a loaded question."

Amy was enraged. "This is not a joke."

"No," he agreed, "I can see that." He put down his mechanical pencil and leaned back in his chair to study her. "What is it, exactly?"

"Just tell me the truth, Jed. Does knowing about my past change everything for you?"

"Are you asking me if I still want you now that I know what happened in the caves?"

"It's not just what happened eight months ago, is it? There's also the small matter of a murder that took place twenty-five years ago. Then there's the issue of a few emeralds. And maybe some espionage. We mustn't forget that. Who knows what else is involved? The point is, I'm not exactly a sweet, innocent little ex-cheerleader, am I?"

Jed got to his feet now and walked toward the stairs. His eyes never left hers. "Amy, believe me. I was never under the impression that you were a sweet, innocent little ex-cheerleader." He started up the steps. "From the beginning I knew you were a sweet, innocent little science fiction writer who has an imagination about three sizes too big for her brain. I always knew it was the imagination that would get you into trouble."

"What's that supposed to mean?" Uneasily Amy backed a step or two Jed didn't slow his ascent.

"It means you think too much."

"Jed, wait, we have to talk about this . . ."

He reached for her, catching hold of her wrist before she could escape. Slowly, inexorably he drew her close. "I don't think this is the time for talking. Sometimes a man has to act."

"Don't go all macho on me. I want to know the truth. I want to know what you really think of me."

"I'm going to show you what I really think of you."

He used his grasp on her wrist to tug her closer and then, before Amy could protest, Jed scooped her up in his arms. The movement was accompanied by a barely stifled groan. Amy heard it and was instantly alarmed.

"Jed, your ribs."

"Forget my ribs." He carried her down the hall to her room.

"You shouldn't be carrying me like this. You'll hurt yourself."

"I'll survive. You can fuss over me later."

"Oh, Jed, I didn't mean you had to . . . That is, I only wanted to find out if anything had changed between us because of what you know about me now."

"Nothing has changed between us." He walked through the bedroom door and tossed her lightly down on the bed. "We'll get that part clear first and then we'll talk." He started unfastening the buttons of his shirt.

"Jed, are you sure? I only want to know the truth. Just tell me the truth."

"The truth about how I feel about you? Open your arms and I'll show you the truth, Amy." He stepped out of his clothes and eased down beside her, his body strong and warm and powerful in the tropical moonlight. "Turn off that overactive imagination for a while and concentrate on how you feel, not what you think."

With a sigh of feminine surrender, Amy opened her arms and took his advice.

"But, Jed . . ."

He reached for her, shutting off the uncertain protest with a rough, hot kiss. Amy sighed softly, and Jed acknowledged his victory with a groan. He sprawled along the length of her, his weight crushing her gently into the bedding. She felt his knee edging between her legs and her thighs parted.

"You aren't going to have any doubts about how much I want you," Jed muttered. His hands moved over her, exciting, probing, possessing. He was lying between her legs, his throbbing shaft pressed against her inner thigh. He reached down to moisten himself in the dew that was forming at the entrance of her soft sheath. "And there aren't going to be any doubts about how much you want me, either, are there?"

"No, Jed." She arched against him, shivering when he used his fingers to stretch the opening and prepare the way for his penetration. *"Please."*

"God, Amy, I want you so much. Sometimes I think I'll explode with wanting." His voice was a ragged whisper of need as he guided himself to the secret channel between her legs. He hesitated a moment longer, stroking the blunt end of his manhood through her dampness until he was wet and slick with the evidence of her desire and then, as if he could wait no longer, he drove himself into her.

Amy clutched at him, the muscles in her thighs straining as she wrapped herself around his body. Jed filled her completely, pushing out all the fears and uncertainties that had been plaguing her all evening. There was nothing left but Jed's undeniable desire. It flowed into her, mingling with her own and setting a torch to the already smoldering flames.

Amy gave herself up to the blaze, satisfied with the knowledge that on this level at least, nothing had changed between herself and Jed.

A long time later Amy stirred in Jed's arms. A balmy ocean breeze caressed her relaxed, nude body, evaporating the last of the sensual dampness from her skin. Jed lay sprawled in luxurious splendor beside her, his leg over one of hers, his arm cuddling her close.

"Jed?"

"Hmm?"

"Are you awake?"

He chuckled softly. "I'm awake."

She ignored whatever was amusing him. "There's something I want to ask you."

"Ask."

"How long have you worked for the government?"

Whatever he had been expecting in the way of questions, apparently it wasn't that. Amy felt him grow alert.

"Eight years, give or take a few months," he finally replied. "Why?"

"That's a long time to be doing such dangerous work."

"It isn't always dangerous. It's just that once in a while things go wrong."

Amy took her courage in both hands. "Is that how you got into this job in the first place? Because something went wrong eight years ago? Did it have anything to do with your brother getting killed?"

He was silent for a moment and then slowly turned his head to look at her. "So. You've put that together all by yourself, have you?"

She couldn't tell if he was angry or merely thoughtful. "You said things changed for you eight years ago. Your engagement ended. Your brother died. And that's when you started working for the government. I just wondered—"

"Lord preserve me from a woman's mind."

"You don't have to tell me, Jed."

"The hell I don't. After all the secrets you've told me? You have a right to some more of mine."

"If you'd rather not talk about it . . ." She let the sentence trail off.

"I can talk about it." He paused. "To you." There was another long pause while he collected his thoughts. "Andy was a government agent, though I didn't know it at the time. My brother was a fine engineer and he used his work as a cover. It got him into a lot of hot spots without a lot of questions. He never came back from his last assignment. I was told he was dead, killed by terrorists while he was shopping for souvenirs in the town near the construction site. I spent a few days looking for the bottom of a few bottles. When the government man showed up at my door I was not in a good mood. He took advantage of the fact and I let him."

"What do you mean?"

"He told me what Andy had really been doing and how he'd been killed by one of the men he'd been sent overseas to investigate. Then this nice man from the agency which had employed my brother offered me a chance at a little revenge. All I had to do was take Andy's place at the construction site and make contact with the crowd Andy had been chasing."

Amy was appalled. "But you had no training in that sort of thing. You could have been killed. That agency had no business sending you in cold on an assignment like that."

"The agency was desperate. As for me, I was more than willing to go."

"Because you wanted to avenge Andy's death."

Jed nodded in the shadows. Then he said dryly, "As it turned out, I had a certain, uh, aptitude for the work. Things went like clockwork. The agency got the information it needed and I got what I wanted out of the deal."

Amy shivered and touched him. There was no need to ask what form the revenge had taken. "And when you came home?"

"When I came home Elaine announced she had found someone else. I never told her the real reason I'd gone out on that assignment. I postponed the wedding plans and let her think it was just another construction site job. But I think she knew or guessed that there was more to it than that. The way she looked at me when I came home . . ." Jed shook his head. "All I know for certain is that by the time I returned there was another man. I couldn't blame her. I didn't think I'd make a very good husband or father after what I'd done."

"You just made that decision all by yourself? Or did you get a second opinion?"

"No, I didn't get a second opinion." Jed's voice roughened. "I figured it out by myself. After Elaine handed me back the ring I was at loose ends for a while. I couldn't seem to settle down. I kept thinking about what had happened to Andy and what I'd done because of it. Then one day the agency man was standing on my front step again. There was a little matter he thought I could handle for his employer. Something for which my engineering background would make a first rate cover. It wouldn't take long, he said. In and out. Very quick. Very neat. I went."

"And after that there was another assignment and then another, right?"

Jed shrugged. "I told you. I seemed to have a talent for it. And . . ."

"And what?"

"And, in the beginning at least, I was naive enough to think I was needed. That I was fighting a small war that had to be fought."

"Of course you believed in what you were doing," Amy said promptly. "You're not the kind of man who would do such things unless you thought they were necessary."

There was a gleam of interest in his eyes. "You seem very sure of that."

"I am sure of it. But eight years is a long time to do such things, Jed."

"I know. A lifetime."

Amy raised herself up so she could look into his face. "I know the feeling, even though for me it's only been eight months. Maybe you and I need new lifetimes."

Before he could respond to that she leaned down to kiss him. Her fingertips trailed slowly down his chest and stomach to the softened shaft of his manhood. She felt him stir under her touch and then he was no longer soft.

"When you touch me like that," Jed muttered thickly, "the only lifetime I'm interested in living is this one. You make my head spin, lady."

"I'm glad." She trailed her fingertips over him, teasing his hard, pulsing masculine flesh. She brushed her mouth against his throat. "I'm very glad I can make your head spin a little, Jed. It's only fair, considering the effect you have on me."

He groaned as she drew a tiny circle on the inside of his heavy thigh. Then Jed reached for her, pulling her down and pushing her onto her back. He loomed over her for a moment, his eyes glittering with desire as he watched the mysterious feminine passion take hold of her. With deliberate provocation Amy ran the sole of her foot down his calf. She clenched her fingers around his hard, muscled buttock.

"Playing games?" Jed asked in a husky voice.

"Games you taught me."

"You've got the makings of a born tease."

"Possibly." Her eyes were brilliant as she moved enticingly under him.

"You're not the only one who can play this game." Jed moved slightly and Amy sighed. He was just barely inside her.

When he didn't go farther, she wriggled invitingly and tried to pull him closer. Jed ignored the summons, nibbling appreciatively at her ear. When he withdrew himself Amy clutched him.

"Jed, please." She lifted herself and Jed obligingly entered her once more. But he didn't make any attempt to finish the job. Amy's grip tightened demandingly. "Come here," she whispered.

"I want to watch you go wild." He repeated the teasing, tantalizing movements.

"I won't go wild, I'll go insane."

"Even better."

"Oh, Jed . . ." She grabbed him, wrapping her legs around him, sinking her nails into him, calling him to her with fierce, husky pleas.

"Wild," Jed muttered as he slowly and completely filled her. "Soft and wild." He stopped playing lovers' games and let the passion take hold.

Chapter Eleven

The sleek, white cruise ship was visible as soon as the Jeep rounded the last cove on the way into town. It was tied up at the docking facility that had once been used by the military.

Amy caught her whipping hair, held it out of her eyes and stared in amazement. "Good grief. Rosie was right. Orleana is getting downright civilized. She said a cruise line had started making the island a port of call, but after all these years of being ignored, it's hard to believe. The village shops must be going crazy with all those tourists descending on them. Hank and Rosie's will be packed."

"Speaking of village shops, where can I pick up some new batteries for the dive light?" Jed asked as he drove along the road bordering the harbor.

He had to slow the Jeep to a crawl as he entered town. Throngs of tourists from the ship were crossing the narrow road with little regard for traffic. Some of the bright, colorful cruise clothing on display was almost as vivid as the fuchsia shirt Amy had tied below her breasts and the island print shorts she was wearing.

"Harry Sanderson runs a general store at the end of the street. He's got a small dive shop attached. You can get batteries there," Amy said as she watched the tourists with fascination.

"Are you sure you want to dive that old bomber today?"

Jed asked as he found a parking place for the Jeep and neatly slipped the vehicle into it.

"That's the fortieth time today you've asked me that question. The answer is still yes." She grinned at him as she alighted from the Jeep.

"Don't get sassy. It's only the thirty-ninth. I just want to make sure." Jed used his left hand on the window frame to lever himself out of the driver's seat.

Amy's grin faded. "Don't worry, Jed. I won't panic on you. I've told you, if I start getting *stressed*, I'll signal you and we'll surface."

He regarded her intently, thick brows drawn together in a frown. "I'm not worried about you panicking on me. I just don't want you rushing things."

"It's time I went back into the water. I feel capable of handling it today. I don't want to put it off any longer."

"All right, if you're sure."

"I'm sure. Go get the batteries. I'll wait for you at Hank and Rosie's." Amy waved toward the direction of the small store at the end of the street, then swung around and strolled toward Hank and Rosie's. She didn't glance back, but she could feel Jed watching her until she disappeared through the doorway of the open air bar.

The place was filled with people from the ship. Amy spotted several guava juice cocktails as well as more traditional island drinks sitting on the old rattan tables as she made her way toward the rear. It was obvious the tourists were thoroughly enjoying the laid back island atmosphere of the bar. The place looked like a scene from a film set in the islands

Amy spotted Rosie working madly amid a cloud of

steaming pots. She waved at the plump woman from the kitchen door.

"Hi, Rosie. Looks like you've got a full house. These folks are really getting off on the South Seas image. Since when did Hank learn how to make frozen banana daiquiries?"

"Since the cruise ship started putting in here once a week. The man learns fast. He can also make a wicked mai tai these days." Rosie grinned, mopping perspiration from her forehead with a tea towel. "You wouldn't believe the kind of stuff tourists want to drink. Hardly an honest Scotch drinker in the bunch. Nothing but daiquiries, mai tais and fluffy pink stuff. One of these days we might actually have to start stocking white wine."

"Oh, I don't know. Looks to me like you're making inroads converting the cruise folk to guava juice cocktails."

Rosie's hearty laugh filled the kitchen. "Speaking of which, how did you survive the other night? Your man have to carry you into the house?"

Amy grimaced, folding her arms as she leaned against the doorframe. "To tell you the truth, my memory of getting into the house is a little vague."

"I'm not surprised. Listen, I got a little loose lipped that night. I guess your mentioning the old days got me remembering. I hope I didn't upset you by telling you some of those things about your mom and dad and the past." Rosie looked anxious.

"No," Amy said gently, "you didn't upset me." Determined to change the subject, she added quickly, "Did your guests arrive? The ones you said had made genuine reservations?"

"Sure did. Got in this morning. That makes three staying

upstairs now. I'm getting ready to feed them lunch, along with some of those folks from the boat. What are you and Jed up to today?"

"We're going to dive the old bomber this afternoon. Jed's buying some batteries for the dive light now. Here, let me give you a hand serving that stuff."

"I appreciate it, honey. Pick up some plates and follow me."

Amy deftly slid two hamburger baskets and a bowl of fish chowder onto a tray and followed Rosie into the dining area of the tavern. Several tables were filled. One man sat alone at the rear, his hands wrapped around a can of beer. Rosie directed one of the hamburgers toward him.

Amy dutifully carried the hamburger to the waiting diner. He was a thin, wiry man somewhere between thirty and forty, though it was hard to tell. It had been difficult to tell Jed's age at first, too, Amy remembered. This man was not bad looking with his light hair and gray eyes, but there was a surly, indifferent quality about him that made her want to serve him as quickly and unobtrusively as possible. Amy summoned up her brightest smile.

"Here's your hamburger, sir. Anything else?"

He looked at her curiously, making Amy wonder exactly what he was thinking. Automatically she stepped back a pace.

"No," he muttered. "That'll be all. For now."

Amy nodded and hurried off with the tray. Rosie was signaling her from a table where two other men were seated.

"Chowder goes there in front of Mr. Guthrie." She indicated the short, heavily built man at the table. "And that last hamburger is for Mr. Renner, here." Rosie gave the second man the full benefit of her laughing grin.

"Call me Dan, Rosie," the man said, his eyes on Amy And my friend here just uses his last name as his first name. He prefers to be called Guthrie, don't you, Guthrie?"

"That's right." Guthrie was ignoring the two women. His full attention was on the chowder and the beer at his elbow.

"Guthrie and Dan are staying upstairs," Rosie explained. "That guy who had the other hamburger is the third guest I was telling you about. He got in a few days ago."

"How about an introduction to your waitress, Rosie?" Renner was smiling at Amy.

Amy smiled back. She couldn't help herself. Renner was the kind they called drop-dead-good-looking. He obviously knew it, but he seemed to find the fact amusing as much as anything else. His smile invited Amy to share the little joke nature had played by endowing him with so much attractive charm. That smile implied Renner himself didn't take it too seriously and neither should anyone else. It was a very disarming expression. Renner had a wealth of jet black hair that fell across his forehead in a rakish wave and vivid blue eyes that mirrored his smile.

He was dressed in a dashing version of tropical khaki shirt and trousers with lots of snappy pockets, epaulets and buttons. To be fair Jed was wearing similar clothing, but on Jed the clothes looked comfortably worn and faded. Renner's appeared to have come straight from a Rodeo Drive boutique. His smile said he found his clothing amusing, too.

"I'm Amy Slater. My folks have a place here on the island. I just dropped in to visit Rosie and decided to give her a hand serving lunch."

Renner blinked. The voltage of his smile went up another few notches. "No kidding? You live here?"

"No, I just visit a couple of times a year. My parents are

the permanent residents, although they're gone for a few weeks. How long are you staying, Dan?"

"Just a few days, then we're heading back to Hawaii. We heard the diving was great around here. I'm a novice, but I'm trying to get in as much experience as I can on my vacation."

Rosie interrupted to clap Amy on the back. "While you two are yakking, I'm going to get the rest of my food dished up. Take your time, Amy. I can handle the rest."

Amy glanced around quickly. "I don't mind helping, Rosie."

But Rosie was already halfway back to the kitchen. Renner made another bid for Amy's attention.

"Do you dive?" he asked.

Amy smiled. "What? Oh, yes. The diving really is great around here. A friend and I are going to the north end of the island this afternoon to check out the wreck of an old bomber. You should be sure and see it before you leave."

"Thanks. We'll make a point of it, won't we, Guthrie?"

Guthrie nodded once and continued spooning his soup.

Renner ignored his companion. He kept his attention on Amy. "Any chance we can get you and your, uh, friend to show us some of the good dive spots around here? We could use an insider's knowledge."

Amy hesitated, looking for a convenient excuse. She didn't want to dive with anyone except Jed until she knew she was back in control of herself underwater. "I'm afraid we've already got this afternoon planned. But Hank, the guy who owns this place, can give you some tips."

Renner looked mildly chagrined. "I can take a hint. Maybe some other time?"

"I'm not sure," Amy said hesitantly. "My friend and I are going to be busy for the next few days."

"Say no more, I get the picture. It would be too much, I suppose, to hope that this, er, friend is female? When Guthrie's not eating soup, he's really a pretty decent guy. Any chance of a double date in scuba gear?"

Amy laughed and shook her head.

Jed heard the sweet, clear sound of her laughter as he walked into the tavern carrying a paper bag from Sanderson's dive shop. He glanced around at the roomful of colorfully dressed tourists looking for Amy's even more colorful fuchsia shirt. He spotted her talking to a dark-haired man who looked to be about her age. The man was seated at a table with another, slightly older man, but Jed ignored the second male. It was the first one, the one with the carefully styled black hair and the expensive bush shirt who was making the pass at Amy.

Jed's reaction was immediate and startlingly intense. Every nerve in his body reacted fiercely to the sight of Amy laughing with another man. The possessiveness he felt took him by surprise.

He realized with a start that part of the problem was that he was accustomed to having Amy completely to himself. During the time he had known her—even when they had been playing the game of being friends—he had never had to deal with the potential threat of another man.

Oh, there had been that brief moment when he was calling her from the L.A. airport and he had wondered if she was with someone else, but that jarring thought had quickly been forgotten when she'd agreed to meet his plane. Caliph's Bay was a small place and Amy lived a quiet, private, almost reclusive life. She had never even dated anyone else in town.

For the past three months Jed had had her virtually to himself. She was always at home when he called, available for dinner or willing to invite him over for an evening, and finally, after three long months, willing to share his bed.

It occurred to Jed that he'd gotten pretty damn spoiled. Where had he picked up the notion that he actually had exclusive rights to Amelia Slater?

In the next instant he realized it didn't matter where he'd gotten the idea; it was firmly embedded in his mind. Amy belonged to him.

He shouldn't have let her leave the house with that shirt tied just below her breasts like that, he decided as he watched her. It left her neat little midriff fully exposed.

Jed heard her laugh again and started forward. He walked up behind her just as the blue-eyed man spoke casually.

"I understand the cruise ship has a standing invitation to the locals to go aboard in the evenings, spend a little money at the bar and enjoy the entertainment. Any chance you'd ditch your diving friend and join me tonight? Rosie says they usually have a good band. Apparently she and Hank go aboard when the ship is in harbor."

"I'm not surprised," Amy began politely. "There's not a lot of night life here on Orleana, but as far as tonight goes—"

"As far as tonight goes," Jed interrupted smoothly, "Amy is busy. Her diving buddy isn't about to get himself ditched." He put his arm around Amy's bare waist. She glanced up at him in surprise.

"Oh, there you are, Jed. I wondered what was keeping you. Did you get the batteries?"

Her voice was a bit too bright and Jed knew why. She had sensed the potential for trouble and was determined to head it off at all costs. He knew instinctively that Amy would hate finding herself at the center of an uncivilized scene between two growling males. Ruthlessly he took advantage of her natural desire to avoid a rude exchange of masculine insults. Jed smiled down at her a little grimly.

"I've got the batteries. Are you ready to leave?"

She nodded quickly. "I'm ready." Then her manners got in the way. She paused to introduce him to the two men seated at the table.

"Glaze." Renner's smile went down a few watts but stayed in place. He studied Jed with interest.

"Renner." Jade acknowledged the other man with a cool inclination of his head. It was hardly worth bothering with Guthrie. He seemed concerned only with spooning up the last of his chowder. He did so with a distinct slurping noise that made Dan Renner wince. Jed didn't like the wryly apologetic smile Renner gave Amy on behalf of his companion; it was too much like a private exchange. The man was a nuisance. Jed's arm tightened around Amy. "Come on, honey. Let's get going."

She didn't argue with him but she insisted on stopping by the kitchen before they left. Rosie had dished up the last hamburger and was about to carry it into the other room. She smiled when she saw Jed.

"I hear you two are going diving this afternoon. You take good care of this girl now, you hear?"

"I hear."

"And you bring her out to the boat tonight. Be fun for both of you. I'm gonna make Hank put on a fresh shirt and polish his shoes. That man can dance when he puts his mind to it, you know."

Hank loomed in the doorway behind Jed and Amy. He exhaled gustily. "The woman wears me out on the dance floor. Hadn't danced in over thirty years and then this cruise ship started putting into port every week and inviting all us local yokels on board. Next thing I know, I'm trying to remember how to fox-trot."

"Believe me, I understand," Jed muttered. "I'm not much of a dancer, either. Never was."

"Well, it sounds like fun," Amy said with an enthusiasm Jed knew he wouldn't be able to override. "Save us a seat tonight."

"Will do," Rosie confirmed. "I guess Renner and Guthrie are planning on living it up, too. Heard them say they wanted to take in the night life on board."

Jed glanced back toward the two men. "I hope Renner realizes he's going to have to turn up his own dancing partner from among the passengers. He's not going to borrow Amy."

"Jed!" Amy gave him a quelling glance which Jed ignored.

Rosie laughed zestfully and patted Amy's arm. "Don't fret, girl. The good ones are always a tad possessive. Seems to go with the territory." She paid no attention to the warmth in Amy's face. "You know, that Renner puts me in mind of someone I once knew."

"You've met him before?" Amy asked.

Rosie shook her head. "Oh, no. I'd remember if I had. You know me. Never forget a face. No, there's just something kinda familiar about him. What about you, Hank? Does he remind you of anyone?"

Hank glanced down the aisle of rattan tables, frowning in concentration. "Can't say that he does. Probably just your imagination, Rosie."

"Maybe," Rosie agreed. "Well, you two run along and have fun this afternoon. We'll see you tonight."

Jed nodded, using his hand on Amy's waist to steer her toward the door as she said her good-byes.

"Really, Jed," she announced as she found herself out on the street beside him, "you came very close to being rude in there."

"I can do better than come close. I can get right down to the real thing."

She was clearly taken aback by his words. "Don't you think you overreacted a bit? Dan was only being friendly."

"Sure."

"Sure, what?" she demanded. "That's no kind of answer. Sure you overreacted or sure he was being friendly?"

"Amy, your voice is rising." He opened the Jeep door and helped her onto the seat.

"My voice is rising?" she squeaked. "I can do more than raise it a little, I can scream. Jed, this is ridiculous. Why are you so upset?"

He sighed as he got in beside her and turned the key in the ignition. "I just realized I've gotten spoiled."

When she tried to pin him down on his meaning he switched the conversation to the dive plan.

An hour and a half later Amy watched a sleek blue jack swim lazily through the water in front of her and knew this time she was going to be all right. Her breathing was normal, the water felt good and she was actually beginning to enjoy the dive. Jed was to her left and a little behind her,

swimming easily. If he was watching her for signs of incipi-
ent panic he was doing a good job of hiding his concern. He
appeared relaxed and interested in the underwater landscape.

The bomber lay in shallow water just beyond the reef that
ringed a small cove. Jed and Amy were both carrying dive
lights to explore the inside of the fuselage, but the lights
weren't necessary for anything else. Sunlight filtered
through the beautiful water, illuminating the waving seaweed, the scalloped sand and the flashing schools of endlessly patrolling fish. Everything was clear and gently lit.
There were no terrifyingly dark corridors that led nowhere,
no confining rock walls that threatened to close in on a
diver, no body guarding the only exit.

And Jed was with her. Jed, who now knew everything.
Amy had told him the truth about her worst nightmares and
he had accepted it all without batting an eye.

Amy didn't kid herself about why he had been able to
handle the facts about her past so easily. It was because his
past contained nightmares that were undoubtedly a lot worse
than her own. But hadn't she subconsciously guessed that all
along? He had confirmed those half realized truths the night
before, although he had spared her the details.

It occurred to Amy as she watched Jed glide down to
explore a small reef cranny that she had accepted his past as
easily as he had accepted hers. In spite of what had happened to her eight months before she had a feeling she
should have been far more shocked when she heard the truth
about Jed. After all, for her the terrifying experience with
LePage and the excursion into darkness that had followed
were distinct aberrations in her world. For Jed such things
apparently bordered on the normal.

He wasn't the kind of man she had once thought she could

love. Never in her wildest imaginings had she envisioned losing her heart to a man like Jedidiah Glaze.

Strangely enough, the shadows in him weren't what disturbed her the most, although a year ago they would have been the reason she would have steered clear of him. No, now Amy knew it was Jed's manner of dismissing most of his past and a large part of his future that truly bothered her. He kept both locked away in the farthest corners of his mind, just as he kept the shadows imprisoned. Amy sensed it was his ability to do so that had helped him survive. It had been her inability to do just that which had threatened her sanity.

She understood Jed's commitment only to the present, but she wondered what hope there was for a love that existed within such boundaries. She wasn't even sure that in Jed's case the emotion could be labeled love. It was probably more in the nature of a short-term sexual bond that could be severed quite easily. Unfortunately for her, her emotions were far more complex. She was in love, and there was nothing else she could label it.

Amy pushed aside the unanswered questions and concentrated on her diving. Kicking forward, she led Jed around the reef toward a large, hulking shape on the ocean floor. The twin tails of the B-25 were still intact, although their once sleek outlines were marred by decades of marine growth. The sea had done its work on the invading object from the outer world. It accepted it and used it for its own purposes. The bomber was now home for a variety of plants and aquatic creatures.

Amy swam around it first, letting Jed have a good look at the empty nose where the gunner had once crouched. The glass was long gone, but it wasn't hard to imagine how it had looked. Amy thought briefly of the unknown young man who had sat there at the front of the craft, so vulnerable and exposed, in order to do his job. She had always told herself that the crew of the plane had managed to bail out before the bomber went down. It was probably a fairy tale, but she preferred it to the more likely truth that everyone on board had been killed.

A creative imagination, Jed said, had its drawbacks. Sometimes he was right. She couldn't bear to think of the crew of the bomber trapped in the plane as they watched their doom rise to meet them. It was one thing to create that sort of scenario on a word processor, quite another to imagine it happening in real life.

Amy turned away from the gunner's seat and swam toward the broken fuselage. She was aware of Jed keeping an eye on her now. He was trying to be unobtrusive about it, but she knew he was wondering if she would find the interior of the plane too reminiscent of the interior of a cave. Amy was wondering the same thing. She switched on her dive light.

A wave of relief swept through her, and for the first time Amy realized she had been more tense than she had thought. This wasn't a cave. It wasn't anything like a cave. Her imagination had been a little overactive on that subject, too. Sunlight pierced the shattered, twisted skin of the craft in several places. Amy glanced around, bouncing her light off the encrusted interior walls of the plane as she hovered just outside a jagged tear in the metal.

Jed appeared on the opposite side of the craft, his light pouring through what had once been the hatch. The twin beams of the dive lights caught a school of colorful wrasses. They were propelling themselves through the cavernous interior of the plane with the distinctive rowing motion of their pectoral fins. They seemed unperturbed by the human intruders.

Gingerly Amy swam through the tear in the fuselage and went toward the cockpit. Jed followed. Their lights played over what remained of the panel and the pilot's seat. Amy was about to turn around when she spotted an untidy little pile of empty shells beneath the seat.

Swimming closer, Amy dropped down and aimed the dive light up under the skeleton of the instrument panel. She saw what she had half expected to find. The tip of a tentacle was just barely visible. The shells piled up below the pilot's seat were the remains of several meals. She had found an octopus' den.

Experimentally she moved her wrist back and forth in the water, inviting the den's resident to view the shiny metal casing of her dive watch. It was a toss-up for a minute or two, but eventually the creature's curiosity overcame its natural timidity. A tentacle whipped out to wrap around Amy's wrist. It was a very small tentacle and Amy wanted to laugh. She glanced back and saw Jed watching. Behind the mask she saw the amusement in his eyes.

Gently she reached out to stroke the tentacle. But the instant she touched the octopus it panicked and withdrew completely into hiding. The game was over.

Amy swung slowly around in the water, following Jed back out of the cockpit. As they slipped past the entrance a moray poked its head out from under a jumble of wooden crates. Amy backed off, giving the creature room. Morays weren't aggressive, but they had no compunction about biting a stray hand or foot that wandered too close to their territory.

Amy was about to swim out through the hatch when she

caught Jed's questioning gaze. She signaled she was fine and kicked easily back out of the plane.

She *was* fine, she realized. A small burst of relieved euphoria caught her and she swung around to wait for Jed. He appeared after a moment and seemed to understand her mood. Side by side they headed back toward shore.

As they waded out of the surf Jed shoved his mask back on his head and asked, "Everything okay?"

"Peachy," Amy said blithely. "Terrific. A-OK. Wonderful. Great."

"Good. Tomorrow or the next day we'll go after that box in the caves."

Amy's euphoric mood splintered. "No, Jed. I've told you there's no need to drag that thing out of there."

"Have a little faith in me, sweetheart. I know what I'm doing."

"Why, you overconfident, arrogant son of a—"

He leaned down and cut off her words with a quick, salty kiss. "I enjoyed the dive. You're a good partner underwater. Come to think of it, you're pretty good out of the water, too. Terrific in bed, in fact."

Amy saw the unabashed sexual humor in his eyes and didn't know whether to yell at him or give him a disgusted, cold shoulder. It was obvious he wasn't going to argue about the box in the caves. He was going after it and if she didn't go along, he'd probably go by himself. Quietly she turned away from him and began unbuckling her gear.

Jed watched her mood shift and stifled a sigh of regret. He was genuinely sorry to have caused the change, but there wasn't any help for it. The business with the box in the caves had to be handled sooner or later and it was his nature to take care of loose ends as soon as possible. It made him distinctly uneasy to know Amy's secrets had been so precariously hidden for so long.

She'd handled herself well in the water today, he thought as he silently helped pack the gear. She had been relaxed and efficient. Jed realized he was taking a certain pride in the fact that she seemed back in control. Had confiding her secrets to him relieved some of her stress? It was undoubtedly his ego at work, but he liked to think he'd helped Amy. It satisfied the side of him that wanted to protect her.

As if her secrets were all that horrendous, Jed thought wryly as he swung the tanks into the back of the Jeep. But death and fear could be relative matters. For someone like Amy, the events that night at the caves constituted a true nightmare.

Whenever he thought about how close she had come to getting herself killed by LePage, Jed had a few nightmares of his own.

"What you have to understand, Amy," Jed said as he climbed into the Jeep beside her, "is that that damn box can come back to haunt you in more ways than one. Leave it where it is and it might do more than keep you awake nights."

She turned to eye him uneasily. "What are you talking about?"

"That box has already gotten two people killed, Wyman and LePage. Don't look at me like that, Amy. I'm glad it was LePage lying on the bottom of that pool the next morning, not you." He saw her wince. "Yeah, think about it. He had plans to be the one who discovered your 'accidentally' drowned body that morning."

Jed knew he sounded cold, but he was determined to do whatever he had to in order to make an impression. Amy was too gentle to be involved in this mess, but the world rarely respected such innocence. Amy was involved and the only way to free her was to make her face her involvement.

Amy wasn't looking at him any longer. She was staring at the road ahead. "All right."

He gave her still profile a quick, startled glance. "What's that supposed to mean?"

"It means all right. If you're absolutely sure it's the only alternative, we'll go after the box."

Jed exhaled deeply. "It's the only way, Amy."

"I hope you know what you're doing."

He took one hand off the wheel, reached out and caught her fingers in his. He squeezed gently. "I do. When it comes to this kind of thing I've got sound instincts. Cleaning up loose ends is one of the few things I'm good at."

"Actually," Amy said with a grave, thoughtful air, "you're good at a few other things, too."

He cocked a brow interrogatively. "Such as?"

"Building bird cages."

"Oh, that."

"Yes, that. And don't you forget it."

Jed shrugged. "I keep telling you, it's just a hobby."

"Maybe."

He didn't know what to make of the stubborn look on her face, so he shrugged again and put his hand back on the steering wheel. She trusted him, he thought with deep satisfaction. She wasn't pleased with his advice, but she trusted him.

An hour later Jed was still luxuriating in the unexpected pleasure Amy's trust had given him when he realized he might have been deluding himself all day.

Someone had very carefully and discreetly gone through

the contents of his room. Whoever had done it had paid particular attention to the flight bag he had unpacked and left stashed in the closet. As usual, Jed had left the last eight pairs of the zipper's metal teeth unzipped. The searcher hadn't caught that little detail. There were only six pairs left unconnected at the end of the zipper.

Someone had recently come looking for some answers about Jedidiah Glaze.

Chapter Twelve

Amy had just gotten out of the shower, one towel tur-
baned around her head and another wrapped around
her body when she realized she was not alone in her
bedroom. Jed was lounging in the doorway, a remote,
watchful expression in his eyes. She paused, one hand se-
curing the knot of the towel as she met his gaze.

"Is something wrong, Jed?" she asked uncertainly. She
realized he hadn't looked at her in quite that way before.

"You'll have to answer that one. If you've still got questions, Amy, I'd rather you asked them straight out."

The edge of his low, dark voice cut into her. Amy instinctively took a step backward. "I don't understand. Tell me
what's wrong."

"Nothing's wrong—except that I made the mistake of
thinking I had your trust." He moved into the room with a
prowling stride that made Amy take another step toward her
closet. "Didn't you believe anything I said last night?"

"Of course I did. Why on earth are you acting like this?
Jed, what is it?"

He stopped a short distance away from her. "Find anything of interest in the flight bag? Say a passport in another
man's name? Or a nice, neat, reassuring government identi-
fication card proving who I am? A gun, perhaps? Or maybe
a mysterious telephone number? With your imagination, you

should have been able to attach some kind of significance to a phone number."

Amy's palms grew damp. "Are you saying someone searched your belongings?"

"That's what I'm saying." He took another step forward, forcing her to retreat an equal pace. "You could have just asked me, Amy. I'd have been glad to show you what was in the flight bag. Not that it would have done you any more good than going through it on your own. It was empty, wasn't it?"

She felt a wave of panic and frantically beat it down. "I don't know," she managed. "I didn't go through your flight bag." Her back was against the slatted door of the closet. Jed leaned over her, his hands planted on either side of her to form a cage. This close and in this mood he was extraordinarily intimidating. Amy lifted her chin defiantly. 'Did you hear me? I haven't touched your things."

He said nothing for a long moment, pinning her with his eyes. "Just tell me the truth, Amy. It won't matter. I may not like the fact that you've got qualms about me, but I can sure as hell understand your having them. It's just that I thought we worked them all out last night."

"I thought it was your qualms about me we were working out last night," Amy said bluntly. "You were so quiet and distant all day after I told you what happened to LePage, and then when you didn't seem to want me, I was sure—"

"Stop babbling. If I spent a lot of time being uncommunicative yesterday, it was because I had a lot of thinking to do. I was working through all the possible problems we've got because of that box sitting in those caves. But you must have known damn well I wanted you. Didn't I make myself perfectly clear?"

"Well, yes." She felt helpless. "But that was after... after you'd spent hours acting as if you didn't know what to think of me and I—"

"And you came up here and searched my flight bag?"

"No, dammit, I did not search your bag! I give you my word of honor on that, Jed Glaze. My word happens to mean something to me."

He was silent, studying her as if he were trying to decide whether to keep up the pressure. Then Jed drew a deep breath and his arms fell away from the wall. He shoved his hands into his back pockets and paced toward the open window.

"I believe you. If I'd thought it through instead of just reacting, I'd have realized right away it couldn't have been you. You're not a pro. You'd have left all kinds of tracks. Whoever tossed my room was reasonably proficient."

"Gee whiz, thanks."

He paid no attention to her. "That leaves us with a problem."

Amy gasped as it all clicked in her mind. She walked over to the bed and sank down, feeling weak. "Yes, I see."

"If you didn't search my room, who did?"

She cleared her throat. "That's a very good question. I haven't seen any signs that anyone was in the house." She shot to her feet. "My father's study."

Jed turned around. "What about it?"

"There's a safe in it. Surely if anyone searched the house he would have tried to open the safe."

"I don't think it was that kind of search, Amy. I doubt if anyone went through the place on a random basis. I think the guy found the one room he wanted."

"Your room? But why, Jed?"

"Maybe someone wants to know if I'm following in LePage's footsteps," he said calmly.

"*What?*"

"There was a point during the past few days when you were asking yourself a similar question, wasn't there?" he reminded her. "We've got to get that box out of the caves, Amy."

Amy was pacing the room in a distracted manner. "You keep saying that. I've already agreed. But I can't believe someone is after that box, Jed. It's been eight months since LePage . . . died. Why would someone move in on the box now, at this particular time?"

"Because your parents have finally left the island?" he suggested. "Theoretically, with your mother and father off the island for a few weeks, this should have been an ideal time to search for the caves."

"But we're here! It's not as if the place is vacant." Amy was concentrating intently. "How do you know your room was searched? Is something missing? Were things tossed around?"

"It's nothing obvious, honey," Jed said patiently. "Just half a dozen unzipped teeth on my flight bag. Normally I leave eight unzipped."

Amy was astounded. "Six little teeth instead of eight? Good heavens, Jed, that's hardly evidence for a search. You could easily have miscounted. Why would you be counting zipper teeth in the first place?"

"Habit "

"Oh, come on, there was no reason for you to have taken precautions here. How can you be certain you left that bag unzipped just so far and no farther?"

He ran a hand through his hair and said again, this time a little wearily, "I've told you. Habit."

Amy threw up her hands. Then she grabbed her kimono and slipped into it. "Let's take a look at this famous flight bag." She headed for the door without waiting for him to follow. She was aware of Jed coming after her, shaking his head as if she just didn't understand.

Amy marched into the room to see the bag wide open. It was empty, as Jed had said. Amy studied it before spinning around to confront him. She eyed him suspiciously.

"This is it? This is all the evidence of a search you've got?"

In spite of his obvious concern about the situation, Jed began to look faintly amused by her interrogation. "Yes, ma'am. That's it. One empty flight bag that should have been zipped to within eight teeth of the end of the zipper."

"Which is now totally unzipped so we can't even count teeth."

"Right," he agreed.

"Are you absolutely, positively certain about the number of teeth, Jed?"

"If I weren't I'd probably crack under all this pressure you're applying. You sound like a police detective trying to break my story."

She was offended. "It's just that I can't quite believe someone was in the house today. We don't have any crime on Orleana. Oh, a few fights down in the village, perhaps, but that's about the extent of it. Who could have done something like this? From what you've told me, it would take a fairly sophisticated sort of intruder."

"There's a whole cruise ship full of strangers sitting in the harbor, Amy."

Her eyes widened. "Good grief, you're right."

"I'm glad I've finally made an impression. You'd better go get dressed."

"Dressed? You still want to go out this evening? Even though you think someone was in here going through your things today?" She was taken aback by his apparently casual attitude.

"Why not? Whoever got in here today is long gone, and no one's likely to try stumbling around in the jungle looking for the cave entrance tonight. It'll be safe enough for us to spend a few hours on board the ship."

"You're very sure the box is at the bottom of all this, aren't you?"

"Let's just say I'll feel much more secure when I know that box is out of the caves and empty of all its secrets Run along, Amy."

"You're sure you want to go out tonight?"

"I'm sure."

She gave him one last, doubtful look and then did as he suggested.

After he and Amy were seated in one of the ship's three lounges later that evening, Jed realized he wasn't sure he wanted to spend the evening on board after all. The guy who had made a pass at Amy that afternoon in Hank and Rosie's was seated along with his buddy on the opposite side of the room. He caught Amy's eye and waved, and she politely acknowledged the greeting. Jed turned to Hank who was sitting beside him. The big tavern owner and his wife were sharing a table with Jed and Amy.

"What did you say his name was?"

"Who?" Then Hank grinned with good-natured understanding. "Oh, you mean Renner. His friend's name is Guthrie." Hank leaned closer. "Don't worry. Amy isn't the wandering type."

Jed glanced at Amy who was talking animatedly with Rosie. "I know. But I get the feeling Renner is." Just gazing at Amy made his body tighten in pleasant anticipation. The feeling of possessiveness went deep, deeper than he had even suspected this afternoon. It went right to the bone.

Tonight she was very appealing with her hair on top of her head in a deceptively casual knot that left wisps trailing temptingly down her nape. The style seemed to highlight the faint slant of her eyes, making her look more like a sorceress than ever. She was wearing a lemon yellow island dress of polished cotton. It had a deep, curving neckline that exposed a fair amount of her soft skin and it fell in a long, narrow column to her ankles. The skirt was slit high on the side to facilitate walking. The design also facilitated a tantalizing glimpse of leg. Jed realized just how far gone he was when he caught himself actually thinking of telling Amy to uncross her legs so the yellow dress wouldn't reveal quite so much of her shapely calf. It didn't take a creative imagination to guess how she'd treat that suggestion.

Jed sighed and ordered another round of drinks for everyone at the table. He was valiantly sticking to white wine this evening and was aware of Amy's silent approval. Hank and Rosie weren't being nearly so circumspect. They were both sampling martinis. The drinks were served with a flourish by a white-jacketed waiter just as the band appeared onstage. The lights in the lounge dimmed and the music swelled to a lively number based on a rock beat. Conversation dropped to a minimum and the dance floor began to fill.

Jed caught Amy watching him expectantly and belatedly

realized she was waiting for him to ask her to dance. He listened to the driving rhythm of the music and groaned silently. She was tapping her fingertip on the surface of the table. Jed sought for a reasonable excuse.

"Uh, the floor's kind of crowded. How about waiting for the next one?" he offered.

"You're not getting out of this that easily." Amy got to her feet.

"Sweetheart, have a little pity on me. This isn't my kind of music. I'm a little old for this type of dancing."

"Stop looking for excuses." Her fingers closed around his wrist, but before she could coax him to his feet, Renner's voice interrupted. He had come up behind Amy.

"If it's a partner you want, I'm game," Renner said easily. "No need to drag your friend here out on the floor. Let's let the older crowd enjoy their drinks in peace while you and I give the band a try."

Jed considered the various and assorted pleasures that would be his if he were to plant his fist in the center of Renner's face. Then he saw the anxious expression in Amy's eyes. She'd hate him if he caused a scene. Realizing his options were limited, Jed got to his feet.

"The *older* crowd," he informed Renner, "can still manage to get around." He dragged Amy toward the dance floor before she or Renner could say anything. When he reached the polished wood floor he yanked her into his arms and found her laughing silently up at him. The unholy amusement in her green eyes made him long to exert some authority.

"The *older* crowd," Amy repeated whimsically. "What a quaint phrase."

"One more word on that subject and I'll haul you out on

deck to give you a little demonstration of how old I feel right now."

"Is that a threat?" she asked brightly.

"You're enjoying this, aren't you?" he accused, trying to hold her close and still find the beat of the music. It was tricky. Most of the other couples were moving about the floor in a freewheeling fashion.

"Are you jealous, Jed?" she asked softly, her eyes luminous in the dim light.

"I'm feeling provoked."

"Oh." She pursed her lips in a disappointed pout. "Is that all?"

He groaned and hauled her closer. "Do you want me to feel jealous?"

"Well, I know how I'd feel if that blonde sitting near us put the moves on you."

"What blonde?" He was honestly confused until he glanced around and saw someone tall, golden haired and slinky looking toward him with predatory eyes. "Oh, *that* blonde."

"Yes," Amy agreed a little too sweetly, "that blonde."

Jed grinned. "She looks a few years older than you. Maybe she likes the slow dances."

Amy found the top of his shoe with the heel of her dressy yellow evening sandals.

"Ouch! Okay, tell me how you'd feel if the blonde had made a pass at me," Jed invited.

"I'd go for her throat. Then I'd go for yours."

"Hmm." He pulled her tightly against him as the last of the rock music faded into a slow, sensual piece. He nestled his cheek against her hair, inhaling the soft, clean fragrance.

"Now you know how I feel when I see Renner trying to move in on you."

"We're even, huh?" She smiled against his shoulder.

"Not quite. The blonde hasn't made a pass at me yet. Don't I at least get that much out of this before we say we're even? *Ouch!* Amy . . ."

Satisfied, Amy took her heel off his toes a second time and relaxed. Jed forgot about trying to find the beat and gave himself up to the pleasure of feeling Amy's small breasts pressed against his chest. His fingers strayed down the sexy curve of her spine to the fullness of her buttocks, shaping her with lingering enjoyment. She always felt so good, he thought. He could feel her moving with him, following the lead of his body as he guided her slowly through the crowd of dancers. She was so sleek and soft and warm. His lower body was stirring, growing taut and aware.

"I think you really are a sorceress, just like the heroines in your books," he murmured.

She wound her arms around his neck and looked up at him with dreamy, seductive eyes. "No," she said gently, "I'm not the one with the magic. You are."

He saw the melting sensuality in her eyes and took a deep, steadying breath. "I think we'd better sit down."

"Why?"

"Because we can't lie down."

"Oh, I see." Her smile became very intimate.

"My biggest concern at the moment is that everyone else will be able to see, too. Let's get off this floor before I embarrass myself." He guided her back to the table without waiting for an affirmative response. Hank and Rosie watched them return.

"You two didn't stay out there long," Rosie observed.

"I'm afraid the nightlife on board a cruise ship is a little too much for Jed," Amy said blandly.

Hank chuckled. "Is that right, Jed? You'd better get ready to defend your territory, then. Renner's already licking his chops."

Rosie spoke before Jed could respond. "You know," she said with dawning satisfaction, "I just realized who Dan Renner puts me in mind of. It's not so much his looks, although that's part of it. It's the way he's flirting with Amy in front of Jed."

Jed picked up his wine. "If he flirts with her much more, he's going to put you in mind of a squashed bug."

"Jed, for heaven's sake," Amy said admonishingly.

Jed just looked at her. Then he glanced across the room and noticed Renner was sitting alone at the table he had been sharing with Guthrie. Guthrie had moved to the bar. "All right, Rosie, tell us who Renner reminds you of."

"Something about him," Rosie said slowly, "makes me think of Michael Wyman."

Amy nearly choked on her white wine. She coughed and sputtered until Jed reached around the table and slapped her casually between the shoulders. Her eyes grew very wide as she stared at Rosie. Amy wasn't the only one staring at the plump woman. Hank was also looking at his wife as if she'd just put a live hand grenade in the center of the table. But it was Jed who demanded clarification first.

"Michael Wyman? Slater's old partner?"

Rosie chuckled, pleased with the small sensation she had caused. "That's it. Wyman had that same shade of hair, as I recall. and there's something about his looks that's vaguely familiar. Those eyes... 'Course, it's been nearly thirty years. But it's more than that. Wyman was charming the way Renner is. Know what I mean? There was a kind of mischief in Wyman. A dangerous mischief," Rosie added with a sidelong glance at Amy. "Like he'd cause trouble if he could, just for the hell of it, then stand back and watch everyone fly into a tizzy."

Out of the corner of his eye, Jed saw Renner ask the tall, cool blonde to dance. He watched the pair move out onto the floor and then realized Guthrie had not returned to his seat. Nor was the other man dancing. He was walking away from the bar, heading toward the doors that opened onto the deck.

Eight years of learning to trust instincts and gut reactions made Jed watch Guthrie carefully. The sexual tightness that had come to life on the dance floor began transforming into another, familiar kind of physical alertness.

"Jed?" Amy's attention had swung from Rosie's announcement to Jed. "What's the matter?"

He turned back to her, aware that he looked and sounded considerably different than he had a moment before. He could see the concern in her eyes change to wariness. He got to his feet with a decisive movement. "I think I can handle this slower stuff. Let's try another dance, honey."

He saw the confusion in her face, but she didn't argue with him. Without a word she followed him back out onto the dance floor. Jed took her into his arms, his eyes on Guthrie as the man wove through the crowd.

"I want you to stay here with Hank and Rosie, understand? And I don't want you dancing with Renner while I'm gone."

"Gone where?" she demanded.

"I'm going to follow Guthrie."

"But why?"

"I'm not sure. Curiosity, I guess."

"Curiosity? What kind of an answer is that, for heaven's sake?"

"The only one I've got at the moment. Follow my lead when I take you back to the table."

"But Jed—" Amy's protest was short-lived. He was already leading her back to their table.

"Amy just remembered she needs something she left in the Jeep. I'm going to run down to the dock and get it for her. Be back in a few minutes. Keep an eye on her for me, will you?" He nodded at Hank.

"Heck, we'll watch her. Wouldn't be the first time we've baby-sat Amy." Hank returned the nod in a relaxed fashion.

"I'll be right back. Amy, remember what I said about not dancing with Renner."

"Ah, you never let me have any fun."

Beneath the sassy words, Jed heard her underlying worry. She was sitting tensely, her fingers wrapped too tightly around the stem of her wineglass. He couldn't do anything about either the tension or the worry, not at the moment. He lightly touched the bare curve of her shoulder and then left.

The lounge was dark and full of people who were determined to enjoy themselves. Weaving a path between the crowded tables, Jed managed to make his way to the door just as the band went into a classic rock tune. The glittering vocalist struck a pose reminiscent of the early Elvis Presley and began belting out a familiar song. Amy would undoubtedly recognize it, Jed decided as he stepped out on deck.

There was no sign of Guthrie at first. Jed stood quietly in the shadows, letting his eyes adjust to the change in light. There was a pool at the far end of the deck and beyond that a quiet indoor seating area. As Jed watched he saw a person

who could have been Guthrie open the door to the other
public room and disappear inside.

There was a second set of elevators at that end of the ship,
Jed remembered. It would be easy for Guthrie to make his
way down through the decks until he reached the one which
had access to the dock. From there he could leave the ship.
If he was planning to leave the ship.

Jed moved swiftly to follow. Guthrie sure as hell wasn't
heading for the rest rooms. Jed thought of Renner dancing
back in the lounge with the blonde Amy hadn't liked.
Rosie's words kept flickering on and off in his mind like a
faulty neon light. Renner reminded her of Michael Wyman.

There were two facts that had to be put into the equation.
The first was that Wyman was dead. The second was that
even if he were alive, he would be considerably older than
Dan Renner. But the implications were fascinating.

Deciding to concentrate on the task at hand and worry
about sorting through implications later, Jed stepped into the
elevator and punched the button for the exit deck. Guthrie
had used the other elevator. Jed figured he shouldn't be more
than a few seconds behind him.

He was right. He stepped out of the elevator in time to see
Guthrie saunter through the open hatch and take the gang-
way down to the dock. A group of tourists returning from
the island got between Jed and Guthrie for a moment. When
the crowd had cleared, Guthrie was almost to the end of the
dock. From there he could walk the few blocks to his room
at Hank and Rosie's. Jed found the shadows he needed and
fell into step behind his quarry. Guthrie never once looked
back.

Then again, why should he? Jed wondered as he remained
a discreet distance behind the other man. Maybe Guthrie

simply didn't like dancing. Maybe he was bored with Renner's company. Maybe he'd developed a headache. There were a lot of innocent explanations for Guthrie's decision to leave the ship.

There were also a few not-so-innocent reasons why Guthrie might want to leave. Jed speculated on where Guthrie had been that afternoon while he and Amy had been diving the bomber wreck. Perhaps Guthrie had spent the time letting himself into the Slater home without an invitation.

Guthrie took an unexpected turn to the right, one that led up the short hill from the waterfront toward a jumble of weathered buildings and narrow, tangled alleys. Jed had seen this section of the small town earlier in the day and knew it wasn't Orleana's residential section. Some of the tin-roofed structures had obviously been around since the military had run its refueling depot there. A few were still used as storage sheds, but many were vacant. The narrow streets had once been paved but no one had bothered to keep up the tradition. There were more potholes than pavement, and nothing resembling a sidewalk.

There was also nothing resembling a street light. Orleana wasn't big on such amenities.

Curiouser and curiouser. Figuring out what sort of business Guthrie might have in this part of town made for an interesting puzzle. This certainly wasn't the direct route back to Hank and Rosie's.

Guthrie turned another corner, slipping down a narrow path between two metal sheds. The faint moonlight spotlighted him for an instant and then he was lost in the darkness. Jed listened intently, hearing the small, distant crunch of gravel. Guthrie wasn't making any effort to conceal his movements.

Jed, on the other hand, was doing his best to conceal his own presence, but the effort it took was virtually second nature. He was aware of his own caution but he didn't have to work at it very hard; it came naturally. His soft-soled shoes made no noise on the uneven path. He paused before crossing in front of a screen door that was swinging wide on rusty hinges. Deep gloom hovered behind the old door. The distant sound of laughter from the waterfront floated up the hill on the soft, balmy air.

Jed felt the silent chill that stirred every hair on the back of his neck a split second before he felt the faint change in the air behind him. He swung around instantly, prepared to let the movement carry him all the way to the ground if necessary.

The man came out of the narrow alley between two buildings, the knife held low and ready for a gut-opening thrust.

Jed barely had time to realize his attacker was not Guthrie before he let the momentum of his own turn carry him down and to the right.

The knife ripped at him as he fell, slashing his left arm. Jed knew he'd been cut, but the rush of adrenaline blotted out the pain before it even got started. The luxury of pain would come later, when there was time to concentrate on it. Jed grabbed for the man's leg as he lunged to the side.

The knife came around in an arc that was designed to end in Jed's neck. The assailant swore as he felt himself being tumbled off balance. Jed hit the ground and rolled, carrying the man with him.

There was a soft, muffled cry of rage from the assailant and then Jed was on top of him, driving a hand full of stiffened fingers into the vulnerable places of his neck and upper lip. The man shrieked with agony and then there was silence.

Jed sat up slowly, trying to see his victim's face in the shadows. Then he felt the wetness of his arm and clamped a hand over the wound in his shoulder. Blood welled between his fingers. Jed glanced down at the wound and sighed.

Amy would undoubtedly fuss.

Chapter Thirteen

*A*my did more than fuss. She lost her temper.

The moment the waiter approached the table to announce politely that she was being paged by someone ashore, Amy knew there was trouble. When she discovered the message was from Dr. Stearn she rounded on Hank and Rosie.

"I knew I should never have let him go off by himself like that!"

"Who? Dr. Stearn?" Rosie watched as Amy frantically searched her purse to find money for the last round of drinks. Amy had insisted it was her turn to buy.

"Not Dr. Stearn." Amy dropped the bills on the table. "Jed."

Hank was helping Rosie to her feet, preparing to follow Amy. "But the message was from Stearn."

"Which," Amy pointed out with grim logic, "can only mean he's got Jed in his office, and since the message wasn't from Jed, I have to assume Jed's gone and done something stupid again."

"Again?" Rosie's confusion was laced with genuine concern as she followed Amy. Hank had already stepped into the lead, using his considerable bulk to open a path through the crowd.

"Never mind, it's a long story. Oh, Rosie, if he's badly hurt I'll strangle him. I swear it."

Hank spoke gruffly as he ushered both women into the elevator. "Wouldn't that be redundant if he really is hurt? Calm down, Amy. No need to go off like a cannon over this. We don't know that this message of Stearn's has anything to do with Jed." Hank had clearly voted himself the voice of reason, what with Rosie and Amy choosing to anticipate the worst.

"Something's wrong, Hank. I know it. It's got to be Jed." Amy was in no mood to be soothed. Her intuition had combined with her imagination and she had no doubt at all but that Jed was in serious trouble.

Ten minutes later Hank pulled the Slaters' Jeep into a space in front of Dr. Stearn's clinic. Lights were blazing inside. "Looks like we're not the only ones who got an invitation." Hank nodded toward a second vehicle parked nearby. It was an old battered Ford.

"Kelso," Rosie said, recognizing the car. "I wonder what he's doing here."

"This is getting worse by the minute." Amy bounded out of the Jeep, holding the hem of her yellow dress above her knees. Ernie Kelso had been the closest thing to an official representative of the law Orleana had had since the Navy had shipped out. He had been duly elected to his post largely because no one else on the island wanted to be bothered locking up drunks and settling minor arguments between fishermen. Kelso didn't mind doing either as long as he was sober and as long as he got his monthly check. No one was sure just where Kelso had come from, but after ten years on the island he was finally beginning to be accepted as a local.

Amy raced toward the screen door of the clinic. She grabbed the rusted metal handle, yanked open the door and rushed into the waiting room like a small whirlwind. Hank and Rosie followed at a more sedate pace.

The door to the examination room was open. Three men

were inside. One was Dr. Stearn, the other was Kelso and the third was Jed. He was sitting casually on the end of the examining table, bare to the waist. There was a short, neat row of stitches on his left arm. Blood still oozed gently from the wound. Stearn was in the process of unwrapping a gauze bandage when his clinic door was thrown open. All three men turned to look at Amy.

She had eyes only for Jed.

"I knew I should never have let you leave the ship alone. What on earth happened to you? You had to go and get into trouble, didn't you? You can't be trusted on your own, you know that? You're a menace to yourself and others. Of all the stupid, idiotic, crazy things to do. You just take off and leave me sitting there without a word of explanation and the next thing I know I'm being called to the doctor's office. If you think you're going to get away with this sort of behavior indefinitely, Jedidiah Glaze, you can damn well think again. I will not tolerate it, do you hear me?"

Jed listened to the tirade with absorbed interest. "I knew you'd fuss," he said affectionately when she stopped for breath.

"Fuss? You call this fussing? I am infuriated, Jed." She tried to approached the examination table, but Dr. Stearn was in the way. She peered over his shoulder as he applied the bandage. "What happened here, anyway? And don't give me some song and dance about a car accident."

Kelso cleared his throat. "Actually, it was more like a knife accident," he said.

Jed raised his eyes heavenward in silent dismay as Amy turned on the paunchy, balding, older man. "A knife accident?" she asked, her voice dangerously soft.

"Yeah," Kelso nodded enthusiastically grateful for her

quick understanding. "Seems like your, uh, friend Glaze met with a slight accident up in the old warehouse area. You know that group of sheds and buildings on the hill where the Navy used to store stuff?"

"Of course I know it." Amy glared at Jed. "What were you doing there, Jed? There's nothing up there but a bunch of deserted old sheds."

Jed sighed, watching Stearn secure the bandage. "That's where Guthrie went when he left the ship."

Hank frowned and asked quietly, "Guthrie pulled a knife on you?"

"Jesus," Rosie breathed.

"Guthrie attacked you?" Amy yelped.

"No."

That stopped the three new arrivals as they tried to sort out what had happened. They backed off and Amy tried again.

"Then how did you get that slice on your arm?" she demanded.

Dr. Stearn finished his bandaging and stepped back to admire his handiwork. "It was a knife, all right."

"I knew it!" Amy turned on Jed again. He smiled winningly, but she ignored his placating expression. "Stop dragging this out, Jed. I want to know what happened and I want to know right now."

Kelso stepped in to rescue Jed. "According to the ID in the guy's wallet, his name is Vaden."

Rosie glanced at Kelso. "He's staying at our place. Hit the island last week."

"How did you get his wallet?" Amy zeroed in on Jed again. "Was there a struggle? Did his wallet fall out or something?"

"I removed his wallet when I took Vaden into custody," Kelso explained in a formal voice.

"Took him into custody?" Amy gave Kelso a perplexed frown. "How did you find him so fast? How did you even know it was Vaden you were looking for in the first place? Jed doesn't know him. Neither do I. Who identified him for you?"

Kelso glanced at Jed, who was paying no attention. "Vaden didn't, uh, leave the scene of the crime."

Amy's beleaguered brain finally got the message. She swung her widening eyes back to Jed who tried another placating smile. "Oh, my goodness," she said weakly.

Hank asked calmly, "Vaden still alive?"

Amy shivered, never taking her eyes off Jed's face.

"He's alive," Jed stated briskly. "Didn't you hear Kelso say he took him into custody?" He nodded at Stearn. "Thanks. What do I owe you?"

Stearn held up one finger after another as he ticked off the expenses. "Office visit, anesthetic, stitches. Make it sixty bucks."

Jed nodded agreeably and reached for his wallet.

"Anesthetic?" Amy repeated wryly. "For this tough, macho guy who follows strangers into dark alleys and gets into knife fights for fun? You had to give him anesthetic?"

"Just a little topical stuff," Stearn assured her, accepting the cash from Jed.

"I have this thing about pain," Jed explained as he got off the table.

"Then maybe you're in the wrong business," Amy muttered. She darted forward to take his good arm. The frightened anger went out of her as she realized he was probably all right. "Oh, lord, Jed, if you make a habit of terrorizing me like this, I'm going to . . ." She didn't finish the threat. She couldn't finish it because the only logical conclusion was to leave him if he continued to play with guns and knives. And how could she bring herself to kick him out of her life?

"I would like to take this opportunity," Jed announced grimly, "to point out that this was not my fault."

"Hah. You should never have followed Guthrie into that warehouse district."

Kelso ambled to the window and stared out into the darkness. "Why did you follow him, Glaze?"

Amy froze as she realized where all these logical questions would lead. If Jed started explaining about Guthrie, how could he avoid explaining his suspicions? And if he got as far as his suspicions, he would have to explain the box in the caves. The secrets would be out.

Jed seemed oblivious to Amy's unnatural stillness. He did seem to notice the way her fingertips were digging into his arm. In fact, he had to gently pry himself free of her grasp so he could put on his shirt.

"Sheer stupidity," Jed said calmly, buttoning his shirt. "I left the ship to get something Amy had stashed in the glove compartment of the Jeep. Something, uh, personal, if you know what I mean. I saw Guthrie walking along the docks in front of me and then he suddenly turned to go up into that warehouse area. I couldn't think of any good reason why someone would head in that direction." Jed shrugged. "I got curious and followed. Vaden jumped me from one of the alleys."

Kelso listened to the story in silence. It was impossible to tell whether he believed it. But they weren't on the mainland and he wasn't a big city police detective. Things were done differently on Orleana. There were basically three unwritten laws on the island. The first law maintained that men sometimes ended up in out-of-the-way places like Orleana Island because they had secrets. Kelso, himself, had taken advantage of that law. It was also understood that, unless he caused trouble, a man was entitled to keep those secrets to himself.

The third and most rigidly applied law was that in the event of trouble, locals were given the benefit of the doubt. The burden of guilt was always on the off-islanders. Because of Jed's connection with the Slaters, he was considered a local.

Amy breathed a sigh of relief when she saw Kelso nod. "Guess I'd better go talk to Guthrie. Vaden sure as hell isn't going to tell us much. You think those two know each other?"

Hank shook his head. "Nah, I don't think so. Guthrie's a friend of Renner's. The two of them hang around together. Diving buddies. But neither of them seems to know Vaden. Vaden just sort of hangs around by himself. A loner. I was wondering how much longer he was going to stay on the island. Didn't seem to be enjoying himself much."

"He'll be enjoying himself a lot less after tonight," Kelso predicted as he walked to the door. "Gonna have a mighty sore throat for a while. See you folks later." The screen door slammed behind him.

There was a long moment of silence in the clinic room. Then Stearn said casually, "Well, that'll be the end of that."

"What do you mean?" Amy asked uneasily.

Hank grinned. "Hell, Amy, old Kelso ain't hardly what you'd call a real cop. You know that. If he were, he wouldn't have wound up out here on Orleana, would he?

He'll ask Guthrie a few questions, Guthrie will give him a few answers and that'll be about as far as it goes. Hell, maybe that's as far as it should go. Guthrie's probably not involved anyway. He's just a tourist who took a wrong turn on the way back to his hotel."

"What about Vaden?" Rosie asked suddenly.

"Vaden's a drifter." Hank shrugged. "You know the type, Rosie. We've had enough of his kind here through the years They just hop from one island to another, maybe deal a little dope, take a few odd jobs, work a fishing boat now and then. He probably needed some extra cash and decided to pick on one of the tourists from the cruise ship. Maybe he saw Jed leave the main road and very obligingly wander off into a nice, deserted area. Too good an opportunity to miss He followed and tried to take him." Hank cocked his big bearded head at Jed. "This ain't exactly downtown L.A., but even out here a man's got to take a few precautions."

"I got the point," Jed said dryly. "Literally. You ready to leave, Amy?"

She nodded quickly. "I'm ready." She turned to Stearn "Does he need any medication? What about an infection?"

"He'll be fine. Have him stop by in a day or two and I'll make sure everything's healing okay. Take him home now and give him a shot of brandy."

Amy nodded and seized Jed's arm to lead him out to the Jeep. "Good night Hank, Rosie. I'll see you in a day or so It was a lovely evening up to a point."

"Drive carefully," Rosie said easily as Amy helped Jed into the passenger seat and walked around the front of the vehicle to climb into the driver's side.

"I will," Amy promised. She held her hand out toward Jed.

Without a word he dug the keys out of his pocket and handed them to her. Amy started the engine and, with a last wave at the trio in the doorway behind her, she spun the wheel of the Jeep.

"This is getting to be a bad habit," she muttered as she turned onto the winding road that led out of town.

"What is?"

"Driving you home after you've gotten into trouble playing with guns and knives. Jed, you gave me a terrible scare tonight. What happened?"

"Just what I told Kelso. I saw Guthrie leave the harbor area and take a detour through that maze of sheds, so I followed. I lost him when Vaden jumped me."

"You could have been killed!"

"No. Vaden was too slow."

"Don't you dare try to treat this casually. This is not a casual matter," Amy stormed. In her agitation she jerked the wheel of the Jeep a little too hard going around a corner. The vehicle strayed precariously toward the jungle. Jed grabbed his door handle.

"For Christ's sake, Amy, watch what you're doing or you're going to finish what Vaden started tonight."

Amy ignored him. "Why did you make that excuse to leave the ship in the first place?"

"Take a guess."

She sucked in her breath. "Because Rosie said Renner reminded her of Michael Wyman?"

"Right. Renner reminded her of Wyman and Guthrie is obviously associated with Renner. What did Renner do after I left to follow his friend?"

"Nothing. Danced a few more dances with the blonde."

"Did they leave together?"

Amy shook her head, trying to remember. "No, I think they were both still there when the waiter brought me Dr Stearn's message. In fact, I'm sure of it. Jed, what's going on? There's no way on earth Renner could be Wyman. He's much too young. And Wyman's dead, anyway."

"I know."

"Are you sure that this time it isn't your imagination that's taken a turn toward the bizarre? Vaden's attack on you was probably exactly what Kelso thinks it was, a case of a down-and-out drifter trying to take some easy money off a tourist."

"And Guthrie's nocturnal wanderings up in the old ware-house district?"

'Who knows? Maybe he lost his way back to Hank and Rosie's."

"Sure."

"You really think something's going on here, don't you?" she asked quietly.

"I have a suspicious nature."

"Maybe we should leave, Jed."

"Not without the box." He probed his bandaged arm with his free hand. "And it'll be a day or two before I can go after it. I don't want to go down into those caves until I have the full use of both arms."

"You shouldn't do any diving untill that wound is com-pletely healed."

"We're not going to wait that long, honey. Things are moving too quickly I just need a day or two."

Amy gripped the wheel more tightly. "If only we knew for certain just what things are moving. So far we've got noth ing but eight zipper teeth to go on."

"I resent that. What about my little adventure tonight?"

"I'll bet Kelso's explanation is the right one. Vaden will turn out to be just a dumb, dangerous drifter."

"And the fact that Renner reminds Rosie of Wyman?"

"Jed, it's been twenty-five years since Rosie saw Wyman. She said that if she hadn't been talking to me about him just the other night, she would never have thought twice about the vague similarity."

"You're forgetting the one really awkward problem in all this," Jed said coolly.

"What's that?"

"LePage. Somehow he knew about the box. That means that someone else knows. And that makes everything else that's happening very interesting."

Amy fell silent. Finally, she said, "You're very tenacious, aren't you? Once you latch onto something, you don't let go."

"Not until it's finished," Jed agreed. "I'm an engineer, remember? We like to see our projects through to completion."

"Even if you run into people like Vaden in the process?" Amy retorted bitterly. "What did you do to him tonight, Jed? Kelso said the man was going to have a sore throat."

"I've picked up some unmarketable but occasionally useful skills during the past eight years, Amy. You don't want to hear about them."

Amy heard the new weariness in his voice and refrained from asking any more questions during the drive back to the house.

Jed didn't break the silence as she pulled into the drive and parked the Jeep. He followed her into the house and sank down into one of the cushioned chairs in the breezy living room.

"I'll get the brandy Dr. Stearn ordered," Amy said, turning away to fetch it. She didn't like the grim, drawn expression on Jed's hard face. Stearn had implied that Jed was not badly hurt, but she was determined to get the patient to bed as soon as possible. Jed needed some rest.

"Come on upstairs," she coaxed as she returned with the brandy. "You can drink this while you're getting ready for bed."

Jed studied her from under his half lowered lashes as he sprawled in the chair. "You really are sweet when you fuss over me. I think I could get addicted to it."

"Don't be ridiculous. I'm not fussing, I'm just exercising some common sense, unlike a certain male whose name will go unmentioned for the moment. Come on, up the stairs, hero. You look beat."

"Too much dancing." He took the brandy from her hand and downed half of it before he reached the first step. "I won't be able to sleep, you know, unless I'm in your bed."

"Is that a fact?"

"Yeah, it's a fact." At the top of the stairs he turned deliberately toward her room. Amy didn't argue.

A few minutes later she had him neatly tucked into her bed. She stepped back to examine her patient with a worried gaze. He lifted his lashes and she was startled to see the smoldering sensuality in his eyes.

"Come to bed, Amy."

She felt herself responding to the heat in his eyes. Without thinking she took a step toward the bed. Then memory returned. She knew that particular expression. She'd seen it before in Jed's hazel eyes. She stopped.

"What is it, Amy?"

"It's the violence, isn't it?" Amy asked, her voice husky

with a curious kind of pain. "It does something to you. You get off on it. You looked at me like that when you got back from your . . . your trips."

Jed's hand moved so quickly Amy didn't have a chance to step out of his range. He captured her wrist. "It's not the violence. It's you."

Her fingers wriggled uselessly in his firm grasp. "I'm not so sure. There's supposed to be some sort of psychological connection between sex and violence, you know. Especially in a man's brain. Something to do with hormones, I think."

"Just another weakness in the male brain," Jed murmured, drawing her closer.

"Jed, it's not funny." She gave him a pleading look. "I don't think I want to be used as a . . . a release for the sexual tension violence seems to generate in you. It's not exactly flattering, you know."

"Amy, you're talking nonsense. Have I ever been violent with you?"

She shook her head quickly. "No, but—"

"I wanted you very badly whenever I came back from an assignment. I won't deny it. For the past few months I seem to have been functioning in a perpetual state of wanting you badly. But I waited, didn't I? I waited until you wanted me. Until you weren't nervous of me any longer."

"Yes, I know, but—"

He gave up trying to argue the subject. Jed yanked Amy gently down onto the bed. She sprawled across his body and was instantly aware of his arousal. He was covered only by the sheet, and his powerful, smoothly muscled body was emanating a warm and vital energy.

"Jed, your arm." Anxiously she tried to lever herself off his chest.

"Forget my arm." His voice was thickening as he wrapped his good hand around the back of her head and held her still. "Why the hell do you think I had Stearn give me a little local anesthetic? I can't feel a thing in my arm. But I sure as hell ache somewhere else." He found her mouth, sealing what remained of her protest behind her tremulous lips.

Jed ignored the twinges that got through the fading anesthetic. The fierce, heavy ache in his groin was far stronger than the discomfort of his wound. The need for Amy had been throbbing in him since she'd burst through the clinic door, all anxious eyes and scolding tongue. He realized dimly that part of him thrived on her concern. He was growing accustomed to it, dependent on it, addicted to it, possessive of it.

It had annoyed him to hear her link his need of her with his reaction to violence. Didn't she understand that *anything* could trigger his desire for her? Her smile could be just as effective. Having her fuss over him was enough to start a tantalizing fantasy rolling in his head. Hell, just watching her walk across a room could inflame the slow burn that was always present in him these days.

"It was probably the dancing that did it this time," he informed her, his lips seeking the delicate spot behind her ear. He liked the way she shivered a little when he kissed her there.

"The dancing that did what?" She closed her eyes and sighed softly as he stroked her back.

"That got me hot."

"We barely got out on the floor."

"Doesn't take much," he murmured. "Not where you're involved."

"Oh, Jed."

"Mmm." He felt the familiar exhilaration start to flow in his veins. Her response always intoxicated him. Didn't she realize the extent of her power over him? Probably not, Jed decided. There was a sexy innocence about her that she would possess when she was ninety-five. It was built into Amy and it captivated him.

She moved on him and Jed lifted his hips slightly beneath the sheet, wanting her to feel his need. Amy moaned softly and clutched his shoulders. Jed couldn't stifle his muttered exclamation as her clinging fingers sent a spasm through his bandaged left arm. Instantly Amy was squirming to free herself, her expression alarmed.

"Oh, my God, I didn't mean to hurt you. I'm sorry. We shouldn't be doing this. You should be going to sleep. You need your rest."

He closed his hands firmly around her waist, holding her still. "Hush, Amy," he ordered roughly. "You can't leave me in this condition. I'll go insane."

"But your arm," she protested anxiously. "You shouldn't exert yourself."

"I've already told you, forget my arm. Make love to me, Amy. I need you tonight. I promise not to overdo it. I'll just lie here like a good patient and let my nurse take care of me. How's that?" He watched in silent amusement as her eyes filled with a new kind of curiosity. It was a curiosity that was blended with a budding, feminine excitement. Deliberately Jed encouraged the new sensual twist. "Go ahead, honey. Make love to me."

There was a warm flush on her cheeks as she stood up and slowly began to undress. Jed lay still as promised, and watched, enthralled, as she silently slid out of the long yellow dress. It was obvious she was deeply aware of his unwavering attention. Obvious, too, that while she was a bit self-conscious about it, the knowledge that she was getting him even hotter was doing things to her. Exciting things.

"You're built like a sexy little cat," he murmured, his eyes on her small, deliciously curved breasts as they came into view. "Sleek and soft and responsive as hell."

She didn't say anything, but her eyes glowed and as she stepped away from the pool of bright yellow her fingers went to the waistband of her panties. Jed felt the gnawing hunger begin to eat at his vitals as she carefully removed the scrap of flimsy gold fabric. She lost a small fraction of her nerve as the dark triangle below her gently curving belly came into view. Jed got only a teasing glimpse of the soft, curling hair that hid her secret places, but he didn't really mind. When she turned away from him he was treated to an equally enticing view of lushly rounded buttocks.

Amy made a small production out of picking up the dress and laying it over a chair. Then she spent a few more excruciating seconds putting her underwear into the closet hamper. By the time she turned out the light and walked toward him through the shadows, Jed thought he would explode.

"You're sure this isn't going to be too much for you?" she asked softly as she slipped into bed beside him. Her small palm rested on his chest.

"Even if I thought it was going to be too much, I couldn't admit it. The code of the Macho Ethic forbids admitting that kind of thing." He groaned as she drew her palm delicately down his chest to the part of him that was straining upward against the sheet. "Jesus, Amy."

She smiled at him, and even in the dim light he could see her pleased excitement. She liked this, he thought with deep satisfaction. She liked turning him on; liked having him respond. That was exactly the way he wanted it.

Her fingers closed gently around him and Jed lifted himself against her hand, his eyes closing in a pleasure that was almost painful.

"Jed?"

"Don't stop, honey. Keep touching me. I can't get enough of it."

She leaned over to kiss his throat as she began to tease him more deliberately with her fingers. Jed twisted his right hand into her hair, pulling the golden brown stuff free from its pins so that it tumbled across his chest. She was subjecting him to a sweet torture and he didn't know how long he could stand it. She cupped the fullness of his manhood and began to trail a string of light, exploratory kisses further down his chest. As her hot, silky mouth drew closer to the apex of his thighs, Jed felt his control start to slip. His hand tightened in her hair.

"Jed?" Her voice was different this time, soft and questioning as her lips paused over his navel. She tried to trace a return path back up his chest.

Jed decided quite suddenly that he couldn't let her. Not just yet. Not until he'd found out what it felt like to have her soft, warm mouth a few inches lower. His grip in her hair urged her to continue.

Amy hesitated a moment under the pressure of his hand as if she wasn't quite sure what to do next.

"Please, Amy." The muttered plea sounded harsh in his own ears, but Amy responded to it.

He felt the warm dampness of her mouth as she worked the tip of her tongue down his body. Jed held his breath as Amy reached her goal. Then she kissed him intimately with soft, exquisite butterfly kisses that teased and tormented. Jed felt his entire body threaten to explode. The cool edge of her teeth was an exciting counterpoint to the delicious warmth and wetness of her mouth. Amy's hand cupped the fullness at the base of Jed's trembling manhood, her fingers caressing him until he knew for sure he was going to explode.

"Amy..." He lifted his hips, demanding more of her. He knew she could taste the tiny drops which were escaping from his thrusting shaft, but she didn't seem to mind. She worshipped him with her tongue. Jed wanted to shout his pleasure into the skies.

Then, as if she sensed he could wait no longer, Amy began moving back along the length of his body until she was astride him. Still cradling him in the palm of her hand, she eased his heavy shaft into her. As she sank down onto him, enveloping him completely, Jed shuddered. It was too much. He couldn't wait any longer. He surged upward, holding onto her hips with both hands. He heard her gasp softly.

"I'm sorry, Amy. I can't wait, honey. I can't *wait*." He groaned as his body took complete control, demanding release. He pumped himself into her, flooding her with the warm evidence of his passion. And then as he gave himself up to the hot climax, he heard Amy's small cry as her muscles tightened around him. It was almost unbearable. The shimmering release took him to the edge of consciousness.

She wanted him, Jed realized. He'd never been wanted or needed in his life the way Amy wanted and needed him. And she didn't try to hide it. She held back nothing when they made love. She gave herself completely, with an honest, innocent passion that awed him. He couldn't resist such magic, even if he wanted to. Amy reached him in a way no other woman could. She touched him on some level he didn't understand. He didn't care how her magic worked and he didn't want to waste time analyzing it. He only wanted to lose himself again and again in the wonder of her.

Amy was all that mattered.

Chapter Fourteen

The distant murmur of Jed's voice woke Amy the next morning. She stirred amid the tangled sheets, yawning luxuriously.

"Jed?" She waited for his response and when there was none, she turned on her side. The bed was empty beside her. The faint murmur came again. This time Amy pinpointed the location. Jed was talking to someone downstairs. Wondering who he might be conversing with at this hour of the morning brought her to a sitting position. The sheet fell away from her bare breasts and warm memories of the night flooded back. Before Amy could dwell on them she heard Jed's rare chuckle. The small laugh sounded cool, lacking any real humor. There was no answering voice.

Amy finally realized that Jed was talking on the phone. Perhaps her parents had called. She stretched and got up from the bed to find her kimono. Belting it around her waist, she padded out of the room and into the hall. As she reached the top of the stairs, the low murmur of his voice began to separate into distinct words.

"Skip it, Faxon. Do this favor for me and we'll call it even." He paused. "Yeah, I know, but that's the best I can do. I'm working with limited information. Anything you can get will be useful." There was another pause and then Jed's easy, humorless laugh. "Hell, no, I'm not working. I'm on vacation, remember? The info I'm asking for is just because I feel like playing a few games. *Private* games."

Amy descended a few more steps, listening with unabashed interest. She could see Jed standing at an open window, the phone in his hand as he looked out over the sunlit sea. He was wearing only a pair of chinos. His chest and feet were still bare and his hair wasn't yet combed. In the morning light he looked strong and healthy and vigorous. The bandage on his arm just seemed to add to the overall impression of raw male power.

He listened to something the other person was saying and then he said in that nonchalant, very knowing voice that men used with each other when they were talking about women, "You've got the picture, Faxon. I am not fooling around on some lonely island all on my own. We're talking the perfect vacation paradise here. Plenty of sun, sand and—" He glanced back over his shoulder at that moment and saw Amy watching him from the staircase. "And a good friend to share it all with."

The sweet, loving memories of the night that had been in Amy's head when she awoke began to dissolve in the harsh light of day. Sun, sand and a *friend*. If she hadn't been standing at the top of the stairs would Jed have made that sun, sand and sex? Probably. She had to remember that a man like Jed would view this affair very differently than she had. She had to keep in mind that she was the one in love. Jed had never said or implied anything to give her the impression he even knew what love was, let alone that he felt anything connected with the emotion.

Jed's eyes never left hers as he finished his conversation with the person called Faxon. "Sure, this is just the sort of thing I need to get me back into shape. Everything's healing up fine. I'll be ready to go back to work soon, but don't tell Cutter. You can't blame me if I try to stall a bit." He paused again, listening. "All right, give me a call when you get the data. You've got the number. Take it easy, Faxon, and thanks." Very gently Jed replaced the phone in its cradle, his gaze still locked with Amy's.

Amy was trying to adjust to the last part of the phone call. Back to work soon. He was planning to return to those mysterious, dangerous assignments as soon as he was completely healed. The interlude with her was just that: temporary, a way of filling time between assignments. Her place in his universe was already established and he meant to keep her in her proper orbit. *Nothing had changed for Jed.*

"Who was that?" she asked with distant politeness as she slowly descended the stairs.

"Faxon." He didn't move, but he was watching her warily, as if trying to assess her reaction to the conversation. "He handles the files at the agency. He owes me a couple of favors."

"I see." She had reached the bottom of the staircase and wasn't sure where to go next. The kitchen seemed a reasonable target. Coffee sounded good. She started in that direction.

"I asked him to find out what he could on Michael Wyman." Jed watched her disappear into the kitchen. He followed, halting in the doorway. "You never know. There might be something on file. After all, Wyman was involved in a company that had plenty of government contracts for military stuff. A security check was probably run on both partners as well as most of their employees at one time or another. It would have been routine procedure."

"Your agency would have access to that kind of information?"

"The agency wouldn't have been involved in the security clearance check, but Faxon has ways of getting data from the files of other government agencies. He's got a talent for it. As long as the stuff's on a government computer somewhere, he can get it. The man knows computers inside and out."

"Whatever might be in the files would be old information by now," Amy observed coolly as she measured coffee into the pot. She kept her back to him.

"As I said, you never know what might turn up. It's worth a look. If nothing comes of it, we're no worse off than we were yesterday. The same damn questions will be bothering us."

Amy nodded politely. She turned on the coffee maker and stood looking out the kitchen window. "It's a beautiful day, isn't it? But then, it always is on Orleana. The perfect vacation paradise. Plenty of sun, sand and *friendship*. The ideal place to recover from a few picturesque wounds."

"And pick up a few more while I'm at it," Jed said meaningfully.

Instantly Amy was swamped with remorse. She remembered his injured arm and swung around anxiously to glance at it. "Oh, Jed, I didn't mean that the way it sounded. How are you feeling today? Is your arm okay? Any signs of infection?"

Something in his eyes relaxed. A slow grin softened the natural hardness around his mouth. "I like it when you get that stricken look in your eyes. So concerned and anxious. You make me feel wanted." He walked toward her with a deceptively lazy stride and planted his big hands on her shoulders. Then he dropped a possessive, lingering kiss on her mouth. "It's a temptation to play injured hero just so I can see that look in your eyes."

"That's called manipulation," she managed accusingly.

"Even worse. It's called greed." He released her to reach for a golden yellow papaya that had been ripening on the windowsill. "The truth is, I have absolutely no right to use the injured hero routine."

"You're not an injured hero?"

"Nope. I'm an injured idiot. Only an idiot would have been taken by surprise the way I was last night." Jed paused on the verge of sinking the knife into the papaya and said thoughtfully, "That's twice in one month. You know, Amy, I think I'm slowing down."

Amy seized the opportunity to say stoutly, "Then it's time ιo consider a new line of work, isn't it?"

He looked at her as if she hadn't spoken. "I'll cut the papaya for breakfast. Go back upstairs and get dressed. Unless, of course, you'd rather scratch the papaya plans and have something else for breakfast?" There was a deliberately friendly leer in his voice.

Amy pretended not to see the sexy amusement in Jed's eyes. The phone rang as she headed for the stairs. She halted on the bottom step, turning back to answer it, but Jed was already walking out of the kitchen to pick up the receiver. Perhaps he was expecting Faxon to return his call very quickly. Amy watched Jed's face as he spoke.

"Oh, hello, Kelso. Yeah, I'd appreciate an update." Jed listened intently and then said quietly, "I see. I'll have to think about it." There was another long pause and then with a crisp farewell he hung up the phone and met Amy's questioning glance.

"Well?" she prompted anxiously.

"That was Kelso."

She waved aside the obvious. The detached watchfulness was back in his eyes. "What's going on, Jed?"

"Not much. Kelso says Vaden hasn't said much and it doesn't look as though he's going to. He's obviously been in this sort of situation before and knows that his best bet is keeping his mouth shut. Kelso wants to know if I'm going to press charges. He recommends I don't."

"On what grounds?" Amy demanded, incensed at the idea.

Jed mumbled something unintelligible and stalked back into the kitchen.

"What was that?" Amy called after him.

"I said, Vaden's only comment this morning was that he was the one who was attacked. He claims he pulled the knife to defend himself."

"But that's ridiculous!" Amy hurried after him.

Jed shrugged as he went back to work on the papaya. "Who's to know for certain what happened? Vaden and I were the only ones present at the time. We both got hurt. What's more, we're both off-islanders, so who cares?"

"I care. Besides, Vaden may be just an island hopper, but you're a guest on this island. My father's guest, for pete's sake."

Jed inclined his head in mocking acknowledgment. "Thank you, but I'm afraid that at this stage the protection of your family's name extends only so far. I'm still an unknown quantity, at least as far as Kelso is concerned. He'll honor my privileged status only up to a point. Face it, Amy. The easiest thing for Kelso to do is write off last night's events as a classic example of a couple of tourists having a little too much to drink and getting into a quarrel. They both got hurt but no one was killed. No property was damaged and nothing was stolen. No big deal."

"Dammit, I will not allow Vaden to get out of this so easily. He used a knife on you, Jed!"

"Don't get so excited, Amy. These things happen."

"How can you stand there and say that? How can you treat it so lightly?" She was rapidly losing her temper.

"I give you my word, I didn't treat it lightly last night."

That stopped her for an instant. "Just how badly is Vaden hurt?"

"He'll recover. He's already got his voice back, although Kelso says he can barely talk. And the bleeding has stopped." Jed casually scooped the little black seeds out of the papaya.

"The bleeding has stopped?" Amy repeated weakly.

"His nose was bleeding when I last saw him." Jed placed the fruit neatly on two plates and looked at her. "Are you going to get dressed before we eat?"

She stared at him, afraid to ask what he'd done to Vaden that had temporarily deprived the other man of his voice and left his nose bleeding. Aware that her mouth was open, she abruptly closed it and started once more for the stairs. "Whatever it was, he deserved it," she muttered.

"What did you say?" Jed called after her.

"Nothing. I'll be right down. Are you going to press charges, Jed?"

"No. It's not worth it. But I'd like to convince Kelso to keep Vaden out of our hair for a few days. Go on, Amy. When you come back, I'll tell you what Kelso said about his interview with Guthrie."

Amy scurried up the stairs, dashed into the shower and

then pulled on a pair of scarlet shorts and an exotically printed blouse. She was downstairs in record time. Jed was pouring the coffee.

"All right," she announced. "Tell me about Guthrie." She reached for a piece of toast as she sat down.

"Guthrie was absolutely stunned to find himself involved in this whole affair." Jed sat down across from her, his amusement obvious. "He told Kelso he had no idea I'd followed him up the hill into the warehouse section."

"So what was he doing in that section?"

"Claims he was trying to find a local legend. Ever heard of a lady of the night named Matilda Hawkins? Apparently she runs a small business operation out of a converted warehouse."

Amy hesitated and then realized who he was talking about. "Mattress Matty? But she retired years ago. Business was never the same for her after the Navy pulled out. She lives in a room that overlooks the main street in town."

"Apparently her legend lives on," Jed said dryly. "Guthrie claims some locals told him all about Mattress Matty and implied the business was still, uh, thriving. He went looking for a little action. Guess the nightlife on board the cruise ship wasn't sufficiently exciting. Maybe he's not much into dancing, either."

Amy wrinkled her nose. "I can see some of the local characters deciding it would be a great joke to send a tourist on a wild goose chase looking for Matty. So that's how Guthrie came to leave the ship, hmm? What about Vaden?"

"Kelso's convinced his original assumption is the right one. Vaden was just lying in wait, hoping to take a few wallets off a couple of unwary cruise ship passengers. When

I left the ship and headed up into that deserted warehouse district, I became a very tempting target."

"Yeah?" Amy demanded caustically. "If Vaden was looking for tempting targets, why didn't he pick on Guthrie?"

"Who knows? Maybe he didn't see him. Or maybe I looked easier."

Amy put down her unfinished slice of toast. "Jed, this is all very, very strange."

"Yes," he said. "I agree."

Dan Renner shot out of the shaky wicker chair where he'd been sitting and began pacing the small inn room with his usual sizzling impatience. Guthrie watched him in laconic silence. He'd known from the beginning it was a mistake to actually take the client along on the job. Clients were notoriously unpredictable, emotional and inclined to hysteria. Clients didn't understand true professionalism.

"This whole thing is falling apart," Renner accused furiously. "It's cracking like an eggshell. What the hell is happening? You and Vaden were supposed to be good. You were supposed to know how to handle this kind of thing. Neutralize Glaze, you said. That was the simplest thing to do. Get him out of the way and then concentrate on using the woman to get the box. What happens? It's Vaden who gets neutralized. Shit. Now we're sitting here waiting for Vaden to spill his guts and drag everything out into the open. It's like waiting for a time bomb to go off. Christ. What next?"

"Vaden won't talk."

Renner swung around, his eyes glittering. "How do you know that?"

"I've worked with him before. He's a pro. What's more, talking would only get him into real trouble and he knows it.

His best bet is to stick to the story he gave Kelso. He and Glaze had both had a little too much to drink, got into a fight in the parking lot and went up to the warehouse district to settle the matter. They both got hurt, but since it was Vaden who was unconscious, it was Glaze who got to give his story to Kelso first. Because Glaze was connected to the Slaters, it was Vaden who spent the night in jail. He knows if he keeps his mouth shut he'll be out in a day or so. Kelso can't hold him for long."

"What about Kelso pinning you down? That doesn't exactly give me a warm, comfortable feeling, Guthrie."

Guthrie was unconcerned. "I had the Mattress Matty story ready, didn't I? He bought it."

"But now there's a link between you and Vaden. That's bound to start someone thinking."

"The only link is the one in your mind. Kelso's not going to make any connections. I doubt if that man's done much original thinking in twenty years. You saw him yesterday. He's hooked on rum. Vaden and I each gave him perfectly acceptable stories and the easiest thing for Kelso to do is believe them. He's the kind who will take the easy way out, believe me."

"What about Glaze?" Renner asked challengingly. "He sure as hell will think there's a link between you and Vaden. And because I'm connected to you, he'll figure I'm involved, also."

"Maybe. Maybe not. Doesn't make any difference. If we're right and he's after that box, too, the last thing he'll want to do is make waves with the local authorities. He'll stick to his story. Not much else he can do."

"And the woman?"

"You saw the two of them last night. Glaze has her eating

out of his hand. She'll believe whatever he tells her." Guthrie leaned back in his chair and stretched his legs out in front of him. "It strikes me that the best thing for us to do now is sit tight and wait for Glaze to do all the hard work."

Renner scowled at him. "What do you mean?"

"Glaze has the inside track with the Slater woman. From what you've told me that was going to be LePage's approach last year. Sounds workable. Let Glaze talk the woman into showing him the location of the caves. Hell, let him go down and get the box, for that matter. No sense risking our necks if we can get him to do it for us. We'll keep an eye on him. Get to him before he leaves the island."

"Then what?"

"Then I think it would be best for all concerned if Glaze and Ms. Slater have an unfortunate accident while doing a little cave diving." Guthrie smiled. "Hell, everyone knows how dangerous the sport is."

Renner hesitated and then slowly nodded his head. "Yes, I think that would be the neatest way to tie this up." He was profoundly grateful to have Guthrie with him. It was Guthrie who would do the killing. Guthrie was the professional.

"There's just one thing," Guthrie said coolly.

"What's that?"

"We'll have to watch ourselves around Glaze. He took Vaden last night. From what Kelso told me, he could have killed him easily. Apparently, Glaze deliberately stopped just short of finishing Vaden."

"So? Vaden blew it."

Guthrie shook his head. "You don't understand. Vaden is fast. Very, very fast. But last night Glaze was a little faster."

* * *

Amy uncurled from the chair where she had been making notes on the last half of *Private Demons* and went to peer over Jed's shoulder. He was completing the bird cage design he'd started a few days earlier. The precision of the drawing and the neat block printing Jed used for making notes made Amy shake her head in wonder.

"I would never have the patience for such detailed work," she observed. "It's perfect. Every little hinge, every connecting point, every bend in the wire. It's all there on paper."

Jed gave her an amused glance. "I wouldn't have the patience to construct a hundred thousand word story out of thin air, even if I had the imagination to do it. So I guess we're even."

"Are you going to build this cage when we get back to Caliph's Bay?"

"Think it would sell?"

"In a flash! Jed, I think there's a huge, untapped market for your cages. Putting them on display in one little gallery in Caliph's Bay isn't even scratching the surface. You need to get them into other shops, maybe some pet stores. People spend hundreds, sometimes thousands of dollars on exotic birds. They wouldn't flinch at the idea of getting a beautiful cage to go with the bird."

"The Caliph's Bay Gallery handles my total output as it is," Jed reminded her calmly. "I don't have time to build enough cages to put into other outlets."

Amy braced herself and then took the plunge. "You would have the time if you quit your government job."

There was an acute silence. Jed was watching her but his gaze was unreadable. Amy held her breath.

At last Jed said slowly, "It bothers you that much?"

"It could get you killed one of these days."

"It's what I do, Amy."

"It's what you did last month and last year and seven years before that, but nothing says you have to keep doing it."

Jed stood up slowly until he was towering over her. His hands closed around her shoulders. "Tell me something," he asked softly, "when I've cleaned up the mess you're in here, are you going to call off our affair because of the way I make my living?"

Amy drew a shocked breath. "Is that what you think? That I'd let you use your . . . your peculiar talents to help me and then, when I was safe again, tell you good-bye?"

"You never wanted to know what I did for a living. But now you do know. Sooner or later you're going to have to deal with it and with me." His words were low and slightly roughened by an emotion she couldn't define.

"Jed, stop it, I'm suggesting you quit your job for your own sake. It's dangerous. There's no future in it."

He gave her a slight shake. "Would you leave me because of it?"

"Jed, please, you've got it all wrong," Amy wailed.

"Would you leave me because of my job?"

Amy stepped back, out from under his painful grip. Her eyes were burning with a clear, green flame. "No, dammit, I wouldn't leave you because of your job. I think it's a terrible job. I think it's done some terrible things to you and will probably continue to do terrible things to you. But I won't leave you because of it. We're *friends*, remember? Friends don't desert each other because they disapprove of each other's jobs. There. Are you satisfied? I think we'd better change the subject. How about a walk down to the cove?"

"Amy, wait—"

"I'm going to put on my sandals." Amy retreated up the stairs. She felt his eyes on her until she disappeared down the corridor toward her bedroom. Friends, she repeated silently. That was a joke. Friendship didn't begin to cover what she felt for Jed, although it was certainly part of it.

She found her sandals and stepped into them, thinking once again of how she would never have become friends, let alone lovers, with a man like Jed Glaze eight months before. But then, she was a different woman than she had been eight months before.

Jed was waiting for her at the bottom of the stairs, his expression stark and intent.

"Amy," he began as she lightly descended the stairs, "do you mean it?"

She frowned. "Mean what?"

"What you said about my job not making any difference. That our friendship is going to hold after we leave Orleana."

"I mean it." She eyed him quizzically. "Why should it make any difference in our friendship?"

"Because you're not the kind of woman who gets involved with a man like me," he told her through clenched teeth.

"But I am involved with you," she pointed out sweetly, her sense of humor revived. "Therefore, we have to assume that there is either something screwy with your reasoning or else you don't know me quite as well as you think you do."

He was silent for a few seconds. "We're learning a lot about each other these days, aren't we?"

"A great deal. Are you ready for that walk?" Without waiting for confirmation, she headed toward the door.

Jed followed, falling into step beside her as they left the veranda and headed toward the path that led down to the cove. "Thanks, Amy," he finally said quietly.

"For what? For not threatening to break off the affair because you won't promise to quit your job?"

"For accepting me the way I am." He was close beside her but he didn't touch her. His attention was on a wheeling sea gull. "Not everyone would or could."

"Is that why you've gotten so good at playing chameleon?"

He gave her a strange sidelong glance. "Chameleon?"

"You seem to be able to slip into certain social roles whenever you want to. You do it the way a chameleon changes colors, instinctively. The way you handled my parents, for example. You let them treat you as though you were an earnestly aspiring, financially secure suitor for my hand. Connie at Caliph's Bay Gallery and just about everyone else in town thinks you're a struggling, eccentric artist who has to do some engineering on the side in order to make ends meet. Hank and Rosie think you're a friend of the family who happens to be sleeping with me and whose intentions, they hope, are honorable. Dr. Stearn thinks you're a suitably macho, world-weary type who knows how to handle himself in a knife fight."

"So?" Jed challenged softly. "You want the real Jed Glaze to stand up and show himself?"

Amy smiled and shook her head. "There's no need. I've decided that the real Jed Glaze includes all of the above and maybe a few more interesting persona I have yet to discover."

Jed reached out and took her hand, lacing her fingers through his. "You want to watch out for that imagination of yours, woman. Sometimes it takes control."

"You want to watch out for that streak of cynical realism that runs through you, Jed. Sometimes it takes control."

"Maybe your fantasies make a good counterbalance for my realism."

"Maybe." They walked in silence until they reached the sandy cove and then Amy said gently, "There's just one thing I'd like to make very clear."

"Yeah?"

"Yeah." Deliberately she mocked his laconic tone. "I would never call a halt to our relationship because of your job, but that does not mean I approve of it. I still think you should quit."

"Let's talk about something else," Jed suggested coolly.

"Such as?"

"Such as going down into the caves."

Amy nodded unhappily. "I was hoping you'd want to put off the dive for a while until your wound healed."

"I'll take my chances. Vaden's knife didn't do that much damage. It looked worse than it is. A little blood goes a long way. By tomorrow or the next day I should be ready to go back into the water. I'll put a plastic bandage around my arm if it makes you feel any better. That should keep most of the water out."

"You're determined to do this dive, aren't you?"

"It has to be done, Amy. I've already explained that you can't leave that kind of loose end lying around. It's already attracting trouble."

"Vaden?"

Jed nodded. "It's too much of a coincidence that he picked me to roll last night."

"Maybe he was working alone. After all, LePage came alone. Maybe Vaden was a friend of LePage's and therefore knew about the box," Amy suggested urgently as her agile brain went to work creating a scenario that would provide an excuse to postpone the dive indefinitely. "It makes sense. He just decided to make a try for the box himself. But he blew it because you stopped him. With him in jail we can relax. Even if Kelso releases him, he'll kick him off the island. Kelso doesn't let troublemakers hang around long."

Jed's mouth curved briefly. He freed her hand and ran his fingers teasingly through her windblown hair, shaking her gently. "Like I keep saying, lady, you've got a truly creative imagination."

Amy winced, her expression rueful. "You don't buy that version?"

He lifted one broad shoulder dismissingly. "I'm not sure. It has a certain inherent logic except for the fact that it doesn't tell us how LePage or Vaden or anyone else knew about the box in the first place."

"Details," she scoffed.

"That's what I'm good at," Jed reminded her. "Dull little details."

Amy surrendered to the inevitable. "All right. When do we plan the dive?" She was unaware of the slight shiver that went through her as she accepted that the return to the flooded caves was now imminent.

But Jed felt the tiny tremor. He also saw the bleak determination that replaced the normal warmth in her eyes. He wanted to take her into his arms and tell her they didn't have to make the dive. He longed to hold her close and assure her that she was safe, that he could protect her without retrieving the box. But he couldn't make that kind of promise. The evidence of brewing trouble was all around them, and there was no way in hell he could ignore it.

Jed came to a halt in the sand and caught Amy by the arms. "Honey, if there was any other way to handle this, I'd use it. Believe me?"

She smiled up at him with a woman's acceptance and understanding. Her fingers touched the side of his face, as light as a graceful strand of seaweed reaching out to caress him underwater. "I believe you, Jed. We'll do this your way."

Chapter Fifteen

"**C**hrist, I can't believe you went down into those caves that night with only one dive light. You should have had at least one extra light as a backup. Preferably two. Do you realize what could have happened if the batteries had failed in the single light you had?" Jed paced slowly around the pile of diving equipment he and Amy had laid out on the living room floor. Tanks, regulators, dive lights, line and reel, fins, diving knives, buoyancy compensators and a few other assorted items were all neatly arranged for his inspection. Two days had passed since the Vaden incident.

With typical Glaze attention to detail, he'd already been over every item on the floor twice. He'd made Amy go over everything with him both times and was now starting in on a third inspection. Jed Glaze, it turned out, was a great believer in knowing a diving buddy's paraphernalia as well as he knew his own. Especially, it seemed, when it came to the business of cave diving. He gave credence to the old axiom that a diver's life could depend on his buddy's equipment.

Amy was torn between amusement and the distilled remnants of nightmares as she listened to his admonishing question. "Trust me, Jed, I was well aware of what might have happened."

"Dive lights fail all the time, just like flashlights."

"I know, Jed."

"Swimming around inside a cave without a light would be like—" He broke off abruptly.

Amy finished the sentence in a surprisingly neutral voice. "Like swimming around inside a tomb. The thought crossed my mind more than once that night, Jed."

"And you went into that cave on a half filled tank of air. No safety margin at all. If something had gone wrong you wouldn't have had a minute's worth of reserve supply."

"I know, Jed."

He muttered something that sounded both violent and disgusted as he bent down to unsheathe the diving knife. "Why the hell am I lecturing you? It's not as though you thought you had a lot of choice. But dammit, Amy, you took a hell of a risk that night."

"The caves didn't seem a whole lot worse at the time than looking down the barrel of that gun LePage had. It was only afterward that I realized it was the caves that terrified me. I think that after I decided I had to hide the box, I just sort of turned off something in my nervous system for a while. It let me function without thinking about the fear. But afterward I never had nightmares about the gun, only about the caves."

Jed resheathed the knife and crouched down beside her. His gaze was steady and intent. "I can try going in alone. You can wait at the entrance pool. I'll see if there's any chance of finding the box based on your description of where you hid it."

Amy shook her head, committed now. "No. Absolutely not. You're not going into those caves alone. If ever there was a situation that demanded the buddy system, this is it. Besides, I can't tell you for certain how to find the right tunnel. I know I swam past two or three entrances before I finally set the box down inside one. The only thing I re-

member clearly is a distinct bend in the main passageway."
She suddenly realized what was probably worrying him.
"Afraid I'll panic on you?"

He half smiled and shook his head. "Are you kidding?
After the way you handled yourself that night LePage pulled
a gun on you? No. You are one gutsy lady. When the chips
are down, you're not the kind to panic. I'd trust you at my
back any day."

His rough approval warmed her. "That first day when we
went diving in the cove I didn't handle myself well."

"It was your first time back in the water after the experience eight months ago. You were bound to be nervous. You
did fine when we explored that bomber."

She nodded. "It was easier the second time."

"If you get anxious this time, we'll get out, give you some
time to relax and then try again later. There's no rush. The
box can't be very far inside the caves. You wouldn't have
had the time or the air to have gone far."

Amy took a breath, remembering her fear of running out
of air that night. She didn't tell Jed because she knew it
would only upset him, but the truth was by the time she
returned to the entrance pool that night she had been out of
air. She'd barely made it back out of the cave.

"Speaking of air," Jed went on as he got to his feet and
resumed his prowling inspection, "we'll stick to the standard
safety formula for this kind of diving. We won't use any
more than one third of our supply going in. We'll assume
we'll need another third on the way out, which leaves an
additional third for emergencies. When either one of us uses
up the first third of our air supply, we both turn back. Understood?"

Amy nodded obediently and then unsuccessfully tried to

stifle a small grin. "Why do I get the feeling you're going to be the captain on this dive?"

"Probably because I'm the one who's supposed to be good at details," he retorted. "Now hush up and pay attention."

"Yes, sir."

He ignored her too-obedient tone. "We'll have backups for everything—regulators, lights, the works. We'll strap the knives to our forearms instead of our legs. Less chance of having them snag on something that way. To cut down on snagging problems we'll reverse the fin straps and tape them. We'll also tape down anything else that might stick out and get caught. The last thing we need is for one of us to get equipment tangled on a projection of some kind inside the caves."

"I understand." Amy glanced at the array of diving gear. "You know, Jed, the thing I worried about most that night was kicking up silt. The visibility was good, I remember that much. The water was very clear, but..."

He nodded grimly. "But the visibility could have gone down to zero in a few seconds if you'd accidentally loosened some silt with a fin or brushed the tank against the ceiling. The stuff could have clouded the water and left you as blind as you would have been if you'd lost the light." He ran his fingers through his hair. "Damn, Amy, whenever I think about it—"

"Don't think about it. Believe me, I try not to." For a moment she felt as though she were the one who had to push the project forward in the face of an overactive imagination —this time Jed's. "We'll be careful. We'll do everything by the book this time, follow all the rules. We'll play it nice and conservative and we'll put you in charge, how's that?"

"Maybe I ought to do this alone."

"We've already been through that."

He sighed. "You're right. Okay, back to basics. I'm satisfied with the line. It's in good shape, light colored, won't float. We both stay on it at all times, even if the visibility is one hundred percent. If the water clouds up in a hurry and one of us doesn't have hold of the line, we're in trouble."

"Don't worry, I'm not about to let go of the line." Since Jed would be going in first, he would have control of the reel of nylon line they would use. The line would be tied off at the cave entrance and would be reeled out as Jed swam along the corridors. It not only marked the path back to the entrance, it would be the only means of finding the entrance if something went seriously wrong. The one piece of emergency equipment Amy had thought to use on her first dive in the caves was the reel and line LePage had brought along. She had clung to it with a death grip as she'd frantically kicked her way back out to the entrance pool.

Jed sat back on his haunches. "I want you to draw me a diagram of what you can remember about the caves and also what you remember about that little chart you said LePage had with him that night. I don't suppose you kept that map, did you?"

Amy shook her head. "No. I stuffed it into the box with the emeralds and the letters and the photos. It was just one more piece of evidence I was trying to hide. It wasn't very elaborate, Jed. It showed the first few feet of the main entrance tunnel and I think it marked a couple of side tunnels, but that was about all. When Wyman hid the box the first time, he apparently put it close to the pool entrance, just inside the first branching tunnel. At least that's how it looked on that little chart."

"But that's not where you put it when you hid it?"

"No. I wanted to put it as far back in the cave as I dared. I wanted that box to stay hidden forever. It was all I could think about that night." Amy looked at him. "Jed, if we do find it, we've got to destroy everything inside. The letters, the photos, *everything*."

"We'll take care of the dangerous stuff," he promised. "That's the whole point of this little expedition."

Neither of them mentioned the half dozen emeralds. As far as Amy was concerned, they were inevitably linked with the rest of the box's contents and therefore came under the heading "dangerous stuff." But she wasn't certain Jed viewed them in the same light.

Jed got to his feet once more and walked over to the table he had been using to sketch his latest bird cage design. He picked up a piece of paper and handed it to Amy, along with a mechanical pencil.

"I want you to sketch as much as you can remember about those caves, honey. Start from the entrance. You said there was a small amount of breathing space above the waterline just inside the entrance?"

Amy nodded, remembering. She reached for the paper and pencil. "It doesn't extend more than a couple of feet. After that the cave angles downward slightly and it's completely filled with water." She glanced up at him anxiously as she started to draw. "I'm not very good at this kind of thing. Drawing, I mean. My sense of perspective is poor. The last art class I had was in third grade."

"Just do the best you can." He crouched beside her, peering intently at the blank sheet of paper as she started a sketchy rendering of the rocky pool that formed the entrance of the cave.

Amy was painstakingly drawing the dark, yawning mouth

when the fragile lead of the mechanical pencil snapped. Patiently Jed took the pencil from her, adjusted the lead and handed it back. Without a word, Amy went back to work. Jed watched her for a moment and then shook his head.

"Don't draw it from that angle. You're trying to sketch it as though you were swimming into it. Give me a cutaway view. You know, from the side." He momentarily took the pencil back from her and showed her what he meant.

"I told you I wasn't very good at his kind of drawing," Amy complained, retrieving the pencil. She started over again, eventually producing a gently sloping corridor that twisted suddenly to the right. Uncomfortably aware of Jed gazing over her shoulder, she attempted to sketch in what she could remember of the two branching caves she had noted that night.

"How far did you swim before you passed the first side cave?" Jed asked.

"I don't remember. I wasn't paying attention to that kind of detail. I just recall seeing the dark opening on my left and thinking that it wasn't far enough. I swam past the second side cave a short time later."

"How much later? A few seconds? A couple of minutes?"

"Jed, I don't remember! I just kept swimming, thinking I had to go deeper into the cave before I hid the box."

"All right, all right, don't get upset."

"I'm not upset," she answered, her anger flaring.

He cocked one dark brow in mocking skepticism but said nothing. "Keep going. Do you remember anything else about the caves? Stalactites? Stalagmites?"

Amy had a fleeting mental image of jagged swords hanging from the ceiling and thrusting upward from the floor. Her mouth tightened. "Yes. The main passage was fairly wide but the interior was very jagged and uneven. The caves were formed by lava flows and later filled with sea water."

Jed tapped the paper. "That means we'll have to be extra careful about snarling the equipment or accidentally kicking an obstruction."

Amy went back to her drawing, frowning intently now as she tried to push aside the nightmare images and reduce her recollections to a simple sketch. "After I'd passed the second passage I knew I couldn't swim much farther. There wasn't a lot of air left in the tank."

Jed's look was grim. "Don't remind me."

"It was shortly after that second side cave that I turned into a third branching cave. The entrance seemed wider than the others. I went a short distance and put down the box, turned around and swam back out."

"You're sure you only passed two side passages before you swam into the one where you hid the box?"

"I think so, but Jed, you know what it's like in a cave. Darker than midnight. I only had a single light and it wasn't a very big one. It's possible I just didn't notice a couple of small side passages. I had no intention of ever trying to get that box back out of the cave. I wasn't exactly trying to chart the place for future reference."

He ignored the sharpness in her voice. "I know. Okay, we'll start searching side passages after we've passed the two you remember." He straightened, reaching down to tug her up beside him. "Are you ready?"

"As ready as I'll ever be."

He searched her face for a moment, then nodded abruptly without saying anything. He turned to collect the diving equipment that had been set out on the floor.

* * *

Amy tried very hard not to look into the depths of the entrance pool as she climbed over the jagged rocks and into the water. But her imagination combined with her too-vivid memories, and out of the corner of her eye she saw the place where LePage's body had lain. Memories of his dead stare illuminated by the light that awful night crowded too close. She shook herself free of them, reminding herself that she had to concentrate on the job at hand. Jed's life as well as her own could easily depend on how alert she was during the dive.

In the full light of day, she could easily see the floor of the rocky pool. Getting into the water wasn't nearly as treacherous as it was at night. But as soon as they put on their fins and swam into the dark, gaping mouth of the cave, the warm, clarifying light of the sun became useless. The darkest of all possible nights was waiting just inside the entrance.

The intensity of the darkness was increased by the fact that one had to swim through it. The water gave the utter blackness another dimension.

The dive lights provided a narrow path through the water, a corridor of visibility that cut a swath of safety through the midnight depths. When Amy glanced to the side, down or back, the lighted path disappeared, leaving only the endless, watery blackness.

Amy kept a firm hold on the nylon line Jed let out from the reel in his hand. The line had been tied off around a rock in the entrance pool and again just inside the passageway. Jed paused every so often to tie it off again as he swam. Whenever he had to touch a projection inside the cave he did so gingerly, his cautious movements reflecting his respect for the fragile nature of the cavern surfaces.

Amy listened to the sound of her own breathing and was satisfied with the relatively normal rate. She couldn't deny she was somewhat tense, but she was in control of herself. She tried to assume an analytical frame of mind, forcing herself to concentrate on the details of the passage.

The first thing she realized was that her memory for the cave's details was exceedingly poor. She recalled the jagged teeth of the stalactites and stalagmites, for instance, but she hadn't remembered that there were so many of them. The cave was wider near the entrance than it had seemed that night in October. Of course, there was more illumination on this dive. Perhaps that accounted for the different perspective.

Visibility was excellent along the beams of light. Occasionally tiny pale creatures appeared suspended in the alien sun of Amy's dive light. Amy guessed they were small shrimp, or some other sea creature that had adapted completely to the endless night. She knew if she captured one and examined it she would undoubtedly discover it was blind. Senses other than sight were crucial to survival in a world of complete darkness.

Ahead of her Jed paused. Amy slowed, assuming he was going to tie off the line again. Instead he signaled her to swim closer. When she did so he aimed the beam of his light against the left wall of the passage. An entrance to another corridor came into view. Jed held up one finger, silently asking if this was the first of the two branching caves Amy recalled. She nodded. Jed turned and began swimming forward again.

Amy flicked the beam of her light down the corridor to her left as she swam past. She suppressed a shudder and heard the regulator record the increased tempo of her breathing. Taking a firm grip on herself she tried to relax. She was still in control.

A little farther on, Jed paused again, this time pointing out a second side cave. Amy nodded and again Jed went forward, the nylon lifeline spinning out behind him.

When Jed paused at a third side passage, Amy stared at it uneasily. According to her memory, this should be the one she had gone down that night with the box, but it looked different. The entrance seemed narrower. And where was the bend in the passage she thought she recalled? She looked at Jed and conveyed her uncertainty. He acknowledged it and turned into the passage. It was just wide enough to admit a diver and his tank. Amy swam in behind Jed.

Beyond the cramped entrance, the cave passage broadened to more comfortable proportions. There was room to turn around easily. Amy swung her light in a searching arc, finding nothing familiar. Surely after so many nightmares she should remember the passage fairly well. Perhaps it was the wrong one, after all. She could have easily missed seeing the narrow side entrance that night and instead gone on to another branching cave.

She was about to signal to Jed that this wasn't the right cavern when her dive light picked up an odd reflection near the roof of the passage. Instead of being able to see the jagged surface of the roof, all she could see was a sort of flat, silvery mirror. On a hunch, she swam up to it, aware that Jed was watching.

Cautiously Amy put her head through the flat reflection and discovered her hunch had been correct. She surfaced to find herself in air instead of water. Jed's light wavered beneath her as he swam to join her.

Amy spit out her regulator and shoved back her mask as

Jed surfaced beside her. She was intrigued in spite of herself by the discovery.

"Take a look at this, Jed." She bounced her light off the portion of the cavern that was above water. It wasn't more than ten feet across, but there was a ledge jutting out just above the water line. Amy swam toward it.

"I assume this isn't the cavern where you hid the box?" Jed's voice was tinged with impatience.

"No, but isn't this wild? Who would have guessed there was a breathing space down here? It must have been created when these caves were first flooded. This cavern didn't fill completely with water. It doesn't smell too bad. Maybe there are some fissures in the rocks overhead that let in a little fresh air."

"Amy, we're not here to explore these caves. Let's get going." Jed started to lower his mask.

"Just a second," Amy called, "I want to see how broad that ledge is." She swam over to it and raised her hand to grasp the edge of rock.

"Watch where you put your hands. You can't see what's up there."

"There's nothing up here," Amy assured him as she used her grip to hoist herself a little higher in the water until she could just barely see over the edge of rock.

She swept her light across the surface of the ledge and found herself staring into the empty eyesockets of a human skull.

Amy's scream ricocheted off the cavern walls, filling the small space and echoing horribly.

"Amy! Oh, God . . ." Jed kicked forward, grabbing for her as she shoved herself away from the ledge and floundered awkwardly in the water. "Amy, what is it? What's wrong?"

He braced her with one hand, using his other to keep himself afloat. He flashed his light toward the ledge.

"A skeleton, Jed. Up there on the ledge. It's Wyman," Amy gasped. "It must be."

"Are you okay?" he demanded.

Amy nodded mutely, still struggling to steady her nerves. Jed released her and swam toward the ledge. Hoisting himself up with one hand he surveyed the rocky surface.

Amy watched in horror, wondering how Jed could calmly study such a grim scene. One glimpse had been more than enough for her. When he eventually dropped from the ledge and swam back to her he looked strangely thoughtful.

Amy swallowed, trying to make her question sound rational. "What do you think happened, Jed?"

"Offhand I'd say someone was afraid the body might somehow float out toward the entrance of the cave. Whoever killed him apparently decided to leave him on that ledge so the currents wouldn't pull the body out into the open. See this water line? High tide doesn't reach the ledge."

"Oh, God, Jed, it really did happen, didn't it? Just the way LePage told me it happened. My mother must have killed him and then hidden his body in here. What are we going to do?"

"About that skeleton? Nothing. It's been lying there for twenty-five years. It can go on lying there forever. Come on, we've got a job to do." Jed adjusted his mask and dived beneath the surface.

Amy glanced nervously back toward the ledge and then put the mouthpiece of the regulator between her teeth. She lowered her mask and went under the water. Her light instantly picked out Jed. He was waiting for her to precede him back to the main corridor. Since they were retreating along the nylon line, the order of who went first was reversed. Amy took a grip on the line and kicked forward, telling herself she would not think about the skeleton. Jed followed, reeling in the nylon.

Amy reached the narrowed mouth of the passage and slowed to edge her way carefully past the entrance into the wider main corridor.

Suddenly the water seemed to shudder around her. She felt the vibration of the falling gravel and debris even as the nylon line went taut in her fingers. The water began to cloud almost instantly as loosened silt floated around her. In seconds Amy's light was useless. The beam barely penetrated the blinding fog of swirling debris.

Amy's light grasp on the nylon line became an unshakable grip. If she released it she would never find it again in this silty soup. And if she lost the line, she was probably as good as dead. Her sense of direction was gone. There were no reference points to tell her which way to turn in the corridor. She couldn't even tell which way was up and which was down without the line. She couldn't see more than a few inches in front of her face.

All of the problems she was facing registered in an instant, as well as the probable cause. Something, perhaps merely the change in water pressure caused by her swimming past a weak point, had started a slide. The falling materials had kicked up an incredible cloud of silt. But the biggest shock of all came when she tugged gently on the nylon line and got no answering response from Jed.

The line was still rigid in her grasp. Amy prayed that meant Jed was still holding onto the reel on the other side of the gravel fall, but she knew it could also mean that the reel had been trapped beneath the falling debris. Jed might have been trapped as well.

Cautiously, vividly aware of the possibility of jarring more of the interior loose, Amy swam back along the line. She kept the light on because, useless as it was, it was better than the terrifying, oppressive darkness that would descend on her if she switched it off. She aimed it at the line and found she was barely able to pick out the white nylon in front of her.

She didn't have to swim far before she found the jumble of materials that now sealed the narrow entrance of the passageway through which she had just emerged. Carefully she tried tugging again on the nylon, aware that she might loosen more debris in the process. There was still no response.

Fear unlike anything she had ever known was welling up in her. If Jed had been caught by the fall and knocked unconscious he might already be dead. If he was alert but trapped by debris, she had to get to him before he ran out of air. They must both be rapidly reaching the bottom of the first third of their supply. Jed had been very clear about the fact that they had to turn back when they got that low. They would need almost a third of the supply to retreat from the cave. That left only the remaining third to keep him alive while Amy cleared the passageway.

She went to work immediately, increasingly careless of the danger of causing another slide. So much damage had already been done that it seemed pointless to worry about the next possible disaster.

Groping through the silty water she encountered a small mountain of gravel blocking the entrance to the branch cave. She set the dive light down on the floor of the cave. Keeping one hand on the line, she used her free hand to claw at the pile of fallen debris. The thick water swirled around her but no more gravel fell.

Amy didn't try to read the tank's pressure gauge. There was no point tracking the depleting supply of air. She had to keep working until she'd freed the line and discovered what had happened to Jed. It took all her willpower to control the images her mind insisted on conjuring up. He had to be alive on the other side.

She was working blindly but steadily on the gravel pile, trying to convince herself she was making progress when she thought she detected a small tug on the nylon line. Relief rushed through her. Instantly she tugged back. This time the response was definite and deliberate.

Jed was alive.

Amy redoubled her efforts. Moments later she felt another distinct change in the tension of the line. This wasn't a signal from Jed. It felt as though a weight had been lifted off the line itself.

Amy groped hurriedly, following the line to the point where it disappeared into the loosened gravel. She could still see virtually nothing, but she was encouraged by the fact that her fumbling fingers were picking their way easily through the debris.

A few minutes later her gloved hand encountered Jed's. She couldn't see it or his face, but when his fingers closed briefly around hers Amy knew everything was going to be all right.

Having reassured herself that he was alive, Amy made herself slow down and finish the clearing process with greater caution. She realized Jed was doing the same on his side of the slide. Together they widened the gap until Jed could wriggle through.

Amy groped for the dive light and tried to pick out Jed's large frame as he swam into the tunnel beside her. She caught a glimpse of his shiny metal tank, but that was about all.

He reached out a hand until he touched her. She felt the firm pressure and knew he was ordering her to start moving back toward the corridor entrance. She realized from the continuing tension in the line that he still had the reel. Typical Jed Glaze style. The man was good at the important little details. Amy clung to the nylon and started swimming.

She had to go far more slowly on the way out because of the lack of visibility. It would be all too easy to blunder into a projection and either injure herself or cause another slide. The endless cloud of silt still roiled in front of her dive light.

It was the sunlight pouring into the water that eventually told Amy she had reached the outer pool. The water was just as murky, but the murkiness was not the endless darkness of the cave interior. Amy found the original tie off point and surfaced. She knew without looking at the pressure gauge that there couldn't have been more than a few minutes worth of air left in her tank. A few seconds later Jed broke the surface beside her. Amy drew a deep, shaky breath.

"Jed Glaze, I have never been so terrified in all my life. Don't you ever, ever do anything like that again, do you hear me?"

"I hear you. I was just about to give you the same lecture." His mouth tilted at the corner as he raised his mask. "Let's get the hell out of this pool so we can go back to the house and yell at each other in comfort. There's no point making another try for the box now. It's probably going to take a day or two for this water to clear."

Chapter Sixteen

*T*he skeleton was swimming slowly, inexorably, toward Amy. Jed could see the blind intent in those empty eyes. The teeth were set in a mocking grin, and pale, boney fingers moved in a curious, paddling motion that drew the thing through the black water. The long leg bones drifted in the slow current.

Amy was trapped in an underwater shower of rock and debris. She couldn't move as Wyman's skeleton approached. Her legs were pinned. She was running out of air, and in another moment long, dead white fingers would close around her throat, choking off what remained of her waning air supply. Amy wasn't watching the swimming skeleton; her eyes were on Jed, silently pleading for help.

But Jed was also trapped, snarled in a deadly tangle of nylon line, regulator hoses and equipment straps. His weight belt had far too much lead in it. It was pulling him down, making it almost impossible for him to reach his knife so he could cut himself free and get to Amy.

He had to get to Amy, which meant he had to free himself first. But somehow he knew he couldn't untangle himself unless Amy helped him. And Amy was about to confront Wyman's skeleton.

"Jed! Jed, wake up. You're dreaming. Please wake up."

Jed came slowly out of the nightmare, aware of Amy's hands on his shoulders. He could hear her clear voice and the part of him that was still dreaming seized on the sound, seeking a way out of the murky, endlessly dark water of the cave passage.

"Come on, Jed, it's just a dream. Open your eyes and look at me."

Jed opened his eyes and found himself in Amy's moonlit bedroom. She was kneeling beside him on the bed, shaking him gently, talking to him. In the pale light he could read the concern in her eyes.

Jed blinked, groaned and sat up slowly. He forced himself to take a deep breath, aware of the perspiration on his skin. He was oddly embarrassed.

"Sorry about that," he muttered. He rubbed his eyes, trying to clear away the image of the skeleton reaching for Amy. "I must have read too much of your manuscript."

"*Private Demons?* When were you looking at that?"

"I read part of it before we left Caliph's Bay, and earlier today I glanced at some of the notes you've been making," he confessed. He leaned back against the pillows, willing away the last of the disturbing dream. He looked up at Amy. "Do you mind?"

"No, I'm just a little surprised. You never mentioned that you wanted to read it."

"Back in Caliph's Bay I read the last few pages the night you had that bad dream. I wanted to see if you'd written anything so unsettling that it actually gave you nightmares. But it wasn't your book that was causing the dreams, was it, Amy?"

She sighed and lay back down beside him. "No. If anything *Private Demons* was a way of trying to work out some of the anxiety. I doubt it was my book that gave you that nightmare, Jed. It was what happened this afternoon in that cave, wasn't it?"

"No, not exactly, although that was probably part of it." He searched quickly for a way of avoiding the discussion. "Remember we agreed once that sometimes it was better not to talk about bad dreams?"

She turned on her side, pillowing her head on her arm. Her gently tangled hair fell in a seductive curve over her shoulders. Jed had made love to her earlier and afterward she had put on her nightgown. He found her taste in night-wear amusing, as well as very appealing. She had a way of doing that, he realized. She was both sweet and sexy, inno-cent and seductive, gentle and spirited. And she had a woman's strength, the kind of inner strength that a man could depend on. Jed felt his body begin to tighten in a familiar sexual awareness. As usual, he wanted to both pro-tect her and ravish her.

Amy seemed oblivious of the subtle change in him. Her mind was clearly on other things. "I've been thinking about what happened in that cave."

"Don't," he advised.

"I can't help it. You may be able to put certain things out of your mind, but I can't. Tell me the truth, Jed. Was it my fault?"

"The slide?" He turned his head on the pillow and looked into her clear, anxious eyes. "No, it definitely was not your fault. It wasn't my fault, either, as a matter of fact. It was just one of those things that can happen in an underwater cave. It's one of the reasons cave diving is so damn hazard-ous. Whatever you do, don't start blaming yourself for what happened today." He was silent for a moment, then said aloud what he had been thinking most of the afternoon and evening. "You cut it very close, though, Amy."

"You mean when I was swimming through that narrow opening into the passage? That's what I was afraid of. I don't think I hit anything or brushed the tank against the wall of the cave, but maybe I did. Maybe that's what started the slide."

He rolled over, pinning her beneath him and gently cutting off her self-incriminating words with a palm over her mouth. Above his hand her eyes were wide and questioning. "That's not what I meant when I said you cut it close. I meant that you hung around a little too long trying to dig me out. You used up your entire safety margin of air. You were into the third of the supply you were supposed to save for the return trip. Another couple of minutes and you might not have made it back out."

She pushed his hand off her mouth. "I couldn't leave you there," she said simply. "I was afraid you were trapped by the slide. I had no way of knowing whether you could get free to swim back to that ledge."

He stared down at her, reading the truth in her eyes. "Ah, Amy," he muttered thickly, "what have you done to me?"

"Done to you? I haven't done anything to you."

"That's what you think." He bent to brush his mouth against hers. He arched his body, letting her feel his growing arousal.

She smiled tremulously and wrapped her arms around his neck. "I get the impression you want to change the subject."

"How did you guess?"

"A woman's intuition."

"Is that right?" He pressed himself against her again, liking the feel of her soft, warm thigh. "I'm impressed." He kissed her slowly, deepening the caress with a slow intimacy until she willingly parted her lips.

When he heard her faint moan he felt his own excitement and anticipation quicken. She was so responsive, Jed marveled, not for the first time. So incredibly responsive. He'd never had a woman respond to him the way Amy did. He was getting addicted to her and he knew it. Sooner or later he was going to have to confront all the ramifications of that addiction.

But right now he just wanted to make love to her, sheathe himself in her clinging warmth, find the sweet peace of mind he always found in the aftermath.

Slowly Jed withdrew from her mouth and began to trail a hot, damp stream of kisses down her throat to her breasts.

"Oh, Jed," Amy whispered, her fingers twisting in his hair as she lifted herself against him. She sighed when he teased the peak of one breast with his tongue and then used his lips to gently tug her nipple erect.

He flattened a hand on her stomach and slid his fingers down through the soft, curling tangle between her legs. "You're getting warm and soft already," he breathed.

"You're not soft." Her voice was filled with gentle, seductive wonder. She ran her palms over the contours of his shoulders and down his back. Then she touched him more intimately. "Not soft at all."

"Not around you," he agreed. Already he was aching with the force of his desire. It was a sweet, hot ache that could be tolerated only because he knew eventually it would be satisfied. In the meantime it left him feeling lightheaded. He trailed the string of nibbling kisses lower, past her cute little navel and down her thigh. Carefully he pried apart her legs with his hand. When he found the exquisitely sensitive center of her excitement with his lips, Amy gasped. Her nails sank into his skin and her legs shifted with a new restlessness.

She tried to draw back slightly from the intimate contact, as if she wasn't certain it was what she wanted. But Jed felt the instant response of her body and knew she did want it. She just needed a little convincing. He was more than willing to convince. He curved his hands around her lush derriere and anchored her while he continued to tantalize her in new ways. Amy's slender, supple body tightened and her cry of mounting pleasure was a siren's song in his ears.

"Jed, that feels so . . . so good. I can't stand it."

"Show me how good it feels, sweetheart." He continued to tease her with his tongue and slowly inserted one finger into the dew-filled channel. Amy went wild beneath him, pleading for a release that he knew was soon going to swamp her senses.

When it came, the tiny convulsions tightening her around his finger, Jed gave up trying to restrain his own raging need. He flowed up along her body, driving himself into her softness just in time to feel the last of her release pull him deeply into her. His own reaction was almost immediate. In another few seconds he was arching savagely against her, calling her name aloud as he found his own satisfaction.

Amy clung to him as he came slowly down to earth. When Jed opened his eyes he found her smiling dreamily up at him.

"You were asking what I do to you," she drawled. "I'd say it's more a question of what you do to me."

He shook his head, too pleasantly exhausted to argue. Reluctantly he withdrew from her warm body and settled himself beside her. "Go back to sleep, honey. We both need the rest. In case you've forgotten, we had a rough day."

"I haven't forgotten," she replied, the sensual amusement drained from her voice.

Jed cursed himself for bringing up the subject. He stroked her hair in an effort to soothe her. "Go back to sleep," he said again.

"Jed, I was thinking about that skeleton," she said slowly.

"That's the last thing you need to think about tonight." His words were a little rougher than necessary, and Jed knew it was because the scenes from his nightmare were still hovering at the back of his mind. "Forget the skeleton. It's twenty-five years old and it can't hurt you now." He wouldn't let it hurt her, he swore silently.

"What if someone else ever found it?"

"No one's going to spend much time investigating a twenty-five-year-old death, Amy. And no one's going to automatically assume it's Wyman. He went down at sea, remember? No one doubts the story. If anyone ever did find the skeleton, it would be assumed that some poor diver snuck into the caves and got lost. He managed to find the ledge but there was no way he could swim back out."

Amy shuddered in his arms. "What a horrible thought."

He smiled wryly. "I just made that little scenario up on the spot. Not bad for an engineer of somewhat limited imagination, huh?"

"Maybe you're right. Maybe you have read too much of *Private Demons*."

"Could be." He stroked her gently until she fell asleep.

But it was a long time before Jed found refuge in sleep. He lay awake, staring up at the ceiling and thinking about what the woman in his arms was doing to him. His world was shifting on its axis and he didn't know what to do about it.

For the past eight years he had gone from one assignment to the next, never looking back or too far ahead. It was like living in an outtake from a full-length feature film—the past and future portions of the film went on without him. Cutter told him the work he did was important, and to some extent Jed accepted that. They told him there was a need for his kind of soldiering in a world that was in many ways still ruled by the ancient laws of the jungle. Jed was a natural predator. In some ways. He had a talent for the kind of work the agency wanted him to do. From the beginning his senses had adapted easily to the skills necessary for his survival. Too easily, perhaps.

At first he had been motivated by a burning need for justice. He would have done whatever was necessary to get the man who had killed Andy. But somehow he had become trapped by the lethal success of his first mission. There had been nothing at home to keep him from taking another assignment. And another one after that. Eventually the work became the focal point of his world.

Until Amy entered the outtake he was supposed to be inhabiting by himself.

Amy had befriended him. Then she had become his lover. And then he had realized she needed him.

The closer he got to Amy, the more involved he got, the more Jed realized that she was going to stretch the narrow perimeters of his well-defined world. He wasn't sure what would happen when the bubble of isolation in which he lived finally burst.

He was trapped. He had to get free so he could protect Amy. But only Amy could free him. He was trapped.

Jed went to sleep with the twisted circle of problems still unresolved.

The phone was ringing the next time Jed opened his eyes. He squinted briefly at the morning light pouring into the room and listened to the next jarring summons from the phone. Beside him, Amy stirred and stretched.

"Phone," she mumbled into the pillow.

"Yeah."

"Better get it," she said encouragingly as she snuggled down under the sheet.

"I take it I'm elected?" Jed eyed her indulgently as he got up, reached for his pants and padded barefoot toward the door.

"Right. You're elected."

But she was yawning and he knew she would be up in another few minutes. Amy was a morning person. It was one of any number of her traits he was discovering since they had arrived on Orleana. Fortunately, he was also a morning person. Jed fastened his pants as he went down the stairs. He managed to capture the phone on what must have been the sixth or seventh ring.

"Say hey, Glaze, I was just about to give up on you. How's it going out there in paradise?"

Jed yawned. "Hello, Faxon. It's about time you called."

"Geez, all I ever get are complaints."

"Some people are born to collect complaints."

"Uh huh. And some people are born to hand them out, I suppose. Well, we also serve who only sit and stare at a computer screen. Are you interested in learning a few pertinent and amusing facts about one Michael J. Wyman or would you rather spend the government's telephone money complaining?"

"It's a temptation to waste a little government money, but I'll take option number one." Jed walked toward the window, trailing the long telephone cord behind him. "Give me what you've got on Wyman."

"Well, to begin with, he's supposed to be dead."

"I knew that much."

Faxon was obviously crestfallen. "You did? Why didn't you tell me? You didn't bother to mention that little fact when you called. Do you have any idea of how hard it was to start pulling records when I didn't even know the guy was dead?"

"Sorry, Faxon. My mistake."

"That's why you're in fieldwork rather than internal operations, I suppose," Faxon grumbled.

"You're probably right. Fill me in on the rest. I'm waiting with baited breath." A small sound on the stairway made him turn around. Amy was walking down the steps, pulling her kimono sash tight as she did. She was listening intently. She looked so good in the morning, he thought.

Faxon's voice was a little thin over the line. "For starters he was, as you said, partners with Slater in a West Coast aerospace firm that had a lot of government contracts. Some of the work was classified as confidential and some was secret. Clearances were run on a lot of the staff, including Wyman and Slater. Do you know how tough it was to dig up those old clearance records, Glaze?"

"No, but I'm sure you'd tell me if I gave you the opportunity. However, I'm not going to be that dumb. Just give me the results."

"That's another problem with you field types. You're only

interested in the final data. You don't give a damn about what it takes to retrieve it."

"Tell Cutter I said you should get a raise."

"I'll do that. By the way, Cutter has a message for you. Remind me to give it to you before we hang up."

Jed was suddenly irritated. "This was supposed to be between you and me, Faxon. It's private business. Did you tell Cutter what I was asking you to do?"

"Nope. Just told him you'd called to check in and say you were healing. That's it, I swear. Why? Is this stuff that sensitive?"

"No, but it's no longer government business and I'd just as soon keep the Feds out of it. Go on with the report."

"Well," Faxon continued, his voice businesslike, "Slater passed his clearance with flying colors. Interesting military record, by the way. Seems he did some small jobs for Intelligence while he was stationed in the Pacific. Nothing major, but he had some training and he was reliable. Wyman, on the other hand, was a different story."

Jed cocked a brow at Amy as she came toward him. "I'm listening."

"The guy was brilliant. Probably a genius. He was also a sports freak. Sailing, scuba diving, skiing, flying, surfing, you name it. According to the clearance report, he was lucky in love, too. Never lacked lady friends. Had a problem with money, though."

"What kind of problem?"

"Chronic lack thereof. But then, who isn't a little short?" Faxon asked generously. "In Wyman's case it was cause for some minor questioning. The operative in charge of conducting the clearance raised the issue as a potential source of concern. Sailboats, private planes and ladies didn't come cheap even then, I guess. The matter was discussed, but it was noted that there was no real problem at the time. If Wyman wanted to live at the end of his credit limit, that was his worry."

"All right, he got his clearance, so I assume there were no major questions raised about risky associations. No drinking problems? Drugs?"

"Not from what I can tell. As you say, he got his clearance."

"Then give me what you've got on the private side," Jed said. "What about women?"

"I didn't get any help from the clearance report," Faxon said, "but I am not a man to give up easily. I knew you'd want service above and beyond the call of duty."

"Did I get it?"

Faxon groaned. "Unfortunately, I owed you an especially big favor. Yeah, you got your service. Based on the old addresses and other data I got off the clearance form, I went looking for the usual things: birth certificates, marriage licenses, military service records."

"Any marriages?" Jed asked suddenly.

"No, but there was a rather long-term association with a woman named Vivien Anne Renner. She died a little over a year ago."

"Children?"

"She had a son."

Jed closed his eyes, thinking carefully. "Name?"

"First name is Daniel. He'd be, let's see . . ." Faxon hummed to himself as he worked on his computer. "Twenty-six now. By the way, Wyman is listed as the father on the birth certificate, but Daniel apparently uses his mother's last name. As I mentioned earlier, his parents were never married. Judging from the date of Wyman's death, it looks like the boy probably never knew his dad."

"What happened to Vivien Renner?"

"Booze and pills."

"And her son?"

"He works in a stock brokerage firm in L.A. That's about all I've got on him. I wasn't sure how far you wanted me to go in that direction."

"Anything else on Wyman?" Jed braced himself with one palm against the windowsill. Amy was standing beside him, studying his expression. He could feel her frustration at hearing only one side of the conversation.

"I'm not sure," Faxon said slowly.

"What the hell's that supposed to mean?"

"It means I'm not sure. I told you he got his clearance without any real problem, but the cross-referencing program turned up a mention of something called the Orleana Project. That clicked because that's the name of the island where you're staying. I tried running a query on the project, but so far I haven't gotten any answers. It looks like it's non-computer accessible archive material."

"What's that mean?" Jed asked impatiently.

"It means that no one's ever entered the material into the computer data bases I'm searching." Faxon was obviously disgusted at the very notion of anything remaining in hard-copy. In his dream world, all data—however obscure—was in a computer data base somewhere and could, therefore, be accessed by anyone blessed with his superior capabilities. "It *means* that the stuff's still in hardcopy somewhere in some-body's central files."

"Whose central files?"

"Ah, the sixty-four dollar question. It's going to take

some digging. The computer is a nice, neat, silent way to ask questions, but once I have to start going through real people I won't be able to guarantee privacy. I thought I'd better let you make the decision. You want me to make some inquiries?"

Jed hesitated. "Not yet. I will if I have to, but I'd rather avoid it if I can. Go ahead and give me Cutter's message."

"Our esteemed high honcho boss wants me to inform you that he's found out what went wrong on your last assignment."

Jed grunted. "Better late than never."

"I understand things were a wee bit close for you last time out." Faxon cleared his throat. "I assume everything vital is still functioning?"

Jed glanced at Amy. "I get by. Give me the rest of the message, Faxon."

"Sure. In a nutshell, Cutter has a lead on the guy who sold you out to those two jokers who got you in that alley. He says he wants you to go in and make sure we've tagged the right guy. Once you've made sure, he wants the situation cleaned up. He wants all this done ASAP, naturally. The man's a menace. Cutter wants to know when you're going to be ready to finish the job you started."

A curious tension unfurled in Jed. Suddenly he couldn't take his eyes off Amy's questioning gaze. She couldn't possibly have overheard what Faxon had said, but he knew she sensed the change in the conversation. She knew that what Jed was talking about now concerned his job.

"Tell Cutter—" Jed began, but Faxon interrupted to finish his message.

"Cutter also said to tell you that this doesn't just involve you. The guy who sold you also made another sale last week."

"Who?"

"Ramsey and Dickens."

"Shit." Jed gripped the phone more tightly. "Either of them make it out?"

"No. They're both dead. Cutter thought you'd be interested."

"Cutter's right." Jed's eyes were still on Amy. And he was trapped.

Amy, what am I going to do? What have you done to me?

"So, do I tell the old man you'll be back at work a little sooner than planned?"

"Tell Cutter I'll sell the salesman for him, but I need a few more days in paradise."

"Cutter will be thrilled," Faxon assured him dryly. "In the meantime, do you want anything more from me?"

"No thanks, Faxon. Go play with your computer." Jed quietly hung up the phone.

Amy was on him before the receiver clicked in the cradle. "That was your friend? The one who was going to check on Wyman for us?"

Jed nodded. "That was him."

"What about that comment about Cutter? And what's a salesman?"

"Never mind that. The important thing is that Wyman had a son."

That distracted her. "A son?" Her mouth opened in amazement.

"Right. Wyman was apparently sleeping with a woman named Vivien Renner. Shortly before his death, she gave birth to Daniel. Michael Wyman is listed as the father on

Renner's birth certificate, although Vivien gave the boy her own last name."

"The blond floozy!"

"What?"

"Rosie mentioned a blond woman who tried to seduce my father. I'll bet it was this Vivien Renner," Amy said. "I'll bet Wyman put her up to it for some reason. Probably just to cause trouble. Rosie said Wyman was jealous of my father. Rosie also said Wyman was the kind who liked to cause mischief." She turned around and began to pace the length of the living room. "So Renner is Wyman's son. And after all these years he shows up on Orleana. Something of a coincidence, I'd say."

"Uh, yes, it struck me the same way," Jed said wryly.

"What do we do now?"

"We get that damn box out of the cave," Jed said.

"But what about the silt that's clouding the water?"

"We'll monitor it. As soon as it's reasonably clear, we're going in. In the meantime we're going to buy ourselves a little protection." He reached for the phone.

"What kind of protection?"

"What's the number of Hank and Rosie's tavern?"

She gave it to him and then demanded, "What are you going to do?"

"I'm going to ask Hank to do me a favor." Jed was already dialing. The phone was answered on the other end before Amy could ask any more questions. "Hank? It's Jed Glaze. I need a favor."

"Sure," Hank promised easily. "Like I told you once, any friend of the Slaters is a friend of mine."

"All I'm asking is that you keep an eye on Dan Renner

and his friend Guthrie. Give me a call if they leave town, will you?"

"That should be easy enough. What's up?"

"I'm not sure, but I'm still not convinced that Kelso was right in thinking Vaden was working alone the other night. I just thought it would be wise to keep tabs on Renner and Guthrie."

"You got it. I'll give you a holler if they leave town."

"Thanks, Hank, I appreciate it. Does Kelso still have Vaden under wraps?"

"Far as I know. He said he could keep him locked up for a few days on drunk and disorderly charges."

"Good. I'll talk to you later, Hank." Jed replaced the receiver again and looked at Amy. "Let's go check the water in the caves."

"Before breakfast?"

"I'm in a hurry," he told her.

"I noticed," she grumbled. But she turned toward the stairs to go get dressed. On the first step she paused and turned once more to ask, "But what about Cutter and that business of selling a salesman?"

"It's nothing. I'll explain it all later. Move, Amy."

She moved, but it didn't do much good. The water in the caves didn't clear until late that evening.

Chapter Seventeen

"You don't think this could wait until morning?" Amy asked as she buckled her weight belt. She wasn't expecting Jed to agree to a delay, and she wasn't disappointed.

Jed pulled on his diving gloves. "No. Things are coming together too fast. I don't like it. I just wish to hell we'd been able to get that box out yesterday. Having Michael Wyman's son on the island is not conducive to my peace of mind."

"Do you think Guthrie's working with him? Vaden, too?" Amy was only partially aware of his answers. She stood looking at the night shrouded entrance pool, thinking it looked very much the way it had that night in October. The moonlight was fretful and scattered, just as it had been eight months before. A storm was gathering out at sea.

"Being an engineer, I'm inclined to assume and design for the worst possible case. Whatever can go wrong will go wrong. Yeah, I think Vaden, Guthrie and Renner are all connected. Vaden, at least, is tucked away in jail. And Hank's keeping an eye on Guthrie and Renner. With any luck they won't move on us until we try to leave the island. Why should they do the hard work if we're willing to do it for them?"

"If you're right, how *are* we going to get off the island?"

"Very carefully." He picked up his fins. "Are you ready?" Automatically he checked her equipment one last time.

"I'm ready." She wouldn't think about how much this night dive reminded her of the experience last October. After all, Amy thought as she clambered down over the rocks and into the pool, once inside the caves it was night twenty-four hours a day. She could always tell herself the sun was shining brightly just outside the entrance.

Beside her in the water Jed put on his fins and adjusted his mask. "Let's go."

He was all business, Amy realized as she turned on her light and dived under the pool surface. He had been all business all day, in fact. There had been no light moments, no teasing, no time set aside for sketching bird cages. Jed had walked down to the pool to check the clearing water every hour. In between checks he had been nearly silent. Amy had sensed his controlled impatience, his icy tension that seemed to sizzle just under the surface. He reminded her of a large hunting cat pacing its den, waiting to go out on a kill. She wondered if this was the way Jed behaved when he was on one of his terrible assignments.

They passed through the gaping cavern entrance and angled down to follow the passageway. The beam of her dive light revealed water that had cleared almost completely. Amy kept one hand in contact with the nylon line that was spinning out behind Jed and wondered again about the conversation she had overheard that morning.

Faxon, she knew, was the computer whiz, the one who had pulled up the information on Wyman and Renner from the data bank. She seemed to recall Cutter's name from the first telephone conversation. Jed had told Faxon to give Cutter the message that he was almost ready to go back to work. Cutter must be Jed's boss.

Jed had promised to "sell the salesman" for Cutter. Amy

had seen the chilled, remote look on his face when he had made the promise. She didn't want to think about what the words might mean.

Jed was right: Things were closing in. One of those things was his job. When this was all over, Amy thought, she would be forced to watch him return to the pattern of frequent absences, phone calls from the airport asking her to pick him up because he was too injured to drive, a future that he never discussed and for which he never made plans.

It was ironic, Amy thought, that Jed was rapidly taking steps to restore her own future to her. He had broken the time loop with the past in which she had been caught. But nothing had changed for him. Amy knew she would give everything she possessed to free him as he had freed her.

Maybe he didn't want to be free. Jed was well adapted to the way he lived. The potential for violence didn't seem to bother him. He didn't question his own lack of interest in the future. As far as she could tell he tuned out everything but the present. He seemed content to keep their affair relegated to a separate portion of his life.

Who was she to try to change his world?

Amy swam cautiously around a collection of delicate stalactites hanging from the ceiling, following the white nylon line. At least thinking about Jed kept her from dwelling on what had happened before in the cave.

Jed paused briefly when they reached the fall of gravel that had trapped him the previous day. He played the light over the debris and Amy saw that there was still room to squeeze through the narrow entrance into the corridor that led to the skeleton's cave. She shuddered at the memory of hollow eyes and teeth that had been grinning for twenty-five years. Amy was relieved when Jed turned to swim further along the main corridor.

The passageway twisted to the right a few feet beyond the gravel fall. The curve in the corridor struck a familiar chord in Amy's brain. Jed stopped to tie off the line. He looked at Amy, silently asking if the scene appeared familiar. She shone the light on the walls of the cavern and nodded uncertainly. This had to be the right direction, but her memories of the cave's layout were vague.

But as soon as she followed Jed around the curve in the corridor, a few more stray recollections clicked into place. She kicked forward a little harder and touched Jed's leg. He glanced back inquiringly and she signaled vigorously that this section was familiar.

When they aimed the dive lights on the side wall of the cavern they saw the opening that led into another branch tunnel. Amy's breath sounded momentarily harsher in her regulator as she realized it was the corridor where she had left the box. She pointed to it and Jed obediently swam forward.

The metal box was sitting right where she had left it eight months before. It was nestled into a small gouge in the cave wall, sharing the space with a cluster of tiny blind fish. The pale creatures scattered as Jed put his gloved hand into the opening and pulled out the box.

Amy stared at it, all the terrifying images she associated with these caves crowding back into her mind. Two men, Wyman and LePage, had died because of this box. In that moment it was easy to believe that one of them, Wyman, still haunted the caves, protecting his treasure.

Because of this box she had almost been killed. Because of this box she had looked into the staring eyes of a dead man. Because of this box the past had intruded on the serenity of Orleana Island.

It took all of Amy's willpower to respond to Jed's rough demand for attention. When she met his eyes through the mask she understood he was ordering her to carry the box out of the caves.

Belatedly she realized there was no other practical alternative. Jed had his hands full with the dive light and the reel.

She carried the damn thing in, she could carry it back out, Amy thought. She took it from Jed and turned around to leave the side corridor ahead of him. A few minutes later she was in the main passageway, aware of Jed swimming strongly behind her, reeling in the line.

The box wasn't really very heavy. How much could six emeralds, a pile of letters and a few damning photographs weigh? But Amy felt as though she were holding a live grenade. She retreated eagerly along the white line, anxious to get out of the cave before the thing in her hand exploded.

Amy rounded the deep bend in the main passage and found herself blinded by the full glare of another dive light in the distance.

For an instant she couldn't figure out what it meant to be staring into an oncoming light. It was not unlike being in a railroad tunnel and encountering the glare of a train light. Full realization set in just as Jed yanked violently on her leg.

Startled, Amy glanced back, wondering what he wanted. She tried to point out the oncoming diver and then realized he was well aware of the intruder. When he yanked again she realized he was urging her through the narrow entrance that led to the skeleton's cave.

The last thing she wanted to do was return to that morbid

cavern, but Amy quickly made another discovery about her friend and lover: When Jed Glaze gave a command, he expected to be obeyed. Even as her mind protested, Amy found herself swimming through the small hole in the wall.

Half expecting to elicit another dangerous shower of gravel, she was vastly relieved when nothing happened. When she glanced back she saw that Jed was following her. He urged her forward, handing her the reel of line because she was now in front. He took the box from her.

Unable to think of any convincing arguments under the circumstances, Amy grimly swam forward into the darkness. She began watching for the flat, silvery mirror that indicated the air pocket.

How far away had the other diver been? She'd seen nothing but the glare of his light, and distances were tricky to judge underwater. Objects were magnified by about twenty-five percent, making them seem closer than they actually were.

Still, she calculated that they had a little time before the other diver found the point where the nylon line vanished into the branching passage. Jed obviously wanted to spend that time getting to the only source of air inside the flooded caves.

It made sense, Amy thought, but she dreaded the prospect of getting up on the ledge where the skeleton had been all those years.

She found the air pocket and surfaced. Jed was beside her at once.

"Up on the ledge," he snapped. "Hurry."

"What are you going to do?" she asked breathlessly as she swam toward the skeleton's resting place.

"Prepare a welcoming committee."

"Jed, who is it?"

"How the hell should I know? Guthrie, maybe. Or Renner."

"But Hank was going to keep an eye on both of them." Her hand rammed painfully into the cave wall just under the ledge. "Uh, we're here. I take it you want me to climb out?"

"As fast as possible. Move, lady." He was already lifting the box out of the water and setting it on the ledge.

Amy heard something crunch as the metal box struck the rock. Probably just a little loose gravel, she told herself bracingly, not bones. Taking a deep breath she put her light on the rocky surface and reached up to plant both palms on the ledge.

"Watch your head." Jed gave her a strong boost that lifted her high out of the water.

Amy closed her eyes in brief horror as she found herself looking down at the rib cage of the skeleton. The glare from her dive light shone up through what had once been the chest cavity, revealing the rows of bones.

She managed to turn herself into a sitting position on the very edge of the ledge, her legs dangling over the side into the water. Jed heaved himself up beside her and casually kicked the bones out of the way to make a space for himself.

Amy was quietly grateful when the skeleton disappeared into the darkness at the back of the ledge.

"Now what?" she whispered.

"Now we turn out the lights. No sense pinpointing our location for him. Ready?"

"No, but I never will be, so you might as well do it." Amy braced herself for the dense blackness that descended immediately.

The darkness inside the cave was like no other darkness

on earth. There were no shadows, no tiny chinks of light, no hint of a moon, just total, endless *nothing*.

Amy groped for Jed's hand and found it just as a tiny glimmer of light appeared underwater far down the passageway. The other diver had entered the side passage.

"Get your feet out of the water," Jed muttered softly, rising to his knees on the ledge.

He felt her changing position and knew she was curling herself into a kneeling pose. It wasn't easy maneuvering out of the water with the full weight of the diving equipment bearing down on them. Amy was wearing nearly twenty pounds of lead in the weight belt alone. The additional burden of the tank and assorted gear made a very uncomfortable package out of the water.

He knew what it had cost her to get up onto the ledge with the skeleton, but she hadn't hesitated. Amy was good in a crisis he realized, not for the first time. She did what had to be done and worried about the emotional trauma later. He'd worked with too many men who came apart during the actual crisis not to appreciate her inner fortitude. Amy was a good friend to have at his back.

Jed watched the dive light flicker back and forth in a sweeping arc under the surface. He eased his knife out of the sheath on his forearm. The timing would have to be just right. He wondered if the intruder would see the silvery mirror that indicated the air pocket. With any luck the bastard wouldn't make the discovery and realize what it might mean until it was too late. It would seem to whoever was swimming down below that his quarry had simply disappeared in the dead end passage. Beside him Jed heard Amy draw in her breath. He could feel her tension as well as his own and knew she had figured out what he planned to do. He heard a soft noise in the darkness and realized Amy had taken her own diving knife out of its sheath.

"If you use it," he whispered, "just be sure you get a look at your victim first. I'm tired of being stuck with knives."

"Oh, Jed, have a little faith."

He grinned briefly in the darkness and then shushed her as the light under the water came closer. His silent laughter vanished. It had to be now.

Jed adjusted his mouthpiece and mask. Then, using a giant stride that would take him out and over the intruder, he jumped into the water.

The other diver heard the splash and tried frantically to dodge out of the way. Jed saw the dive light swing crazily upward to pin him but it was too late. He was already on top of the man, his knife slicing through the regulator hose. A furious bubbling ensued and the intruder panicked.

The dive light spun lazily in the water and dropped to the floor of the cave. The beam shone uselessly along the bottom, leaving the two men to conclude the battle in darkness.

Jed swam back out of the way of the frantically struggling diver. He used the pale gleam of light on the floor of the cave to orient himself toward the surface, then kicked out swiftly. "Turn on a light," he called to Amy when his face was above water.

Instantly she did so, sweeping the beam along the top of the water.

Jed swam toward her, reaching up. "Let me have it."

She thrust the dive light into his fingers and he whirled to pick out the writhing diver. Whether by luck or because of the new light, the intruder had found the air pocket. His head bobbed out of the water just as Jed swung the beam toward him. He was gasping desperately for air.

"Bastard!" Vaden hissed.

Jed realized Vaden was still clinging to something under the water. He flicked off the light and shoved himself abruptly to one side just as Vaden fired the speargun under the surface. The spear hurtled uselessly against the wall of the cave, missing Jed's thigh by a reasonably healthy margin.

"Dammit, I'm getting tired of people trying to take potshots at the source of my love life." Jed dove deep, switched on the light and swam up behind Vaden. Keeping his grip on the light, he circled the man's throat with his arm and let Vaden feel the point of the knife against his neck. Vaden stopped struggling.

"I shoulda killed you the other night, Glaze."

"You weren't fast enough. I hope you work cheap, Vaden, because your employer sure isn't getting his money's worth out of you." Jed gave him a push toward the ledge. "Get out of the way, Amy. We're going to show Vaden our little picnic spot."

She flicked on another dive light and edged aside as far as she could. "What are we going to do with him?"

"Leave him here with Boney while we see what's going on out front. Get into the water, Amy. Bring the box and the reel with you."

She did as he instructed, sliding down over the edge of the rocky ledge. When she was clear Jed methodically stripped Vaden's knife and gear, dropping the equipment to the bottom of the cave.

"Okay, Vaden, your little swim is over. Get up on the ledge.

"What the hell do you think you're doing, Glaze? You can't leave me here."

"What's to stop me?" Jed asked with casual interest.

"You stupid bastard, don't you realize it's all over for you?" Vaden hissed as he crawled onto the ledge. "They'll get you when you leave the caves."

"You'd better hope they don't. If I don't come back for you, you won't be leaving here at all. There's no way in hell you could hold your breath long enough to make it to the main corridor. You'll probably drown somewhere between here and the entrance to this passage. Now, why don't you tell me exactly what I'll be facing out front? Try to keep the details reasonably accurate if you want me to come back for you."

Vaden, as Jed had guessed, was at heart a practical man. He valued his own skin above everything else. After a few seconds he started talking. The information was given grudgingly, but it was supplied. Under the circumstances, Jed was inclined to believe most of what he was being told.

"Guthrie's out there with Renner," Vaden muttered.

"Weapons?" Jed asked.

"Guthrie's got my .357 Mag and he's good. Renner's got a cute little Beretta, but I wouldn't worry about it too much. He just bought it for show, I think. Probably thought it looked good with his Italian designer sportcoat. Look, Glaze, you and me, we could work something out. Let me have the woman's tank and I'll go out of here with you. Between the two of us we can take Guthrie and Renner. Leave the woman here. You can come back for her later."

Jed smiled faintly. "Sorry, but in a situation like this, I'd rather have someone I can trust backing me up. You know how it is, Vaden. I hope you're not afraid of the dark." He turned around. "Okay, Amy, let's get going."

"Goddamn! Wait a minute. You can't leave me here without a light," Vaden yelled.

"Your light's on the bottom. If you want it, I suppose you could try diving for it." Jed glanced down and saw the faint beam shining in the watery depths. Then he signaled to Amy. She handed him the reel and ducked under the surface, the box and dive light in one hand.

When they reached the entrance to the main passageway, Jed instructed her silently to leave the box there. She hesitated a fraction of a moment and then obeyed. When it was safely settled near the gravel fall, they swam on out into the main corridor and headed toward the entrance pool. Jed took the lead, handing the reel to Amy. He wanted his hands free in case Guthrie had decided to see what was keeping his partner.

When they were almost at the entrance, Jed turned off his light. Behind him Amy took the cue and did the same. They coasted forward along the nylon line, waiting for the point where they could lift their heads above water.

Jed reached it first and surfaced silently. Amy swam up beside him. The darkness was not so intense here because they were only a few feet from the entrance. Jed listened to the light, spattering sound of raindrops on the pool's surface. The storm was drifting closer to the island. It wouldn't last long but it could become very intense for a short period of time.

In the meantime, the rain might add an extra dimension of

cover. The light, soothing noise was interrupted by Renner's harsh voice.

"What the hell's keeping Vaden? He should have found them and taken care of Glaze by now. You guys are supposed to be such hot shit. I'm paying you enough. But all I get is incompetence."

"Settle down, Renner. Give him time. We don't know how far into the caves he had to go before he found Glaze and the woman." Guthrie sounded concerned in spite of his calming words.

"This whole thing is blowing wide open," Renner muttered. "I should have handled it myself."

"You are handling it yourself, remember? You're giving the orders," Guthrie mocked.

"Dammit, who is Glaze, anyway?" Renner asked. From the sound of his voice, it wasn't the first time he'd put the question to Guthrie.

"I've told you, I don't know who he is. My guess is that he knew LePage and got his information from him."

"That's what I've been figuring, but now I'm not so sure." Renner spoke slowly, as if he were mulling over the details of his assumption and found something lacking.

"What else could he be but another free-lance who got a line on the emeralds through LePage?" Guthrie demanded. "Stop worrying about it. When this is all over he'll be out of the picture. He's probably out of it by now, come to that. I've told you Vaden can take care of himself."

A flashlight moved along the edge of the pool. Jed caught a glimpse of a shadow behind it and realized Renner was pacing agitatedly around the water's edge.

"What if Vaden's already taken care of Glaze and has decided to open the box and hide the emeralds somewhere inside the cave?" Renner mused angrily. "I can see it now. He swims out of there with the box, then he acts astounded when we open the thing and find out it's empty."

Jed shoved Amy gently back out of the way and then moved a little closer to the mouth of the cave. He was careful to keep himself out of sight behind a shield of rock. If Guthrie or Renner shone the flashlights in his direction they wouldn't be able to see more than a couple of feet past the entrance, but Jed didn't want to take unnecessary chances.

As Renner's agitation increased so did Guthrie's. They continued to toss verbal barbs at each other while they waited for Vaden.

"You should have gone in there with him," Renner grumbled.

"We agreed that someone who knows what he's doing should watch the entrance. It's not like Vaden's unarmed. He's got the speargun."

"You told me the range on the speargun is short, six or eight feet maybe," Renner reminded him. "Beyond that, you said, it's not very accurate and it doesn't have much punch."

"Six or eight feet is enough to give Vaden the advantage. Don't forget, Vaden and I saw Glaze go into the water earlier. He wasn't carrying anything except the light and the reel."

"But there are two of them down there. Glaze and the woman."

"Believe me," Guthrie drawled, "the woman isn't going to be any problem. Glaze is the only one we have to worry about."

"Okay," Renner snapped, "so I'm starting to worry already. So what the hell are you going to do? Vaden's been gone too long and you know it. He must have run into trouble."

There was silence instead of the usual mocking reassurance from Guthrie. Then he said slowly, "By now Glaze and the woman must be nearly out of air, assuming Vaden hasn't finished them off. They were in that cave a good fifteen or twenty minutes before Vaden went in after them. I know they only have single tanks. I saw 'em myself."

"What happens now?" Renner hissed. "Do we just wait for Vaden to reappear?"

Guthrie moved along the edge of the pool. Jed could see the shifting pattern of shadows. A few more minutes crept past. Jed saw Guthrie aim the beam of his flashlight at his wristwatch.

"I think you're right," Guthrie announced calmly. "Vaden should have been out by now. And Glaze and the woman have run out of air. Maybe Vaden blew the whole thing, just like you said. Maybe Glaze got him. That means all three are dead."

"And the box is just sitting down there." Renner swung the flashlight in a savage arc toward the cavern entrance as if willing Vaden and the box to appear. "We've got to get that box, Guthrie. I've waited too long, made too many plans. I want it. I'm not leaving this island until I get it."

"I'll go down and take a look."

Jed listened to the clink of equipment as Guthrie strapped on his diving gear. He edged farther back into the shadowed cave entrance. He sensed Amy waiting silently behind him and wished he could tell her what was going to happen next. But he didn't dare utter a sound.

There was silence from the two men at the pool's edge.

The rain began to spatter more heavily on the water. Then came the sound of Guthrie making his way into the pool.

"Guthrie!" Renner called just as the other man went into the water. "No tricks, you hear me? I'll be waiting out here and I've got the Beretta."

"Don't shoot off your big toe with it," Guthrie advised. He disappeared under the surface.

Jed sank down into the water, gathering a length of the nylon line into a loop. He waited, watching as Guthrie's light flicked on and cut a narrow path through the gloom. In another few seconds the other man would be swimming past Jed's hiding place.

The light moved through the water until its source was directly in front of Jed. He moved out behind Guthrie to drop the loop around the man's throat.

It was like landing a thrashing, heaving, desperate shark, but it was all over very quickly. Not quite as quickly as it would have been if he'd used his knife, Jed decided, but he resisted the temptation now for the same reason he had resisted it earlier with Vaden. The simple truth was that Jed didn't want Amy to watch him get his hands bloody. Jed waited until Guthrie went limp and then he pulled him to the surface. Guthrie groaned as Jed used the nylon to bind his hands behind him.

"Hold his head out of the water, Amy, or he'll drown."

"Guthrie!" Renner's startled shout was evidence enough that he realized something had gone wrong. The flashlight played erratically around the cave entrance. "What's going on? Where are you?"

"Guthrie's a little tied up at the moment," Jed called back. "But I don't think we need to worry about him. We've got some business to discuss, you and I."

"Glaze? Where are you? Come on out and don't try any tricks. Where's the woman?"

"Amy and I are both here. But what really matters is that we're the only ones who know where the box is. I hear you sell stocks and bonds for a living. As it happens, I'm pretty good at dealing with salesmen. Interested in making a deal for the emeralds?"

Chapter Eighteen

"Y ou want to deal, Glaze? Sure, we can deal. On my terms."

There was a high-pitched edge to Renner's voice that Amy couldn't quite identify. It was as though the man was halfway between blind rage and hysteria. Treading water behind Jed, trying to keep Guthrie's lolling head out of the water, Amy had the distinct impression Renner was capable of killing, either from panic or out of sheer fury at the way his plans had gone awry.

"Amy and I know where the emeralds are, Renner. But to get them we'll need to refill the tanks. We're out of air. There's a compressor at Slaters'."

"You'll bring out the emeralds, is that it?"

"That's it," Jed said evenly. He stayed in the protective shadows of the cave entrance.

"In exchange for what?" Renner yelled.

"I'll settle for an even split of the stones."

Amy glanced at Jed. In the dim light seeping through the entrance she could just barely see the hard lines of his profile.

"Who are you, Glaze?" Renner shouted. "Who the hell are you? How did you get into this? How did you know about the woman? About the caves? About everything, dammit?"

"We can talk about that after we've made the deal. What do you say, Renner? I'll even throw in a couple of freebies."

"What freebies?"

"I've already given you one. I took care of Vaden for you. I'll do the same for Guthrie here."

"He's not dead?"

"Not yet. I got the impression you hired him and Vaden to do the garbage work for you. Well, you got what you paid for, Renner. The world is full of incompetents. But for a split I'll take care of all the outstanding problems here. And you've got a lot of them. Believe it. If you want to get out of this with the rocks and your skin, you'd better think about doing business with me."

Amy waited tensely, wondering what would happen if Renner refused to accept the deal. She and Jed couldn't stay in the cave indefinitely. The water was warm as ocean water went, but it wasn't body temperature. After a while it would begin to sap their internal heat.

There was only one option and Jed was going for it. He had to convince Renner to let them out of the cave; had to convince the other man that he needed Jed and Amy if he wanted the emeralds.

"All right, Glaze. The two of you can come on out of the water. We can work something out, I think."

Jed was silent for a moment, clearly turning the possibilities over in his mind. Then he said quietly to Amy, "This is as good as it's going to get. Let's try it. He's nervous, but he hasn't worked himself up to the point of pulling the trigger on that Beretta. At least not quite. Definitely an amateur. He's never done this kind of thing before. He hired Vaden and Guthrie to do the dirty stuff for him. It's one thing to employ someone to do it for you, but doing it yourself is something else. Go ahead. You'll be safe. Renner's not afraid of you. I'll bring Guthrie."

Amy glanced at Jed once more, trying to see his eyes in the shadows, but it was impossible. She handed Guthrie over to Jed and started forward into the outer pool. The rain was still falling lightly. She could feel it as she swam out into the open. There was a glare of light from one side of the pool and she knew Renner stood behind it, holding a gun.

He kept her in the spotlight for a few seconds, watching as she stripped off her fins and began to climb out of the rocky pool. Then he yanked the beam back to the entrance of the cave to cover Jed.

"Take it nice and slow, Glaze. Why don't you leave Guthrie in the water?"

"He's unconscious. He'll drown."

"So? You were going to finish him for me, weren't you?" Renner taunted.

"That's part of the deal," Jed agreed. "But if I do it now, I have one less bargaining chip. I think I'll keep Guthrie around for a while."

Amy looked back over her shoulder as she got to her feet. Jed was swimming slowly forward, keeping Guthrie's sagging body in front of him. She glanced speculatively at Renner and realized his attention was focused on Jed. Obviously he didn't consider Amy any kind of serious threat.

Now that she was only a few feet from Renner and the flashlight was pointed away from her, she could see the man more clearly. The rain had slicked his hair and thoroughly dampened his shirt. His face was rigid in the shadows and he held the pistol with a grip that appeared far too tight. Admittedly, she had only confronted one other person in this sort of situation, but it didn't take too much experience to recognize the fact that Renner was in the thrall of a dangerous anxiety. It would take very little to push him over the edge into outright panic. If he panicked, he would probably pull the trigger.

A small, muffled sound from the foliage behind her captured Amy's attention. Automatically she looked around and saw a large man lying on the ground. He was tied and gagged.

"Hank!" She started toward him. Renner's voice stopped her in her tracks.

"Leave him alone. He stays where he is. Stupid fool tried to follow us. Vaden and Guthrie got him."

Hank silently shook his head at Amy and she reluctantly turned back to watch Jed as he began his climb out of the pool. It wasn't easy because he was trying to handle Guthrie and all the equipment the other man was wearing at the same time. Even so, it seemed to Amy that Jed was making a great deal of work out of the project. He outweighed Guthrie by several pounds and Amy knew the strength of Jed's sinewy build.

"Hurry up," Renner snapped.

"If you want speed, try giving me a hand with Guthrie," Jed advised calmly. He was about halfway out of the pool.

"Wait a minute," Renner said suddenly. "Just hold it right there. Put Guthrie down on those rocks and don't come any farther. I've got to think."

Amy saw the new level of tension that was seizing him and a wave of fear went through her. Renner was slipping over some invisible edge. She could almost see it happening. As quietly as possible she continued to fumble free of her diving gear. She had the tank off now and was holding the heavy weight belt in one hand. Renner still wasn't paying much attention to her.

"What's there to think about, Renner? Except the emeralds, of course," Jed asked easily. He had stopped climbing out of the pool but he hadn't released Guthrie.

"Yeah, the emeralds. I've got to get a few more answers." Renner shot a sidelong glance at Amy. "You're pretty good at this cave diving business, aren't you? And you know where the emeralds are. It occurs to me I don't really need Glaze as long as I've got you. And you'd be a hell of a lot easier to handle."

Amy froze as she heard the new direction of his thoughts. There was silence from the pool. Wildly she sought for a way to deflect Renner's logic. She started talking, writing the scene off the top of her head as if she were sketching out an idea to use in a book.

"You don't need him to get the stones for you," Amy agreed. "But you better find out just who Glaze is before you kill him. You don't want to leave any loose ends, do you?"

"Who is he?" Renner demanded, swinging his attention back to Jed, who was waiting quietly in the shadows of the pool. "A friend of LePage's?"

"Not exactly a friend," Amy murmured with a coolness she was far from feeling. "But you're close. LePage was the source of the information about the stones. Haven't you figured it all out yet, Dan? Jed's an employee, like Guthrie or Vaden, but he's in a league neither of them will ever be in. Jed's first class talent."

"Who hired him?" Renner's tone was shaky with nervous agitation. "Tell me, dammit. Who hired him to get those stones?"

"Now you're asking the right question," Amy said approvingly. Idly she swung the weight belt from her right hand. The movement was barely perceptible in the darkness. "The answer is that he's working for a gentleman who goes by the name of Cutter. Mr. Cutter, it seems, is a collector of fine stones, especially emeralds. Mr. Cutter has been collecting them for years. He's rich, powerful and quite untouchable. He has friends in high places, as the saying goes. Very high. He can afford talent like Jed. What's more he can afford to have you conveniently removed if he learns that you got between him and the emeralds. If Jed's offering to split the profits with you, then you can assume he's speaking on behalf of Mr. Cutter. Cutter will trust Jed to make a deal and he'll probably honor it. But if he thinks he's been cut out completely, he's likely to be very angry. Cutter knows all about you."

Renner's eyes snapped back to her for an instant before returning to Jed. "How do you know all this?"

"Let's just say Jed talks in his sleep. The advantage of taking Jed up on his offer is that he can deliver. He can cover up this whole mess for you. With Cutter's help, he can make sure your connection to the emeralds is never known. No one will find out, for example, that you're Michael Wyman's son."

"Sonofabitch. How did you know?"

"I didn't know. Not until Mr. Cutter found out and informed Jed. I told you, Cutter has friends. He also has access to all kinds of information. Who knows what Mr. Cutter would learn if he started really investigating you, Renner?"

"Shut up, damn you!" Renner was distracted and frantic now. The Beretta was wavering in his hand, as if he couldn't decide who to point it at.

"Better take Jed up on his deal," Amy said. "Everything will turn out fine if you do."

"No!" Renner shouted. "Everything's not going to turn out just fine. Everything's going to hell! I've got to get rid of all of you as soon as I've got the stones and the photos. That's the only way out of this. I've got to get rid of everyone who knows about this!"

"What about Cutter?" Amy asked softly.

"I'll make a deal with him, myself," Renner announced as if he'd just been struck by a revelation. "That's what I'll do. I'll make a deal with him, myself. I don't need Glaze." The Beretta steadied, the wicked snout pointed at Jed.

Amy knew her story hadn't worked. Renner was too frightened of Jed. He was going to kill him. She saw the way Renner steadied himself, clearly preparing to pull the trigger.

She lifted the heavy weight belt that had been swinging lightly from her hand into a quick, short arc that brought it crashing down across Renner's hands.

There was an explosion and Renner yelled. Before he finished the scream, Amy whipped the lead-filled belt back up to strike the side of his head.

Renner screamed again and staggered to the side, raising his hands to his head. He reeled and then tumbled head first into the pool.

"No!" Amy shouted. "You can't die like that. Don't let it happen again!" It was like a repeat of the nightmare in October. Amy watched, stunned, as Renner sank into the water. Then she grabbed the flashlight that had fallen from his hand and raced to the edge of the pool. She started down the rocky slope.

"Amy, don't worry, he's all right." Jed had released

Guthrie and was already heading back into the water to re-trieve Renner. "He's alive, Amy. See? He's moving."

Jed was right. Renner was surfacing, albeit in a dazed manner. He got his head out of the water just as Jed reached him. Amy breathed a shaky sigh of relief. The thought of another drowning death in this pool, regardless of the cir-cumstances, was more than she wanted to deal with after all she had been through.

Renner was sputtering and holding his head where the weight belt had struck him. "Bastards," he hissed. "All of you. Those emeralds are mine. My father made the deal for them. They're *mine*, don't you understand?"

When she realized that Jed had a grip on Renner and was dragging him up the side of the pool, Amy abruptly remem-bered Hank. She whirled around, grabbed her diving knife and began freeing him.

Hank groaned as she pulled the gag off his face. He shook his head and sat up. "Jesus, Amy, I'm sorry about this. I really screwed up, didn't I?"

"We're the ones who should be apologizing," Amy de-clared stoutly as she finished untying him. "We had no busi-ness getting you involved."

"She's right," Jed remarked as he secured Renner. "I'm the one who screwed up. I didn't think keeping an eye on Renner and Guthrie was going to be so hazardous to your health."

Hank rubbed his wrists and chuckled. "Well, to tell you the truth, I got myself into trouble because I decided to do a little more than just keep an eye on them. When Guthrie and Renner left the inn this evening, I phoned Kelso to see how long he was going to keep Vaden under wraps. The fool told me he let Vaden go yesterday because he couldn't think of a good reason to keep him in jail any longer. He'd ordered Vaden off the island, but apparently Vaden snuck back here last night or this morning. I tried to call you, but there was no answer."

"We were probably already on our way here," Jed remarked.

Hank nodded. "I remembered what you said about thinking Vaden might have been working with Guthrie. I decided to follow Renner and Guthrie. I managed to find them because a couple of fishermen had seen them down by the docks." Hank groaned and got to his feet. "Probably shouldn't have tried to play hero. I'm not as young as I used to be. Was a time I could have taken a pair like Guthrie and Vaden, but not any more. They realized I had followed them and set up a neat little trap in a storage shed. I fell right into it. Next thing I know, we're on our way here. The only reason I'm alive is because Renner had some bright idea I might be useful to him."

Jed picked up the flashlight and asked quietly, "How did they know where 'here' was, Hank?"

"Apparently when Vaden got out of jail he headed out here to keep a watch on the house. I heard him tell Renner he'd seen you two go into the caves yesterday afternoon. I gather something went wrong?"

"There was a slide. Clouded up the water." Jed began collecting gear. "We couldn't go back in until tonight."

"I think Renner had some notion of sitting around and waiting until you and Amy came out of the caves with the emeralds, but by the time we got here Guthrie and Vaden had convinced him they could handle it better their way. I got the feeling Vaden wanted to settle a private grudge with you, Jed. He'd didn't like the way you took him the other night. He told Guthrie to watch the entrance while he followed you inside. He thought you were unarmed. Guess you surprised him, huh?"

"He's still nursing his surprise," Jed said.

Hank arched his heavy brows. "That right? He's been down in those caves a heck of a long time."

"He's sitting down there on a ledge that's above water, waiting for someone to get him out. He might have sat down there a long, long time if Amy hadn't given us such an enthralling sample of her creative powers. I always did say she had one hell of an imagination." Jed smiled at her in the shadows.

"She's got a pretty fair right hand, too," Hank added admiringly. "Where did you learn that trick with the weight belt, Amy?"

"I write fiction for a living, Hank. It's very educational."

"The thing about that story you gave Renner," Hank went on thoughtfully, "is that it sounded damn plausible."

"Good fiction often sounds plausible," Amy said smoothly.

"No offense, Glaze," Hank said bluntly, "but I'd like to know just where you fit in."

"Believe it or not," Jed said calmly, "I'm just an innocent bystander who got dragged into this." There was a short, meaningful pause. "Where do you fit in, Hank?"

Hank sighed. "I'm the one who sank Michael Wyman's boat twenty-five years ago." He glanced at Amy's shocked expression. "Somebody had to do it, Amy. Your Dad needed a little help, you see. And me and your dad had been friends for years even then. Hell, we used to dive together in the old days. You wouldn't remember. He gave it up before you were born. Your dad never really liked diving. It was your mother who loved it."

Amy was so stunned she couldn't think of anything to say. She just stood and stared speechlessly at Hank. It was Jed who took control of the situation, as usual.

"Let's get back to the house and figure out just how we're going to clean up this mess. I have a feeling we might need a little more of Amy's creative imagination. And maybe a drink."

"What about Vaden?" Amy asked anxiously. "You can't just leave him down there."

"No, I suppose we can't. I guess I'd better get some air in a couple of these tanks and go fetch him," Jed said in resignation.

A long while later Amy stepped out of the shower, pulled on a vividly colored muumuu and went downstairs to find Jed and Hank waiting for her. They were each holding a glass of Scotch. As she approached, Jed handed her a glass of white wine. He had changed into a pair of khaki slacks and a shirt. He searched her face intently.

"Are you okay, Amy?"

"I'm fine." She glanced around the room. "Where are the others?"

Hank spoke up, lounging back in his chair. "Jed and I figured we'd leave Renner, Vaden and Guthrie together in your mother's pantry for the time being."

"While we sort out the story we're going to give Kelso," Jed added by way of explanation. "Sit down, honey, this is going to take a while."

Amy sat and took a fortifying sip of her wine. Her eyes were on Hank. "Tell me what happened all those years ago,

Hank. I have to know. I've got too many bits and pieces of the puzzle. If I don't find out the truth, I'll go crazy."

"That's the problem with her kind of imagination," Jed put in as an aside.

Hank nodded understandingly. "I don't see why I can't tell you the whole thing. It's true, the government slapped a top secret clearance on the Orleana Project as they called it, but that was twenty-five years ago, and what are a few government secrets between friends? The main reason the subject's never been discussed much is because your dad didn't want it talked about. It was his wishes I respected, not the government's. But since you already seem to know a lot, you'd better know it all."

"Tell me about my father and Michael Wyman."

"They were friends and partners, Amy," Hank said gently, "until they started getting successful. Wyman couldn't handle the fact that it was your father's business sense that was making them rich. He couldn't stand to share the glory. He wanted, no, he *needed* to be the star attraction. He was like an artist who demanded full credit for the completed painting, if you know what I mean. He started drinking. Started spending pretty wildly. Took more chances in the sports he favored."

"What did my father do?"

Hank shrugged. "Tried to weather the storm, I guess. But I don't think he ever realized just how wild and dangerous Wyman really was. Or how much Wyman came to hate your father. Then one day the government agents showed up on your father's doorstep. They told him they suspected Wyman was in the process of making a deal with the Russians. There was money involved. A lot of it, they told Doug. It seems they had an agent working for them on the inside. He told them Wyman was to be paid in emeralds and that the plans for the new aircraft wing design were to be exchanged for the stones in Hawaii. The government wanted your father's cooperation in case they screwed up the bust. They wanted Doug to make sure the wing design plans were altered, just in case. Doug agreed to do that much, but he wanted no part of trapping Wyman."

"Did he believe Michael Wyman was really setting up the deal?" Jed asked.

Hank shook his head. "No, I don't think so. He didn't want to believe it. But I guess the government men showed him photographs of Wyman having secret meetings with a man the agents identified as a Russian spy. Doug flew to Hawaii about the time the transaction was supposed to take place. I think he wanted to see for himself if Wyman really showed up to go through with the deal. But the government men fouled up the arrest. They moved in too late. Oh, they managed to get the Russian at the airport, but they missed Wyman. To tell you the truth, I think Doug was secretly glad Wyman escaped. After the bust fell through, Doug decided that as long as he was as far as Hawaii, he'd fly on to Orleana to check up on the house."

"He got here and found Wyman waiting for him, right?" Jed asked.

Hank nodded. "Right." He looked steadily at Amy. "Wyman was desperate, Amy. He knew the agents were hot on his trail. He had the emeralds but they weren't any good to him until he could get them sold. But he was afraid to emerge from hiding long enough to risk trying to sell them. He needed help and he turned to his old friend."

"My father."

"Doug said he couldn't help him, that he'd be better off

surrendering. Wyman turned nasty. He threatened to blackmail your Dad. I'm not sure what he used and I never asked.
But it must have been something pretty foul. Your Dad drew
the line at that. He'd put up with a lot from his old partner
but he wouldn't let Wyman blackmail him. There was a
struggle out there by the caves. Wyman had brought a gun
along. It went off during the fight and Wyman died. I never
understood why Wyman and Doug were at the caves when
the fight occurred. Your dad said Wyman had dragged him
out there but the struggle took place and Wyman got killed
before Doug found out why Wyman took him there. We
always assumed he'd been planning to kill Doug if he didn't
cooperate. Maybe Wyman thought he could make the death
look like a diving accident." Hank broke off to glance at the
metal box on a nearby table. "Now I can guess why Wyman
headed for the caves with Doug. He'd already hidden the
box and probably intended to show Slater just what sort of
blackmail material he had."

"But things never got that far," Jed concluded. "Wyman
died before he told anyone about the box in the caves."

"He must have told someone," Amy pointed out. "Because Renner knew about it."

"True." Jed was thoughtful for a moment. "Maybe the
girlfriend. What was her name? Vivien?"

"Vivien," Hank mused. "I remember her, I think. Sexy
little blonde Wyman brought to the island once. Yeah, that
was her. Vivien. I don't think I ever heard her last name."

"Finish the story, Hank." Jed cradled his glass between
his palms and stretched his feet out in front of him.

"Not much more to tell. The night Wyman died, Doug
came to me and told me what had happened. We decided to
contact the agents who were supposed to have handled the

Hawaiian setup. There weren't many private phones on Orleana in those days. I had one of the few on the island. Doug called the number he'd been given by one of the agents who originally asked for his cooperation. The government men gave instructions that we were to sit tight and not say a word until they arrived."

"That must have been a little easier said than done," Jed observed wryly. "What the hell did you do with Wyman's body? I can imagine how unpleasant things would have gotten in this heat and humidity."

Amy winced, thinking about it. "How awful. What did you do?"

Hank took a sip of his Scotch. "Packed it in ice from your mother's freezer. Christ, what a night that was. Fortunately the government men arrived early the next morning. They told your dad they wanted the whole thing hushed up completely. It would be better, they said, if Wyman just disappeared. Your father agreed."

"Because he didn't want the press getting hold of the story," Amy said with sudden insight. "Not only would it have been bad for the firm, which was going to have a tough enough time surviving as it was, but he probably feared that whatever Wyman was using to blackmail him might come out into the open." She remembered the letters from her mother that were in the box. And the photos. Which of those two damning bits of evidence had Wyman used? Amy had a hunch it must have been the letters. She didn't want Hank knowing about them. "Once the reporters started investigating, there was no telling what kind of scandal might have developed."

"Exactly," Jed put in blandly. "The simplest thing to do was have Wyman disappear under normal circumstances.

Lost at sea. But dumping a body at sea is always a risk. Bodies sometimes wash ashore, and in this case there would be the bullet hole to explain. If Wyman's body ever surfaced that would be the end of the lost at sea story. So Slater took the body down into the caves."

"Right. And I took care of the boat," Hank admitted. He looked at Amy. "Your dad figured he could keep people out of the caves for as long as it mattered. After all, he owned them. The government agents hushed up the whole thing, swore Doug and me to secrecy and left the island."

"What about the emeralds?" Amy asked.

"Nobody was too worried about them," Hank assured her.

"Why not? They were worth a fortune."

"Not unless the price of green glass has skyrocketed in the past twenty-five years," Hank said with a small grin.

"Glass!"

Hank nodded. "Afraid so. Remember I told you the government had an inside man working on the deal?"

"Yes?" Amy prompted.

"Well, he told his contacts that the Russians had been planning to cheat Wyman all along and had the glass cut into classic emerald shapes. Wyman left Hawaii with six perfectly cut pieces of green glass. Even if the agents had known he'd hidden them in that box, I doubt they would have bothered trying to find them."

"I think it's time we took a look in that box," Jed announced. He rose lithely from the chair and headed for the table before Amy could think of any logical excuse not to open the box.

"Jed," she tried, thinking of the letters, "I don't think we should open it. Let's just throw it away and be done with it."

"Remember what I told you, honey. No loose ends." He

examined the locked box. "Where's the key Renner had on him?"

Amy got to her feet, accepting the inevitable. "I'll get it."

Ten minutes later Jed raised the metal lid. Amy glanced around his arm, trying to see inside. Hank hadn't moved from his chair across the room. He was placidly sipping his Scotch, watching them.

The letters were still tightly sealed in the waterproof pouch. Jed didn't lift them out of the box. But he did pull out the packet of stones and the photos. Amy watched anxiously as he fanned the photos out on the table. Her father as he'd looked years ago was as recognizable as he had been back in October when she'd first opened the box.

"Jed, please," Amy begged in a tight voice. "We've got to destroy these."

Jed scooped them up and studied them. "There's no need to worry about these, Amy. They're fakes. Bad ones at that. Wyman must have been in a hurry when he made them. Look, you can still see the lines where he tried to put them together."

She stared at them. "Wyman doctored these photos of my father talking to that man?"

"And did such a bad job of it, most people wouldn't be fooled for a minute."

"Unless," Amy suggested weakly, recalling her hurried examination of them in October, "someone was viewing them in the middle of the night with only a flashlight."

Jed glanced down at her as he tossed the photos to Hank. "Under such bad light, I guess they might look real," he said gently. "Especially if someone had other things on her mind at the time." He closed the lid of the box, leaving the packet of letters still inside. "What do you think, Hank?"

Hank was examining the photos. "You're right. They're bad. But this explains what Wyman tried to use to blackmail Doug." He shook his head again. "So what the hell are we going to tell Kelso?"

"I think," Jed said thoughtfully, "that since the government created this mess, we ought to let those nice folks in Washington, D.C. clean it up. I'll call my boss, Cutter."

Hank looked confused. "Cutter? Your boss? But I thought Amy made up that story about you working for someone named Cutter."

Jed grinned. "Truth," he declared, "is sometimes a lot simpler and more straightforward than fiction." He reached for the phone.

Chapter Nineteen

A couple of hours after Renner, Vaden and Guthrie had been delivered to the tiny cell that served as Orleana's jail, Amy sat down in front of the metal box, reached inside and pulled out her mother's letters.

Hank Halliday had gone home to Rosie to be severely scolded by her for his unexpected disappearance. Kelso and any other interested townspeople who bothered to inquire were given the story Cutter had advised Jed to use. Renner, Vaden and Guthrie were three off-islanders who had gotten together to rob the Slaters' home. Several locals shook their heads and declared gloomily that the incident was one of the many problems Orleana was going to face as the island became more popular. The price of being discovered, as it were. Things had been different in the past.

"I'm not so sure just how different they were," Amy said quietly as she sat looking at the small pile of envelopes in her hand. "There seems to have been plenty going on here twenty-five years ago."

Jed watched as she tapped the envelopes against the table. He was sitting in a chair near an open window, making no effort to view the contents of Gloria Slater's letters to Michael Wyman. "What are you going to do with those, Amy?"

"Burn them. I should have done it that night in October, but I wasn't thinking clearly."

Jed shrugged. "I'm not so sure about that. You had to work fast that night and not leave any evidence of what had really happened. A fire, even a small one, might have raised some awkward questions if it had been discovered. Where would you have built it? In your dad's barbeque grill? I can just see your father finding charred remains of envelopes in the grill the next time he lit the coals. No, on the whole, you probably did the best thing by hiding the box in the caves again."

"But the best thing wasn't good enough. It left loose ends."

"Sometimes that's the case," Jed said gently.

Amy rose from the chair. "Let's go build a fire."

Jed didn't argue. He got to his feet and followed her out onto the veranda where he started a small blaze in the pit of the barbeque. When he had it going he stood back and waited for Amy to toss the letters into the flames.

She did so, burning the letters steadily until only one remained in her hand. She hesitated, clutching the final letter to Michael Wyman. "I only read one of the letters that night, Jed. Just enough to know for certain my mother had written them and that she thought she had fallen in love with Wyman. I have no right to read any of the rest, but I wonder about this last one . . ."

"Why?"

"I don't know. Maybe because it's so short. Only a single page." She held up the envelope. "Do you think it might have been a good-bye letter to Wyman?"

"You're hoping she broke off the relationship of her own accord? Amy, I know she's your mother, but she's human. Don't get your hopes up."

"There's something different about this letter. I can feel it."

"Don't ask me for permission to read it, Amy. It's not my business," Jed said.

Amy set her teeth and pulled the single page out of the envelope. She had to know. She had gone through so much for the sake of these damn letters, she had to know the truth about this last one. She scanned the single paragraph and grateful relief washed over her.

Jed watched her changing expression and smiled faintly. "Good news, I take it?"

Amy nodded vigorously, stuffing the last letter back into its envelope and tossing it into the fire. "I had a hunch it would be. My mother is a strong woman. I knew that in the end she would have done the right thing. She told Wyman she'd been a silly, discontented idiot. She said that even though she was having problems with Doug, deep down she loved him and would never leave him or the children. She asked Wyman to understand and forget her foolishness. It wouldn't happen again."

"Feel better knowing that?"

"Much. I'm not sure why, but I do. It's nice to know she didn't intend to run off with him. He was such a bastard. I wonder if my father ever knew?"

"About his wife's temporary aberration? Probably." Jed poked the coals, making sure the last of the letters went up in smoke. "I'd sure as hell know if you were falling for someone else."

Amy blinked in amazement. "You would? How?"

"I don't know how exactly. I'd just know. We've gotten too close to each other, Amy. Secrets like that would be impossible to keep for long."

Amy was afraid to comment on that. Did Jed realize just what he was saying? she wondered. What he was admitting? Probably not. Some psychologists said men seldom analyzed their own emotions or reactions the way women did; men were inclined to accept their feelings, even act on them, but not dissect them.

Amy coughed delicately. "Do you think Wyman used the doctored photos or the letters that night to try to blackmail my father?"

"My guess is he used both. He probably wasn't sure if the letters would work. There was always the chance Slater would simply dump his wife and say the hell with her. Wyman had the photos as double insurance. A man might walk away from a woman, he'd figure, but he wouldn't walk away from his career."

"Oh."

Jed went on, as if he hadn't heard her dismay. "But Wyman was judging Slater by his own standards. Your father was different. I've had to make a lot of snap judgments about what motivates people under pressure in the last eight years, Amy. I've got a fairly good track record."

"How do you know you've got a good record?" Amy couldn't resist the question.

"Because I'm still alive."

Amy swallowed at the unarguable truth of that statement. It said so much about the kind of life he led. "I see. So what do you deduce about how my father might have acted under the pressure of blackmail?"

"Do you really want to know?"

Amy hesitated and then said in a small rush, "Yes, I really want to know."

Jed put down the barbeque tool he had been using to stir

the flames. "He would have told Wyman to go to hell and find his own way off the island if Wyman had threatened him with the photos. But if Wyman used the letters, your dad would have been furious. He would have done whatever was required to stop Wyman."

"And that's what the struggle was about that night?"

Jed looked down into the last of the flames. "I imagine so."

"You seem very sure of your reconstruction of the scene," Amy said a bit tartly.

Jed glanced up, his eyes gleaming in the faint light that shone through the windows of the house. "Maybe I'm sure of it because I know that's what I would have done under the same circumstances. I wouldn't have let any man walk away with letters like those if the letters had been written by you, Amy."

He didn't have to spell it out, Amy thought. She got the point. Without a word she moved into the circle of his arm and together they watched the fire die.

"I'll empty the ashes tomorrow," Jed told her. "There won't be anything left in the barbeque pit when your father gets home."

Amy nodded. "Do you think it was Vaden or Guthrie who searched your things the other day?"

Jed shrugged. "Vaden, probably. He seemed to be handling that kind of thing for Renner. It didn't do him any good. There was nothing to find."

"Maybe finding nothing at all made him even more nervous," Amy speculated.

Jed grinned. "Now you're thinking like a pro. That's probably exactly what happened. And that's probably why he decided to get rid of me in that alley."

"Thank you, Jed. For everything." Amy leaned her head on his shoulder, reveling in his strength.

He smiled into her hair. "I'm the one who should be thanking you. You saved my hide tonight. Renner had worked himself up into a full-blown case of hysteria. He was going to pull that trigger. And then there was the little matter of digging me out of that rock fall in the cave. Did I ever thank you properly for that?"

"You wouldn't have been in either one of those situations if I hadn't been in a much bigger mess."

"We'll call it even, since I more or less invited myself into your mess."

"Speaking of messes, do you really think your Mr. Cutter can clean this one up?"

"No sweat. It's the sort of thing Cutter's good at. When I called him back an hour ago to find out how things were going he told me he's already got most of the pieces in place. Faxon has turned up enough on Guthrie and Vaden to put them away on other charges. Seems like they're both wanted for gunrunning."

"What about Daniel Renner?"

"Renner, it appears, is going to have his hands full trying to explain a few matters to the Securities Exchange Commission. His wheeling and dealing has come a little too close to the line in too many cases, according to Faxon's data. There are also rumors of some past drug dealing. On top of everything else, he's going to have to explain to the government what he was doing consorting with known gunrunners. Renner may or may not be able to stay out of jail, but it's a cinch he's going to be busy for quite a while."

"You don't think he'll mention the emeralds?"

"The *fake* emeralds," Jed emphasized. "No, I don't think

he will. It would only complicate his life more. The last thing he'll want anyone to know is that his father was dealing with Russian spies."

"I feel sorry for him, Jed."

"I gathered that when you handed him that packet of glass stones," Jed said dryly.

"I warned him they were fakes," Amy reminded him. She recalled Daniel Renner's beaten expression as he was being led out the door by Hank. It had hurt her, somehow, in spite of everything. Renner's inheritance from the father he'd never known had turned out to be worthless. "Maybe I shouldn't have done it. At the time I wanted him to have something from his father. But I think it was the last straw for Renner. After all he'd gone through, he discovered his father had left him nothing but a few bits of green glass."

"I wouldn't waste too much sympathy on him," Jed advised.

"I'm not. Still . . ."

"Forget it." Jed turned her around so she was facing him. He grinned down at her. "That tendency toward softness is just a natural weakness in the female brain, I suppose. Goes along with the tendency to fuss. Are you going to tell your parents what happened?"

"I think it's better if there aren't any more secrets, don't you?" Amy asked. "Except for one, of course."

"You're not going to mention the letters?"

She shook her head. "No, there's no reason to mention them. After all, my father apparently never actually saw the box or its contents. He might not know for certain those letters existed. He could have assumed Wyman just made up the tale in a last-ditch attempt to blackmail him."

Jed nodded. "Wyman, for obvious reasons, didn't mention the letters to Vivien Renner, either. He'd hardly want his mistress to know about other women in his life. He did tell her, according to Dan Renner, about the photos. Renner thought he could use those pictures to threaten your brother's political future. It wouldn't do an up-and-coming politician much good to have his father accused of espionage. No, I think you're right. The only person who actually knew about the box besides Wyman was Vivien Renner. According to her son, Wyman had sent Vivien a small map showing where he had hidden the box. He told her about the emeralds and the photos and mailed her a duplicate key. Maybe he wanted her to know about the so-called treasure in case something happened to him. Who knows? She might have told him he had a son and that might have meant something. At any rate, she entered the information in her diary, along with that little map Renner was using and then turned to the bottle. Everything stayed hidden until she died and her son got hold of the diary, the map and the key."

Amy put her arms around Jed's neck. "I kept one of the glass bits as a souvenir. It's strange. When this all started, the last thing I wanted out of it was a souvenir. Eight months ago I never wanted to see that box or anything in it again. The damn thing has been haunting me since October. But now it doesn't seem to matter any more. I think I've seen the last of the nightmares." She stood on tiptoe and brushed her mouth lightly against his.

Jed's arms tightened around her. "Good, because I can think of much more interesting things to do at night than dream about underwater caves and swimming skeletons."

"Swimming skeletons? I never actually dreamed about a swimming skeleton."

"Forget it. Let's concentrate on some of those more interesting things I mentioned."

"Such as?"

"Come over here and I'll show you." Jed caught her up in his arms and carried her to a nearby lounger. He began to undress her. His gaze was shimmering with sensual intensity by the time he tossed the muumuu aside.

When he had finished undressing himself, he stood for a moment looking hungrily down at her. In that instant Amy knew with the full strength of a woman's intuition that his longing was more than physical. He might not be able to put it into words, but Jed was reaching out to her in ways he probably didn't even understand. Amy opened her arms.

Even as he came to her, it crossed Amy's mind that she might be deluding herself about Jed's shrouded emotions. A woman in love could easily fool herself, she thought. But this was Jed, her best friend and the only love she wanted. Surely she wasn't wrong about him.

His mouth came down on hers and Amy stopped thinking about Jed Glaze's complex feelings and needs. When he held her like he was doing now, she lived completely in the present.

There would be time enough later to worry about the future.

When the last of the sweet, hot need had been assuaged, Jed lay still beside Amy, holding her close while reality slowly seeped back. He gazed out through the veranda pillars and thought about what had to be said. He couldn't put it off any longer. Cutter had been very forceful when Jed had talked to him the second time that evening. There was a need for immediate action. Cutter would clean up the mess on Orleana, but Jed was expected to finish cleaning up another mess in another part of the world. Jed had delayed telling Amy as long as possible.

She stirred in his arms, sensing the change in him. She was awfully good at that, Jed mused. She seemed to know exactly what kind of mood he was in at any given time.

"What is it, Jed?"

He stroked her hair, wishing he could avoid the conversation altogether. It had been easier a few weeks ago, before he'd come back from that last disastrous assignment, before he had learned about Amy's private demons, before he became her lover. In those days he simply said good-bye and left. He called her when he got back and that was that; no questions, no demands for explanations, no pleas, no lectures. Everything had been simpler then. Still, he was beginning to realize the price he had paid for that simplicity. Why had he been so unaware of his own loneliness for the past eight years?

But everything had changed now. The loneliness, at least when he was with Amy, had vanished, but there were new complications. Not the least of which was trying to tell her he had to leave on another assignment.

"I have to go back to work, Amy." Jed braced himself. He knew it was best to get it over with quickly. He only hoped she wouldn't cry. He didn't know what he would do if she cried. Probably cry with her, the way he was feeling these days. Ridiculous.

"I know."

Her simple response startled him. "How do you know?"

"I heard you talking about having to . . . to sell the salesman yesterday, remember? And tonight, when you talked to

Cutter the second time, I could tell when you got off the phone that he wanted something from you."

"I should leave tomorrow. I can fly out of Honolulu. But I'll be back as soon as possible, Amy." Perhaps she wouldn't cry after all, he thought in relief.

"Fine. I'll see you when you get back. I think I'll fly home to Caliph's Bay tomorrow, too. I've had about enough of island life for the present. And I'm anxious to get back to *Private Demons*."

He shifted, frowning slightly as he listened to the casual tone of her voice. Jed told himself he was glad she wasn't crying, but he hadn't expected her to be so easygoing about the matter, either. "I'll try to wrap this up as soon as I can, honey."

She was silent for a moment before asking softly, "What's a salesman?"

Jed set his teeth. "In this case he's a renegade agent who's selling out his own people to the opposition. He sold me out on my last trip."

"Was that why you were shot and cut with the knife?"

He wondered at the almost total neutrality of her voice. Where was the usual fussing note it acquired when she talked about his wounds? "Yeah. Now he's gone and sold a couple of other agents. They weren't as lucky as I was. They're both dead."

"My God." The curiously neutral note vanished.

Jed held her more closely. "I have to get him, Amy. Cutter thinks he's found out who the salesman is and he has to be taken care of before he does any more damage."

"I think," she said very steadily, "it would be better if we didn't discuss this any further." She snuggled against him, her palm fluttering lightly down his bare chest. She bent her head and kissed his shoulder. He could feel the tiny, tantalizing nip of her teeth. Jed shuddered. He was leaving tomorrow and he didn't know how long he'd be gone. This was going to be his last night with Amy for some time.

His last night with Amy. The words seared his brain even as he gathered her close once more. He was thinking about getting back to her and he hadn't even gotten on the plane yet. He was missing her before he even left.

"What the hell have you done to me, sweetheart?" he asked roughly as his body leaped in response to her gentle caresses.

"I'll tell you tomorrow," she promised.

He wondered what she meant and then he stopped wondering about anything except the huge, seemingly unquenchable need she aroused in him.

He sought and found the sweet, dampening place between her legs, glorying in his ability to make her respond to him. Gently he stroked her silky skin, stoking the fires within her until she was a living flame in his arms.

"Sorceress," he breathed as he covered her body with his own.

"Magician," she accused and then pulled him to her, drawing him into her warmth, surrounding him, clinging to him.

Jed held her still as he entered her, aware of her firm nipples against his chest, her thighs as she wrapped her legs around him and the exciting way she said his name.

He needed this, he realized dazedly. He needed Amy more than anything else in the world. He poured himself into her completely as if he would merge with her and make himself a part of her. She was his, she belonged to him and he wanted to make certain she knew it in every fiber of her being before he left.

They arrived at the Honolulu airport the following afternoon shortly before three o'clock. The business of getting packed, making reservations and closing up the house had kept Amy and Jed so busy that Jed hadn't had time to initiate any more discussion about his job. As he carried the baggage through the terminal he realized something was bothering him, but he wasn't sure how to put it into words. It occurred to him that he almost wished Amy would fuss more about his departure.

Stupid idea, he thought. The last thing he wanted was a scene. She was keeping it nice and simple for him. He should be grateful.

But he realized as they waited in the airport lounge for his flight to be called that he didn't want her to keep it quite so simple. She acted as though he were leaving on a routine business trip.

Well, that was exactly what he was doing.

"My flight doesn't leave until later this evening. I think I'll go into Waikiki and do some shopping. I haven't been there in a long time," Amy remarked chattily.

Jed had a sudden image of her running loose around a tropical paradise inhabited by thousands of tourists, many of whom were male. Jesus, he thought, he really was spoiled. He was used to having her to himself in paradise. "I'm not so sure that's a good idea," he said gruffly. "Hawaii isn't what it used to be. They've got crime problems here just like everywhere else now."

"Don't worry about me, Jed. I've been here lots of times. I know my way around. There's a great little restaurant in one of the big hotels on the beach. I think I'll have dinner there before I board the plane."

"You're going to get a meal on the plane," he reminded her irritably. Visions of beach boys joining her for dinner danced in his brain.

"Yes, but airline food is terrible. I'd much rather eat before the flight."

"Listen," Jed said abruptly, "you're going to be getting home in the middle of the night. Be careful on the drive from the airport."

"Yes, Jed," she agreed meekly.

"Maybe you should stay overnight in San Francisco and fly to Monterey the next day," he decided thoughtfully.

"Waste of money," she declared.

"I'm not so sure. You'll be tired and it will be late. There'll probably be fog on the road to Caliph's Bay."

"Probably. I've driven in it before."

"Yes, but—"

"Jed," she interrupted firmly.

"What?"

"Stop fussing."

He stared at her. They were calling his flight. Too soon, he thought. He needed a little more time with her. "Was I fussing?"

She grinned up at him. "Yes, I believe you were."

"Oh." He didn't know what else to say. He felt oddly shaken. They were boarding the last rows of passengers now. He couldn't delay much longer.

"Perfectly understandable, of course," Amy said blithely.

"What's perfectly understandable?" Things were getting confusing. Amy wasn't behaving the way he had expected her to behave and he didn't comprehend his own feelings.

Jed was suddenly filled with a restless impatience at everything around him.

"Your fussing," Amy explained.

"Why is it understandable?" he almost shouted. Heads turned. Fortunately most of the passengers were already on board.

Amy went on her toes to kiss his cheek. "You're fussing for the same reason you made love to me the way you did last night. For the same reason you insisted on involving yourself in that situation on Orleana. For the same reason you don't want to get on this flight. Because you love me."

"Amy!"

"You may not know it yet, but you do, Jed. When you come back we can talk about it—along with a few other things."

"What other things?" She was edging him toward the gate and he wanted to stay but he couldn't. He was committed to this assignment. He couldn't back out now. Lives hung in the balance. But all the same he didn't want to leave. He had other things to talk about. Amy just said so. He gripped her shoulders. "Amy, what other things?"

"Well, there's the matter of combining our two households. We'll have to decide if we can both share my cottage or if we'll have to buy a bigger one. Then there's the business of getting your bird cages out to some other galleries. The time has come to expand with your cages, Jed. They're too beautiful to just sit in that little gallery in Caliph's Bay. We're going to have to make a decision about children, of course—"

"Children!"

"Certainly. It's a major decision, but on the whole I'm inclined to go for it. Just one or two. I've told you before, I think you'll make an excellent father. We should plan for that possibility when we buy a new cottage. Also, I'm going to want space for a garden. I've decided to put one in next spring. Do you like gardening, Jed?"

"I've never done any," he heard himself say weakly. She was still shoving him gently toward the gate. An airline attendant was reaching out to take his boarding pass. "Amy, wait—"

"Don't worry, Jed. We can talk about the future when you get back. I'll be waiting. I love you." She blew him a kiss as he felt himself being sucked through the gate. Jed managed to get to his seat and fasten his seatbelt without calling too much attention to himself, but he felt far from normal. His head was spinning and his fingers shook slightly. He gripped the arms of his seat and tried to spot Amy through the window. He couldn't see her. The jet was already easing away from the gate.

He listened to the roar of the engines and thought about what it meant to plant a garden. Amy was planning for next spring and the summer harvest that would follow.

The garden was nothing. Hell, Amy was planning on having a baby. *His* baby.

Amy loved him and she was planning a future.

Back in the departure lounge Amy quietly succumbed to the tears that had been waiting to fall since she had first realized Jed was going out on another assignment.

Chapter Twenty

T he call from Douglas Slater came just as Amy was finishing the last chapter of *Private Demons*. She knew as soon as she picked up the phone that she wasn't going to have to explain what had happened on Orleana. Slater had already heard the tale from Hank Halliday.

"Hell, Amy, I kept calling the house trying to get you and when I didn't get an answer, I finally called Hank. Then I had to track you down in Caliph's Bay. To say I am a bit stunned at the moment is putting it mildly. Are you all right?"

"I'm fine, Dad."

"What about Glaze?"

"He's fine, too."

"Let me talk to him. I want to ask him a few questions."

Amy smiled briefly at her father's boardroom tone. "Sorry, he's not here at the moment."

"Where is he?" Slater demanded.

"Out of the country. He's been gone for over a week." Amy glanced at the calendar on the wall. She glanced at it frequently lately. She had added a new worry to her already brimming load wondering if anyone in Jed's agency would think to notify her if something happened to him. After all, she wasn't his wife. Just a friend. And a lover. Did the government notify friends and lovers when things went wrong? She forced the question out of her mind.

Slater paused. "Hank said he worked for the government."

"That's right."

"I suppose, given the situation you encountered, it's just as well the man knew what he was doing. All right, I've already heard about Renner, Vaden and Guthrie. Tell me about LePage. All of it this time, Amy. No more secrets."

"Dad, this is a transatlantic phone call. It's very expensive. Maybe this should wait until you get back to Orleana."

"I'm paying for it so don't worry about it. Tell me what really happened the night LePage died, honey."

Amy drew a deep breath and told him everything. Everything, that is, except about the letters. As she did so she studied the small piece of green glass she was keeping in a little bowl on the windowsill.

"Christ almighty," was all Douglas Slater said when she was finished. "To think you'd been living with that all these months. No wonder you resisted going back to the island."

Amy couldn't think of anything to add to that.

"Hank said you pulled a box out of the cave? Something Wyman hid down there before I got to Orleana and found him?" There was a different, perhaps wary note in Slater's voice now.

"That's right. It contained a packet of the stones the Russians apparently used to pay off Wyman. There were also some doctored photos of you meeting clandestinely with some Russian spy. I burned those."

"Did you?" Slater let silence flow over the line for a moment. "That was probably a good idea. The bastard told me he had some photos but I didn't believe him. How could he? I'd never been near any Russian spies. It never occurred to me he might have faked a few shots. Typical Wyman piece of mischief."

"Yes, I guess so. Well, they're gone. I gave five of the glass stones to Renner, by the way. Kept one for myself as a souvenir."

"It must have been quite an adventure. I'm just damn glad you had Glaze with you. I had a feeling he was the kind of man who knows how to take care of his own."

"Yes," Amy agreed. "He does."

There was another moment of silence from England and then Douglas Slater said carefully, "You did the right thing burning those photos, Amy. Was that all there was in the box? The photos and the emeralds?"

"That's all," Amy said firmly.

"I see." Then Slater said deliberately, "Amy, honey, I just want you to understand that if by some chance there had been anything else stored in that damn box, I'd want it burned, too. Completely."

Amy caught her breath. "I understand, Dad. Believe me, I burned everything in that box except the green stones."

"Good." Slater sounded curiously satisfied. "I've always known you are the kind of woman who can be depended on when the chips are down. As I told Glaze, you'd go for the devil's throat if you thought that's what it would take to protect someone you loved."

Amy's fingers tightened on the receiver. "Did you really say that to Jed?"

"I really said it."

"What did he say?"

"He agreed with me." Slater chuckled. "But then, he understands that kind of direct approach. He'd do the same thing if necessary. Hasn't he proven it? I think he's going to make a good husband for you. Listen, your mom's just coming out of the shower. I've already given her the gory details. I'll put her on so you can say hello."

"Fine. Dad, before you get off the line . . ."

"Yes, Amy?"

"I love you."

"I love you, too, honey. Don't ever forget it. But please, no more shocks like this one. A father can only take so much. Here's your mother."

Gloria Slater came on the line. "Amy, dear, what a dreadful experience. You're quite certain you're all right?"

"I'm fine, Mom."

"Thank goodness you had Jed with you through all that. I really do like that man, Amy."

"So do I."

"I rather thought you did." Gloria gave a small, knowing laugh. "I have a feeling we'll be attending another wedding in the not-too-distant future."

"I'm not sure about that, Mom. Jed hasn't said anything about marriage. Don't get your hopes up." Or her own, Amy added silently. She decided not to mention that she'd actually gone out and bought a couple of Vivaldi records the day before. Talk about getting one's hopes up.

"We'll see," Gloria said easily. Then she sighed. "To think that awful Michael Wyman was still causing trouble after all these years. The man certainly had a talent for it. I'm just sorry you had to be touched by it, Amy. Wyman was a complete and utter bastard, you know."

"So I've heard. Don't worry, I believe it. Tell me, how's London?"

Her mother launched into an account of the trip and Amy relaxed, listening attentively. Everything was all right.

* * *

Jed was chagrined to discover his fingers were a little unsteady as he dialed the phone. He closed his eyes when it began ringing on the other end, waiting tensely for the clear, warm, refreshing sound of Amy's voice. The receiver was lifted on the third ring, just as he had begun preparing himself for the possibility that she might be out. Jed opened his eyes and found himself staring at the AT&T symbol.

"Amy? It's me."

"Jed, you're home!"

"Almost. I'm in L.A. I'll be getting into Monterey at . . ." He fumbled with the ticket. "At seven-fifteen."

"I'll be at the airport."

Jed began to relax for the first time since he'd gotten on the plane in Honolulu. "You don't know how glad I am to hear you say that. I've missed you, sweetheart."

"I've missed you, too. Jed, are you . . . are you okay?"

He grinned like an idiot. "Still structurally sound."

"Jed!"

"No, I mean it, love, I'm fine." He took a breath and then took the plunge. "I'm in great shape to start that family you were talking about before I left."

"Jed," she said again, this time quite breathlessly. "Do you mean it?"

"We'll discuss it when I get home. I've got to run, Amy. They're calling my flight."

"Jed, wait a minute. Tell me exactly what you meant. I've got to know."

"I love you, Amy. See you at seven-fifteen." He hung up the phone, still grinning, and picked up the flight bag at his feet. It was kind of fun to turn the tables on her once in a while. Let her stew about his last message until he got there, just the way he had stewed about her last message on the way out of Honolulu.

She loved him. She was planning his future for him because she loved him.

The cage door was open and Jed was free.

Jed had just time enough to buy a bunch of yellow chrysanthemums before he got on the plane.

Amy was waiting at the airport. He found out later that she had arrived a good forty minutes early. She had apparently spent the time pacing the arrival lounge until the jet set down. When Jed finally walked through the door she was in his arms before he knew what hit him.

"It's about time you got here," she said as she clung to him.

"I know," he replied gently. "Believe me, I know." He hugged her so tightly she gave a tiny yelp.

Then she laughed up at him, her love in her eyes. "Come on," she said, "let's go home."

Jed needed no further urging.

Much later that night Amy stirred amid the tangled sheets, felt the vacancy beside her and opened her eyes. Jed was standing at the window, his strong, lean body silhouetted in the vague moonlight.

"Jed? Is anything wrong?"

"No, Amy. Not any more." He turned to look at her, his eyes warm and caressing. "I guess I'm still in another time zone. I can't sleep."

Amy remembered the intensity of his lovemaking earlier and shook her head, smiling faintly. "I would have thought you'd be exhausted."

He ignored that and instead met her eyes. "I love you, Amy."

"I'm glad," she whispered. "Because I love you. With all my heart."

Jed went back to the bed, sitting down beside her and pulling her into his arms. "I missed you so damn much. I was a fool not to realize how much I need you."

"Don't feel bad. I spent quite a while suppressing the fact that I needed you. We were just friends, remember?"

"I remember. Amy, I quit my job."

Her head came up so quickly she nearly hit his chin. "You did what?"

"When I finished this last assignment I told Cutter I wanted out. I quit. Don't look so surprised." He smiled. "Didn't you want me to quit?"

"Yes, but I wanted you to do it for yourself, not just for me."

"I did do it for myself. Eight years in that business is long enough. I want my future back, Amy. And I want you in it. Do you understand?"

She hugged him. "I understand. Was this last assignment very bad, Jed?" she asked gently.

"It went smoothly."

"That doesn't tell me much."

Jed groaned. "There was a time when you never asked questions."

"Things have changed, friend."

"Yeah, I guess they have. All right, I'll tell you what happened in a few short sentences and then we won't talk about it anymore. Agreed?"

"Agreed."

"I sold the salesman back to the terrorists who were paying him."

"What does that mean?" Then her eyes widened slightly. "Oh, I see. You made his employers think he'd betrayed them, is that it? And they . . . they . . ." She ran out of words.

"They took care of him for us," Jed finished bluntly. "It's all over, Amy."

"Yes."

"Things might be a little tight financially for a while," he said tentatively. "I mean, I've got some money saved and the cages will bring in a bit, but—"

"The cages are going to bring in a lot. I went down to the Caliph Bay Gallery and upped the prices on all the cages you had there. Two of them have already sold," she told him smugly. "And when I put them into a San Francisco gallery, the prices are going even higher."

He laughed ruefully. "I was about to say I was going to try to get back into engineering. I can do it on a free-lance basis, short-term assignments for companies in need of temporary engineering help. It might mean some travel or we might have to move, but you could come with me. If that doesn't work out, I might be able to do some security consulting work."

"Whatever," she agreed blissfully. "In the meantime we won't starve. There's my writing and there's also something else." She pulled herself free of his arms, slid out of bed and hurried into the living room.

Jed followed curiously. "What are you up to, sweetheart?"

She plucked the green stone off the windowsill and handed it to him. "You are looking at a nice little financial cushion, Jed Glaze."

He frowned, turning the stone over in his hand. "What kind of cushion?"

"Maybe fifty thousand dollars worth of cushion. Mr. Albright wasn't certain." She laughed at the expression on Jed's face.

"Who's Mr. Albright?"

"A jeweler I looked up last week. On a whim I had him check out that rock, Jed. It's real."

His fist closed around the emerald as he stared at her in astonishment. "You're joking."

"Nope. Apparently the Russians really did pay off Wyman. The government's inside man was wrong."

"And you gave the other five stones to Renner," Jed yelped.

"Daniel Renner is Wyman's son. If anyone deserves them, Renner does. But I figure you and I are entitled to that one for all our trouble."

Jed looked torn between laughter and shock. He flipped the gem into the air, caught it and reached for Amy. The laughter won out. "Amy, my love, I have a feeling the next sixty or seventy years with you are going to be very interesting."

VISIT US ONLINE

@ WWW.HACHETTEBOOKGROUP.COM.

AT THE HACHETTE BOOK GROUP WEB SITE YOU'LL FIND:

CHAPTER EXCERPTS FROM SELECTED NEW RELEASES

•

ORIGINAL AUTHOR AND EDITOR ARTICLES

•

AUDIO EXCERPTS

•

BESTSELLER NEWS

•

ELECTRONIC NEWSLETTERS

•

AUTHOR TOUR INFORMATION

•

CONTESTS, QUIZZES, AND POLLS

•

FUN, QUIRKY RECOMMENDATION CENTER

•

PLUS MUCH MORE!

Bookmark Hachette Book Group
@ www.HachetteBookGroup.com.